"Can you see me in this light?" Petunia asked.

Longarm blinked and told her, "I can barely make out my own hand in front of me when the lightning flashes. Might that be important to you for some reason?"

She said, "We'll catch our deaths in these wet duds before the day dawns cold as the clay. I'm going to strip my wet hide bare and bundle my goose bumps up in dry blankets. The *Kituhwa* are going to kill us if they find us alone like this in any case and I may as well get comfortable whilst I await my fate!"

Longarm forced a chuckle and said, "Go ahead and strip, then. It's not a bad notion and I have my own bedroll lashed to my saddle. What do you reckon they'd say if they caught us both naked as jays in two separate bedrolls?"

She laughed sort of wildly and replied, "Nobody knows what those crazy night riders say to folk before they kill them. Nobody they've killed has ever told anybody else . . ."

DON'T MISS THESE
ALL-ACTION WESTERN SERIES
FROM THE BERKLEY PUBLISHING GROUP

THE GUNSMITH by J. R. Roberts
Clint Adams was a legend among lawmen, outlaws, and ladies. They called him . . . the Gunsmith.

LONGARM by Tabor Evans
The popular long-running series about U.S. Deputy Marshal Long—his life, his loves, his fight for justice.

SLOCUM by Jake Logan
Today's longest-running action Western. John Slocum rides a deadly trail of hot blood and cold steel.

BUSHWHACKERS by B. J. Lanagan
An action-packed series by the creators of Longarm! The rousing adventures of the most brutal gang of cutthroats ever assembled—Quantrill's Raiders.

TABOR EVANS

LONGARM

AND THE BLUE-EYED SQUAW

JOVE BOOKS, NEW YORK

LONGARM AND THE BLUE-EYED SQUAW

A Jove Book / published by arrangement with
the author

PRINTING HISTORY
Jove edition / January 2000

All rights reserved.
Copyright © 2000 by Penguin Putnam Inc.
This book may not be reproduced in whole or in part,
by mimeograph or any other means, without permission.
For information address: The Berkley Publishing Group,
a division of Penguin Putnam Inc.,
375 Hudson Street, New York, New York 10014.

The Penguin Putnam Inc. World Wide Web site address is
http://www.penguinputnam.com

ISBN: 0-515-12705-1

A JOVE BOOK®
Jove Books are published by The Berkley Publishing Group,
a division of Penguin Putnam Inc.,
375 Hudson Street, New York, New York 10014.
JOVE and the "J" design
are trademarks belonging to Penguin Putnam Inc.

PRINTED IN THE UNITED STATES OF AMERICA

10 9 8 7 6 5 4 3 2 1

Chapter 1

This horse breeder with more imagination than common sense had crossed a Spanish Barb with a Lippizan Carriage Gray to produce a handsome dapple gray mare they called Tabitha, after that lady in the Good Book, Acts 9:36–43, who'd suddenly risen from the dead to unsettle everyone considerable.

Tabitha stood sixteen hands at the withers and appeared to be steady as a Lippizan and as intelligent as a Barb until you tried to ride her. So the Army Remount Service had bought her, cheap, as a band mount. Army bands all rode dapple grays. Partly for show but mostly because the cooler Nordic breeds rode steadier when you had to blow a tuba or beat a drum that close to any horse's head.

Tabitha hadn't worked out as a band mount. So they'd demoted her to guidon duty and then, after she'd bucked off a score of guidon riders and busted more than one flag staff, they'd decided she might make a fair brood mare, until she'd busted the jaw of a thoroughbred stud, stomped one hostler, and bitten the arm of another to the bone.

So she'd been ordered sold or, failing that, shot, the day she met up with U.S. Deputy Marshal Custis Long in the training paddock out at Fort Gibson in the Indian Territory.

They'd been introduced by Remount Sergeant Martin Mulholland after some heated discussion as to why on earth the U.S. Army should have to issue riding stock to a damned civilian riding for the Federal Justice Department for Gawd's sake.

The burly Sergeant Mulholland prided himself on his poker

1

face, for a humorist with Mulholland's brand of humor would have had himself some trouble getting an intended victim aboard a mount like Tabitha at gunpoint if his full intent had shown in his innocent pussy-cat eyes. But Longarm, as he was better known to friend and foe alike, had been dealt many a hand of poker from the bottom of the deck and forked himself aboard many a bronc after leaning-some on a reluctant wrangler. So he was ready for whatever the handsome gray mare had to offer as he circled the paddock with her once and found her long and lanky gait as steady as if she'd been a clockwork toy wound up for a spoiled rich kid to ride.

Then, passing Mulholland and his two slyly grinning stable hands near the paddock gate, that big wind-up spring snapped under him and all hell broke loose as the dapple gray he'd been riding suddenly seemed to decide it was time they parted company.

Tabitha bucked with inspiration as well as double-jointed fury. So Longarm was tempted to just roll clear at the top of a crow-hop and quit whilst he was ahead. For it was easier for a man to land on his boot heels when he knew when he would be getting off, and there was no way in hell he was ever going to ride this explosion on the hoof all the way to the Cherokee capital at Tahlequah, a good thirty miles to the northeast, aboard a horse unwilling to carry him that far at ground level.

But Longarm had never liked bullies, even after he'd grown too big to be afraid of most of them, and that son-of-a-bitching Mulholland was grinning like a shit-eating dog whilst both his stable hands were laughing right out loud. So Longarm decided to ride her out.

It wasn't easy. The big gray crow-hopped, sun-fished, and shook at the peak of some rises like a duck-hound coming out of a glacier lake in January.

When that combination didn't seem to open the space betwixt Longarm's pants and the familiar saddle he'd brought along from his own outfit, out Colorado way, Tabitha cranked her powerful muzzle down and around to see if she might bite his right toes off, boot and all. But Longarm spoiled her fun by kicking her smack betwixt her flaring nostrils hard, more than once, until she gave that up in favor of a sincere attempt to scrape his left knee off against the whitewashed upright planks of one paddock wall.

Longarm had ridden mean broncs before. So even though she'd been a cut above clever by choosing his mounting-leg to maim, Longarm showed her he could ride a bucking bronc as well whilst standing in the off stirrup with his left knee crooked around the cantle as he held both reins and hornless fork in his left hand to whup her about the head with the coffee brown Stetson in his big right fist.

"No fair!" shouted a gawky stable hand of mayhaps nineteen summers as Tabitha corkscrewed away from the wall and Longarm dropped his left leg back down to grip her big barrel better.

Neither Mulholland nor the older and wiser cavalryman to his right saw fit to protest Longarm's sensible grabbing of some leather. For a rider who said he never grabbed leather was a wondrous liar or a man who'd always wondered what it might feel like to ride a bucking bronc.

Mulholland and his top hand had both ridden broncs in their day, and both had been thrown ere this one by that big old double-jointed gray the pestiferous civilian lawman seemed to be riding pretty good at the moment. So, though it burned like fire to allow it, Mulholland found himself yelling, "Ride her, cowboy! Ride her hard, whup her ass and teach the sass some manners!"

Sergeant Mulholland hadn't been out to save his stripes with that momentary lapse of his usual manners. But it was a good thing for him the field grade officer bearing down on them, afoot, would later recall the burly sergeant's shouts of encouragement. For Major Roger Midfern, provost major of the Fort Gibson Military District, was fuming like a geyser fixing to spout by the time he joined the cavalrymen around the paddock gate to demand in an ominously calm tone, "What's that civilian doing aboard that condemned man-killer, *Trooper* Mulholland?"

The erstwhile Sergeant Mulholland was an old soldier and, as every old soldier knows, there are three and only three answers any soldier with a lick of sense ever gives a field grade officer who is chewing him out. They are, "Yes, sir!", "No, sir!", and "No excuse, sir!"

So the last one would have been Mulholland's only sensible option if he hadn't been frozen in a stiff brace with mortification as Longarm loped the spent gray mare their way, reined in, and called out in as calmly determined a tone, "Begging the major's pardon, that display of spirit enjoyed by man and beast alike was all my fault. The sarge and his hands told me flat out I didn't want to pick this particular mount from your remuda. They warned me she could get frisky and, as we just saw, she surely can. I'd be U.S. Deputy Marshal Custis Long from the Denver District Court, by the way. My travel orders authorized me to requisition two cavalry mounts, here, to carry me and my possibles as far as need be in Cherokee Country. Don't ask me what in blue blazes I'm supposed to be doing in Cherokee Country. A Chief Dennis Stuart, President of the Cherokee Legislature, asked the Bureau of Indian Affairs to send for me, by name, in connection with some mysterious goings on that they don't want to bother the army or Judge Parker over to Fort Smith about, no offense."

Major Midfern sniffed like a subsiding geyser and called back to the still-mounted Longarm, "His Cherokee name is Oo-na-du-ti, which means Bushy Head, and by any name he thinks he's too clever by half. We know what's eating the devious breed. But we're not supposed to know about it and we'd better talk about it in the privacy of my office, assuming you're through playing with that impossible mount."

Longarm took a deep breath and let some of it out to sound a tad more calm than he felt as he replied, "Aw, she ain't so so much a sinner as a misunderstood critter who's been sinned against, Major. She only bucks when she's spooked, and now that I know how easy it can be to spook her, I reckon I'll just use her on the trail away from any spooky distractions and ride a steadier bronc I ain't picked yet the rest of the time. Do you want to wait a few minutes whilst I choose me that second pony, or would you rather I join you in your office for that private talk about Cherokee matters?"

The older army man wrinkled his nose and decided, "Make it in less than half an hour, at the officers' club, unless you want to talk to me after a formal retreat formation and my own private supper at home with my family."

Longarm never asked why he hadn't been invited home for

4

supper with total strangers, but the army man felt obliged to add, "My mother-in-law is visiting us from back east and she'd be inclined to get excited when the topic of Mister Lo, the poor Indian, comes up."

Longarm nodded soberly and said the officers' club within half an hour sounded easier on all concerned. So the provost marshal curtly told the abashed Sergeant Mulholland to take good care of their fellow federal employee, turned on one heel, and marched off as if he aspired to be taken for a toy soldier with a ramrod up its ass.

Longarm let him get a ways off before he gingerly dismounted just inside the gate, soberly warning, "I'll kill you if you snap that cute tin clicker again, Mulholland."

The remount sergeant never did. He stood there smiling as if butter wouldn't melt in his mouth as Longarm got safely to the ground to pat old Tabitha's velvet flaresome muzzle, soothing, "Easy, girl. He ain't fixing to click that big mean beetle bug at you no more. It was just a little joke he was playing on a greenhorn. He never meant it as a joke on you, personal, you sensitive critter."

The burly sergeant asked what he was talking about as the taller but leaner lawman in the tobacco tweed suit, cavalry boots, and Colt .44-40 worn crossdraw and double-action opened the gate with his free hand to turn the calmed Tabitha over to the senior trooper and say, "I'd be obliged if you'd pick me out another trail mount and fix it up with this saddle and bridle. I somehow feel certain I won't have as much trouble next time. So I'll let you pick the other one out for me."

The stable hand took the reins. But his sergeant demanded, "What's all this bullshit about some sort of beetle bug, lawman?"

To which Longarm replied, firmly but not unkindly, "We both know what you did just now. You heard the major tell me he was expecting me to join him pronto. So I ain't got time to decide whether I ought to arrest you or just beat the shit out of you before I have to leave for Tahlequah and we'd best leave her at that unless you really aim to push it, soldier."

As the one stable hand was leading Tabitha away Sergeant Mulholland told the other to go with him and come back directly with Red Rocket saddled for their obviously drunk or deranged visitor.

Longarm didn't mind private conversations. So he said nothing before the two of them stood alone by the open gate of the empty expanse of weathered tanbark. Then he unbuckled his gunbelt and draped it over the gatepost, quietly asking, "Might this reassure you if you'd care to dance, little darling?"

Like most born bullies, Sergeant Mulholland could get friendly as a chastised pup when it looked as if he might be whupped for pissing on the hall runner or mistaking a tall tanned gent with eyes the color of gun muzzles for a safe man to push. So he shook his head hard and protested, "Nobody said nothing about no trip to Fist City with a gent the major's waiting for in the officers' club! I ain't packing one of them toy beetle bugs that kids can click sneaky in a schoolroom, if that's what you're talking about!"

Longarm said, "That's what I'm talking about. I heard you click it as I passed this very gate aboard an otherwise natural mount who's inclined to spook mighty wild at the sounds of metallic clicking. I reckon something that clicked the same way caused her some anguish in her younger days. If horses could talk I'd ask her what it was about such sounds that unsettled her. But since she can't talk, I can't ask and suffice it to say I'll just have to keep it in mind that Tabitha is inclined to go *loco en la cabeza* at such sounds. Just like you've been keeping it in mind for whatever reason you've been spooking her so's nobody in this outfit has wanted to ride her."

Mulholland protested, "That's crazy. Tabitha bucked me off the day she got here! Ask any man on the post if you don't believe me. Why on earth would any man want to spook a pony he was trying to break in his ownself?"

Longarm shrugged and said, "You'd know that better than me. I hope you're just a poor loser who can't abide the notion of a better rider setting more horseflesh than he can manage on his own. On the other hand, I knew this mess sergeant who managed to sell a whole lot of army rations he'd been told to get rid of as unfit to eat. You have to really work at making army rations smell that awesomely bad. But he concocted this water-soluble formula he could wash off a side of beef or a rasher of bacon once he had a buyer."

6

Longarm saw they were coming back with his private saddle aboard a red pony that stood around fourteen hands on his short but sturdy legs. So he casually reached for his gunbelt and strapped it back on under his frock coat as he quietly added, "That mess sergeant with the secret formula ain't with the army no more. He'll get his D. D., printed on yellow paper, at the prison gate, once he's served his time-at-hard in Leavenworth. I don't know why they bother to print dishonorable discharges on any sort of paper. Do you? I've never in my life met up with anybody who wanted to show me his dishonorable discharge from any branch of the service."

Mulholland licked his suddenly dry lips and protested, "Hold on! I ain't never in this life tried to sell no army mounts to anybody at any price! You heard the major say Tabitha was a man-killer and, all right, you did piss me off a mite by riding her so good, both ways. I was only trying to get you throwed, Lord love you! I ain't been trying to get any innocent cavalry mount condemned unjust. Tabitha *is* a man-killer and it ain't too late to let us fix you up with another mount to go with old Red Rocket, yonder!"

Longarm shook his head and said, "You heard me tell that officer I meant to ride her out on the lonesome trail where nobody figures to click nothing metal at her. I was just about to say, before you clicked that beetle bug in your pants and made her buck like a string of firecrackers, that she rode comfortable with a mile-eating gait a man could get used to out in the middle of nowheres."

As the stable hands led the calmer-looking Red Rocket over for a closer inspection, Longarm added, "This chunky gelding looks as if a man could ride him into an Indian camp without the barking dogs and snot-nosed kids shying him too much. So have him and the bigger gray ready for me when I come back, before that prissy retreat formation, Lord willing and nobody stands me at attention in front of the ladies!"

As he started to turn away, the bemused Sergeant Mulholland asked, "Don't you want to ride Red Rocket around the paddock before you make up your mind about him?"

To which Longarm could only reply, "My mind's made up. I ain't got time to find out whether you've tried to stick me with another outlaw bronc or not. I have a long night ride ahead of me and I told you boys to pick me a steady second mount. So I'm assuming you have and, if you haven't, you'd best all commend your souls to Jesus, for all three of your asses will belong to *me*!"

Chapter 2

Field grade officers didn't belly up to the bar in any officers' club. So Longarm found Major Midfern seated at a corner table with a younger captain, a pitcher of ice water, and a fifth of bourbon.

An extra glass was waiting in front of an empty chair with its back to the dance floor. So Longarm took it when the Major waved at it, even though sitting with his back so exposed made him itch betwixt the shoulder blades.

The junior officer turned out to be a Captain Bleeker, attached to the provost marshal's office to lead military police patrols in the field. Longarm had noticed the darker tan and leaner hips right off. Major Midfern allowed he'd asked Bleeker to sit in because the Cherokee situation kept changing day by day, usually for the worse.

Bleeker said, "Right now we're worried about the Kituhwa night riders. The major, here, tells me you were planning on riding over to Tahlequah after dark?"

Longarm commenced to build himself a bourbon and branch water high ball as he calmly replied, "Two reasons. I was asked to sort of drift in discreet and report to Chief Bushyhead on the sly and, after that, it gets hot as hell in high summer over this way, no offense. But tell me more about them Kituhwa riders."

Bleeker shrugged and said, "They're a secret society. By definition there's not much to tell about any bunch that meets in secret. One of our Cherokee informants tells us they're mostly pure-bloods with a hard-on for the so called Tribal

9

Government Washington keeps recognizing and a sentimental hankering for a glorious past, when the Cherokee made everybody else more uneasy. My point is that the Kituhwa ride by starlight and it's a hard night's ride to Tahlequah with nobody laying for you!"

Longarm shrugged and said, "I don't see why any secret society of sentimental Indians would be laying for this child. I've never in my born days counted coup on any old-time Cherokee and nobody but the tribal leaders who sent for me are supposed to know I'm coming."

Major Midfern grimaced and said, "Everybody knows you're coming. I used to think white women gossiped before I was sent out here to cope with Cherokee. The man who said two could keep a secret as long as one of them lay dead must have spent some time around here. We've tried in vain to get official word on your mission out of the white agents Bushyhead had to go through. But we knew you were coming, and why you were coming, before you left Denver."

Longarm took a sip, decided it needed less ice water, and proceeded to lace his drink stronger as he mildly asked if some damned body would kindly tell *him* what in blue thunder he was doing there in the Cherokee Strip.

Major Midfern grimaced and said, "There isn't any Cherokee Strip on any map. We'll get back to that in a minute. You asked why Bushyhead sent all the way to Colorado for outside help with a delicate matter. I don't know why the sly old dog chose you in particular. But I know what's eating him. He's got a serious moonshine liquor problem on his hands and Cherokee take it so *personal* when their own tribal police arrest them for bending the white man's law."

Longarm frowned, tasted his drink, and decided it would do and swallowed some of it before he demanded, "I've been hauled all the way from my way cooler federal district to arrest moonshiners running corn liquor to Mister Lo, the poor Indian?"

The two army men exchanged amused glances. Then Midfern told him, "Not exactly. The state of Kansas, directly to our north, just voted itself dry. So drinkable whiskey has just gone from three dollars a gallon to twenty and it's still hard to buy in some counties. So the moonshiners in this case are

Indians, running forbidden fire water to the cowboys, see?"

Longarm had to laugh. So he did. Then he sobered and asked how come the more law-abiding Cherokee hadn't asked for help from Fort Smith to the east, where Hanging Judge Isaac Parker ran a tight ship and had as tough a crew of federal deputies as such bullshit usually called for.

Midfern said, "I just told you. The situation is delicate. There's no way in hell any white lawman, yourself included, is about to track down Cherokee outlaws in Cherokee country without Cherokee help. When some worthless asshole Cherokee such as Sam Starr steals horses from other Cherokee, no Cherokee gives a pig's ass whether Parker's deputies haul him in to stand trial in a white man's court. Few if any Indians would deny a common thief deserves to be punished. After that, things get less certain. Washington will pass laws forbidding Indians to do things Indians just want to go on doing and the Five Civilized Tribes were distilling their own sour mash before President Jackson marched them west across the Mississippi."

Captain Bleeker chimed in, "Your opposite numbers out of Fort Smith have been searching high and low for those Indian moonshiners. For the state of Kansas asked them to. We've had our own patrols out, policing for trouble in general. The treaty of '66 provides that the Cherokee and Osage police to our north have the exclusive right to arrest any and all Indian outlaws on Indian range while we, in turn, get to take in any white outlaws raiding or hiding out in the Indian territory."

He raised his own glass to mutter darkly into it, "That's a laugh."

Longarm shot him a natural puzzled look. So Major Midfern quietly explained, "Sorting the sheep from the goats can be a problem. That same treaty of '66, negotiated after the Cherokee gave Washington quite a scare during the war at Pea Ridge, provides for the Cherokee, themselves, to decide just who might or might not be a Cherokee, or what Bushyhead defines as a citizen of the Cherokee Nation."

Bleeker snorted, "Nation my aunt Fanny Addams! They lost complete self government rights when they sided with the Confederacy to hold on to their own slaves. I don't see why Washington has to coddle the slippery bastards and if I had

11

my way they'd be treated the same as any other redskins!"

Major Midfern sighed and said, "Ours not to reason why and while I want to puke every time I hear that pissing and moaning about the so-called Trail of Tears, what's done is done and we're all stuck in the here and now with the confusing results."

"The major mentioned sheep and goats," said Longarm, hoping to get some sense out of them so he could be on his infernal way.

The provost marshal said, "They call the Cherokee, Chickasaw, Choctaw, Creek, and Seminole the Five Civilized Tribes because, back around the turn of the century, their mostly breed leaders convinced 'em that if they couldn't lick us they should join us. A lot of the eastern nations had taken to white improvements such as the horse and wagon, the plow, glass windows in warmer housing, and so forth. Some credit a Cherokee named George Gis or Guess with introducing his own nation to literacy. It's more fashionable today to call him Sequoia. Some Cherokee I've talked to recall him as a visionary with a serious drinking problem. But some more practical Cherokee did put out their own newspaper, the *Cherokee Phoenix*, with the help of a Congregational missionary, back in New Echota, Georgia, in that lost Cherokee Garden of Eden they still pester everyone about."

"They've done lots of wonders and eaten lots of cucumbers with the help of Tanned Yankees, or white men playing Indian," snapped the well-tanned Captain Bleeker, who added, "You should see all those blue-eyed Cherokee herding Texas cattle over in the Outlet right this minute. I don't even want to talk about Black Cherokee."

Major Midfern must have. He poured more bourbon for himself as he explained, "Like most Iriquoians, the Cherokee were matrilineal back in their original mountain hunting grounds. Our own kind, of course, inherits from the father's side. So white traders turned squaw men produced an unnatural tribal aristocracy of well-born breeds. Few if any pure bloods could compete with a so called fellow tribesman who claimed all the rights of his mother's clan while he got to run his late father's family business."

Bleeker growled, "All the Cherokee chiefs since the late

seventeen hundreds have been part white. That great John Ross they love to brag about was seven-eighths Scotch-Irish, for Gawd's sake, and that much *nigger* wouldn't show when you went to shave in the morning!"

Major Midfern said, "The poor persecuted Cherokee hung on to their Negro slaves as they suffered all the way west, after accepting money for their land and travel expenses from the government. They naturally had to free their slaves after the war, the same as everyone else. But as the former property of Cherokee masters, said slaves were one and all declared free Cherokee by the Bureau of Indian Affairs. We figure at least one third of the so called Cherokee, enjoying all the advantages of their martyrdom, don't have a drop of Indian blood to call their own."

"The major is speaking of the so called Nation or proper reservation to the northeast," Captain Bleeker pointed out. He drained his glass and added, "It gets even sillier over in the Outlet, where those Tex-Mex cowboys are grazing beef meant for white tables on Cherokee grass at a few cents a head per month. My men and me have seen more white whores than Cherokee out yonder and we're talking about a whole lot of land being held tax free by absentee landlords who keep accusing us of robbing them!"

Rising to his feet, the junior officer asked his major's permit to get his MP troop ready for the pending retreat formation.

Midfern let him go and turned back to Longarm to say, "That makes two of us. I haven't much time left to talk you out of riding out for Tahlequah alone, after dark. Why don't you let us put you up for the night in our BOQ and send you on your way in the morning with the mail wagon and its guard detail?"

Longarm shook his head and answered, "That ain't my notion of any discreet approach to the gents who sent for me, no offense. But, seeing it was you who corrected my notion there might be a Cherokee Strip and allowed we could talk about that later, it's later and I'm still sort of confused."

Midfern made a wry face and said, "Welcome to the Indian territory, where confusion is the intent of all self-serving Indian agents, said Indians, and anybody else who can elbow his way to the pork barrel."

The older army man took out his watch, scowled at it as if he'd been hoping it was later, and leaned back to begin, "When President Jackson told the Supreme Court to go to hell and told the Five Civilized Tribes to head out this way, he overlooked the Osage who were already hunting and dwelling out this way in the sincere conviction it was their own Horse Indian range. All of it. Nothing from Wakan Tanka about sharing it with Indians or part-Indians from back east."

Longarm nodded and said, "I got to work with the Osage police in connection with an earlier case. You're right about the Great Mystery they follow. Osage could best be defined as friendlier Sioux-Hokan speakers than their Dakota-Lakota-Nakota cousins further north. How did Old Hickory manage to keep his Osage brothers from becoming as famous as, say, Red Cloud or Crazy Horse?"

Major Midfern said, "By paying them off and giving them their own reservation, centered on their traditional meeting grounds just to the northwest of here. The Cherokee had been promised more land than you could fit between the Osage along the Verdigris River and the Arkansas line. So Washington set aside an even bigger block, most of it prairie, running east and west just south of the Kansas line. Its official name is the Cherokee Outlet. The original notion was for the Cherokee to occupy it once they'd filled the eastern reserve up. Each Cherokee family has been granted the right to claim a full section of land, or four times as much as whites are allowed under the Homestead Act. But, so far, their original allotment stands mostly empty and not one Cherokee clan or family organized along Christian lines has seen fit to settle in the Outlet. Some whites passing through it call that Cherokee land the Cherokee Strip. Others confuse the term with that narrower strip of unincorporated federal land, between Colorado and the Texas Panhandle with Indian territory, while still others would have it that the north-south original Cherokee grants should be called their strip, because it's obviously shaped like a sort of strip along the Arkansas line."

Longarm nodded and said, "I reckon I won't call nothing a Cherokee Strip, then. How come some call the part most Cherokee live in either a nation or a reserve?"

Midfern shrugged and said, "It depends on whom you ask.

All five of the original civilized tribes were reduced to agency status after abusing their original rights to greater self-determination by siding with the Confederacy. The Osage, who'd never claimed to be civilized under their own full-blood leaders, were smart enough to fight for the Union against Kansas rebel raiders. So who do you expect to wind up with all that reserve land in the so called Cherokee Outlet, in the end?"

"White men," said Longarm, who read more than he let on around the office, before he demanded, "Are you saying the Cherokee Nation and the Cherokee Reservation are the same thing, as far as Uncle Sam sees her?"

Midfern shook his head and said, "No. We're talking about an Indian reservation with limited self-government, subject to continued common sense on the part of the elected tribal legislature and administration. What the Indians want to call it is their own beeswax, confusing as it all may sound to outsiders."

Longarm started to pour himself more bourbon, decided he'd better start out sober in the dark with one pony he'd never ridden and the other a certified lunatic, and told the major, "Thanks to you and Captain Bleeker I ain't half as confused as I was when I showed up this afternoon. You cleared away a wondersome ammount of cobwebs when you declared the Cherokee powers-that-be an *elected* government. For I'd hate like hell to send my own lawmen after the popular kith and kin of registered voters if I didn't have to and, if I had the Great White Father to pin the donkey's tail on, I wouldn't have to!"

He reached for a smoke instead of another snort as he thoughtfully added, "But how come I'd send all the way to Colorado for a lawman who wouldn't know how to order a meal in Cherokee? Assuming neither you army MPs nor our other deputy marshals out of Fort Smith would be able to catch anybody on Cherokee range without Cherokee help . . ."

Major Midfern sounded certain as he said, "That's easy. You'll be even less likely to succeed. Did I fail to mention how poor old Chief John Ross wound up at this end of the Trail of Tears in a two-story mansion, served by house slaves, while others worked his two hundred acres of tobacco or herded his livestock on the open range all about?"

To which Longarm could only reply, "Nope. But I'm starting to see why ladies and gents born with blue eyes might claim Cherokee blood, and there's always been more money in alcohol than tobacco."

Chapter 3

The peacetime army held Retreat, or lowered the flag and called it a day at five in the afternoon. So Longarm had plenty of daylight left to work with as he rode off the military reservation with the army band playing wistfully behind him. It was hard to say why old soldiers got lumps in their throats every time they heard Retreat being sounded. Such lumps seemed to get bigger as one got farther away from the army in time and distance. Retreat-call likely reminded old soldiers of how young they'd felt riding off post into the nearest town or how unfair it seemed for most civilian jobs to keep all noses to that grindstone until six or later.

Longarm was glad he was off post, riding Red Rocket and leading old Tabitha, by the time that band cut loose. Albeit in truth the skittish gray mare didn't seem to worry her fool self about the sounds of fifes, drums, or bugles. Longarm made a mental note to watch for cricket chirps on the trail ahead as he led her, bareback, on a long lead for such time as the smaller pony he was riding needed a break.

So far, Red Rocket carried a rider at a steady three-mile-an-hour walk, with neither more effort nor spirit than he might have pulled a plow in light soil. So it was Tabitha he was more concerned about when a locomotive whistle blasted unexpectedly just off to their right.

But nothing happened, even as Longarm gripped the lead line tighter and braced himself to play a plunging pony like a sailfish fighting the hook in frisky weather. Tabitha wasn't spooked by train whistles, either. It sure beat all how a man just never knew when a woman or a pony was fixing to cloud up and rain all over him, or vice versa. When she wasn't having a fit, old Tabitha, like many a gal he'd met up with in his time, could be fine company. So he was looking forward to riding her some more out on the open range ahead.

Meanwhile they were coming to the railroad tracks and telegraph lines serving the military post and such from the north. So Longarm kept a good grip on that lead line and a sharp eye open all around for anything that might go twang or plunk. The eastbound train's caboose was closer to them as they approached the crossing. That locomotive had sounded down at the far end and now its bell was chiming for everybody to get a move on, damn it. The mellower clangs of the big brass bell didn't seem to spook Tabitha either. He saw some freight handlers loading a canvas-covered Studebaker wagon with heavy looking wooden crates. That had to be what was holding the train up. Longarm didn't care. He'd arrived aboard an earlier passenger combination and there wasn't any railroad depot over to Tahlequah, bless all five civilized tribes.

So he'd have just crossed over and ridden on, left to his own devices. But suddenly a husky-looking gal wearing a tall crowned black hat, a man's denim outfit, and a brace of Manhattan .36s came out of nowhere with a coiled mule skinner's whip in hand to wave it up at him as he called, "Don't snap that whip, ma'am. I'm leading a proddy pony who turns into a box kite every time she hears a sudden pop!"

The big gal, who wasn't bad looking under the brim of that ugly hat, grinned impishly up at Longarm to reply, "I know old Tabitha of old. They tell me you just rode her. You're headed over to Tahlequah on that secret mission, ain't you?"

To which Longarm could only reply with a sigh, "I thought I was. I'd be U.S. Deputy Marshal Custis Long, as if you didn't know."

She said, "I'd be Petunia Squirreltail and I'm trucking a load of jam jars over to the general store in Tahlequah. If you have a minute we might take that trail together, with night coming on and there being safety in numbers."

Longarm knew he'd make way better time alone. Then he reconsidered what she'd said she was carrying and how, back home in West-By-God Virginia, the moonshiners up amid the second growth hardwood had sold their corn whiskey by the jar. So instead of making some polite excuse and riding on, Longarm ticked the brim of his own hat to the lady and gravely replied, "I heard about them night riders, ma'am. Could you use any help getting that wagon loaded?"

The oddly named white gal, for she hardly looked Indian to Longarm, allowed the train crew she'd paid extra had just about finished down the track. She added, "If I was you I'd lead old Tabitha on a ways lest she spook when the couplers clatter, starting up again. Me and my mules will be along directly if you'd care to wait for us under them blackjacks a furlong up the road."

Longarm allowed he might and rode on as far as the windrow of blackjack oak someone had drilled in along a fence line facing the wagon trace. As he reined in, two bitty colored kids drifted over to the bob wire strung betwixt the tree trunks to gaze up in wonder at him.

That was to say, they appeared to be colored kids, a boy and a girl, until the raggedy boy called out to demand, "Might you be an *Ontwaganha* or *Tsalagi*, mister?"

To which Longarm could only reply, "I ain't sure, sonny. What might either of them critters you just mentioned be?"

The kid who sure looked colored smugly answered, "You have to be an *Ontwaganha*. Any *Tsalagi* would know what an *Ontwaganha* was!"

The little girl whispered something in a lingo Longarm couldn't follow and the two of them ran off, laughing. Their Black Cherokee elders had doubtless told them to beware of white men, if that was what an *Ontwaganha* might be.

Longarm got out a three-for-a-nickel cheroot and just had it lit when that train in the middle distance started up with another toot. Tabitha didn't spook, and Longarm saw Petunia Squirreltail along the far side to the crossing. So he just stayed put and enjoyed a few drags until she drove her six mule team abreast with him without stopping and he fell in beside her wagon without asking how come. He'd had to start a team from a dead stop with a heavy load in his day.

Petunia seemed too busy to talk until they'd made it to the crest of the gentle but tedious rise beyond that first farm. Then she held the ribbons looser and called up, "You'd ride as easy and the two of us could talk way better if you'd care to join me on this lonesome perch, Custis."

He doubted the unsprung wagon seat would be easier on any ass than a well broke-in saddle aboard a steady mount. But she was right about how tough it was to converse casual whilst shouting. So he fell back and, sure enough, old Petunia reined in just over the crest and shoved the brake lever with one booted foot so's he could dismount and tether the two cavalry mounts to the tailgate of her freight wagon.

He figured as long as he was at it he'd unsaddle Red Rocket and let the wagon carry his heavily laden McClellan. It gave him an excuse to peek inside when he had to open the canvas, drawn nearly shut, across the rear cover-bow. But there was nothing to be seen in the wagon bed but a couple of dozen sturdy crates marked, "FRAGILE NO HOOKS DON'T DROP!" as he drew his Winchester '73 from its saddle boot and jogged around the off side to join the big raw-boned but not bad looking gal on the front seat.

Petunia started the team, easy, without having to snap her whip on the down slope. She seemed to be riding the brake lever with one denim-sheathed leg, as a matter of fact, and there was something to be said for wearing pants whilst driving a freight wagon, as scandalous as it might seem to Queen Victoria and her pals.

Petunia said that tobacco he was smoking smelled good. So he got out another cheroot, lit it for her, and stuck it bewixt her lips as she drove on with both dainty fists sort of busy.

She thanked him and said, "I've been thinking about that spooky mare you brung along for some strange reason. Everybody knows Tabitha spooks at snapping sounds. They don't have to be too loud. It's the quality, not the quantity she can't abide. So what if we was to stuff her ears with say some milkweed silk? The milkweeds are ripe with pods all over the nation and—"

Longarm cut in to say, "I've already considered having a vet do her eardrums with a more sanitary needle. But I'd rather not, if it can be avoided. It seems sort of mean to make a pony go deaf on purpose."

The lady teamster innocently asked, "How come? Lord

knows she can't be happy in a world so filled with clicks and clacks and don't we cut a stud horse's balls off just to gentle him down a mite? Speaking for myself, I'd much rather spend the rest of my born days hard-of-hearing than without no tender feeling betwixt my legs!"

Longarm laughed. But his ears were burning as he admitted that made two of them. He'd never met a mule skinner who didn't talk sort of down-home. It likely went with cussing so much whilst spending so much time alone on the open range.

Since it was still broad day, they were both wearing buttoned up pants, and he wasn't sure whether their traveling together had been her own notion or as directed by somebody else, Longarm tried to get them back to more polite conversation by bringing up those colored kids and the odd words they'd flung at him, back yonder.

Petunia corrected his pronunciation and explained the subtle but important distinction betwixt *Ontwaganha* and "White Man."

She said, "It translates more properly as stranger. Anybody who's not *Tsalagi*, or Cherokee, as it's said in English. *Tseroki* was what we called our country back east. The folk who belonged to the seven clans of the forty-three towns of *Tseroki* called themselves *Tsalagi*. But don't worry about it. Anybody in the nation you might want to talk to speaks English. They have to, if they mean to be important out our way."

He asked, "You mean to get a square deal from the BIA?"

She laughed bitterly and replied, "The day we get a square deal off the top of the deck will be the day I walk on water and turn water into wine. My people find it easier to learn English than all three of the so called Cherokee dialects. Four, if you consider the mixed up tribal members who came out here before the *Nuna da ut sun'ee* and sort of made up their own blend of *Tsalagi* before the rest of us had to join them."

Petunia sighed and said, "My elders took the *Nuna da ut sun'ee* west but I was born out here. So, like a good many of us, I can count off *Saquo, Tali, Tsoy* in the lingo, say my prayers and most of the dirty words in the same. But after that I seldom have call to say anything in *Tsalagi* to anybody on or off the reservation, see?"

"I'm commencing to," Longarm replied, blowing a thoughtful smoke ring at the off rear mule's brown rump before adding, "It reminds me of other second or third generation immigrant folk I've met up with in my travels. Homesteaders with Swedish names barely manage some baby talk Swedish when they're feeling sentimental, and Irish cowhands like to talk dirty in the Gaelic until somebody who really speaks the Gaelic tries to talk to them. I know this ain't none of my beeswax, Miss Petunia, but was it your mom or your dad you got that light brown hair from?"

She sounded unconcerned as she answered, "Hard to say. I have red, white, and likely black roots on both sides. I just told you we define folk as my kind of folk and your kind of folk. Think of being *Tsalagi* or Cherokee as belonging to a *nationality* rather than a complexion. I know the BIA defines us as Indians. I have my own BIA Allotment Number to prove it. But holding one drop of Indian blood don't make you all Indian any more than holding a dash of white or black blood makes any born Cherokee a white or black *Ontwaganha*. I don't see why you fool *Ontwaganhas* can't understand that."

Longarm said, "I'm trying to understand it. I just find the legal ramifications sort of complexicated. How might you paid-up members of the Cherokee Nation tell a black or white citizen who ought to be here from a black or white drifter or even an outlaw."

She shrugged and said, "How do you *Ontwaganhas* tell any white or black stranger from a neighbor? How do you tell an immigrant from a native-born registered voter?"

"We snoop," said Longarm with a sheepish smile. Then he asked her why she was driving so fast down another slope they'd come to. But she just snapped the ribbons to lash the rumps of her leaders as they started rolling even faster. So Longarm stood in the dash to grab the forward bow and leaned out for a look back at the ponies he hoped he might still see tethered to the tail gate.

He could. Both Red Rocket and spooky old Tabitha seemed to be enjoying the downhill romp as Petunia drove lickety-split up the left fork of the tree-shaded junction she'd been aiming for. Longarm asked why as she reined in under some low box elder branches, set the brakes, and rose from her seat to face backward as she drew one of her six-guns and said,

"Riders trailing us. They looked like *Kituhwa*. Nobody else wears feathers and fox tails on their wool hats at this late date!"

Longarm picked up his Winchester and levered a round of .44-40 in the chamber as he rose to peer over the cover-bows at her side, saying, "Pulling up to let the dust settle might or might not have been a good move. We're just out of sight from that fork and the dust is still high betwixt them tree branches. Run that word, *Kituhwa*, past this child again. I think that's what some officers I just talked to called a sort of Cherokee secret society, right?"

Petunia wrinkled her freckled nose and said, "Picture your own Ku Klux Klan and then make them meaner and crazier on the subject of race relations."

He said, "Nobody is crazier than the Klan about race relations and didn't you just tell me you Cherokee fold didn't worry yourselves as much as some about such matters?"

She repressed a shudder and explained, "*Kituhwa* worry a heap about most everything. The full-bloods who founded the society seem to want to turn the clock back. They say it's time to purge the nation of all newfangled *Ontwaganha* notions and go back to the old ways we followed before the *Nana da ut sun'ee*, in the hills of *Tseroki*!"

She drew one of her five-shot Manhattans as she calmly continued, "That was when they really civilized us. You'd call it the Indian Removal Act. We called it the Trail of Tears. The *Kituhwa* have never called it anything else, or forgiven anybody the least bit."

Chapter 4

Whilst Petunia held the ribbons with the brakes on, Longarm and his Winchester made their way back to a better field of fire over the tailgate. He lay belly down across the crates with both elbows braced over his saddle as he covered the rear. Red Rocket and Tabitha had drifted over to the low-slung tree branches to inhale some leaves, box elder growing greener than most grass, this late in the summer. As the spooky gray mare rolled one curious eye at him, Longarm confided to her in a soothing tone, "I ain't pointing this gun at you. I'm still sort of working on who I might be pointing it at."

The sun shone low and bloodshot from between some ominous purple thunderheads to the west. So Longarm started to ask the suspicious mare if she thought she'd be able to make out fox tails pinned to any rider's broad brimmed hat at any distance against such a glowering sky. But he never did. Tabitha wouldn't have been able to follow his drift and he didn't want old Petunia, up forward, to suspect he might suspect her of making phantom riders up from thin evening air.

A million years passed slowly by and then, by the Great Horn Spoon, they did hear hoofbeats coming closer and closer, then passing on up that other road they'd been traveling. It sounded like half a dozen riders or another wagon team moving at a slow steady trot.

Longarm made himself count to five hundred Mississippis before he stirred in the now-dead silence to crawl back over the crates to join Petunia in the front again, soberly saying, "Whoever that might have been, they took the other road. That

24

would be the post road from Fort Gibson to Tahlequah, right?"

The tall white Cherokee gal put her gun away, released the brakes, and snapped her ribbons to head on up the back road as she explained, "This route will take us there almost as fast and way safer. The *Kituhwa* ain't inclined to night-ride the back roads unless they're paying a call on somebody in particular. There's this crossroad up ahead we can follow east after we've only passed Tahlequa to our east by three miles or less."

Longarm shrugged and let her call the tune, allowing the lady had to know her own country best. This was the simple truth once you stared hard at it. Nobody had asked if he'd been through these parts at all before and he didn't recall this particular neck of the woods from any earlier cases.

So he just sat smoking with his Winchester across his thighs as she drove on with the sun sinking ever lower and the scenery taking on that sentimental shade the world gets toward sundown.

He'd noticed that time over by Younger's Bend that despite all the pissing and moaning about a Great American Desert the new lands ceded west of the Mississippi to the Cherokee were almost as well timbered and watered as their older eastern ranges. For the western foothills of the Arkansas Ozarks extended across Cherokee holdings as far as Fort Gibson, where the Neosho ran into the Arkansas River. The more open range west of the Neosho was rolling long grass praire with wooded draws. Since they were northeast of the Neosho the rolling country all around was well endowed with blackjack, box elder, choke cherry, locust, wild plum and such, with alder and willow tanglewood in the boggy draws.

The stirrup-deep grass betwixt tree stands was mostly bluestem and the range was in good condition depite the season and the widely scattered range cows they spooked in passing. Most of the cows seemed to be Black Cherokee, a thrifty cross betwixt the Texas Longhorn and heavier Black Angus beef stock. As the shadows lengthened and critters who'd been denned all day came out to play in the cooler shades of evening, Longarm spotted more than one flock of quail and some fine fat deer that would have tempted him sore if there'd been time to dress and hang some venison properly.

25

The sky ahead was a dark enough blue for the brighter stars to wink on one at a time as, off in the gathering dusk, a rainbird was bitching at them, or about the weather. Neither Longarm nor the gal born and raised in the Indian territory said it was starting to feel like rain. It was usually city folk who made such comments to country folk, and they were under the canvas hood of her freight wagon if that rainbird turned out to be correct about those clouds to the west.

Longarm was more interested in that load in the back, once it seemed they weren't being followed along this less-traveled wagon trace. When he asked her who on earth would want so many jam jars all at once, she told him, "I said I was delivering them to the Tahlequah general store. They sell heaps of jars this time of the year, with harvest time coming on. It was our Iroquois uncles who taught us the secret of preserving fruits and berries, after they'd learned it from the Black Robes. We *Tsalagi* were converted by less practical missionaries than the Black Robes. But our Iroquois uncles were willing to pass the secrets of the more clever Black Robes on to us."

"Like distilling whiskey?" Longarm just had to ask.

The white Cherokee gal shook her head and innocently replied, "We learned that from our Scotch-Irish kith and kin along the Tennessee. The Black Robes made wine they drank instead of the Black Drink when they wanted to talk to their own *Nayehi*. *I* only pray to *Eithinoha* when I'm *scared*. My mother prayed to Jesus and He didn't do a thing for her when she took sick with the consumption. So I'll just stick with the Great Mother both my granddams trusted in, if it's all the same with you."

Longarm said he didn't care who anybody prayed to as long as they didn't require his participation or cash contributions. When he said he'd heard some Scotch-Irish and High-Dutch missionaries had been sent to do good amongst the Cherokee she said some had made out mighty good indeed.

She said one white sky pilot with a Cherokee wife had left an estate of four hundred cows, one hundred horses, and fifty slaves, along with his parish, to his half-breed missionary son and heir. He'd already heard how the Ross family had bred themselves mostly white as they'd accumulated Indian honors and white wealth. The sainted John Ross had cashed in his chips before Longarm had started riding for the Justice Department. So he had no call to doubt the blue-eyed chief had done as well as he could by his fellow Indians and the less said about how well his brother Lew Ross had done as a slave trader the better.

He asked Petunia how many other important Cherokee had pure white names and she came up with Adair, Gunter, Penn, Rogers, Taylor, and Vann before she had to stop, think, and decide, "The Bushyheads, Path Killers, Redbirds, and Ten-Killers are as likely to have blond hair or blue eyes, while some *Tsalagi* with pure Indian names such as Pushmataha may be just as white, or black. I told you before that we think of it more as citizenship than race."

"I see you make Bushyhead one name, like Townsend," observed Longarm just before asking, "How come them *Kituhwa* you say you saw seemed to be following you, me, or us in general if our complexions don't matter to anybody in these parts?"

She grimaced and said, "Oh, the silly things could be out to keep me pure. I know that sounds silly. I just said they were silly. But I fear they consider me a *Tsalagi* maiden and we all know what you are, you fresh *Ontwaganha!*"

Longarm said, "You're right. It's just plain silly and I hope that was an owl-bird spitting on the toe of my boot just now. For if it wasn't we could be in for some wet weather ahead!"

She said she hoped it rained like hell and gave all those night riders the galloping consumption. They hadn't driven much farther when her wish seemed to be coming to pass. The sunset sky went from blood red to black as a bitch, with the rain coming down in sheets you could only see when lightning flashed as it chewed at the canvas above them and filled the exposed wagon boot with warm spit.

They drove on in spite of the storm until the next draw they came upon was exposed by lightning as a newly invented river. Petunia said it was no use trying to ford before the rain let up and Longarm was in no position to argue. So he helped her lead her mules into a wind-breaking willow grove, unhitch them from the heavy wagon, and tether them securely with nose bags of cracked corn. He would have tethered both his borrowed cavalry mounts the same way. But Tabitha had busted loose to run off through the storm. He could only hope she'd wind up back at Fort Gibson as he made the only panic-stricken Red Rocket as comfortable as he could manage amid the rain-lashed willows.

He was feeling mighty rain-lashed himself as he joined the soaked to-the-skin Petunia in the wagon bed on top of the jam jar crates while the wind kept trying to tear the canvas top off. Her teeth chattered as she tried not to cry and gamely managed to say she meant to go easy on her prayers to *Ga-oh* in the future. He'd been wondering what Cherokee called the Thunder Bird.

He suggested, "Look on the bright side. Ain't no night riders likely to come looking for us here, wherever in tarnation here might be. Do you have the least notion where we've just wound up, surrounded by all this confusion?"

She said she had a fair notion where they were, but didn't see how they'd be able to go on or turn back with this gully washer in progress. She added, "We're never going to make it to Tahlequah under cover of darkness and you know what they're bound to say when I drive in by broad daylight with an *Ontwaganha* as good looking as you! Can you see me in this light?"

Longarm blinked and told her, "I can barely make out my own hand in front of me when the lightning flashes. Might that be important to you for some reason?"

She said, "We'll catch our deaths in these wet duds before the day dawns cold as the clay. I have a sleeping bag and a change of underthings stored behind the seat. I'm going to strip my wet hide bare and bundle my goose bumps up in dry blankets. The *Kituhwa* are going to kill us if they find us alone like this in any case and I may as well get comfortable whilst I await my fate!"

Longarm forced a chuckle and said, "Go ahead and strip, then. It's not a bad notion and I have my own bedroll lashed to my saddle. What do you reckon they'd say if they caught us both naked as jays in two separate bedrolls?"

She laughed sort of wildly and replied, "Nobody knows what those crazy night riders say to folk before they kill them. Nobody they've killed has ever told anybody else."

Longarm could hear the sibilant wet whisper of wet cloth

peeling off damp limbs and it was a caution how shemale it suddenly smelled under the flapping canvas wagon cover. He crawled back to where he'd left his saddle and unlashed his own roll to spread it out across the load before he started to shuck his own wet duds.

He draped his gunbelt over the saddle, put his watch, derringer, wallet, and such in the crown of his upside-down Stetson and got his shivering bare hide betwixt the summer-weight flannel blankets atop the canvas ground cloth and waterproof tarp. The crates under him were not much harder than the grassy ground outside might have been, had it been dry enough to consider, so he was already feeling better when it occurred to him that somebody had crawled over in the dark to join him, naked as a jay and still goose bumped, to hear Petunia tell it.

No natural man would have fought a naked lady off as she tried to crawl into a bedroll with him. So Longarm never did, but even as Petunia slithered down the length of his bare flank, her pubic hair wet as a sponge all the way, Longarm felt obliged to ask her if she thought he was made of wood, adding, "I thought I heard you say some of your own boys don't approve of outsiders playing slap and tickle with Cherokee maidens."

She giggled and threw one bare thigh across his middle to snuggle even closer as she confided, "They're going to accuse me in any case. So why have the name without the game? Don't you think I'm pretty?"

Longarm kissed her, as most men would have, and then before he could roll over on top of her, Petunia had grabbed his dawning erection as if to use it as a saddle horn whilst she rose to mount him, gasping with girlish glee as she impaled her rapidly warming flesh on all he had to offer.

It almost went soft inside her when she moaned, "Oh, this makes me feel so *uwodu* and I was so afraid I'd never get to fuck the famous Longarm!"

He couldn't go soft as she leaned forward to brush his bare chest with her turgid nipples whilst she slid her clinging innards up and down as fast as if she was sitting on a trotting pony. But as soon as he had come in her that way and rolled her over on her own back to spread her thighs wider and come

29

in her some more, he chuckled fondly, kissed her French, and demanded, "Fess up, honey. Were you just out to count coup on my notorious pecker or have we really been dodging them night riders I've yet to lay eyes on?"

She moaned. "Don't take it out! Let me just clasp it and cling to pleasant memories if you don't want any more! There was somebody over on that main road who might have been following us. You heard them go by yourself."

He held most of his weight politely on his elbows as they both let nature and her internal pulsations take their course. He said, "That ain't what I asked. I'll confess I wanted to fuck you as soon as I saw you if you'll admit you took this back road in hopes I might!"

She sighed, bit down harder with her amazing vaginal muscles, and said, "I can't say in all honesty whether I was out to fool you or fool myself. I was pretty sure those other riders might have been *Kituhwa*. They have been out in force, stirred up by all this talk about Kansas Militia threatening to invade the Nation. But I reckon that if I hadn't spied dust above the trail behind us and we hadn't been stuck out here by this gully washer, I'd have likely come up with some other excuse. For you're so right about the reputation this wonder inside me has in tribal circles! Is it true you once shacked up with two Kimoho sisters out Colorado way and had them both begging for mercy before you were done with them?"

Longarm cocked an ear and commenced to move his cock some more as he calmly replied, "That rain seems to be blowing over. The creeks all around ought to fall about as fast as they riz. But I reckon we have time to see if I can make you beg for mercy."

But, in the end, she never did. A big strong gal who spent a lot of time with her crotch spread lonesome on an unsprung wagon seat could take a hell of a lot of pounding down yonder before it got uncomfortable. But, fortunately, she moved her hips and clung so tight with her old ring-dang-do that trying to satisfy her hungry flesh could be pure pleasure.

Chapter 5

The summer squall blew itself out as abruptly as it had blown in. But the rain-soaked range had some draining to do before they could drive on. So Longarm suggested a night fire to dry their duds. But Petunia said the flames might attract worse pests than moths. So it seemed possible she'd been sincere about those night riders.

They draped their wet cotton and wool over willow branches to see how the night winds might manage without help. Old Petunia's bare hide sure looked pretty in the moonlight and she must not have found his muscular body too awful to contemplate. For they warmed up again outside the wagon when she said there was a position she'd always meant to try, ever since she'd climbed apple trees as a little gal with an imaginative nature.

She swore she'd never done it that way before with anybody else. Longarm didn't ask what else she might have done with anybody else as he stood leaning into a gnarly crab tree to run his old organ grinder in and out as Petunia hung wide open with her ankles hooked in widely spread forks of the lower branches as she sort of swung the rest of her like a playful monkey hanging by its hands.

Later on, as they shared a smoke and cuddled warmer back inside the wagon, Longarm decided that whether she was working for the customers in the market for so many quart jars or not, he'd learned more in the process from her than she could be learning from him. She'd already known he was a well-known lawman her principal chief had sent away for.

He'd felt no call to deny that, or to say much more than that he wasn't sure why in thunder old Dennis Bushyhead had requested him by name from the Justice Department.

Petunia, in turn, didn't seem to be holding anything back as they smoked, screwed, and shot the breeze like pals. But the more he got out of her the less he saw how anybody expected him to catch anybody the army, the tribal police, or the more experienced federal lawmen riding out of Fort Smith couldn't catch.

Petunia soothed that he wasn't expected to catch anybody and the more he got out of her about the so called Cherokee Nation the more sense her cynical notion made. For Longarm was a keen questioner as well as a friendly bedmate and some of his more casual questions got him unguarded answers to string together in patterns even a paid-up citizen of the Cherokee Nation might not have been fully aware of.

As was often the case in recording the travails of Mister Lo, the poor Indian, there was more to the story than wicked white men fucking noble red men, albeit old Andrew Jackson had sure paid the Cherokee off in wooden nickels after they'd fought under him against the Creek Red Sticks at Horseshoe Bend, before Old Hickory ran for president as a war hero.

Governor Wilson Lumpkin of Georgia could only be described as a land-grabbing shitface as well. But after that the Cherokee had shit in one another's faces pretty good.

The kindly Roman philosopher who'd advised in Latin to divide and conquer had had somebody like the American Indian in general or the Five Civilized Tribes in particular in mind. Divided into rival factions and rent by family feuds before white squaw men had organized them into little frontier republics, the Indians who'd decided that if they couldn't lick the white man they might be able to join him, had been wide open for the dirty politics that went with both ways of life.

As unjust as the Indian Removal Act had been, the Trail of Tears had been even rougher than Old Hickory could have hoped for when a heap of the money Washington allotted for travel expenses wound up in the private purses of protesting tribal leaders, who'd doubtless felt that they were entitled to a little extra for the loss of their own eastern plantations.

The white or mostly white Petunia Squirreltail didn't seem

aware of her own racial feelings as she dismissed the mostly full-blooded *Kituhwa* society as jealous troublemakers. She allowed she couldn't say just who'd been behind all those political assassinations ordered by rival chiefs as the Cherokee Nation rebuilt itself in the Indian territory carved out of West Arkansas and the Osage hunting grounds. Longarm was willing to buy her protested ignorance. He knew those old unsolved murder cases were still in the federal files. He wasn't as sure as she was that they'd sent for his help in solving more recent troubles because they knew full well he'd never solve shit, and thus none of the tribal leaders would have to worry about his house and barn going up in smoke, or somebody waiting for him in the outhouse with a sawed-off shotgun. She said things had calmed down wondrous since the feuding and fussing betwixt Cherokee Union and Confederate vets just after the war. She told him she'd ridden over to watch, as a young gal, while the imposing brick mansion of Chief John Ross had burned for hours. Their principal chief had changed sides again when he'd seen the Union figured to win. So Rebel Cherokee under Stand O-Watie had paid him back for running off to Washington to cut a new deal for the Cherokee with Abe Lincoln.

Longarm said he'd never seen why the Cherokee had sided with first the English during the Revolution and then the Confederacy during the war betwixt the states, seeing how the British Lord Dunmore and then the Old South's own Old Hickory had been so mean to them.

She explained things hadn't been that simple. Few if any full-bloods had been offered officer's commissions by King George or Jeff Davis and a slave owner in the Indian territory had had as much to lose as anyone else to a Union victory.

Longarm allowed she'd convinced him the tribal leadership aspired to civilized notions and got her to grudgingly admit the former slaves had only been accepted as sort of half-ass Cherokee by the full-bloods, who hadn't kept slaves in the Golden Age of a downtrodden nation. But she insisted and Longarm ruefully had to agree a heap of full-bloods went out of their way to be nice to Black Cherokee because they knew that pissed off a heap of White Cherokee. He didn't ask Petunia whether Red, White, or Black Cherokee were running

33

moonshine to the white folk up Kansas way. She kept telling him all those quart jars were intended for tomato preserves, apple butter, and such.

He never found out how she felt about falling asleep in his company. When she got to fretting about her reputation, long before the usual cold gray dawn, Longarm took advantage of her expressed concern by strolling bare-ass down to the creek bed, wading out to the thigh-deep middle, and returning to report the water had fallen enough for a man to ford on horseback, if she'd like him to go on ahead and let her show up later with her duds on and reputation intact.

She said he was a darling man for being so understanding and they abused her reputation for the last time in a soft bed of lovegrass by the side of the wagon trace. They called it lovegrass because livestock loved its sort of vanilla scent. By the time they were done with that particular patch Longarm's knees and her big curvaceous rump sort of smelled like ice cream parlors.

Hauling on his still clammy duds didn't give a man's balls half the pleasure. But he did what he had to, kissed old Petunia a fond farewell, and saddled old Red Rocket to ride on alone.

The two of them were still soggy but warming up a mite when the sunrise caught them near the crossroads Petunia had told him to watch for. The eastbound wagon trace they turned on to looked to be a mite more traveled by others heading in or out of the Cherokee capital to the east. They started spooking more range stock than quail or jackrabbit as the sun rose higher in a crystal-clear sky to dry the two of them some. The first signs of civilization that wasn't grazing on bluestem and lovegrass were the ever more noticable tree stumps. The far-ranging woodcutters had spared a lot of popple, cottonwood, and such, but hickory and oak grew within an easy wagon-haul from town at its own peril.

They came to a bob-wire fence, since you seldom saw split-rail fencing where trees were of any other value. Longarm had grown up in the more heavily wooded hills of West-By-God Virginia, so he could sort of feel for Smoky Mountain Cherokee who didn't get to snake split-chestnut rail fencing instead of expensive bob wire, out this way.

They rode past fewer trees of any description as the trail

wound betwixt fenced-in corn fields. He noticed Cherokee grew their corn the same as most white settlers, complete with scarecrows. The more "primitive" nations planted squash-vines betwixt the rows to shade out weeds and ripen as a second crop. They often planted beans to sprout later and climb the harvested corn stalks instead of other poles. But at least the Cherokee seemed smart enough to let tumbleweed and brush windrow along their fence lines. A lot of tidy white farmers worked like beavers to make certain there'd be no shelter for bug-eating birds within easy reach of their crops.

They'd had a wetter than usual greenup that year. So the summer's crop was almost ready for what promised to be a bountiful harvest. He spied woodsmoke rising over sun-silvered roof shingles in the middle distance to either side of the trail. Structures close enough to get a better look at seemed to be constructed of substantial log or frame and if there was anything "Indian" you could see from the road it had to be the lack of paint or even whitewash.

Longarm had noticed in his travels how few Indians held with painting wood. A heap of white settlers had dispensed with the usual brick red or flat white you saw east of the Mississippi, once they'd noticed how paint weathered out this way. So there was hardly more than an overall feel to the country all around to say the folk who farmed it might not all be lily white. The few distant figures he spotted working out in their fields could have belonged to most any race favoring bib overalls and hats of black wool or bleached straw. Nobody had any feathers stuck in their hat bands and the only hint from any distance that they might not be regular country folk was their apparent lack of interest in a passing rider.

It wasn't true that Indians talked less or acted more surly than your average white stranger. They were simply more in-clined to wait and see whether you wanted to mess with them or leave them the hell alone.

The sun was higher and way hotter by the time Longarm spied a church steeple down the road ahead. He'd long since shucked his frock coat and shoestring tie to ride on in his shirtsleeves and tweed vest. He thought about getting his badge out to ride in with some authority pinned to said vest, lest he catch the usual hazing a white man could expect as he rode into an Indian camp. But some of the cabins he'd ridden past had been built closer to the road and none of the mostly dusky but otherwise natural-looking men, women, or children he'd passed had paid him either interest or discourtesy. The one yard dog that had barked at him and Red Rocket had been severely hushed, in English, by an old lady shelling peas on her front porch. He couldn't tell whether they in turn had taken him for a nosy white man or just a down-home rider none of them knew to howdy. Longarm had no Indian blood, as far as he knew, but others had commented on his naturally dark hair and deep suntan, and it wasn't true no Indians at all could grow face hair. Pure Indians, like pure Chinese, tended to have more hair on their heads and less on their faces than most whites. So it made it easier for them to get by with whispy mustaches or just pluck out all their face hair and forget it. But as many an almost pure Chihuahua Mex vaquero could prove at a glance, a gent of Indian ancestry could grow a mustache if he really aimed to.

After that, as old Petunia had confessed, as hairy as most pure white gals, the Cherokee were no longer one hundred percent anything. So as he rode into the outskirts of Tahlequah, Longarm saw plenty of old boys with face hair, some of it red, and not a soul asked him who or what he might be as he walked Red Rocket along what seemed to be the main market street toward a big barnlike town hall, council house, or whatever near that church steeple.

As he did so he saw that otherwise the Cherokee capital looked a lot like any other western settlement of modest size. The shop signs to either side of the dusty street were in plain English for the most part. With here and there a line or two added in that curious Cherokee alphabet made up by the late George Guess or Sequoia. The plain English allowed there were barbershops, blacksmiths, hardwares, hat shops, and so on, run by literate Cherokee or part-Cherokee proprietors. The buckboards and stock-saddled ponies tethered along either side of the street were no different than one might expect in such a natural-looking town and the folk shopping or just spitting and whittling along the plank walks were dressed as plain or fancy as white folk of the same social position on a weekday. Some of the ladies were decked out in the latest fashions, whilst more than one prosperous farmer or merchant made Longarm feel a tad shabby with his coat rolled up with his bedding and the collar of his hickory shirt wide open. The more obvious cowboys and plowboys along the walks or riding past were dressed no more like Indians than one might spy on the streets of Dodge or Denver. There were always a few beaded hat bands or fringed vests to be seen in cattle country.

Most of the locals did seem darker and more quiet than you'd expect in your average county seat. But some few had lighter coloring than he did. So Longarm felt more comfortable about just being himself as he neared what seemed the center of town around a tree-shaded square in front of that big barnlike building. He saw said square was crowded and there seemed to be some sort of a fuss going on. So he reined in closer to a notions shop and dismounted to tether near a watering trough so's Red Rocket could water and he could sort of drift in slow and easy whilst he scouted the mood of that buzzing bunch of Cherokee.

He saw one such gent coming his way from the crowd, looking sort of worried. So he chanced just asking the apparent cowhand what was going on over yonder.

If the Cherokee recognized Longarm as an outsider he never showed it. Petunia had already explained why they mostly spoke plain English to one another. The Cherokee said, "A back-shooting. A bad one that's likely to cause us some trouble with the *Ontwaganha.* Some silly sons of bitches just gunned a federal deputy old Oo-na-du-ti sent away for. They got him as he reined in near the municipal corral and there's likely to be hell to pay with Little Big Eyes!"

Longarm knew Little Big Eyes was what most Indians called Secretary of the Interior Carl Schurz. So he asked if the Cherokee could tell him who that dead federal lawman might have been.

The Indian cowboy answered, "Sure. He was famous and they'd sent away for him, like I said. They called him Longarm and he was supposed to be pretty good. But now he's been shot in the back and lays dead as a turd in the milk pail, for all the good he'll do us, now!"

Chapter 6

Longarm had drifted through milling crowds before. It was easy to blend in as long as a man kept his mouth shut, his ears open, and his hands polite. From time to time he heard a word or phrase of what had to be Cherokee. The lingo was more guttural than Lakota or Cheyenne, with words ending in what sounded like grunts. But being a mixed mob raised with three or more distinct versions of officious Cherokee, a lot more English than Cherokee was spoken to save time and avoid the misunderstandings you could get when folk from England tried to talk English with folk from, say, Scotland. Longarm knew better than to try and fake any Indian words, himself. The "cigar store" Indian most every white man thought he knew was Algonquin, because those Indians invited to Thanksgiving Dinner by the pilgrims had spoken that lingo. But nary a Sioux-Hokan, Uto-Aztec, Na-Déné, or even Western Algonquin speaker had the least notion what words such as moccasin, papoose, pow-wow, squaw, tomahawk, wampum, or wigwam meant and, worse yet, tended to think white folk were mocking them when they were subjected to such outlandish talk.

Making his way to what seemed to have been the scene of his own death, Longarm was able to solve some of the puzzle right off. One of the ponies dancing walleyed in the dusty confusion of the municipal corral across the square from that big council house was the spooked gray mare Tabitha from Fort Gibson. Longarm had been wondering where she'd run off to after she'd busted loose in that storm the night before.

Leaning both elbows over the top rail of the corral, Long-arm waited until a duskier cowboy loafing nearby seemed used to him being there before he asked in a desperately casual tone, "Might that gray be one of the ponies that dead lawman rode in with this morning?"

The Cherokee nodded soberly and said, "Yep. He was riding a bay and leading that spooky gray. She's been acting like that ever since her *Ontwaganha* master stopped a buffalo round with his back an hour or so ago. I didn't see it happen. But I was there when they picked him up and carried him over to the clinic. I don't know why they carried him over to the clinic. Anyone could see he was already dead."

Longarm cautiously replied, "So I just heard from my pal, Casper Bluefeather from up the creek. Casper said the gent's name was Long something?"

The Indian said, "Longarm. He wasn't one of us, despite the name. The *Ontwaganha* called him that because he was said to enforce the long arm of the law. His real name was just Long, I heard."

The real Longarm casually said, "Such papers and warrants as a lawman would have been packing would likely give his one true name, right?"

The Indian shrugged and said, "I reckon. You say a Casper Bluefeather told you all this? You say you know folk named Bluefeather, up to the north of here?"

"I thought that's where old Casper said his folk lived," Longarm answered in a desperately casual tone, getting his elbows down to say something about meeting somebody else so he could break the conversation off before he put another foot in his mouth.

He retraced his steps to where he'd tethered Red Rocket and led the pony afoot to the livery stable at one end of the municipal corral. Red Rocket had earned a good rest with plenty of fodder and water and, after that, a man on foot blended into a crowd easier.

The older man running the livery looked more colored than Indian. Longarm neither asked what he might be nor volunteered more than one of his favorite fake names. It served Reporter Crawford of the *Denver Post* right for writing all those tall tales about Denver's answer to Buffalo Bill and, after that, Crawford Long had been the sawbones who invented painless surgery just in time for the war betwixt the states. So Longarm had always hoped they might be distant kin and found the name easy to remember when he felt shy about giving his own.

The colored Cherokee hostler allowed they'd be proud to board Red Rocket indoors for two bits a day and threw in the use of their tack room for Longarm's saddle, bridle, and possibles. Longarm held on to his Winchester saddle-gun lest it prove too great a temptation to the stable mice. He paid for a couple of days in advance to save having to settle up when or if he had to ride on in a hurry.

As the older man made change for him from the till, Longarm tried, a mite slyer, for a better description of his recently murdered alter ego. The hostler said he'd been talking to the famous Longarm just before he'd died.

He volunteered, "Near as anyone's been able to figure, the killer or killers was laying for him up in First Adventist with a big fifty. He'd just ridden in from Fort Gibson and left his two ponies out back when that single fatal shot rang out and down he went with a bitty blue hole betwixt the shoulder blades, and his heart and lungs blowed out the front of his shirt. Poor *junaluska* never knew what hit him."

"You say he'd just come up from Fort Gibson?" Longarm asked as he wondered how he'd pose the next obvious question.

The hostler replied in a know-it-all tone, "*Gwo*, Jim Deadpony said they'd been expecting him to show up. Jim was the lawman who identified the remains when somebody sent for the law. Jim said he'd ridden with Longarm over by the Osage Strip a spell back."

It wouldn't have been prudent to say he'd never ridden anywhere with any Indian lawman called Jim Deadpony. So Longarm settled for asking if they still had that telegraph wire strung along the main post road to Fort Gibson. He wasn't surprised when the colored gent nodded and said, "Sure they do. How did you think our *Degalawivi Tsalagi* stays in touch with the *chagee assaracol*?"

Longarm had only recognized one word out of four and so he decided to quit whilst he was ahead. Whatever the Chero-

40

kee Something stayed in touch with at Fort Gibson, some sly bastard had been able to wire ahead that he'd be headed for Tahlequah with one bay and one gray. After that one white stranger could likely pass for another and whoever they'd shot in his place had doubtless met up with the spooked and strayed Tabitha out on the range, whilst its original rider had been saying fonder farewells to old Petunia Squirreltail in other parts. So Longarm owed his own life and considerable revenge to the total stranger who'd only been trying to return a strayed mount to its proper rider and, after that, what could have possessed some other total stranger to say the man they'd shot by mistake was another stranger entire?

"The cocksucker called Jim Deadpony never laid eyes on either one of us before!" Longarm decided as he paused in a puddle of tree shade outside to light a cheroot and gather his thoughts.

He knew he had to gather them good in such time as he still had to work with. According to that friendly Petunia, there'd been plenty of gossip about the tribal council sending away for outside help with that moonshine bunch. Nobody made enough moonshine to matter unless they had at least a few friends in high places. So somebody had been watching for a famous federal deputy to show up at that army remount station at Fort Gibson. After that things seemed even clearer. The sneak stationed over by Fort Gibson had seen him ride out aboard Red Rocket, leading the bigger dapple gray, and simply wired ahead, describing a tall white man in the company of two such ponies.

That left the questions of who in blue blazes they'd really shot and whether this Jim Deadpony had been in on it or simply a blowhard who wanted folk to think he'd been pals with a more famous lawman. It might work as well either way. Longarm was always meeting up with survivors of the Little Big Horn or that killing in the Number Ten Saloon up in Deadwood. That didn't make such bullshit artists logical suspects in the deaths of either George Armstrong Custer or James Butler Hickok. This often tedious world was filled with windy jaspers who'd seen a heap of wonders and advised General Pickett personal not to make that charge at Gettysburg.

The Cherokee lawman's reasons for identifying the wrong

remains of a white lawman were less important than whether the killer or killers thought they'd killed the right man or not.

It worked more than one way. Jim Deadpony could have made a dumb but honest mistake. He could have been simply showing off by jumping to conclusions. Or he could have known full well his pals had gunned the wrong man and lied on purpose, raising a whole lot of other damned suspicions!

After that he didn't know how much time he had to work with. The only person he might be able to trust in the whole infernal territory was the chief who'd sent for him, he hoped.

As he strode on, unsure where he was headed, Longarm decided he'd have to trust old Dennis Bushyhead unless he just meant to turn around and light out with his tail betwixt his legs. He didn't like to think he scared that easy, and it made no sense for old Bushyhead to send away for an outside lawman if he was so afraid of outside help that he'd order said outsider killed!

So his best bet was a beeline for Chief Bushyhead. But he didn't know the chief on sight if he managed to meet up with him before the other side learned they'd made a mistake!

It hardly seemed prudent for yet another stranger answering to the same general description of tall, tanned, but pure white to tear about with a cradled Winchester asking too many dumb questions. He knew he'd be able to blend in as long as the sunny streets stayed crowded. But it wasn't getting any earlier and he had to find his way to the chief or find some place to hole up tight before suppertime thinned the crowd and left him standing out like a big white bird!

He didn't risk drifting closer to the big meeting hall, nor did it seem smart to pay his respects on the unknown murdered man that so many local folk seemed to take for himself. He was curious as all get-out about the poor cuss. But just as heaps of lawmen staked out the scene of a recent crime in hopes some curious culprit might circle back, a killer who suspected he might have killed the wrong man could be smart enough to wait and see who came by to pay his victim their own respects.

A local rider would know where Chief Bushyhead might be found during his regular office hours. Longarm was trying to be taken for a local rider as he ate some fried *kanahena* and

42

sipped hard cider at a stand-up booth across the square from the council house. *Kanahena* was something like the corn tamales Mexican Indians had invented and the fact that the cider was openly sold hard, meant nobody in town took the BIA notions about Indians drinking all that serious.

A drunken Indian could get as mean as a drunken cowboy. So well-meaning folk back east were former passing rules and regulations on what Indians might or might not drink. Indian agents and army officers called upon to enforce such rules in the real west tended to overlook such softer home-brews as Apache tiswin and Cherokee apple cider. It was almost impossible to prevent fruit juice from turning sort of hard on its way to fermenting natural to vinegar and there were no laws at all against Indians making vinegar. It was hard enough to prevent more scientific medicine men from distilling such mild beverages into hundred proof no-shit firewater.

Longarm figured the hard cider he was washing his corn fritters down with was barely stronger than draft beer and so, being the afternoon had warmed up considerable by then, he ordered another mug from the motherly old squaw running the booth, albeit they were more likely to call her an *agehyva* in *Tsalagi* or Cherokee.

Whatever you called the old gal in the Mother Hubbard and sunbonnet, Longarm casually remarked he'd been told Chief Bushyhead was busy over to the council house and asked if she might know where he lived when he got off duty.

The old woman answered in unself-conscious English that everybody in the nation knew the Bushyheads had a big old spread and a general store down near the old Park Hill Mission, a couple of hours ride to the south. So Longarm tried assuring her he'd known that and only meant to ask where the chief stayed when he was in town.

It might have worked on the old refreshment stand lady. But then a deeper male voice asked, *"Ga detsado vi?"* and Longarm turned to see a bearlike full-blood in the blue uniform and black cavalry hat the BIA issued to its Indian police. The Cherokee lawman had a big brown fist riding thoughtfully on the walnut grips of his Schofield .45 as he seemed to be waiting for an answer.

Longarm smiled sheepishly and confessed, "If you were

43

asking if I was one of you folk I ain't. Name's Crawford and I just rode up from Fort Gibson to see Chief Bushyhead about some grazing permits, over to your outlet in the short-grass country to the west."

The burly Indian stared back at him with no expression and replied, "I'd like to see some identification, Mister Crawford."

Longarm innocently demanded, "How come? It's broad daylight on a public thoroughfare and I ain't been bothering nobody, have I?"

The stone-faced Cherokee said, "That's what I'm trying to find out. Another *Ontwaganha* rider from Fort Gibson was shot in the back a short while ago by a person or persons unknown and I don't know you from the great *une-hlanvihi!* So hand over that rifle while you show me some I.D. and tell me what's so funny, laughing boy!"

Longarm tried to wipe the grin off his face as he replied, "I ain't laughing at you. I'm laughing at me. Or the situation I find my fool self in, leastways."

The Indian didn't seem the least bit amused. He said he was still waiting to be let in on the joke.

Longarm allowed it would be sort of tough to explain. That was the simple truth as soon as you studied on it. For how was he supposed to remark on how comical it seemed to be suspected of his own murder when he didn't want to admit he'd been sent there to investigate a case that seemed to add up to wicked Indians running forbidden firewater to white folk, which was pretty comical all by itself as soon as you studied on it.

The burly Cherokee drew his six-gun with a weary sigh and threw down on Longarm, growling, "All right. Drop that gun. Turn to that tree. Grab some bark and spread your ankles, laughing boy. You may have been told us unwashed savages don't have any authority to arrest outsiders on our own reserve. But we'll just have to see about that, won't we?"

Chapter 7

Longarm figured he was damned if he did and damned if he didn't and a crowd was gathering. A skinny young squirt in the same blue outfit came across the square to join them, walking officiously with a superior air. Longarm knew he'd guessed right about the kid's rank when the kid gargled rapid-fire Cherokee at the older tribal lawman and added, "I've been hunting high and low for you, Mister Bradley! Why didn't you come direct to the chief's office when you got here?"

"I got turned around," Longarm replied, even as he wondered who in blue blazes the younger Indian lawman had him confused with. He hoped to find himself alone with any local figure of authority before he had to give his true identity away.

As if he'd read Longarm's mind, the kid nodded and said, "It's just as well. We had a shooting earlier, and we'd like you to have a look at the victim, seeing you might have met up with him over at the rail stop by Fort Gibson."

Longarm fell in beside the squirt to at least get shed of the crowd around the refreshment booth and that burlier policeman. As the two of them got out of earshot the squirt he'd taken for simple warned him in a lower tone, "Don't say anything else, Longarm. I hope you didn't tell old Will Cash too much back there!"

Longarm had been warned not to say anything and he needed time to go back over the short conversation he'd had with that other lawman.

Not knowing he was supposed to be some gent named Bradley, he'd been in no position to say so and if old Will Cash remembered he'd said his name was Crawford, so be it. The burly cuss hadn't acted as if he'd bought that name, anyhow.

They seemed to be making for a carriage house handy to that big frame church, up another side of the central square. Longarm cautiously asked, "Would you mind telling me what this is all about, seeing you seem to have the advantage on me?"

The young Cherokee said, "Sorry. I'd be Sergeant Deadpony and I was the one who identified your body when they got you, riding in from Fort Gibson today."

Longarm cocked a brow to reply, "They told me how we used to ride together. No offense, but this is the first time I've laid eyes on you. So how did you know that was me they'd shot or hadn't shot?"

The younger lawman explained, "Only way it hangs together, unless we're dealing with a homicidal lunatic. We were expecting you to show up. When I got word a strange rider had been gunned at the municipal corral I hurried over, expecting the victim to be you."

"How did you know it wasn't me?" Longarm demanded.

The Cherokee he'd never met before smiled thinly and replied, "They said you thought fast on your feet. But I *did* know the dead man, right off. His name was Moses Bradley. He was a prospector. He'd been here in the territory before and Chief Bushyhead had asked me to keep an eye on him. As you're about to see, the only thing the two of you had in common was sitting tall and pale-faced in the saddle. But we weren't expecting him. We were expecting you. So add it up."

Longarm already had. He said, "I can go you one better. I rode out of Fort Gibson leading that big dapple gray mare Bradley was leading when he rode in to Tahlequah. She busted loose on me during that storm we had early last night. Bradley must have met up with her out on the open range and, seeing she was dragging that long lead line, gathered it up to be neighborly, the poor cuss."

Deadpony whistled and said, "There goes the notion the killer had to be a pure-blood!"

Longarm started to ask what he meant. Then he nodded and said, "We tend to have trouble telling you boys apart at any distance, too, no offense. How come you told everybody that was me they'd shot if you knew right off it was another white man entire?"

Deadpony asked in a disgusted voice, "What would you have told the killer or killers? That they'd fucked up? Somebody went to a heap of trouble to see that the outside help we'd sent away for never got to help us catch those moonshiners. So why not let them think they nipped your investigation in the bud and—"

"Go on investigating!" Longarm cut in with a wicked grin. But then he felt obliged to confess, "I still don't see why anyone would be so worried about this child's limited powers of investigation. I don't know this country all that well. I don't speak Cherokee worth mention and I don't know all that much about distilling sour mash out on the open range. Back home in West-By-God Virginia we had us some old boys who ran a still a few hollows over. But it could be injurious to one's health to pester them about the details of their operation. So none of us watched them all that close."

As they neared the open doorway of the apparent carriage house the Indian lawman said, "We have another *Ontwaganha* technical expert who claims to know a dozen ways to distill as many kinds of firewater. I want you to meet your other self, first."

They ducked inside. The dark barnlike interior smelled of horse and worse. Mostly formaldehyde. A coal-oil lamp was casting its wan light down into one end of the plank coffin resting on two sawhorses at the far end. A portly breed with a butcher's apron on over his snuff wool suit was standing smugly by with a comb and brush.

Deadpony got rid of him in Cherokee so that he and Longarm could talk in private about the shrouded cadaver reposing in the coffin. The late Moses Bradley had been around forty-five and starting to go bald when someone had shot him in the back a few hours earlier. He didn't look anything like Longarm. But Longarm didn't say so. The two of them had already been over that. Someone had wired from Fort Gibson that a tall white rider would be arriving in the company of a distinctive gray mare and a more nondescript bay. Bradley had ridden in leading Tabitha, and that had been enough for the rascal laying for Longarm with that buffalo rifle.

47

Staring soberly down at the freshly embalmed cadaver, Longarm asked how long they figured they could keep from notifying any next of kin.

Deadpony shrugged and said, "Long enough. He was single and they tell me you can keep a body from rotting as long as you can preserve leather, if you don't mind the saddle-leather color and wrinkles. The question before the house is what you want us to wire your own kith and kin. The rascals who just murdered you are likely to wonder why it never made the newspapers if it never makes the newspapers."

Longarm nodded and said, "We'd best declare me dead, then. I have my own way of wording wires to my uncle Billy in Denver so's he won't have to weep too much for me. You say I was a prospector named Bradley the last time I rode through these parts?"

Deadpony nodded and said, "Prospecting for rock-oil, like they've been drilling for in Penn state. There's seeps of rock-oil all along the Vermilion Valley between us and the Osage. They drilled and struck a tolerable flow up near the Kansas line a few summers back. So Chief Bushyhead hired this unfortunate cuss to survey for such well sites around his own spread, summer before last. Like I told you, the chief asked us to keep an eye on him. So we did. That's how I knew who he was right off."

Longarm nodded thoughtfully and asked, "What do you reckon I came back for, this time? Did I find any oil under Park Hill, last time?"

The younger lawman got into the spirit of the game by saying, "Nope. You told us most of the geology seemed to favor the Osage dome-rocks to the northwest. Chief Bushyhead paid you for your time and trouble anyhow. What do you reckon you were looking for this time?"

Longarm said, "Trouble, if I try to pass for Bradley outright. He must have had some reason for coming back. Somebody else could have sent for him to run another survey. After that, if you knew him, some others in these parts must have known him. I'd better go on being some stranger called Crawford, like I told old Will Cash a few minutes ago."

Deadpony protested, "I just got through insisting you were Bradley!"

Longarm shook his head and insisted, "It's safer to admit you took me for a business partner than it would be to insist I'm somebody most anyone else in these parts might know I ain't! I'll just be another rock-oil scout, waiting for Bradley to show up, so's the two of us can get cracking at whatever in thunder he had in mind when he wired me to meet him here, see?"

Deadpony did. He grinned like a kid fixing to swipe apples, nodded, and said, "That gives you call to loiter most anywhere while you wait for this secretly dead pard to show up. Anyone who hired Bradley to do anything is likely to come forward and ask his business partner where he is! Do you know anything about prospecting for rock-oil, should anybody get around to asking you to try?"

Longarm shrugged and honestly replied, "I know as much about drilling for rock-oil as I do about distilling corn liquor. I reckon I'd manage to fool anybody who didn't really know what I was doing if I sort of went through such motions as I recall. Nobody but the real McCoy ought to know you ain't about to produce either product before you just up and fail to produce a drop of either, right?"

The Cherokee laughed and said they'd better run that wild notion past his chief. So Longarm followed him out into the sunlight again and they cut back across the square, past that big council house, to a two-story building of shingled-over logs.

Things didn't seem as rustic inside. Chief Dennis Stuart Bushyhead had an oak-paneled office something like Marshal Billy Vail's inner sanctum out in Denver. Both were on the second floor and both featured big cluttered desks.

The man seated behind the desk at Tahlequah didn't look at all like Marshal William Vail of the Denver District Court, however.

Dennis Stuart Bushyhead looked more like a prosperous banker with a healthy tan than anything else Longarm could come up with on such short notice.

He'd know the paramount chief of the Cherokee was a breed. The same as Quanah Parker, the progressive chief of the Comanche. But you sort of expected any Indian chief to look sort of Indian and so even Quanah wore braids under his stove-pipe hat. But the middle-aged and portly Dennis Bushyhead wore his right-ordinary graying hair trimmed and combed the same as any other public official. After that he sported the same mustache and goatee as Louis Napoleon or Buffalo Bill above a freshly laundered and starched linen collar with a silk bow tie. His dark summer-weight suit looked tailor-made as well, and there wasn't a peace pipe in sight as the heavyset Cherokee chief half rose to shake and offer his white guest a handsome Havana perfecto from a regular humidor on his regular desk. As Longarm sat down with his Winchester across his knees he saw the mostly Indian-looking details within sight were the maps on the oak-paneled walls, and you had to peer close at them before you read things like "Osage Claims" or "Cherokee Outlet."

Young Deadpony took a stiffer bentwood chair near one corner of the desk as Longarm and the older man who'd sent for him sized one another up.

Dennis Bushyhead said, "I suppose you've been wondering why we sent for you."

To which Longarm could only reply, "That's for certain, Chief. I don't know toad-squat about your mysterious moonshiners. Even if I did, illicit moonshine stills are a matter for the Treasury revenue agents to search out and destroy, ain't they?"

Bushyhead shook his regular looking head and gravely replied, "Not in this case. To begin with, Treasury has handed the plate of worms back to the Bureau of Indian Affairs on the grounds that while it's against the law to sell us hard liquor, we are not required to pay any federal taxes on anything and so there'd be no outstanding duties for the revenuers to claim and blah-blah-blah."

Longarm smiled wearily and agreed. "No government agency takes on a thankless chore when they can possibly palm it off on somebody else. But did those Treasury moonshine hunters try at all before they found out they didn't have proper jurisdiction in the Indian territory?"

The Indian chief nodded soberly and said, "They tried. They rode high and they rode low through the tanglewoods along the Oologah and then somebody stole half their supplies and burned their tents while they were out searching for moonshine stills."

Young Deadpony, having more Indian blood than showed, sounded just a mite smug as he volunteered, "They were hunting for *Tsalagi* in one of the less settled parts of the *Tsalagi* hunting grounds. They were not bad at what they did in *other* parts. We learned some things about making firewater from them before they gave up and, as you say, told us it was not their fight. They were looking for the sort of sign your own moonshiners leave. They found none. I think they were frightened. They were not used to moonshiners who left no tracks, left no spent mash or wood ashes, cut no firewood where they should have cut firewood, and drew no water where good water ran. Those revenuers told us you need good clean limestone water to make good whiskey and I have tasted the white lightning they have been selling up around Coffeyville. They have been making very good stuff. Nobody knows how. A good hunter can move through the woods without leaving sign. A clever thief can raid your camp without leaving sign. People who draw tankloads of water, cut cords of firewood, and ferment wagonloads of corn with barrels of syrup, without leaving any sign are . . . spooky!"

The chief smiled thinly and said something in Cherokee. Deadpony got up and left the two older men alone for the moment. Bushyhead told Longarm he'd sent for their other outside expert and added, "None of our police have had any better luck than those revenue agents and the less said about Judge Parker's riders out of Fort Smith the less I'll ever have to take back. Suffice it to say they're pretty good at tracking other *Ontwaganha* in the Indian territory."

Longarm grimaced and demanded, "Why should this child do any better? I know less about your country, your kith and kin than any other federal riders you've mentioned!"

Dennis Stuart Bushyhead beamed at him to reply, "Quanah Parker and me were talking about that. I told him about our problem when we got together on grazing fees a few days ago, over to Fort Reno. Quanah told me you were one of the few white men he'd ever met who was willing to admit he didn't

51

know all there was to know about Indians. We agreed that made you a man who was willing to learn, and that's likely the reason you've done so well by other nations. So puff your cigar and listen tight while I tell you a tale of confusion!"

Chapter 8

The older man took a deep drag on his own cigar and began, "The big mistake both Indian haters and do-gooders who prefer to hate the U.S. Government have in common is Mister Lo, the poor Indian. It's as if some Indian nation had invented gunpowder and sea-going vessels first to set up trading posts in Spain, France, and Scotland so they could describe the poor primitive European as a benighted individual who fought bulls in kilts while wearing lots of perfume. And let us not forget he shuns pork and shellfish while wearing a cross around his neck and praying towards Mecca five times a day."

Longarm quietly replied he'd noticed different nations had different notions.

Bushyhead nodded and said the Cherokee had heard about Longarm and his spirited defense of those Hopi snake dancers.

He added, "That would cut no ice in these parts. A snake is just a snake to us. Albeit no Cherokee in his right mind would ever shoot any wolf under any condition."

Longarm asked how come.

The Cherokee leader said, "Never mind. Think of the Hindus' sacred cows and let's get back to more important differences between the so-called Cherokee and other Indians."

He rose from his desk to pace the rug, turning out to be tall for his girth as he continued, "I have a better perspective on the problems of the Five Civilized Tribes than some because of the way I got to grow up as an accepted member of both the red and white races. As anyone can see, I have more Scotch-Irish than Cherokee blood. My great-grandfather, John

Stuart, was a British officer captured by the Cherokee in 1760 during a border skirmish. The two sides made peace again before they could make up their minds what to do with him. So they gave him a party and he decided to stay on as a Royal Indian Agent. He married Miss Susannah Emory of the Cherokee Nation and although it had been the custom for all Iroquoans to take their mother's clan name, John and Susannah's children took the name the tribe had given John Stuart, Oona-du-ti, or Bushyhead. Great-grandfather John had a healthy head of curly blond hair, see?"

Longarm blew a thoughtful smoke ring and asked, "You say your great-great-Cherokee-grandmother was named Susannah? Emory was an Indian name?"

Bushyhead smiled and said, "They told us you didn't miss much. Our Cherokee princess was a breed, of course. She'd taken both her first and last names from her own Christian background. Despite all the crap about Great Spirits and occult visions, people with no recorded scriptures were at a disadvantage when it came to working out any religion that held together worth mention."

Longarm nodded soberly and said he'd noticed nobody had ever managed to explain the exact difference betwixt Changing Woman and White Painted Woman to him. He added, "In other words your Cherokee kin were well on the way to acting more like the rest of us before the Revolution?"

The mostly white Cherokee nodded and said, "Some say all Iroquians arrived on the scene with a more pragmatic approach to life than many other Indian nations. Our western cousins, the Caddo, Pawnee, and Pawnee Picts or Wichita all combined farming with hunting, fishing and food gathering. Nobody who ever fought us or our Mohawk cousins to the north ever called us sissies, but we thought it was smarter to join the whites than to wind up dead trying to lick 'em. So my father was a Baptist minister or a dangerous savage, depending on whether Chief Justice Marshal of the Supreme Court or Governor Lumpkin of Georgia was speaking."

Longarm nodded and said, "I read how they stuck gold on Cherokee land disputed by the state of Georgia."

Chief Bushyhead shrugged his massive shoulders and said, "Ancient history. I was ten or eleven and had nothing to say about it when they moved us out here to the Indian territory. But pay attention while I tell you something many a Cherokee would just as soon forget."

Longarm paid attention as Bushyhead almost whispered, "We were sold out by our own kind. Our elected paramount chief, John Ross, was in touch with powerful friends in Washington. He'd retained the former attorney general, William Wirt, to argue our case before the Supreme Court. We won some and we lost some. The Supreme Court held that we were not a foreign state but a domestic dependent nation, which was half a loaf. Then they ruled in our favor that federal jurisdiction over any and all Indian nations was exclusive. So no Georgia court had any power to order shit."

Longarm nodded and said, "That's when President Jackson told the Supreme Court to go jump in the lake, right?"

The big Cherokee heaved a weary sigh and said, "Wrong. For all his bravado it's doubtful even Andrew Jackson would have risked his own impeachment for his Georgia cronies. John Ross and his Washington cronies were winning, or at least holding the fort. Jackson sent a new Indian commission led by a preacher named Schermerhorn in the summer of '35 to see if we couldn't be talked into dumping such a savage chief as the stubborn John Ross. You can imagine how tribal leaders like my own father reacted to that grand notion. But others were scared and money talks. So, to make a long story short, Jackson and Georgia recognized a rival Cherokee faction led by Major Ridge, a personal enemy of Ross, and guess how tough it was to get *them* to sign the treaty ceding all our eastern reserves to white settlers in exchange for this land out here?"

Longarm whistled and quietly asked, "Wasn't Ridge one of the so called Cherokee chiefs assassinated by somebody who somehow never got caught?"

Bushyhead nodded grimly and said, "The Ridge brothers' clique signing first had broken a Blood Law of the *Tsalagi*. Ross and the others had no choice but to go along with the treaty if they wanted to hold on to any power at all. So they were allowed to live."

He looked off in the distance as he muttered, half to himself, "Our unwritten Blood Laws can be tricky. There are things not even a chief can get away with. But he has to sort of guess at how the more conservative female full-bloods who quietly rule the clans are likely to decide. But we were talking man talk."

Moving over to a wall map, Bushyhead waved a hand at it to continue. "I was raised down this way at Park Hill. I remember our old hills east of the Mississippi as greener. But I can't say growing up out this way killed me. Needless to say I grew up under the roof of a church manse instead of a bark *adanelva*. Cherokee were building houses before John Stuart joined them way back when. I got to hunt and fish as much as most red or white country boys and my mother made me wash for supper before my father said Grace over the same. We did eat plenty of *kanahena* and my mother baked *duga* on a slate because we liked it, not because we didn't know any better. In '41 I traveled east with a tribal delegation to Washington and wound up going to Princeton University. After college I came home to manage our family store and serve as a clerk of the Cherokee Legislature. The constitution of the Cherokee Nation was patterned after that of the United States. I resigned my tribal duties in the spring of '49 to join in the California Gold Rush with my brother, Edward. Ed's still out there, editing a newspaper in San Diego. Nobody out yonder ever asked if either of us might be a primitive savage. So we never said we were, and I have to say it gives a man a different angle on Indian policy when he's accepted as a prosperous white man."

Longarm allowed he'd found it educational to pretend he knew less Spanish than he really did, in Mexican company.

Bushyhead shrugged and said, "We made out all right as white men and when the Civil War broke out there was no way either of us could even write home. Chief Ross was still alive but nobody listened when he tried to tell them it would be suicidal to side with the South."

Longarm said, "Some surely wondered why you seemed so keen to ride with Dixie, seeing the state of Georgia had been so good to you."

Bushyhead grimaced and said, "I was wondering the same thing, out in California. The Osage and some Cherokee did fight for the North. Our more prosperous leaders had gotten used to raising cotton with slave labor. I just told you one leading faction of our nation had *agreed* to move west in exchange for cash and first choice at bottomlands and timber. I wasn't able to get back to my kith and kin before the war was over. When I finally made it I found most everybody ruined by the war. Rival factions had burned one another out. A highly pissed off Union was in no mood to do favors for Chief Lew Downing, who'd replaced the late John Ross. I'd come home prosperous and, better yet, I hadn't ridden for either side in the war, so nobody was really sore at me. I went back into tribal politics and here we are, with the Cherokee prosperous again and me on damned thin ice."

Stepping closer to the map he ran the back of his hand along a big pink patch just south of the Kansas line to say, "If this ever gets outside this room I'm going to have to call you a liar. But this so called Cherokee Outlet reserved for us west of the Osage Reservation is one big pain in the ass. I've been holding tribal title to it by leasing grazing rights to powerful white cattle barons. Without any Cherokee actually living on it, all that shortgrass range was paying us was trouble. Buffalo hunters fighting Kiowa, white squatters fighting one another, and cow thieves using it as a handy range to cool off stolen herds."

"How come no Cherokee live in that Cherokee Outlet?" Longarm asked.

The Cherokee leader replied without hesitation, "There just aren't that many Cherokee. I keep telling everybody we're *civilized*. Primitive hunting and gathering bands need vast and mostly empty space to roam. A man and his good-sized family can barely farm more than a hundred and sixty acres of decent land. Most Pennsylvania Dutch get by nicely on less than a hundred acres. You need more than a quarter-section homestead as soon as you start grazing beef, of course. But to tell the truth my Cherokee constituents prefer farming close to home more than they enjoy camping out on open range. But since the Georgia crackers who were out to screw us knew we were savages, they set aside less land than we'd have really needed as hunting grounds, while ceding us more land than we'll fill up for years as manageable farms!"

He rapped the map with his knuckles as he continued, "So

far, like Quanah Parker's done for his Comanche, I've managed to hold the land grabbers at bay by enlisting the likes of Captain Goodnight and the Thompson brothers on my side. Cows demand so little, other than plenty of grass and water. But this beef boom can't last forever and as the railroads and that homestead act clutter up the west it will only be a question of time before some son of a bitch like Lumpkin of Georgia gets to pissing and moaning about all the land going to waste as Indian Reserve. Those semiarid Indian lands further west may not be quite as tempting. But we're sitting on prime farmland here in the eastern strip of the Indian territory and we're already having trouble with squatters."

Longarm started to sympathize about that ugly old Belle Starr and her brood over near Fort Smith. Chief Bushyhead scowled at him and said, "I thought you were going to listen. That white trash woman young Sam Starr just took up with isn't squatting on Indian land. We know about her. But as far as we're concerned she dosen't exist. Sam Starr is the worthless son of Tom Starr, a full-blood you wouldn't want to cross. Young Sam and his belle Shirley have been allowed to settle on sixty acres Tom holds along the Canadian near Fort Smith. If she prefers to call the place Younger's Bend that's a family matter. Up to here and now, neither she nor young Sam have done anything to any Cherokee. If they ever do, I feel sorry for them. Nobody's ever been able to say who killed Major Ridge and those other treaty signers, either. They call themselves the *Kituhwa*. Before you ask, I have no idea who they are or how they decide who's broken our unwritten Blood Laws. So I just can't tell you whether those moonshiners stirring up trouble for us with the state of Kansas are in good or bad with our *Kituhwa* Society and I've never mentioned them to you, should anybody ever ask!"

Longarm nodded soberly and said, "I can see why you sent Deadpony out to play. Are you saying your own tribal police might not want to catch anybody them Cherokee night riders might *approve* of?"

The Cherokee chief replied, "I don't know. I do know we of the National Progressive Party don't see how we can afford another showdown with us in the role of Mister Lo, the poor Indian. Mister Lo is always going to live on handouts and be stood in the corner whenever he seems naughty. If he's lucky. We don't want to be robbed of all our land a second time. We don't want to go down fighting. So, if only they give us a little more time, we're going to solve our own Indian problem our own way. First we get fee-simple title to at least two hundred acres of land for every Cherokee family. Then we demand full citizenship and cash on the barrelhead to divide fair and square for all the Cherokee land claims left over. Do you think your people will got for it?"

Longarm shrugged and said, "My people may not be the problem. Your people would be giving up their identity as an Indian nation, wouldn't they?"

The elected chief of the people in question nodded and demanded in a resigned tone, "What in the hell have they ever gotten out of being Indians that they couldn't manage better as tax-paying self-supporting Americans? Everybody would rather go hunting and fishing than work on a farm or at some trade. But you keep up with the world or the world leaves you behind. So, like it or not, in years to come we Cherokee will live like other full citizens descended from ancient warriors, red, white or black, unless we want to spend our lives on government handouts between quaint tribal rituals, like animals in a zoo!"

Longarm whistled and said, "You sure sound a lot like our own General Sheridan, Chief. Have you shared your views on future progress with any member of that *Kituhwa* Society?"

Dennis Stuart Bushyhead shook his head and gravely replied he wasn't ready to die just yet.

Then young Jim Deadpony came back to declare, "We have trouble here in Tahlequah, Chief. Somebody just killed that old Irishman who was going to help Longarm, here, locate that moonshine still!"

Chapter 9

Longarm asked who they were talking about as the three of them went out the back door and along a tree-shaded alley. Bushyhead said he'd sent for a barkeep in Fort Smith he'd known out California way. His old drinking pal had hailed from County Kerry and he'd bragged more than once about the making of potheen there'd been no reason to bother the English excise agents about. His name had been Donovan and, after more than one American revenuer had searched in vain for that moonshine still on Cherokee range, Donovan had written to the chief that he had a pretty good idea how they were doing it.

As they ducked into the small coach station hotel by way of the kitchen door Jim Deadpony explained how Donovan had told him there was a way to make potheen or fair Irish whiskey without any still at all. Neither he, Chief Bushyhead, nor Longarm knew too much about such doings. Longarm only knew enough to know it could be dangerous as hell to drink moonshine made by anyone who wasn't sure what they were doing.

When fruits, grains, sugars, and such fermented they broke down into all sorts of chemistry, good and bad for human innards. When you just sort of let things spoil until they were good for getting drunk on you wound up with softer stuff called beer, cider, pulque, wine, and so on. Whether it tasted good or not, there was seldom enough alcohol or other poisons in the brew to kill anybody. But when you commenced to distill fermented starchy sugars into brandy, gin, rum, whiskey and such you increased both the amounts of alcohol and the toxic by-products such as fusel oil, a deadly poison, along with less lethal ethers that would only drive you crazy or leave you blind for good. So a customer in the market for moonshine had to know who he was dealing with, or want a drink mighty bad. Controlling the delicate balance betwixt such a lethal mixture and tasteless grain alcohol, without any still at all, had to be quite an art, if it was even possible.

They went up the back stairs to the room of the man who'd never explain what he'd had in mind, now. The room reeked of vomit, even though the windows had been thrown open. That same undertaker in the butcher's apron was there with a taller and grayer man Longarm was introduced to as the sawbones who ran their tribal clinic. The one member of the hotel staff, a pretty young chambermaid, was the only one there who looked to be a full-blooded Indian. They said she'd been the one who called for the doc when she discovered the body.

The body was that of an older man with a potbelly and a puffy red nose. He lay half out of his hired bed in his soiled pants and puked-up undershirt, mouth agape and bloodshot eyes staring upside down at the far wall in utter horror, as if he'd seen something or somebody doing something awful over that way.

Chief Bushyhead asked the doc what might have left the barkeep in such a distressing state. The Cherokee physician shrugged and said, "I'm not about to autopsy any *Ontwaganha* without permission from his next of kin. But, off hand, a heart stroke or murder most foul works just as well. You puke either way."

Longarm had been introduced as a prospector called Crawford. So he had no sensible call to ask questions. But young Deadpony knew his onions. He turned to the maid as he said, "He'd just come here aboard the stage from Fort Smith. Did anybody else come to call on him since he checked in barely an hour ago, Miss Redbird?"

The maid shook her head and replied, "No. He rang down for room service twice and asked each time for some baking soda and a glass of water. I found him this way when I came up with the second helping. Nobody called on him this afternoon. I don't think anybody but yourself knew he'd checked in."

The doctor asked if the dead man had ordered any other food or drink. The maid said he hadn't. Deadpony asked the doctor what he was getting at.

The older Cherokee said, "It's a long haul from Fort Smith and he'd have had no chance to eat or drink anything this side of Tenkiller's ferry on the Illinois, better than an hour's ride south. Since he ate or drank nothing here in Tahlequah we're talking slow poison, or a bad heart he should have stayed home with. What was he doing up this way to begin with?"

Chief Bushyhead said, "We were old friends from the Gold Rush of '49 and I wanted to talk to him about some other old pals I've been trying to get in touch with on personal business."

Nobody there saw fit to question their chief's right to look up old pals. But the undertaker wanted to know what happened next.

The portly chief sighed and said, "We'd better just keep him on ice until I can get in touch with his next of kin. I believe he had one of his kids working with him over to Fort Smith. We ought to be able to get in touch with them through the saloon where he was the bookkeeper and relief night manager."

The undertaker said he'd have the dead man carried over to his work shed behind the church. The doctor said something about getting back to his clinic. Longarm didn't say anything as he followed the chief out into the hall. Deadpony stayed inside with the undertaker, the corpse, and that pretty maid.

Longarm waited until the doctor had gruffed past them and headed down the front stairs before he asked Chief Bushyhead what he was supposed to do with nobody having any suggestions as to where in the hell he was supposed to start.

The portly Cherokee leader said, "I'm not sure. I was counting on Pete Donovan to offer you some sensible suggestions. You'd be welcome to come out to my Park Hill spread with me, of course. But I'm not sure how long we could hide just who you were and just what you were up to, here in the territory."

Longarm said, "Since my partner, Moses Bradley, hasn't

arrived as yet, I could likely wait for him here at this hotel at least a day or so before too many got to wondering."

The Cherokee chief grinned like a kid and said, "Quanah Parker was right. You do think fast on your feet for a white boy, Mister Crawford. So why don't we try that and, meanwhile, I'll see if I can enlist us another expert on Irish potheen."

Longarm asked what made him so sure those moonshiners were running a particularly Irish brand of corn to those thirsty Kansas farmers.

Bushyhead gestured toward the door of the room they'd left the dead Irishman in and replied, "Pete did. I'd sent him a jar of the stuff I had one of my other pals buy for me up in Coffeyville. That was what gave Pete the notion somebody might be using some really sneaky moonshine methods. He said there was something about the taste that gave the real stuff away. That was what he called potheen made by the little people out in some bog, the real stuff."

Longarm asked the Cherokee if he'd noticed anything wild about the taste of the jar he'd bought on the sly.

The Indian who wasn't officially allowed to sample strong spirits shook his grayin' head and said, "Just tasted like fire-water, to me, and I've tasted firewater made with everything from sour mash to cane sugar. All the whiskey I've ever been served as Irish tasted as if it had been made from barley malt, not corn, by the way. You can tell the Irish from the Scotch malts because the Scotch is more smoky and . . . That's funny, now that I think about it!"

Longarm asked what was so funny, and the older man licked his lips as if to remind them before he decided, "That moonshine we bought up Kansas way was good stuff, for moonshine, but it had this sort of wild and woolly aftertaste. I can't put my finger on it and I thought it was Scotch and not Irish whiskey that left a funny aftertaste. The stuff was clear as branch water and made from corn instead of barley, and I've no idea how Pete came to the conclusion it had been distilled by ancient Druid methods under a mushroom. I have some extra jars out at my place if you'd like to sample some before you ride out after the rascals."

"Ride where?" Longarm demanded with a raised eyebrow as the older man tried to look innocent.

Bushyhead said, "I thought we'd established that. If I don't send somebody it's only a question of time before the Kansas State Guard or the U.S. Army is ordered in and then how do we ever convince Washington we're ready for full citizenship? You people can be so picky about a few scalpings and some of our boys will be boys when outsiders trample their crops and whistle at their girls."

Longarm glanced around to make certain they were alone before he shook his head wearily and asked, "Have you ever had the feeling you were being bullshitted, Chief? You know damned well I'd never catch a Cherokee spitting on the sidewalk outside unless you and your very own tribal police wanted me to. So you don't really want me to do shit and I've come all this way on a fool's errand to make you look as if you really care about them complaints out of Kansas!"

Bushyhead blustered, "That's not fair! I asked Judge Parker over in Fort Smith to send his own deputy marshals after the rascals. Feel free to ask him why he said he had no dog in this fight if you want!"

Longarm said, "I believe you. I've worked with that Fort Smith District Court in the past and they're good. But you knew when you asked that Isaac Parker ain't free to swear out warrants against just any old members of the Five Civilized Tribes. Him and his deputies have all the caseload they can handle, rounding up white outlaws and heap bad Injuns who've committed crimes against whites *in Arkansas*. Old Isaac is under pressure from the newspaper sob sisters for hanging the few such rascals he's hung, so far. You knew his riders would poke about and never make any arrests to be tried in his Arkansas court when you requested his help, with some fine print left out."

Bushyhead got sort of red faced under his coppery complexion but tried to brazen it out before asking what fine print Longarm meant.

Longarm said, "That part in the orders I left Denver under, saying I'd be serving as an officer of your tribal courts. I never got orders to deliver any moonshiners to either Colorado nor Kansas. You Cherokee requested and were granted my professional skills as a lawman of some reputation as a tracker."

The chief nodded and demanded, "So? You're hinting at some devious motives for that simple request for help?"

Longarm snorted, "I ain't *hinting*. I'm *saying*. I wasn't even able to find *you* this afternoon without Cherokee help. I keep saying I don't know your country or your nation half as well as a whole heap of Arkansas and Kansas lawmen of the pale-faced persuasion. But you keep telling me that's what qualifies me. So let me tell you how it qualifies me. It qualifies me as the scapegoat stuck with an unsolved federal case. You sent for me because you had to send for somebody and most anybody else might catch those Cherokee constituents of yours before the next tribal election!"

Dennis Stuart Bushyhead sighed and said, "Quanah was right about that, too. You don't pull punches. But you've over-simplified our delicate situation. Why don't we ride out to my spread and talk it out over supper? You may feel less suspicious about my motives after a good meal and a night's sleep."

Longarm shook his head and said, "I'm paid to be suspicious and you've been acting suspicious as all get-out. So I have a way better notion. I'm going to check into this hotel long enough to wire Denver and wait for a reply from my regular boss. If he tells me to try and pull your chestnuts out of the fire after I tell him in code how hot they seem to be, I'll look you up again in the morning. But don't bet all your chips on Marshal Billy Vail being dumber than Judge Isaac Parker, once he has a clearer picture of this dumb situation!"

Longarm headed down the front steps. Chief Bushyhead followed him down to the dinky lobby, protesting that Longarm had him all wrong and that he meant to send some wires himself.

Lowering his voice, the chief said, "I don't want to talk about it here, Mister *Crawford*. But I think I can get you somebody else to help you with that, ah, geological survey."

Longarm shrugged and said, "I just told you I'll be here overnight. It's going to take time for my boss to make up his mind and after that me and a couple of horses I know could use the rest before I have to take them back to Fort Gibson."

Young Jim Deadpony came down to the lobby, saying something about a dead Irishman's kin in Fort Smith. Bushyhead left with him as Longarm asked the hatchet-faced full-blood behind the check-in counter how he went about hiring a room for the night.

The Indian who ran the place for the white-owned stage line asked if he had any baggage.

Longarm said, "Over at the livery near your municipal corral, save for this Winchester. Why don't I just pay in advance whilst I make up my mind whether to haul my saddlebags over this way?"

The room clerk said that sounded fair and hired Longarm a room, with meals or room service to be extra, for four bits a day. So Longarm took the key and allowed he'd lock his Winchester away before he went out to tend some other chores before bedtime.

It only took him a moment to do so. He found the room small but tidy a couple of doors down the poorly lit hallway from the fuss still going on around that dead Irishman from Fort Smith.

Longarm didn't want to look at the remains again. He braced the Winchester in a corner on the far side of the brass bedstead and got out his matches, albeit not to light another cheroot just then.

He stepped out in the hall, made sure nobody was watching, and dropped to one knee to wedge the match stem into the door crack under a bottom hinge as he locked his hired room up before pocketing the key and leaving by way of those back stairs.

He circled wide, came out of the alley at the far end of the block, and asked directions to their Western Union. Then he sheepishly strode almost all the way back to his hotel's front entrance. For the hotel stood smack between the stage coach stop and the telegraph office.

He wasn't surprised to find a sort of Swedish-looking white man running the place for Western Union. He didn't ask if the clerk had a Cherokee woman or not. He tore off a yellow night-letter blank to carefully word his message to Billy Vail. He didn't have to explain he was using a fake name, seeing he was fixing to sign Crawford to a wire old Billy would know he'd sent. Most of the rest would be as meaningless to his boss as it would be to anybody else sneaking a peek at it. All he had to do was evoke the name of some crooks they'd dealt with in the past, naming them as the local business associates he'd been asked to work with. Billy would be able to read the rest betwixt the lines. Political hacks were always trying to use public servants for their own ends and he knew how Billy Vail felt about that, too.

Sending the night-letter collect, Longarm went back to that livery and got his saddlebags from their tack room, leaving his bedroll and such with the McClellan. He figured he'd ride back to Fort Gibson more comfortable after a change of underwear and socks.

The shadows were starting to get longer and there were fewer folk out on the streets of Tahlequah now. So Longarm scouted up a regular supper of steak and potatoes with mince pie at the stage depot. The waitress and the cook were both pure-bloods. But they were used to serving white folk passing through betwixt Forts Gibson and Smith.

He went easy on the coffee, knowing how tough it could be to fall asleep, alone, in a strange bed. Then he paid up, left a dime tip, and headed on over to leave the saddlebags with the rifle before he made a last tour of the town.

He'd used a white match stem because he'd found they were easy to see in tricky light. So he could see right off that the match stem he had inserted under the hinge as a crude burglar alarm was now winking up at him from the dark hall runner.

Longarm took a deep breath, let half of it out, and held the rest as he drew his .44-40 before gingerly trying to turn the knob of the door he distinctly remembered locking after him.

It turned easy. Somebody had unlocked the door and Lord only knew who, why, or just where they might be at the moment!

Chapter 10

With his saddlebags draped over one shoulder, Longarm tried the latch he distinctly remembered locking. The knob turned smoothly and silently. So Longarm got the saddlebags to whirling with his left hand, kicked the door inwards, and sent his baggage boomeranging in ahead of him and his gun muzzle.

His unexpected guest was headed his way with a lit candlestick in hand. So Longarm had time to see, as it fell to the floor when the swirling saddlebags hit and wrapped around her pretty little head like the wings of a monstrous brown bat, that he'd likely hurt and surely scared the liver and lights out of that Cherokee chambermaid, Miss Redbird!

As her candlestick hit the floor and flickered out, the gal flew backwards, wrapped in brown leather, to land on her back atop that brass bedstead with her long tawny legs flung skyward and apart, as her skirts flew up around her shapely hips. And it was just as well the candle flickered out about then. For she wasn't wearing anything under her black poplin and white linen maid's outfit.

Longarm kicked the door shut after him and holstered his six-gun as he moved across the dark room to comfort her as she struggled out from under the five-foot length of leather packed with possibles to say dreadful things about it, and him, in Cherokee.

He could tell she was crying as well as cussing when he sat on the bedding beside her to sit her up and soothe her some, allowing he'd thought she was a burglar.

She sobbed that she'd only been doing her damned job. Whilst he'd been out that young Sergeant Deadpony had come by with a package for him. All she'd been trying to do was set it on his bed table for him with the note from the Cherokee lawman, damn his eyes.

Longarm held her gently as he got out his matches and thumbnailed a light, reaching out to light the oil lamp by the head of the bed, and, sure enough, there stood a brown bag with a folded square of white bond paper leaning against it.

He told the still shaken gal, "I suspect that's the jar of firewater I was expecting. Could I interest you in a drink to settle your nerves a mite?"

She snuggled closer to murmur, "I'm not supposed to drink on duty. Just hold me a moment more and I'll be all right."

So he naturally kissed her and she kissed back as downhome and natural. But then, as they sort of naturally fell backwards across the bedding she stiffened and protested, "Not so fast! I'm not supposed to do *that* on duty, either!"

So he let go of her and she rolled off the bedstead to her feet, all aflutter, as he asked her what time she got off duty.

She stammered, "Bringing your package up to you was my last chore for the day. But I have to check out and I don't think they'd want me fooling around with any of our room guests."

Longarm got to his own feet but kept his hands to himself as he smiled wistfully down at her and suggested, "Why don't you study on it, then? You'll know where to find me if you get to feeling lonesome. I wasn't planning on going nowheres else after dark in a strange town with no saloons."

She dimpled shyly up at him, knelt to pick up the candlestick she'd had knocked out of her hand, and asked him for a light before she went off into the gathering shades of evening with the same.

Longarm shut the door after her and threw the barrel bolt before he hung up his hat, coat, and gunbelt. Then he sat down on the bed to examine what Sergent Deadpony had dropped off for him earlier.

There was a quart jar of clear liquid in the bag. The hasty note from the young Cherokee addressed him as a Mister Craw-

69

ford and allowed the contents of that jar was the horse medicine he'd requested.

Longarm opened the jar and sniffed. The contents smelled about a hundred proof. Like most moonshine and a lot of other distilled drinks, corn liquor came clear as water because bonded whiskey was, by definition, dated and stored to age, usually in charred oak barrels that had been used, earlier, to age sherry. It was the aging in wood, or sometimes a dash of burnt sugar to get the color just right, that gave bourbon and such an amber glow.

Longarm took a sip from the jar. It wasn't bad for moonshine. But that was not to say it couldn't have used some time in a barrel to take the raw edges off and pick up some mellow aftertastes of charred wine-soaked oakwood. Fresh from the still, white lightning just tasted of water, alcohol, and a hint of the by-product esters that came along for the ride from the sour mash left behind, when the moonshiner knew what he was doing.

Longarm rose to carry the jar over to the washstand and mix a way thinner nightcap from a water ewer in a hotel tumbler. Nobody had complained of blindness up Kansas way as yet. But a man had to keep it in mind that he wasn't sipping bonded whiskey when it came in a jam jar with no label.

As he sampled his watered-down highball he found it easier to detect that aftertaste Chief Bushyhead had described as wild and woolly. Longarm moved back to the bedstead, sat the drink on the table, and got undressed all the way between thoughtful sips.

"More like sheep dip," he decided as he opened one saddlebag to take out a library book he'd brought along for just such tedious occasions.

He drew the covers down, fluffed the pillows up against the brass headrails, and tried another sip as he tried to recall just what you mixed into your average sheep dip. He didn't detect any naphtha or larkspur lotion in the moonshine, which was just as well. The odor of the creosote some sheep men swore by was missing as well. So what was left . . . ?

"The damned *sheep!*" he decided as, rolling some of the watered-down corn liquor in his mouth, he tasted, or in point of fact *smelled* just a hint of wet wool.

He decided it might be safer to smoke in bed as he cracked open the book about Cherokee history he'd added to the other stuff he'd brought along to bone up on. For, like most self-educated men, Longarm read way more than your average college student. A college student had a wise and learned professor to tell him which version in which book had to be the Alpha and Omega on any subject. But when a man was trying to study on his own he noticed you usually got three opinions out of any two experts and a tedious number of experts had written conflicting tomes on the Five Civilized Tribes in general and the Cherokee in particular. That's what you got when a semiassimilated bunch of literate half-breeds got to comparing notes on facts with friend and foe alike—conflicting tomes.

The particular tome he was browsing had more to do with what Dennis Stuart Bushyhead had said about wanting to gain fee-simple land titles and full citizenship, as selfsupporting tax-payers out from under the sometimes bewildering guidance of the Bureau of Indian Affairs.

One persistent tribal myth the Cherokee liked to tell about their troubles with the federal government was that some few brave Cherokee had refused to move west with the bulk of their nation and so they'd run off to hide out in the Smokey Mountains, where no soldiers dared follow. This was, like a lot of lost-cause folk tales, bullshit.

By more than one ruling of the United States Supreme Court the *bulk* of the Cherokee Nation had been defined as a dependent Indian tribe. So most Cherokee had been on the books as wards of the state and off the books as tax-paying free-holders. But, over the years as Cherokee and white settlers had intermarried and combined their holdings under white as well as Indian custom, many a pale Cherokee or dusky white family had been accepted as just folks. A band of about eight hundred pure-bloods settled outside the official Cherokee Nation had made a separate treaty with the federal government in 1819. This Qualla or Quallatown band had been given full title to their lands and were not being dealt with as dependent Indians. So neither they nor anybody else had said anything about them moving anywhere when the recognized Cherokee chiefs they preferred to ignore agreed to go.

The soldiers had left them alone because they'd had enough of a chore moving the Indians Washington had ordered them to move and, in point of fact, the military escort provided by General Winfield Scott had been meant more to protect and assist the people moving west under their own paid-off leaders than most Cherokee cared to recall.

After that, in addition to the independent Qualla Cherokee, another hundred or so Cherokee who'd been slated to go west under their tough Chief Euchella had moved the other way, to join the Qualla Band, and a general more cautious about Indians than the late George Armstrong Custer had graciously decided they deserved exemption as reward for being such good little Indians.

Counting other Cherokee and part-Cherokee who simply lay low until the trouble had blown over, an estimated fourteen to fifteen hundred Eastern Cherokee were now living as Chief Bushyhead aimed for his own Western Cherokee to live, with no tribal relationship as far as Uncle Sam was concerned, whilst free to live as Indian or white as they felt they wanted to. The book said most of those Eastern Cherokee still cultivated hoe-farms and raised stock around the Smoky Mountains.

They'd avoided a heap of trouble for themselves during the war because they'd been content to do their own chores without holding slaves. After that they'd waited out the war, well armed, up in their own remote hollows, where neither side had felt any call to mess with them.

A few of their young men had run off to join one side or the other, reminding Longarm of the way he'd acted as a fool kid off a West-By-God Virginia hill spread. But most Eastern Cherokee had just mustered and bred to where, more recently, some had applied to their western kin for Cherokee citizenship in more wide open spaces.

Longarm caught himself yawning, put out his cheroot, shut the book, and trimmed the lamp. There'd been nothing about moonshining and Longarm felt sure Billy Vail would agree they were being used as window dressing by a political machine anxious to preserve the status quo.

The book had said and Longarm had already suspected, knowing how calling any man a crooked politician could be repeating yourself, he wasn't being told the whole story. That book had intimated the saintly John Ross had taken his own graft envelopes for moving his people west without an all-out fight. Once he had, the persecuted cuss had managed to regain the upper hand over the faction that had outflanked him. Old Ross had never seen fit to explain his part in the sudden deaths of a heap of political rivals.

Longarm yawned again in the dark but had trouble nodding off as he thought back to other tribal politics he'd read about or survived. It sure beat all how a little civilization could savage up your average Indian.

With Tashunka Witko or Crazy Horse as the exception that proved a rule, most of the really bloody war chiefs had been part white or even pure white. Simon Girty, leading Indians against white settlers during the American Revolution, had scared the poor Indians with his cruelty, and Hair-buying Hamilton, the Royal Governor at Detroit who'd paid well for Yankee scalps, hadn't done a thing to soothe the savagery.

Chief Brant of the Mohawks, Osceola of the Seminoles, and the now much calmer Quanah of the Comanches had all been part white or influenced by white mentors. The Na Déné, now known as Navaho, still stayed pretty much to themselves and their traditions of Changing Woman. So Kit Carson had been able to calm them down with one campaign. It was their meaner Apache cousins who wore gold crosses, and gave their ornery kids names such as Victorio and Geronimo so, yep, the smartest things for a white lawman to do in half-breed country would be to mind his own beeswax.

He shut his eyes and tried to think of something that would neither worry him or give him an erection. There weren't that many choices when a man found himself alone in bed, bare ass.

Then, just as Longarm was about to strike another match, there came a gentle knock upon his chamber door, and he doubted like hell it was any fool raven. So he threw off the covers and rose to his bare feet in the dark. He considered fumbling for a towel to wrap around his waist, but the darkness would hide a hard-on as well as any towel; that is, if anybody wanted him to hide his feelings at such a time.

He didn't feel much call to. He'd asked her to think it over and neither one of them would think he was talking about an invitation to a spelling bee. So he just shot the bolt, threw the door open, and reached out in the darkness for two hands full of romance.

She smelled romantic as rosewater and the shemale body odors of a warm day spent in clean crisp calico usually smelled. He figured she'd changed into her regular duds without taking time for a tub bath after she got off for the evening. He didn't see why she felt so oddly stiff as he hauled her in to kiss her some more. She'd kissed back warmer the last time. But she warmed up some as he swept her off her feet, tongued her between her warm responsive lips, and carried her over to the bedstead.

As he lowered her to the rumpled bedding one of her hands brushed his bare flank and she gasped, "Dear Lord! You're naked!"

He spread them both across the bedding and ran his free hand under her calico skirts to find her warm thighs just as bare while he soothed, "I was about to start without you when you changed your mind, honey."

She started to say something. It would have as likely been something dumb about her not being that sort of a gal. So he just kissed her some more and ran his hand up between the thighs she was trying to cross to where it hit pay dirt amid the roots of her soft chaparral. Her warm slit was already wet with anticipation as he probed her with two fingers. He tongued her deeper and, as her thighs opened in surrender, she was that kind of a gal before she could tell him she wasn't that kind of a gal.

He lay naked atop her gingham-clad torso to make certain she'd be willing before he stripped her down as well. From the way she moved her hips in time with his thrusts they were getting there. She dug her nails into his bare back and moaned, "My God, I seem to be getting raped, and whatever you're doing to me, don't stop!"

But he did as he suddenly recognized her voice as well as her body as the sound and feel of a total stranger. She moaned, "What's the matter? I told you not to stop, damn you!"

To which Longarm could only reply, "I'm sorry, ma'am. I thought you were somebody else!"

Chapter 11

He naturally started in again, harder, as most men would have in such inspiring company. She shuddered in climax before him and came again, with him, when he got over his shyness, to shoot his own wad.

He didn't have to ask her to shuck the rest of her duds. She asked him to let her get on top and stripped her bodice and skirts off over her head as she rode up and down his old organ grinder like a merry-go-round pony grinding up and down to lively clockwork tunes. When her passion got her to moving awkwardly on his pole he rolled her on her bare tits and belly to enter her dog style, and she said that was a new one on her, too. Albeit he had his doubts about her never taking it that way and wilder, before, once she got her back arched enough to thrust her soft rump up at him so friendly. He'd noticed, before he'd been certain, that whoever she was packed more ample and softer curves than the chambermaid he'd been swapping spit with earlier.

They wound up back in a sort of old-fashioned position, with him in her as they both lay on their sides, face-to-face, with one of her legs up under his armpit and the other wrapped around his waist. They lay still that way, both having come again. So Longarm figured it was time to say, in as formal a tone as he could manage, "I fear you have the advantage of me, ma'am. You don't have to call me Mister Crawford whilst we're fucking. My friends all call me Duncan. And you . . ."

"I'd be Opal Standstall from up Ochelata way. Our cattle

75

spread is only a few miles from that rock-oil well they drilled at Bartlesville near the Osage line in '75."

Longarm started to ask what in blue thunder he was supposed to care about drilling for rock-oil near her fool cattle spread. Then he remembered he was supposed to be a prospector named Crawford in cahoots with that late expert on the subject, Moses Bradley.

He didn't want to tell a likely customer it had been the oil well man, not himself, somebody had put a Buffalo round in. So he said he had been waiting there for the expert who knew more than himself about rock-oil.

He said, "Old Moe did mention that earlier oil strike up north of Tulsa Town. We'll have to wait until he gets here if we want to know more about it, I reckon. Moe asked me to tag along because I've prospected in Indian country before, no offense. I really know more about panning for color than drilling for oil and do you mind if I light us a smoke to share, Miss Opal?"

She demurely replied, "Go ahead. I've been wondering what you look like, too. When I asked downstairs for Moses Bradley they told me his partner, meaning you, could be found up here."

She moved her hips teasingly and added, "I'm so glad I found you in such a friendly mood!"

Longarm reached out in the dark for a smoke and a light as he gave her another inch of his semierection, took the cheroot between his grinning teeth, and thumbed a light.

It felt a mite odd to gaze upon a strange woman for the first time with your cock inside her. But it didn't feel bad. Opal Standstall had big blue eyes in a high-cheekboned face as dark as the Cherokee maid he'd kissed earlier. After that Opal was softer all over, with heroic tawny breasts to balance her generous but shapely hips. Neither gal had half the white blood Chief Bushyhead could boast. Neither could have passed for white, albeit Opal seemed to have been brought up more white, judging by the crumpled dress at the foot of the bed and the high button shoes and knee-high silk stockings she still had on. Her shiny jet-black hair was pinned up fashionable as any high-toned eastern gal's and he suspected she'd plucked her eyebrows some to get them so refined. She smiled at him in the soft flickering light and said, "I think you're pretty, too. I was expecting somebody older and balder."

He took a drag on the cheroot and placed it between her lips as he thrust another inch of renewed inspiration into her and said, "I'd be pleased as punch with any bald lady tight as you betwixt her thighs, Miss Opal. But before I screw you silly some more you'd better tell me what you really came up here to talk to me about."

She backhanded the cheroot, letting smoke trickle out the flaring nostrils of the Roman nose centered in her dark exotic face and soberly replied, "I've had so much fun fucking that I almost forgot. As I said, I have this cattle spread up by Ochelata. Mostly bluestem on shallow limestone soil. So, like everyone else up that way, we've drilled for well water."

Longarm took a silent drag on the cheroot. Everybody knew you had to drill for water when there wasn't any running past you.

She said, "The water we've been wind-pumping out of the bedrock is barely sweet enough for our herd. You can taste both brine and brimstone in it and, when you let it stand, an oily scum forms on the surface. It costs money to drill through limestone. So we sent for you and Moses Bradley to tell us if we should drill deeper or be content with what we have. Could we get doggy-style again, seeing you want to talk and fuck at the same time, dear?"

Longarm allowed that suited him just fine. So it only took a minute for them to get her on her hands and knees across the mattress with her big brown rump thrust up in line with his own hips as he stood on the rug behind her. He lit the lamp, took a hip bone in either hand, and leaned his head and shoulders back with the cheroot gripped between his teeth as he commenced to give it to her in long lazy thrusts before he asked to hear more about this *we* she kept referring to.

She allowed she was a grass widow keeping the books for her aunt and uncle up Ochelata way. He didn't ask why she'd divorced a husband with a Cherokee name, once she'd declared she'd been to business school and could handle double-entry bookkeeping. A heap of red and white men of the more rustic persuasion tended to beat women who smart-assed them and even educated folk, male and female, had certain doubts

77

about any gal supporting herself at a man's job. Opal didn't say it, but Longarm felt sure some of her kin suspected a gal who could handle a man's job might feel she had the right to feel as bold as any man, and he had to allow they had a point about this particular double-entry expert.

He said it was early, yet, when she asked if he'd like to try some double-entry in the sixty-nine position. He said, "I can't talk with my mouth full and I was fixing to ask you about them other rock-oil wells up your way. Any bulk minerals that cost less than say, silver, eat up a heap of your profits getting them to market. Where do they haul that oil they've already drilled, up around Tulsa town?"

She said, "Drill me deeper, faster. They raft barrels of rock-oil down the Caney to where it meets the Saint Lou and Frisco Railroad a few miles east of Tulsa town. After that it's loaded into those big Standard Oil tank cars owned by young Johnny Rockefeller. Lord only knows where it goes from there."

Longarm did. He said, "Rockefeller has this swamping oil refinery back in Ohio. He buys different grades of rock-oil from all over and refines it into standardized grades of lamp oil, axle grease, naphtha and so on. That's how come they call his outfit Standard Oil of Ohio. As I understand it, he don't own many oil wells, his ownself. He'd as soon control the transporting, refining, and marketing after letting gents like . . . me and old Moe do the work and take the risks of finding it. It ain't that easy to find. That recent strike up north of Tulsa town is the first I've heard of, this far west."

She moaned, "Faster! Faster! I know I said I came here tonight to talk business. But business can wait and my flesh is on fire! I fear I'd forgotten how good this can feel, even with a man you despise. My childhood sweetheart turned out to be a drunk and, once you say you married a drunk, the only question anyone is really interested in is why you didn't leave him sooner!"

She arched her back and lowered her head to chew on a corner of a pillow as she gasped, "This was why! I really need more of this than anybody but a lusty son of a bitch seems able to give me. So give it to me, you lusty son of a bitch!"

He told her not to mention his momma or any other shemale kin while he was being so disrespectful of womankind. But she went on cussing, dirty as a mean little kid who'd just learned what the words meant, as he pounded her to glory, a tad excited by her filthy mouth, if the truth should be told.

It sure beat-all how, no matter what a man told a maid as he was courting her, it was a lot more fun to rut like a hog with a sweet young thing than it would have been to dance the minuet with her.

Opal seemed to feel the same way about romance and when he protested he was still smoking a three-for-a-nickel cheroot for Gawd's sake, she allowed she'd play a solo on the French horn and damned if she didn't do that wild and dirty, too, taking his full erection down her throat as she lay with her head off the bed, chin held high, to let him ram it in and out of her in that position as if he was long-donging her pretty upside-down face. She was pleasuring herself as she took him that way. So he didn't have to worry about her enjoying herself, a heap, when he came in her pretty face whilst she sort of gargled his cock.

He took it out and flopped beside her on the bed, allowing he was sorry he'd lost control at the last and hoped he hadn't hurt her. She propped herself up on one elbow to wipe her mouth with the back of her hand and sighed, "Oh, thank you! That's something I've always wanted to try."

He couldn't help sounding dubious as he asked, "You've never done nothing like that before?"

She said, "I've been practicing with a hairbrush handle. My aunt Ruby learned the trick from a depraved Creek woman. She told me men loved it and it could give a queer thrill to a girl, once she learned to control her impulse to gag as it slipped past the base of her tongue. Circus sword-swallowers learn to relax those same throat muscles and, once you do, you can take a full yard of sword, or cock, if any man born of mortal woman could offer a girl that much. I doubt I could take twelve full inches, the other way."

Longarm chuckled fondly and said, "I'm sorry I ain't got quite that much for us to experiment with. You say your aunt Ruby spends so much time worrying about such matters, Miss Opal? It sounds as if you have a lot of time on your hands up at that cow spread. What does your uncle have to say about all this experimenting with hairbrush handles and other men with freak cocks?"

She blandly explained, "Nothing. We never invited him to play. You see, Uncle Walt and Aunt Ruby are brother and sister, not husband and wife. Standstall is my married name. The three of us were Ridges of the Deer clan. Aunt Ruby likes to make love to most anyone who'll try. But Uncle Walt is . . . sort of queer."

Longarm had to laugh. He asked, "You mean your uncle is queer to suck three-foot dicks or you ladies find him queer because he doesn't want to?"

The lusty Cherokee gal shrugged her bare brown shoulders and told him, "I don't think he has any sex life at all. He's never married. He's never had any male or shemale friends he seemed to want to fool with. He just rides the range all day, whether it's roundup time or not, and sits in his rocking chair most nights until bedtime. Lord only knows what he does in bed, by himself. He never lets anybody go to bed with him. Aunt Ruby's offered. I don't think it would be right, even if he was willing, do you?"

Longarm said he doubted it. He had no call to observe it seemed to be trash whites who went in for incest while most Indians were totally disgusted by the notion. The blood feud between the so called Sioux and Crows had resulted when the Sparrow Hawk clan of a once united nation had sanctioned intermarriage between second cousins. The people now known as Lakota had turned on them and never referred to the nation the BIA had down as "crow" by any other term than "sister fuckers." There'd been nothing in any of those recent books he'd read saying how Cherokee might feel about one big happy family, such as she seemed to be bragging on.

He suppressed a yawn and asked her to tell him more about oil wells.

She seemed to feel it could wait until the real expert, Moses Bradley, showed up to say what a geological survey of her aunt and uncle's cattle spread was likely to cost them.

She didn't sound interested in the subject at the moment, either, as she coyly suggested one last way he hadn't come in her.

Longarm grimaced and said, "I'd just as soon pass on that

kind offer this evening, seeing there's no adjoining bath for us both to tidy up in, after. Why not save that Greek stuff for some time out to the old swimming hole on your uncle's spread?"

She pouted that there wasn't any swimming hole that private within an easy ride of her kith and kin or the hired help. She said her uncle had some colored riders and added, "I'd just die if a darkie saw me taking it in the ass, wouldn't you?"

Longarm said he'd feel awful if anybody ever caught him taking it in the ass. So they did it some more the old-fashioned way and then she said she had to get back to the family she was staying with in town, lest they think she might be up to something naughty.

Longarm didn't argue. That last time had been sort of showing off and he could see why her uncle Walter liked to be left alone at night, if her horny sounding aunt was anything like her. So she swiftly dressed, tidied up her hair, and asked him to trim the lamp so's she could slip out unobserved.

Once he had, she moved down the back stairs, out through the deserted kitchen, and through the dark backyard to where a lean man all in black stood waiting for her in the alley.

As she joined him, the brooding figure asked, "Well?"

She replied with a Mona Lisa smile, "He claimed to be a fucking rock-hound. *Boy* did he claim to be a fucking rock-hound! But they might have been right about him and, in any case, impulsive girls who ride the owlhoot trail with uncaring brutes have to worry about their own good names. So I told him I was Opal Standstall from up Ochelata way."

The far from kindly gunslick she rode with laughed uncertainly and asked, "That man-crazy half-wit living in sin with her own kin? Whatever possessed you to tell any man a whopper like that?"

She demurely explained, "I never told him Sidewinding Walt was said to be rutting with his niece and baby sister. I told him good old Walter wouldn't *care* if a stranger prospecting for rock-oil asked crazy Ruby for a blow job. Do you remember what Sidewinder Walt did to that creep at the Tulsa town stock show, just for asking his baby sister to dance?"

The gunslick who sometimes found himself uneasy in the

company of such a treacherous beauty didn't answer.

She said, "Oh, don't pout. I was only hoping to save you some trouble. But feel free to shoot him yourself if you're feeling left out!"

Chapter 12

The next day dawned overcast and gloomy. Longarm had already seen they got more summer rain over this way. So after a breakfast of eggs over steak he ambled over to the livery to break out his frock coat and rain slicker. He was carrying both over his arm as he headed back across the main square in his shirtsleeves. Before he could make it to the Western Union he was stopped by that burly and surly Will Cash of the Indian Police.

The big blue-clad Cherokee got right to the point. He said, "That kid sergeant who brown-noses the National Party machine told me your name was Bradley. You told me you were named Crawford and they have you down as a Crawford over to the hotel. I'm waiting."

Longarm smiled easily and said, "Jim Deadpony had me mixed up with the other prospector and business partner I'm still waiting for, Moe Bradley. He'd older and not as pretty. But he knows more than me about prospecting for rock-oil."

The local rider scowled and said, "They have looked for rock-oil around here. They have found none. Where is this other prospector if the two of you are supposed to be hunting together?"

Longarm let his annoyance show, since it was a free country, even when Indians were running it. He said, "If I knew where Moe was I'd hardly be waiting for him, would I? I just told you he knows more than me about rock-oil. I know he looked for some down around Park Hill the last time he came through. Mayhaps he wants to look there some more or mayhaps we'll be head up around Tulsa Town where they drilled earlier. Why are you pestering me instead of your own superior, Jim Deadpony? The sarge was the one who identified me, right?"

Will Cash growled, "Wrong. He said you were somebody called Moses Bradley and that *vginili usdi* has yet to see the day he'll be a real lawman's superior! He got those stripes by brown-nosing them Black Republicans and I'll have you know my mother was a turtle!"

It wasn't easy. But Longarm managed not to laugh as he remembered the maternal clans many Cherokee still bragged on had been named after critters.

As if to confirm Longarm's guess, the burly Will Cash grumbled on, "That Deer Clan squirt was made by the BIA just to please Bushyhead, speaking of brown-nosers. That Black Republican who claims he was born *Tsalagi* skips to the tune when the BIA agents fart!"

Longarm mildly asked, "Is it safe to bet a Black Republican is worse than any other brand of *Ontwaganha*, Officer Cash?"

The burly Cherokee muttered, "Damned A. *Ontwaganha* only means an outsider. You, an Osage, or even a Black Seminole would be *Ontwaganha*. A Black Republican is another fucking *species*, see?"

Longarm said, "I'm commencing to. Is it safe to bet you ain't a member of Chief Bushyhead's National Progressive Party?"

The full-blood growled, "Damned A! If it was up to me the traditional Downing Machine would still be running things. Lew Downing was a chief who demanded more and gave less to the fucking BIA. Nobody in Washington loves us for our healthy tans. The one and only way you can hope to get what's coming to you from Washington is when you stomp your heels and show them you ain't afraid of them! But why am I telling you all this? You don't look like no eastern dude. You likely know how the nations who scare folk the most get the best deals from Washington!"

Longarm couldn't resist remarking, "Yeah, I couldn't help noticing them sissy Tanoans still live in their same pueblos and farm their same corn milpas, over Taos way. I reckon they'd have gotten the same great deal Crazy Horse and Sitting

Bull wound up with, in the end, if only they'd shown more fight."

Then, because he really wanted to learn, he quickly added, "Tell me something, Officer Cash. How come there seems to be some dispute as to just who's running you Indian Police, these days?"

Will Cash grimaced, shrugged, and said, "There's the officious chain of command and there's politics. Up until the War Between the States we had full self-government, with our own elected judges, sheriffs, and so on. The people divided into factions for and against the Union during the war. We know who won. It left a lot of people very bitter, red, white, and black. The Black Republicans wanted to take away all of our old self-governing powers and treat us as defeated hostiles. But John Ross begged for us, while Stand O'Watie defied the Union, Ross, and everybody else to come and take the guns away from him and his riders if anyone thought we were afraid! So then there was a new treaty and we were allowed this half-ass government you see today."

Longarm was too slick a questioner to let on he'd caught that one slip about riding with Stand O'Watie and his Cherokee in gray. So he asked in an understanding tone if that meant the tribe was allowed to manage its own civil affairs but had to defer to the BIA when it came to criminal courts and police matters.

The Indian policeman scowled darkly and said, "You know it does. I saw the way you grinned when I tried to arrest you yesterday."

Longarm shook his head gravely and replied, "If it gives you any comfort, you had me worried shitless when young Deadpony came along to save my white ass. I had it on good authority that you boys do get to arrest white outlaws as long as you turn them over to the military or federal courts and, after that, you said somebody had murdered a famous white man?"

The Indian lawman shrugged and pointed back across the square with his big brown jaw to say, "Deputy federal marshal, riding for Revenue, I reckon. Petunia Squirreltail says she knew him from Fort Gibson. She called him Longarm and said he was after moonshiners. Serves him right for messing with

85

an *atsilv-gelohi tsalagi* on his own reservation!"

Longarm asked in a desperately casual tone about Petunia and wasn't at all upset to hear she'd delivered her damned jam jars down the main street a piece and headed out to her own family spread. If she'd been by the undertaker's to pay her respects to his remains she hadn't said anything. It was just as likely she hadn't. It hardly mattered whether she was worried about her own rep or hadn't meant some of those sweet words uttered wet and horny. The important thing was that he still seemed to be officiously dead.

He asked the Indian lawman if they planned to arrest anybody for killing him. Will Cash shook his head and didn't sound too concerned as he replied, "No. It was probably the bunch he was after. We scouted the belfry of First Adventist. But if the sniper was waiting up there he left no sign, and the door to the ladderway was padlocked. Kids are always climbing up in church spires and crying when they find out how frightening it can be to climb back down."

Longarm casually asked, "How come you thought the killer fired from up yonder? Somebody spotted gunsmoke?"

The Indian shook his head and said, "That kid sergeant told us to scout up there because it was so logical. That's what a kid sergeant calls the most obvious place, logical. During the war the artillery was always knocking down logical church spires and factor chimneys. A lookout could get blown off a rocky crag by cannon fire, too. Nobody who knows shit about scouting scouts from the highest point within range. They were probably waiting for the lawman up in the hayloft of the livery or any one of a heap of second- or third-story windows all around, see?"

Longarm nodded soberly, allowed he felt safer with the streets of Tahlequah guarded by such an old soldier, and said he had to see if he had any messages waiting for him at the Western Union.

They didn't shake. But they parted friendly enough and Longarm mosied on to the telegraph office. That same total white man behind the counter had a night letter from Denver for him, addressed to a Mister Crawford. Old Billy Vail or just as likely young Henry, the office clerk who suffered under the delusion that he had a sardonic sense of humor, had composed a clumsy coded message that made for hard reading. But what it boiled down to was that whether the chief who'd sent for him was dealing from the bottom of the deck or not, a person or persons unknown had gunned what they took to be a U.S. deputy marshal and another white man who'd volunteered to hunt Indian moonshiners.

Billy Vail allowed that sudden death of the late Pete Donovan could have been from natural causes or aided and abetted by bad medicine.

Longarm didn't like that notion much. But he had to agree Donovan had died at a mighty handy time for those moonshiners who seemed to know some sneaky Irish way of distilling sour mash.

He wired back that he'd chase his own tail until he caught it, or found some other infernal sign to scout in country he didn't know amid folk who didn't seem to want him to find anything but rock-oil.

Then he asked the telegraph clerk what he'd told those Cherokee lawmen about telegrams from Fort Gibson the evening before that shooting at the municipal corral.

The sort of Swedish-looking Western Union man looked bemused and told Longarm, "Nobody asked this child anything about any shooting. We sent out a heap of wires on it, of course. The chief ordered both the provost marshal at the fort and the federal district court at Fort Smith notified. Then, let's see, they wired somebody in Denver about it. They had us pretty busy in the back. That may be why they never asked about any incoming messages about that famous gunfighter who managed to get himself gunned. They all do, in the end, you know."

Longarm grimaced and said, "Clay Allison managed to run over himself with a buckboard. I didn't think anybody would have wired about that disgusting Custis Long by name. But you'd recall it if somebody wired anybody anything about anybody heading this way with two ponies, a red bay and a dapple gray?"

The telegraph clerk laughed uncertainly and decided, "I surely would. Why would anybody be wiring anybody about the hides of horses?"

Longarm shrugged and said, "I meant to ask. But seeing

that you don't remember any such wire, they must have worded it another way. Tell me something. Do you handle many wires sent in Cherokee?"

The Western Union man smiled incredulously and demanded, "How? I understand Cherokee is written in them sort of Egyptian handy-griddle letters I have yet to see any Morse Code on."

Longarm explained, "A heap of folk understand that. But I have it on good authority that the Cherokee published their own newspaper, the *Cherokee Phoenix* in both English and Cherokee, using regular old Roman letters. They tried having some of Sequoia's squiggles cast as type and it cost like hell. So they just figured out how to spell the same sounds the regular way, see?"

The Western Union man was paid to know how you spelled most any old sound in dots, dashes, or Roman font. So he followed Longarm's drift, but then he said, "Nobody seems to send long messages in anything but plain English around here. I reckon any Cherokee who knows enough to wire anybody anything already knows how to speak English. Most of them do, whether they can read and write or not."

Longarm said, "A friendly Cherokee told me about them having all them different dialects to cope with. Let's try her another way. Might you ever send any Cherokee in the form of Cherokee *names*?"

The clerk look puzzled. Longarm insisted. "I'm talking about a plain English message about corn futures or the price of beef, addressed to somebody with a name like *saquo tali tsoy* and signed by say another such innocent-sounding surname?"

The white telegrapher backed up Longarm's earlier suspicions about his local social contacts by laughing and saying, "Aw, that just means one, two, three, right?"

Longarm snapped, "I don't *know* how to say red pony or dapple gray mare in Cherokee, damn it. I was only asking whether many of the wires you send or receive for Cherokee have Cherokee at the beginning or end of the infernal message!"

"Why?" asked the Western Union man. "Are you a lawman? I thought you were out this way prospecting for rock-oil. What's made you take such an interest in that dead lawman? Did you know him?"

Longarm said he'd never seen the cuss before they'd laid him out in his coffin and that was the simple truth when you studied on it.

He left before he had to come up with any more clever answers. Longarm carried his frock coat and slicker on to the hotel to leave with his other possibles.

After that he asked directions to the one library next door to a school house. A young librarian who looked more colored than Indian said they had plenty of books on rock-oil geology because so many in those parts were interested in the subject of late. So he got her to let him sit by a window and bone up on scouting for rock-oil, lest some interested Cherokee catch him in a whopper. He wrote some of the terms down in his notebook, knowing they'd be easier to come up with as he pictured them in his own handwriting.

Then, as long as he was at it, he found a book on liquor and pored through it for a way to make hard liquor without a still.

They didn't have any to offer. The professor who'd written the tome warned more than once about blinding your customers or driving them mad if you didn't know what you were doing. It was sort of curious, when you thought about it, how distilling hard liquor and distilling rock-oil were so much alike, save for the petroleum stills Mister Rockefeller used being so much bigger. That was what they called rock-oil when they wanted to sound scientific about it: petroleum.

But Longarm had already determined they were shipping the crude rock-oil from north of Tulsa Town back east to be distilled, and it wasn't easy to picture young John D. Rockefeller as a moonshiner. Building a big old complexicated distilling tower in his head was as likely to lead him astray as help him picture what they were hiding down in some timbered draw. So he cut that out.

By then it was gettting on toward noon and his stomach was starting to growl again. So Longarm put the books back on the shelves, thanked the colored Cherokee gal, and mosied back outside to discover it was warming up a tad.

A familiar voice hailed him. He turned to see young Sergeant Deadpony in full dress uniform despite the heat. The Cherokee lawman asked if he meant to meet the coach from Fort Smith, seeing young Pat Donovan would be aboard it.

Longarm had almost forgotten the dead barkeep who knew so much about moonshining had a younger potheen expert in the family. He told Deadpony, "I reckon. I owe the boy that much. Albeit we all know that no two white men are going to find shit out yonder without Cherokee help."

Deadpony looked innocent as he asked, "Who said anything about nobody helping you? Why would we have sent for you if we didn't want you to track down those moonshiners for us?"

To which Longarm could only reply, "I don't know. I haven't been able to get Cherokee-one to tell me!"

Chapter 13

The sun was past the zenith and things had really heated up by the time the coach from Fort Smith rolled in. So Longarm was in shirtsleeves and Deadpony was wilting in his thicker army-blue campaign blouse as they stood in the dusty street watching the dusty and sweated-up passengers climbing stiffly down from the stuffy interior.

All but two of the six passengers appeared to be Indians or close enough. There was a bedraggled but not bad looking white gal with sad brown eyes and hair that might have started out auburn that morning in Fort Smith. Her well-named travel duster of tan poplin and her big straw picture hat were coated with road dust. Longarm idly wondered how come nobody seemed to have met her coach. It was as likely the poor gal was heading on to Fort Gibson and some lucky army swain. Lord willing and the draws stayed dry.

The only other white, for certain, was a gnomish gent in a dusty dark suit and derby. He seemed a tad long in the tooth to be the offspring of the late Pete Donovan. But nobody could be expected to look bright-eyed and bushy-tailed after better than half a day in a leather-sprung Concord. So Longarm stepped over to ask the dusty old fuss if he was by any chance the Donovan kid.

The man in the dusty derby looked confounded. The bedraggled white gal looked insulted as she blazed, "That would be myself. Pat Donovan at your service, and where might me father's body be? For I'll not have him buried in unhallowed ground among heathens!"

Then she caught the look in Deadpony's eye and added in a politer tone, "I was refering to *Protestants*. They told me in Fort Smith there's a graveyard over in Tulsa town where a decent Catholic, red or white, could be after getting a proper funeral mass and a hallowed resting place for his mortal remains."

Jim Deadpony tugged the brim of his hat at her and assured her they were at her service no matter where she might want them to deliver her father's remains. Then he introduced Longarm and added, "Your father had volunteered to help this federal lawman. He said he knew something about the informal distilling of hard liquor?"

Pat Donovan nodded primly and said, "The potheen. It was the pagan Celts who first made the *uisge beatha*, water of life or whiskey as they say in English. The old ways were the safer ways. For while you do get much more with the fancy copper coils and all, you may well poison your custom while you'd be about it, when you don't know just what it is you'd be after trying to end up with!"

Longarm said, "I know about bad moonshine. What I'm really looking for is a way to distill hard liquor without a regular still. For unless somebody's covering up for them, a heap, them moonshiners no Cherokee I've talked to knows a thing about, have to be moving around from place to place, cutting a little firewood here, drawing water there, and dumping their spent mash yonder, in modest amounts. Might this potheen you and your late father mentioned be made like so?"

She said, "Sure and that's why they call it potheen instead of the *uisge beatha* bottled by leave of Her Majesty's excise men. You only make a few gallons of potheen and move on to another part of the bog if you don't care to share the profits with the Queen."

The stagecoach crew had already handed down some baggage. When the shotgun messenger called a warning about her gladstone bags Pat Donovan stepped closer and raised her hands as if to catch them on the fly, which inspired Longarm to grab her from behind to gently but firmly move her out of the way, saying, "Don't go trying to show us gents up, ma'am. I'd be proud to handle your baggage at no extra charge."

He would have, too. But then a shot rang out and her gladstones landed in the dust as Longarm spun around, slapping leather, while Jim Deadpony drew, others scattered, and that dusty little gent in the derby collapsed betwixt the fallen baggage and the big rear wheel of the coach like a punctured hot water bottle, with the blood from his chest wound gushing red!

"Hotel roof!" shouted Deadpony, even as Longarm spied the gunsmoke wafting eastward on the prevailing winds up yonder. Longarm had no call to tell another lawman what they seemed to have agreed upon. So he went dashing inside and up the stairs behind the muzzle of his .44-40 to the third floor. After that he had to look about some until he spied a ladder against the far wall of a smaller alcove. He scaled it and shoved the trapdoor at the top wide open but paused to take one deep breath as he gathered his knees higher so he could pop out of the ladderway like an armed and dangerous jack-in-the-box.

There was nobody to throw down on atop the flat expanse of gravel-covered tarpaper. Longarm rolled over the rim of the hatch and moved toward the alley side of the roof for an asshole-puckering glance over that railingless edge. There was nobody down in the backyard but one of the kitchen crew, staring up at Longarm with a mop in his hands as he yelled, "What's going on up there? We heard a gunshot, just now!"

Longarm yelled back down, "That makes a heap of us. One of your own Cherokee lawmen is out front, covering that escape. Nobody on the kitchen crew saw anybody lighting out the back way?"

The cook's helper allowed he'd just said that.

Longarm moved to the front, calling out to Deadpony not to shoot at his sudden appearance against the sky. The Indian lawman didn't as Longarm gazed morosely down at the scene around the coach and the tree-shaded square beyond. A crowd was gathering. He spied Will Cash and another figure in a BIA uniform moving to back Deadpony's play. So he made his way to the slot betwixt the hotel and the stage line stop it served. There was nobody down in the slot that dropped thirty-odd feet to what would have been bare dirt if it hadn't been littered with old empty bottles, used rubbers, and such. Anybody slithering all the way to ground level would have had to

93

come out within view of the kitchen crew or the crowd out front.

Longarm moved the length of the roof to peer over the remaining edge. That slot separated the hotel from the Western Union office. So the other made more sense. Not that the trail wasn't colder than a banker's heart by this time. For whether the shootist had made his way into either adjoining building or the hotel under Longarm's very boot heels, he'd made it. You could hardly arrest one man for gunning another when you didn't have a witness to say what the son of a bitch looked like, or, for that matter, whether it had been a man, a woman, or a big ass bird!

He mulled that angle over as he descended to ground level and went out front to find Pat Donovan trying to comfort her fellow passenger as his blood spread in the dust to stain both the hem of her duster and one of her gladstones. Longarm holstered his .44-40 and hunkered down beside her to place two thoughtful fingers against the dusty bleeder's throat before he declared, "He's dead, ma'am. Why don't you let me carry you and your baggage inside, out of this hot sun, whilst the local authorities take care of him and his own?"

She didn't resist. She was crying softly but sincerely as Longarm helped her to her feet and shot a questioning glance at Jim Deadpony. The Indian lawman nodded and said, "I'll join you in the taproom as soon as we have a handle on this. You'll, ah, tell Miss Donovan about your oil business, won't you?"

Longarm allowed he would and helped the confounded-looking white gal inside, where they met up with that pretty Cherokee maid, Miss Redbird. Longarm asked her if she'd heard cold water was best to run over fresh bloodstains and she allowed she'd take care of both that bloodstained cloth and the one leather bag out back, at the stock-watering pump, where you could get some serious gushing from on high.

Longarm allowed she'd find them in the taproom when she was done and helped Pat out of her travel duster as the Cherokee gal picked up her bloodstained bag. The summer-weight checked calico dress she'd worn all morning under the duster was just sweaty and clinging to her in a more revealing manner than late Victorian fashions dictated for a young lady of quality. Albeit Longarm knew some fancy gals who'd have paid extra to get their duds to fit like that! Pat Donovan was on her way to being chunky by the time she was say thirty. But since she was closer to twenty at the moment, she just curved in and out as tempting as hell and it was too bad she carried on so religious.

As he picked up her other bag and steered her towards the hotel taproom, she protested, "Shouldn't I be checking in and washing up? Sure could use a long hot soak from me scalp to me toes after such a long hot ride on that dreadful old coach and all and all!"

Longarm soothed, "I know just how you feel and I'm sure Miss Redbird will be able to fix you up with a tub bath and a Turkish toweling. But all sort of gents will be wanting to talk to the both of us, sooner, about that man out front who may have stopped a bullet for either one of us!"

She gasped. "Surely you jest! Who in the name of Jesus, Mary, and Joseph would be taking a shot at *me*?"

Longarm grimaced and said, "Unless we buy a homicidal lunatic or some connections between a stranger coming from Fort Gibson yesterday on horseback and another arriving just now by coach from Fort Smith, I'd say them moonshiners thought they were gunning me when they saw another man riding in with a gray mare I'd left Fort Gibson with. I fear they just plain got your dad when he showed up to meet me here, and it looks as if they didn't want you telling anybody how to make hard liquor that old-time Druid way as well. So let's talk about that."

By this time they were in the taproom and the barkeep came over as Longarm sat the young lady at a table. The barkeep looked as white as they did. He still looked them over some before he drawled, "I can let you folk have near-beer that's gone a tad ripe and soft cider that may have gone a mite hard in the jug, as long as it's understood nobody serves real liquor on this Indian reserve in contradiction to the rules and regulations of the BIA."

Longarm allowed soft cider going hard sounded tastier than near-beer that had lost its sweetness. So the barkeep said he'd serve them some cider he'd been saving for white travelers passing through.

As he left to fill their order Pat said, "I have a riding habit and my dad's Webley RIC .445 in that bag you just slid under this table. So how soon do you imagine we'll be riding out after the murthering *clanna na n'muc*?"

Longarm replied, "I can't imagine me and no shemale doing any such thing, no offense and regardless of what you just called them."

She sort of hissed, "It's sons of swine they'd be and I mean to be putting himself in hallowed ground at Tulsa Town and isn't that closer to the Kansas line where they've been running their potheen and all and all?"

Longarm shook his head and said, "That trading post town of Tulsa where the Cherokee, Creek, and Osage borders meet ain't no closer than the Arkansas town of Fort Smith, where you and your late father's body belong, Miss Pat. I ain't low-rating you as a fighting Irishwoman and I know you want your father's killers brought to justice. So do I, and I work better alone in the field."

She started to protest some more.

He said, "I hadn't finished. I've rid alone, I've rid with men and women who've known how to fight, and I've rid with others I had to watch out for closer. Alone has almost always turned out better. A gun-toting pard to watch your back on the trail sounds grand, until the time comes you have to worry about watching his or her back."

The barkeep brought their drinks. She raised her stein of apple jack to murmur, "*Slainte!* And I'll be riding with you against the *sluagh salach* no matter what you'll be after saying!"

He dryly remarked, "How about just plain no for an answer? They've already pegged a shot at you. After that, it would be certain to give me away if they saw me ride out with a known moonshine huntress! You see, they think they've stopped me and your dad. If they see you headed home with his body they'll think they've nipped our investigation in the bud and I'll be in way better shape to go on investigating, see?"

She sipped some cider, said it was turning to vinegar, and insisted she wanted to help him track her father's killers down.

He said, "In that case stop carrying on like a mean little kid and let me go on pretending to be a rock hound they don't have to worry about. This cider has gone mighty sour, now that you mention it. How would you Druids make hard cider that stayed hard, Miss Pat?"

She sounded certain as she declared, "You pasteurize it. Professor Louis Pasteur over in Paris, France, wasn't a Druid, albeit the ancient Gauls of France might have been, but he'd done wonders for the French wine business with his studies of the yeasts and little bugs that turn sugars into alcohol at first and acetic acid after, unless you put an end to the glorious process of decay. People used to just let natural sugars and wild yeasts have a go at it while they prayed and all and all. Pasteur has taught the wine and cider makers to begin by boiling their first pressings to kill off anything unwanted and then infecting it with yeasts chosen to break sugar down into alcohol and carbolic gas. Since no creature can live in its own wastes, the yeast buds die and the first ferment stops when you get to ten or twelve percent alcohol and it's then a second crew of bugs take over to ferment the alcohol into acid and water, or vinegar, unless you put the wine in a pressure cooker when it's ready to cork and kill *everything* in it and all and all!"

Longarm sipped some sour hard cider, grimaced, and said, "This ain't the stuff they're complaining about, up Kansas way. You were going to tell me the family secret of turning sour mash, or sprouted corn and sugar, gone as hard as it can get by itself, into hundred proof without no regular still."

So she did. She had to tell him twice before he followed her drift and, once he had, he still insisted her late father's tale of the old timey way of making whiskey sounded just plain silly.

She said, "I'll be after making some potheen that way if you doubt my word. Just find me some barley malt or sprouted Indian corn and give me a grand copper tub to cook it and let it ferment a few days and—"

"We ain't got a few days," Longarm cut in, asking, "Could you make us some hundred proof from plain old five percent beer, seeing that's close to the alcohol content of moonshine mash before you run her through the still?"

Pat Donovan thought, nodded soberly, and decided, "I can't

promise it will taste like *uisge beatha*. But I'm sure I can manage a hundred proof and all and all!"

Longarm decided, "You're on. We ought to be able to keep you alive, here in town, for say forty-eight hours and, can you really show us how to make moonshine whiskey without a still, you'll have surely answered us some puzzles, ma'am!"

Chapter 14

Miss Redbird brought the cleaned-off gladstone bag to Pat Donovan and told her the rinsed duster was hanging out back to dry. She seemed overjoyed by the two-bits Longarm tipped her. The white gal told him he had to let her spring for the next round. They agreed it might be wiser to try the "near-beer allowed to ripen some."

But that turned out sort of sour as well. Pat explained you had to add buds from the hop vine or fronds of braken-fern to the boiled wort and yeast right off if you aimed to wind up with decent beer.

The only real difference betwixt the grain and fruit juice or sugar beginnings of booze lay in the malting or sprouting of grains, which were really seeds, if you wanted to wind up with booze. The breeds of yeast plants that lived on sugar, to shit alcohol, could start right off with sweet fruit juice, molasses, and such. You had to break starch at least partways down to glucose or simple sugar before the yeast could bite into it. You cooked starch in costly acid brews to break it down or you could let it start to sprout and then malt the baby buds, or dry them out, before they used their sweet sap up in growing. That smoky taste some whiskeys had came from letting the smoke of the drying kilns flavor the malt. Brewers out for ales, beers, or bourbon kept the smoke away from the drying malt. In either case, once the grain was malted, they put it back in boiling water to kill off everything and start fresh by letting the thin gruel you called mash or wort ferment a spell.

Nobody liked to drink whiskey mash. But beer wort, before

it turned all the way to beer, had a sweet refreshing taste of unfermented malt and you could strain it clear to be served as near-beer, which nobody in the BIA objected to and, of course, near-beer went on fermenting on its way to real beer if you let it, and they'd let it, behind the taproom bar. But Pat pointed out it was going from strong ale to dreadful vinegar because they'd failed to add the hops that flavored beer whilst discouraging those alcohol-eating acid-shitters.

It was just as well she seemed to know so much about brewing when Jim Deadpony came in to tell them he'd made sure neither of their names would appear on the officious report about that shooting out front. He said they'd identified the dead man from papers found on him as a bank examiner who'd booked passage to Fort Gibson, where he'd likely meant to catch a train. Whether north- or southbound out of the Indian territory, the poor old gent seemed to have been an innocent bystander. But Longarm wrote his name down, anyway. In life the bank dick had been known as Leroy Storch from Fort Smith.

Longarm had already warned Pat Donovan he wasn't sure how far they could trust any Cherokee. But they had to confide some in the Cherokee lawman because what they had in mind just wouldn't have been possible on their own. For whether Pat could really make potheen without a still or not, there was no way to boil mash in a hotel room without somebody noticing. So Longarm told Deadpony what they needed, and he wasn't too surprised when the Indian laughed like hell and told them they were both crazy. The only bright spot, there, was that it hardly seemed at all likely Jim Deadpony had ever heard of the method before. So Longarm hoped those moonshiners were really doing things the way Pat and her late father had suggested they could be done.

First things coming first, they checked Pat into her own room upstairs and Miss Redbird rustled her up plenty of hot water for that long tub bath she craved.

While the white gal from Fort Smith was soaking the dust of the Boston Mountain Trail out of her hide Longarm and the Indian went out shopping for the stuff she said she'd need. Deadpony borrowed them a buckboard and they were able to load it around to the back of a general store owned by the

Bushyhead family after swearing a young kinsman of the chief to silence. Needless to say, he refused to take any money when Longarm offered.

After that they hauled the load to a vacant cabin the Indian lawman knew of, off to the south of town and partly hidden from the road by a hedge of Osage orange and lilac that sure could have used some trimming.

As they unloaded the buckboard, Longarm asked about kids. Deadpony said the place hadn't been empty long enough to have any good haunt stories attached to it. An elderly widow woman had put the place on the market so's she could move in with her daughter, just down the road a piece. Deadpony said he'd tell her he was letting an *Ontwaganha* couple use the place a few days. Lest she find out they were brewing on the premises and call the law on them. He explained the old lady and his own momma were both Deer Clan.

Longarm asked if the neighborhood ladies were likely to gossip about him and the young and pretty Pat Donovan. The Cherokee grinned and asked him, "What would you rather have them say about you? That you were some sort of freak or a natural man? Nobody's going to really give a shit about the reputation of any *agehyva Ontwaganha*. But they'd be certain to snoop if they thought you didn't *want* to fuck her, see?"

They placed the big cast-iron pot on the stone hearth next to the big copper wash tub and case of quart jam jars. They left the pile of winter-weight wool blankets on a kitchen table the old lady hadn't seen fit to take away with her. Deadpony said Cherokee kids didn't steal, even when they nosed about.

Then the two of them drove back to town to see about sneaking at least two kegs of serious beer back to the hideout. Pat had said beer and sour mash had about the same alcohol content and they didn't have the time to start from scratch and let malted corn ferment to the first stages of sour, with as much alcohol as there was ever going to be.

There was more than one place in Tahlequah where a thirsty Indian could refresh himself with near-beer "aged" just a mite. As the two of them were covering the two kegs in the buckboard bed with a tarp Longarm was chagrined to meet the familiar eye of a lady who really liked it dogstyle. But the blue-eyed Cherokee gal who'd told him to call her Opal Standstall was coming along the plank walk in the company of a white man dressed in a Mexican charro outfit of black leather and German silver studs and conchos. So Longarm didn't let on he knew her, in the biblical or any other sense as the two of them sashayed past, with old Opal's Roman nose in the air.

It hadn't been the size, the studs, or the Remington repeater of her escort that had silenced Longarm. He'd been brought up respectful of womankind and nobody but a total asshole ever spoke first to a lady with another man escorting her. You could save the both of you a heap of explaining if you left it up to her, entire, whether she wanted to howdy you or not. So he did and she never did, and after they were out of earshot Longarm asked Jim Deadpony if he knew either of them.

The Indian lawman answered without hesitation, "Never seen him before. Looks like a cowboy out to change his luck. If that's the story, he's picked up the right *vgido uwodu*, from what I've heard about *her* Osage ass."

Longarm cocked a brow and tried not to sound too interested as he asked, "Osage? I don't recall just where I might have met the lady the last time. But I got the distinct impression she was one of your own."

The Cherokee shook his head certainly and insisted, "Osage. She's from Tulsa Town. Some say she was run out of Tulsa Town. They call her Tulsa Tess and some say both initials stand for Trouble. She ain't a whore, if that's what you were wondering about. She deals Faro for a living when she's feeling halfway honest. She got in trouble over in Tulsa Town when she teamed up with another tinhorn and just allowed she'd watch the game with the rest of the gals."

Longarm sighed and said, "I've had poor luck at cards with a dealer's gal standing behind me to wish us both luck. You wouldn't know whether the growing boy in the Mexican cowboy suit was the tinhorn she worked with over yonder, would you?"

The Indian lawman shook his head and said, "If I had that much on him I'd run him out of Tahlequah. All you pink people are here in the Indian territory at Indian discretion. But, sad to say, the BIA makes such a fuss when we arrest any of you and can't make it stick in a white man's court of law."

Longarm broke out a couple of cheroots, handed one to the Cherokee, and considered all he'd just found out about his playmate of the night before as they drove back out to that empty cabin amid the lilacs.

Longarm went over the whole affair in his head before he asked Jim Deadpony what he knew about a Cherokee lady called Opal Standstall, a grass widow living with her kin on a cattle spread to the north.

The Cherokee thought, sighed, and asked, "Who told you about poor old crazy Opal and her totally insane bunch? I haven't seen any of 'em this summer and I'd better not. I told Walt Ridge I'd arrest his ass if he came within a day's ride of Tahlequah, the degenerate son of a bitch!"

As they drove into the dooryard of the deserted cabin, Longarm mildly asked if they were still talking about a recently divorced grass widow living with her aunt and uncle up by Ochelata. When Deadpony allowed they were, he said he'd never heard anything about anybody being the sort of degenerates the law was allowed to arrest on sight.

Jim Deadpony flatly stated, "The three of them are degenerate half-wits. Opal's husband threw her out after he'd caught her fucking his redbone hunting hounds, all four of 'em, more than once. She doubtless inherited the condition. Walt and Rose are kin on her late mother's side. Her daddy deserted the hellish brew early on. Old Walt ain't such a public menace because he's living in sin with his own sister and their niece. He's inclined to fall madly in love with other men's wives, or livestock, and wants to fight for their favors."

Longarm whistled and asked, "How come he's still alive to disturb the peace so much?"

The Indian peace officer said, "He fights good. They call him Sidewinding Walt and one of these days we're going to have to gather a big enough posse to take him, dead. He's already advised us he'll never be taken alive and the tribal council is shy about us killing any more members of the Ridge family if it can possibly be avoided."

Longarm didn't have to ask why. His recent readings of local history had included the unsolved murders of both John and Major Ridge in the struggle for tribal leadership west of the Mississippi. The popular view was that the ferocious future

Confederate Cherokee leader, Stand O'Watie, had led the night riders who'd shot Major Ridge on the road and dragged his brother John from bed to leave him bleeding to death from two dozen wounds. Whether this had been done by or against orders of the sainted Chief John Ross or not was still up for grabs. Some said O'Watie would have murdered Ross as well, in his own grab for power, if a bigger mob hadn't gathered around the chief's house to protect him, if he'd really needed protecting. That Mister Machiavelli who'd written so much about politics had likely had some Cherokee blood.

Thinking back to more recent Cherokee doings as they man-handled the kegs of beer inside, Longarm decided aloud, "If that lady you know as Tulsa Tess wasn't really Opal Standstall I've yet to meet the one and original Opal Standstall. I can't say I'd want to. A gal who *really* likes it dogstyle, living in sin with a crazy uncle who's sworn never to be taken alive, just don't strike this child as a gal worth courting."

The Indian laughed and said, "I'd as soon mess with the Tulsa Tess we just saw in town if I cared to live dangerous. At least she's pretty and if her ass is treacherous, she sure moves it nice in broad day. Can you imagine what she'd move it like in bed?"

Longarm wistfully replied, "Yep. Treacherous. You say the real Opal Standstall née Ridge don't have as much to offer?"

Deadpony made a wry face and replied, "Oh, she'd *offer* all she has to any man or beast who cared to mount her fat frame and they say her aunt Ruby sucks. But neither one is pretty as a mud fence and after that you could wind up in a fight with Sidewinding Walt and a blood feud with his clan whether you won or not. Miss Sally Ridge, the *Ontwaganha* wife of old John Ridge, went back to her own kind years ago. But there were heaps of Ridges of the *Tsalagi* or part *Tsalagi* persuasion and they ain't all as stupid as old Walt. So who in the name of *Hino* would want to mess with either dirty-ass Opal or her cock-sucking aunt Ruby?"

Longarm covered the barrels near the hearth with that same tarp to keep them from looking so tempting as he decided, "Some hard-up gent who was out to get his fool self killed. Or somebody who wanted such a pain in the ass to get his fool self killed. The question before the house is whether I'm talking about a lady who discards her lovers with a sardonic attempt at humor or a hard-hearted bitch with more murderous motives."

Deadpony asked who they were talking about, now.

Longarm said, "I ain't sure. Let's get back to town and see how Pat Donovan feels about her own brand of witchcraft."

So they drove on back to the hotel. Once they had, Longarm asked the helpsome Cherokee to get rid of the buckboard, explaining he hoped to draw fewer curious glances if he and Miss Pat simply left the hotel on foot, after sundown, as if for a walk around the square in the cool shades of evening.

Deadpony pointed out that the vacant cabin where they'd left all the gear she'd ordered was a fair piece to walk.

Longarm nodded but said, "All the more certain nobody's trying to follow us, if we see nobody on the path behind us as we mosey on out of town. Miss Pat keeps saying she wants to go tearing out across the open range with me and a two- or three-mile walk might change her mind. What say you ride out after dark if you want to watch the way the Druids did it back in them dark ages."

Deadpony agreed he'd drop by around ten P.M., by which time they'd have some moonshine to show him, or admit they were full of shit. So they shook on that and parted friendly.

Longarm went inside and headed up the front stairs. Along the way he met Miss Redbird, who shyly informed him Miss Donovan had been out of her bath and awaiting his pleasure for some time, now, in her own room. The maid seemed bemused by the two of them booking separate but adjoining rooms. So Longarm suspected she *had* passed by his doorway the night before. He didn't ask her what she might have heard, or whether she'd been by after work to take him up on his earlier invite. If she had she seemed to be taking it all like a good sport.

Longarm went on up and knocked on Pat's door. The gal who opened it with a table lamp glowing behind her really did have auburn hair and she sure smelled tempting after her long hot soak and some scented talcum powder. But she had on that riding habit she'd boasted of. So there was less to be guessed at through her tan whipcord bodice and split skirts than he'd detected earlier through sweat-soaked gingham.

He joined her in her room for privacy as he told her they'd have plenty of time for supper, first. He said, "Me and Deadpony got all you asked for out to a cabin I'd just as soon nobody else knew we were using. Got you fifty-odd gallons of eight percent beer, a cast-iron pot about the right size for a baby missionary, a wash tub even bigger, and them clean white woolen blankets you allowed you'd need to fill a few jars with hundred proof moonshine. Fill us *one* with anything at all like corn liquor and we'll say we're sorry for laughing at you."

She said the end product might be closer to real whiskey, seeing they were starting from a barley malt potion. Then she asked other questions and didn't seem to worry until he got to the part about just the two of them walking out by the rising of the moon, as she put it, all alone with nobody else but the two of them and all and all.

Longarm started to assure her she'd be perfectly safe, alone with him after sundown. But then he wondered why any man would want to say a dumb thing like that to any gal he didn't want tagging along, once she'd shown him the only useful thing he really wanted her to show him, in spite of the way she seemed to be built.

For there were gals who were built and there were gals who went on about hallowed ground and chaperones until a man with a lick of sense just wanted to bid them a fond farewell, whether they knew how to make the potheen or not.

Chapter 15

Miss Patricia Donovan of County Kerry by way of Fort Smith knew how to make the potheen.

Longarm got to help. He had to help, once he'd walked her out to that cabin after dark, softly bitching all the way. For the ancient arts of the dark ages made a man glad the arts and sciences had been advanced to way less work, as well as way less art, since some ancient Celt had gone to so much trouble just to get a warming shot of firewater.

Pat began by having Longarm build a roaring fire on the hearth with windfall carried in from the wood lot out back. As they let the fire die down to a bed of glowing coals she made him tote buckets of well water in to soak those wool blankets and then hang them up to grow a tad cold and clammy as they dried some.

Then they filled that bitty cannibal pot with beer and set it on the coals to barely simmer. She said it would spoil the whole batch if they brought the beer to full boil.

Once the pot of beer was barely steaming, Pat wrung out a wet wool blanket and draped it over the pot as if to keep any vapors from rising further. From time to time she felt the damp blanket with the back of her hand. She said that was tricky and Longarm believed her when she suddenly gave a triumphant little cry, whipped that one blanket off, and swiftly replaced it with the other.

He naturally asked how come. She told him to help her wring that first blanket out over the wash tub. So he did. He could hear the tinkle in the tub but by then it was too dark to see just what he was hearing. So he suggested they toss another stick on the fire.

Pat tasted one of her fingers and said, "Don't be after doing that. For I fear we're boiling too much water off as it is. I think I saw a candle stub up on the mantel, though."

He struck a match on the fireplace bricks and saw she was right. He lit the two-inch stub someone had left there and by the feeble candle flame he could see mayhaps half a pint of what looked like plain well water spread across the copper bottom of the washtub.

Then Pat had whipped the second blanket off the pot and replaced it with the one they'd just wrung out, saying, "It ought to be after getting stronger as we go on. Help me wring this one out."

He did. You could wring mayhaps half a pint out of a thick blanket you'd been steaming over a cannibal pot set atop glowing coals. This time he tasted one of his own fingers, blinked, and announced, "I'll be switched with snakes if this don't taste like whiskey, save for the woolly edge to it, and you're right about the water. We're getting say eighty proof right now. But the thundering wonder is that we're getting any proof at all! How on earth are we doing that, ma'am?"

She demurely replied, "I told you we would. All distilling works by the same natural rules. Alcohol has a lower boiling point than water. So when you gently heat a mixture of alcohol and water, which is what all drinks from ale to wine are, with sour mash only the same darling brew but stronger, the alcohol cooks off first as rising vapor."

Longarm nodded and decided, "I follow your drift! The rising alcohol fumes condense on the cool damp wool fibers to mix with the little water there and you wind up with a sort of booze-soaked blanket! But who'd have ever thought it!"

She shrugged and said, "The bogs of the auld countries keep almost everyone's wool shawls cold and damp and, sure, they had many a night over many a peat fire to experiment with pots of dreadful brews. The point my poor dad was trying to make was that you don't need a fancy copper still set up to make fair potheen and I'd be saying I was just after proving him right! So how many jars of the stuff would you be wanting me to make up for yez all?"

Longarm started to allow he'd seen enough to convince him. Then he decided, "We may as well see how much we can distill from these fifty gallons of beer. Courts can be so picky about details and I'd as soon know just how much mash those other moonshiners have to process."

It was already time to wring out another blanket. But even as they did so Longarm commented, "No offense and I know ancient Druids had a lot of time on their hands, Miss Pat. But you have to allow this method leaves a heap of mass-production to be desired. I doubt we've a full pint in this tub, so far. At the rate we're going we ain't going to put any up-to-date distillery out of business, this way!"

She 'sniffed and replied, "They'd have never invented the pot still if this was the best way to make potheen. You were after asking if we knew another way, calling for neither a permanent address nor hardware that might give the game away to the excise men, and this would be it. For, sure, how would even an English Resident Magistrate convict some poor but honest tinker for traveling the back roads with some auld pots and a few blankets to be sleeping under of winter's eve?"

Longarm said, "When you're right, you're right and there's hundreds of square miles of open range in this occupied Cherokee reserve alone! If somebody after us knew where we were and what we were up to this very minute, we'd be able to finish up here and be on our way to most anywhere else if they started riding right now from either Fort Gibson or Fort Smith!"

She said the potheen makers of Kerry counted on such ease of movement and open space all around.

Longarm grimaced and said, "It gets worse when you throw in all the open space up closer to the Kansas line! When you say open range this far east of the High Plains you're not talking about wide open vistas under rolling shortgrass rises. For all the moaning about Great American Deserts, this stretch of Cherokee country is more than half timbered, and mighty bumpy in some parts described as plains on the maps. But at least you've given this child a better grasp of what he's up against and, for openers, there's just no way I'll even cut their trail without a heap of help from riders who know this country better!"

Pat swapped blankets again as she shyly assured him she rode well and enjoyed camping out on the range in warm weather.

Longarm started to argue. Then he recalled what some kindly old philosopher had written, likely in French, about life being far too short to waste more of it than you had to, trying to talk sense to a woman. So he just took the wet blanket from her, set it aside, and reeled her in for a French kiss.

She stiffened, twisted free, and gasped, "Have you gone daft, you great fool?"

He grinned at her in the dim ruby light and asked, "What did I do wrong? Didn't I just hear you declare you aimed to go out camping on the range with me, honey lamb?"

She flustered, "You did indeed! But I was only speaking of hunting down the killers of me poor father!"

Longarm nodded agreeably and said, "I heard you so declare, honey lamb. Just as I'm sure you heard me say there's miles and miles of miles and miles out yonder to scout tight. There's no telling how many days, and nights, we'll be alone together out yonder under the harvest moon, and both of us are young and healthy with natural, ah, feelings. So, seeing what's bound to happen seems bound to happen, I see no reason to put things off, do you?"

She gulped and confessed, "It's not that I'd be after playing the Holy Mary with you, Custis. I have been ... engaged a time or two in the past. So if I was to know we had some *understanding* ..."

"What's so tough to understand?" he cut in, adding, "The boy gets on top, starting out, as a general rule. You'll find me ready to try most anything that don't hurt. Have you ever started standing up or mayhaps across a kitchen table, seeing that's a dirt floor under us?"

She circled to the far side of the kitchen table, protesting any dacent gorl needed time to think and demanding to know why he wasn't willing to slow down and let nature take its course and all and all.

Longarm didn't circle after her. He just stood on his side of the table, leaning his weight on it, as he calmly told her, "I used to let nature take her course. Then, one mighty long rainy night out in the front range, I found myself alone in a

110

mountain cabin, about the size of this one, as a matter of fact, with this big blonde gal called Hanna."

Pat warily asked if he'd been this forward with that other poor gorl and all and all.

Longarm said, "Forwarder. You see, it was old Hanna's notion we should shuck our rain-soaked duds and dry out, jay naked, on a bear rug in front of the fire."

Pat said it was time they put a few more sticks on the fire under the potheen. Longarm glanced at the dimly glowing coals and shook his head, saying he was trying to explain his reluctance to buy a pig in a poke or ride off into the sunset with a total stranger to his old organ grinder. She said that was a dreadfully fresh way to refer to his privates, if that was what he'd be after blathering about.

Longarm said, "It would be and it ain't hard to please. For I'm a meat and potatoes man in every way and I'd say nine out of ten gals are worth making love to whilst that tenth one can be a nice change of pace. Providing she's at least alive and breathing."

He shook his head wearily as he thought back and decided, "I hate to brag. But I wouldn't need two hands to count off the very few gals who just managed to lie there like a side of beef. So I just can't say what possessed old Hanna to make all the sneaky moves leading up to my seduction. But she did. Step-by-step until there the two of us lay buck naked in each other's arms, with her giving a right convincing imitation of death by natural causes. I naturally asked her what was wrong. I reckon she wanted me to ask her what was wrong so's she could say it was nothing and that I should just go ahead and enjoy myself."

Longarm snorted, "I might have, had not she thrown in the magic words. Don't ever tell a man in that position that you understand no man could be expected to control his fool self in that position."

Pat laughed nervously and allowed she just couldn't understand a situation such as he'd just described."

Longarm demanded, "Did I say I understood it? Such situations are rare, praise the Lord, but old Hanna's odd display of passion was not the one and only time I ever found myself in such a dumb position. I make it, let's see, three such times in my love life to date. Why any gal who disliked slap and tickle that much would chase after a man to freeze stiff on him after they'd undressed for him, and not before, is beyond the understanding of a mortal man. I just can't picture any man chasing after a gal with flowers, books, and candy until she says yes and then just saying he ain't in the mood. But, like I said, some gals are like that. So before I risk you getting me all hot and bothered, once I'm in your clutches with nobody else to turn to . . ."

Then, before she could answer, Longarm dashed over to the fireplace to pinch that candle flame out, hissing, "Stay clear of that window and don't get betwixt them glowing coals and the doorway. I think I heard hoofbeats outside just now!"

Suiting actions to his words, Longarm drew his .44-40 and moved over to the open window to cover the moonlit dooryard, standing well back from the light from outside.

Then young Jim Deadpony rode into the yard and dismounted to tether his mount to a porch rail as he softly called out, "Longarm?"

The taller federal lawman called back, "Thought you might be Frank, Jesse, or Victorio, no offense. Come on in. We have something to show you."

He moved over to relight the candle stub as the Cherokee came in, wearing a puzzled smile.

Longarm took an empty jam jar from the table and tipped the wash tub to dip the jar in the little potheen they'd managed so far as he told the Indian, "Taste this firewater and tell me what you think."

Deadpony did. He sipped at the jar, made a wry face, and decided, "It's awful, but no worse than what they've been running north across the Kansas line. Seems a tad smoother, or weaker, with an even more wild and woolly aftertaste to it."

Longarm gestured at the blanket-covered pot on the bed of coals with the muzzle of his six-gun as he said, "Them moonshiners are starting with a stronger sour mash and their blankets are doubtless more wrung out and sun bleached by this time. Miss Pat, here, was only trying to prove it could be done and I'll allow starting with beer leaves a lot to be desired if you'll admit this would be a good way to set up just long enough to run off a few jars before moving on."

The Indian sipped more of Pat's firewater as Longarm explained the simple-looking but Celtic trade secrets of potheen. When Jim Deadpony declared, "I see what you've been up to. I taste what you've been up to. I'm still having a time buying such a childishly simple method!"

Longarm said, "All trade secrets are childishly simple. That's why the folk who know them keep them secret. The difference betwixt a kid making mud pies and a potter turning a fine Ming vase is knowing what kind of mud to start with and just how you ought to bake it. You have to know what you're doing when you spit and wittle a fine violin, too. Miss Pat's explained how easy it would be to just make a mess with an open pot of mostly water. Ain't that so, Miss Pat?"

But Pat Donovan had kicked open the door to go steaming off into the moonlight without a word or a backward glance.

Longarm moved over to the window to stare after her as Pat walked out to the road and turned toward town, her back stiff and her chin held high.

Turning back to Jim Deadpony, Longarm chuckled and said, "Reckon she'll make it to the hotel all right, seeing she don't seem to crave no company right now."

The Cherokee lawman looked confused and asked, "What happened? What got into her? Was it something I did or said?"

To which Longarm could only reply, with a broad grin, "Not hardly, Sarge. As a matter of fact I suspect you joined the party just in the nick of time!"

Chapter 16

Longarm had no great call to get up the next morning. But if life was too short to waste much of it arguing with women there wasn't much to be lying slugabed when you weren't really tired. So he got up, got washed and dressed, and went downstairs to see what they were serving for breakfast that morning.

Ham and eggs with flapjacks under sorghum syrup sounded good. So he ordered both. As the waiter served his second mug of coffee Longarm asked if that mighty sweet syrup was home grown or freighted in from other parts.

The Cherokee sounded proud as he allowed that very syrup was rendered from "Chinese Sugar Cane" or sorghum out at his own clan-uncle's spread. He never asked why Longarm wanted to know. So Longarm didn't fib to him. They both knew sorghum was closer to a sweet-pulped corn stalk than any sugar cane and, after that, moonshiners had been known to add sorghum syrup to their malted corn mash because it could bring the alcohol content of the final sour results way up.

Pat Donovan wasn't there for him to run that notion past. But Longarm figured chemistry was chemistry, with or without the approval of a gal he'd been trying to teach biology. A rapid-moving and hard-working crew, using the potheen tricks of the dark ages on a stronger mash of Indian corn and sugary sorghum pulp might be able to fill their jars faster than he and old Pat had managed out to that cabin, starting as beginners with a half-ass substitute for sour mash.

After breakfast Longarm lit a smoke and mosied back into the lobby to see if anybody had left any messages for him at the desk. The gal he'd asked right out for a piece of ass had not. But there was a note from Chief Bushyhead, addressed to Mister Crawford, and asking him to drop by the office around ten to talk about rock-oil.

That gave Longarm plenty of time to wire Billy Vail a progress report from the nearby Western Union. He saved a heap of words at a nickel a word by simply saying the "Little People" seemed to be after "potheen" The marshal had told him one time that Vail had been a Scotch name in the old country and if the hard-drinking Billy Vail had to look that up he liked to look things up.

That left him with time for a shave and a haircut across the square from his hotel. The barbershop looked about like any other small-town barbershop, and if some of the others waiting seemed a tad dusky, the barber looked like a Frenchman and they all spoke English, to the extent they spoke at all. It was safe to assume most Cherokee who got regular haircuts were at least half white. But whether they talked more freely among themselves or not, they didn't gossip much with a total white stranger sitting there.

So Longarm picked up a recent copy of the *Cherokee Advocate* to read. It was printed in English in regular Roman font. Longarm knew a heap of Mister Lo's admirers mixed the *Advocate* published in the west with the old *Cherokee Phoenix* published back east before that Indian Removal Act took effect. The short-lived *Phoenix* was more famous, not because it had been such a great Indian newspaper, but because any Indians had published any newspaper at all. The few old copies Longarm had met up with had reminded him of the school papers put out by high school kids taking a course in journalism. This up-to-date *Advocate* seemed to be a regular newspaper, save for some of the articles and a thundering editorial against letting some eastern Cherokee move out to the "Nation" as they called it, and share in the same land titles and tribal rights as the long-suffering survivors of that *nuna da ut sun'ee*, spelled out in Cherokee lest outsiders guess they were still pissed off about that Trail of Tears. There was nothing at all about those night-riding *Kituhwa* who seemed to take such matters so serious. Texas papers in counties still run by the Klan seldom mentioned the Klan, as soon as you studied on that.

There was something about a railroad proposal, with the editors backing their chief's demand for more serious money if they wanted to run the Iron Horse further down the Arkansas valley and fuck up all that bottomland. Then it was his turn and he never got to finish the piece about some black outlaw getting his fool self arrested as a Cherokee in Fort Smith, to the indignation of some racially liberal Cherokee.

Tidied up and smelling of Bay Rum, Longarm crossed back to the hotel, asked at the desk like a man, and learned Pat Donovan had checked out that morning. They couldn't say where she'd gone because she'd never told them.

By that time it was close enough to the time set by Dennis Bushyhead. So Longarm strolled over to his office. He arrived a good twenty minutes early. It was a bitch how tough it could be to arrive anywhere exactly on time when you didn't suspect a robbery in progress. He was chagrined at getting there too early. Back at the home office, he sort of prided himself on letting everybody else proceed him to work in the morning and get comfortable before he had to pester them.

The Cherokee secretary gal in the chief's waiting room told him he'd have to wait. Then, just as he was wondering how to ask her name without seeming too interested, she said something about an errand and left, whether to sharpen some pencils or take a shit.

Longarm didn't care. He was seated in a comfortable chair near a cold fireplace that gave off a cooling draft whilst, next door in the chief's office, they were holding some sort of powwow. He could tell they were arguing in plain English. He couldn't make out the words.

Or could he?

Seeing there was nobody there to ask him what he was up to, Longarm got down on his hands and knees by the fireplace. They were even easier to listen in on once he shut the damper to the flue the hearth on his side of the wall shared with the one in the chief's office. That cut the draft from outside, but funneled spoken words more direct.

So someone was bitching that the Cherokee Freedmen, or

former slaves, were demanding equal shares in some goodies Chief Bushyhead was demanding of the BIA. He didn't seem to feel those infernal Delawares and Shawnee that Washington had moved west to join them deserved to be described as Indians, either.

A familiar voice Longarm recognized as Chief Bushyhead's rumbled in a soothing tone, "I agree that all of us, red, white, and black, would be better off today if that peculiar institution had never been thought up as a way to advance the unfortunates of Darkest Africa. But it was. They're here. Deny *anyone* listed by the BIA as a Cherokee the full rights of all Cherokee citizens and where does that leave those of us with *white* blood? Haven't any of you read those editorials in that *New York Herald* denouncing us as Tanned Yankees out for a free ride on the tax payers of these United States with no Indian blood of their own to lay claim to? An *Ontwaganha* wise man called Ben Franklin warned his own tribe that men who failed to stick together were easy to hang separately. Our land-grabbing enemies are just waiting for us to split apart as we did back east. I move we accept those eastern bands of *Tsalagi* as blood brothers who will make us a stronger nation. As for those Delaware and Shawnee who might have been our enemies before we had *real* enemies, mark my words, we can let them join us as fellow citizens or they will ask the BIA for their own separate land allotment on this reserve and get it!

Somebody in there swore in Cherokee and added in English that the traditional full-bloods were not going to like any of those suggestions.

Bushyhead's voice said, "I know. That's why I called this meeting. I want you boys to back me, over to the council house, when I nominate old Rabbit Bunch as my lieutenant chief at the next session."

There came a babble of confusion. As order was restored the voice that could live without Black Cherokee protested, "You can't really be serious, Dennis! Rabbit Bunch is a backward full-blood who can barely speak English and wears his hair in damned braids!"

Bushyhead insisted, "He speaks *Tsalagi*, loud, and the full-bloods *listen*! Let's not have any hurt feelings or bullshit about seniority, boys. I'm proposing Rabbit Bunch for *political* ends, not *administrative*. A sub-chief who neither reads nor writes English is hardly likely to get us in Dutch with the Great White Father. But unless we present a united front to the *a sgasi ti* this time, he's going to rob us blind again!"

The secretary gal came back in to ask Longarm what he was doing down there on his hands and knees. He soberly assured her he'd dropped some coins through a hole in his pants, went through the motions of picking the last two up, and didn't get to hear any more. But he'd been right about Mister Machiavelli writing guide books to tribal politics.

A million years later the meeting broke up and a half-dozen breeds in stuffy suits with stuffy expressions filed out, paying Longarm no mind when the chief forgot to introduce him to anybody.

As they left, the portly older man herded Longarm into his smoke-filled back room and sat him down by the desk again, saying he was sorry he'd kept Longarm waiting.

Longarm started to bring him up to date on the chemical experiments of the night before. But Bushyhead hushed him and said, "Sergeant Deadpony and Miss Donovan brought me a jar and told me all about that hours ago. I sent Deadpony and an armed escort back to Fort Smith with her and the preserved remains of her father. I'm sure they'll arrive safely and of course I gave her an extra week's bonus."

Longarm didn't feel any call to ask how come the gal had lit out on him so sudden. But he had to inquire, "A week's bonus, Chief?"

Bushyhead nodded and said, "That was our deal. Ten dollars a day and expenses for their help in tracking down those moonshiners. Didn't she tell you?"

Longarm smiled thinly and replied, "She told me she wanted to stick around. I reckon I convinced her she might be asking for needless danger if she just hung around after she'd showed me how to make potheen the old-fashioned way."

He leaned back in the guest chair and added, "I've wired Billy Vail my own request to back out whilst I'm still free of bullet holes or stab wounds. He ain't said yes or no, yet. So let's hear any bullshit you still aim to feed me."

The chief looked startled, then blustered, "What are you talking about? Who told you anyone in these parts was lying to you?"

Longarm replied, "Most everyone in these parts I've talked to. Those who'll admit they've even heard of that moonshine bunch keep saying I ought to just nose about on my own, without a lick of help, because I'm so fucking smart!"

The chief stared owl-eyed, double chins quivering under his French goatee as he protested, "I'm not sure I like your tone, young sir!"

To which Longarm replied, "I'm sure I don't like yours at all. In my day I've been used and abused by men, women, and children. So I can feel it when somebody tries to shove an umbrella up my ass and then open it before I notice."

"Just what are you suggesting, damn your eyes?" the chief demanded.

Longarm said, "I ain't suggesting. I'm saying. And damn your own eyes for wasting my time and getting two other men killed just to make it look as if you gave a pig's ass about those white men getting drunk on Indian firewater up Kansas way! You . . . let's say *nominated* me, a fool outsider, to track down those moonshiners who likely contributed handsome to your campaign fund. You knew when you done it that I'd have less chance than a snowball in hell. But you'd heard I had a rep as a lawman and you had to do *something* to keep the Kansas State Guard or a posse from most anywheres from invading you. You didn't want any white riders from anywhere invading you because every time white outsiders ride through this prime real estate they tend to report back that you poor Indians ain't all that downtrodden, or all that Indian!"

He shook his head in disgust and added, "This whole charade was intended *political*, not *administrative*. I'm supposed to satisfy the state of Kansas of your sincere support by tearing around in circles until somebody kills me. It may seem a harmless political ploy to you. But them moonshiners have swallowed enough of your tall tale to start shooting at folk. Ain't you ashamed of that, at least?"

Chief Bushyhead said, "I would be if one damned thing you just said was true. But speaking frankly as one bullshit artist to another you've missed one important point."

Longarm said he was listening.

The older man said, "On my orders we've kept it a secret that it was an innocent prospector and not you they shot over by the municipal corral. It wasn't easy, but I've gotten the *Cherokee Advocate* to delay any mention of the attempt on Miss Donovan until she's safely back in Fort Smith. They carried the obituary of her father yesterday, on the next to last page, listing the cause of death as natural. Does that sound as if I was trying to calm Kansas down with a lot of bullshit about an ongoing investigation?"

Longarm scowled at the clutter atop the chief's desk as he tried to come up with something better than, "Well, they did run that story about my own murder, on and off your reservation. What if you figured that was enough to calm them Kansas lawmen down?"

Bushyhead asked mildly, "Why would I figure that? Would you care to see the dozen-odd wires from all over, offering to send in rough-and-ready lawmen to avenge you? Jim Deadpony suggested and I thought the two of us had agreed it might throw those moonshiners off guard if they were convinced they didn't have to worry about you any more!"

Longarm grimaced and said, "I'll be the judge of how convinced the rascals might be! After we'd assured them they'd shot me down like a coyote Pete Donovan showed up and promptly died. Whether his death was natural or somebody poisoned him, they fired a plain old pistol round at his daughter when she came in to take his seat at the table. So I just might buy your logic if you'll buy mine."

Bushyhead looked sincerely puzzled as he asked, "What are we talking about? I'm only trying to convince you there'd be no point in my trying to screw the very lawman I'd sent away for. What are you trying to sell me?"

"Somebody else trying to screw us," Longarm soberly replied, raising a hand to keep the older man quiet as he continued. "They knew I'd be riding in with that dapple gray army mount. After they'd been led to believe they'd killed me they must have found out they hadn't. So two assistants in a row had serious health problems. I'm sure the crooks knew the Donovans knew how they've been making potheen on the run and didn't want a man they were said to have killed to hear about it!"

Bushyhead whistled and marveled, "*Gwo!* You're talking about wheels within wheels!"

Longarm shook his head and declared, "No I ain't, Chief. If you ain't been telling them exactly what's been going on, it has to be somebody mighty close to you. For you and me are the only ones who were supposed to know everything and, no offense, I ain't the one who told them!"

Chapter 17

Like the chief had said, there was politics and there was administration. So whether it was pointless for him to stay dead or not, Longarm owed his boss the choice of rewording things to the newspapers or leaving things read the same way, for now.

On his way out, he asked that secretary gal if she could spare him a recent large scale survey map of both Cherokee holdings in the Indian territory. She said she'd have to clear that with her boss and warned him there was a big old ugly patch of Osage reserve smack dab in the middle.

He said he didn't care and it only took her a minute to crank up the brass and hard-rubber Bell telephone set on her own desk to ask something in Cherokee and nod up at him.

Longarm had noticed the set on the chief's desk inside. He resisted the temptation to comment. Indians could suspect you were mocking them when you were trying to admire them and a paramount chief who dressed in fine linen and broadcloth could naturally afford to have the latest in office gear. Old Henry, back in Denver, didn't have as fine a typewriter as the one the Cherokee gal got to play with, along with her new-fangled telephone.

She'd gotten her answer and barely hung up when the inner office door popped open and Chief Bushyhead stuck his head out to tell Longarm in a surly tone, "Of course you can have the most recent survey. Why didn't you ask me, just now? Why did you have to pussyfoot around my back?"

Longarm replied, "I didn't have to. I chose to. I'm a born

sneak, or I only thought about it after you'd shut yonder door after me. How was I to know a lady who worked for you might tell you I'd snuck off with vital tribal secrets?"

Dennis Bushyhead sighed and said, "I see what you mean about trusting strangers when you're having trouble playing your cards close to your vest. Is there anything else you want from the files, seeing we've not a thing to hide from the Great White Father?"

Longarm didn't let on the Cherokee leader had let something else slip. He just said, "As a matter of fact, seeing I might still want to sell myself as that rock hound we made up, might you have anything in your files about mineral leases signed since you all came out this way?"

Bushyhead just looked confused. His secretary brightened and reminded him of that *dalonige adelvo* they'd lost, back near the *Tanasi*. The much lighter-skinned Cherokee hushed her and wearily told Longarm, "Miss Old Path was speaking of the gold, copper, coal, and such the Great White Father moved us away from lest we hurt our little selves playing with dangerous rocks. The army engineers surveyed these new Indian lands for us before they decided they were safe for savages. That was long before Colonel Drake drilled for oil in the limestone country of Penn State, of course. So, yes, oil companies large and small have asked for exploration and drilling rights from all the self-governing tribes out this way. That unfortunate Moses Bradley who got shot in your place ran a survey of my own home spread down at Park Hill a while back. I regret to say I don't seem to be raising beef on top of a salt dome. That's what they call the sort of hill they drill for rock-oil, a salt dome. Don't ask why."

Longarm didn't have to. He'd been reading up on the subject lately. He said, "I've been thinking about Moe Bradley ever since we agreed them moonshiners had no call to kill any moonshine experts coming to help me if they thought I was dead. What if we've been adding one and one to get three? What if the man who shot Moe Bradley in the back knew all the time who he was? Outsiders have already struck rock-oil on Indian land up north of Tulsa Town and I've heard grim tales about ruthless oil men wheeling and dealing drilling rights, oil leases, and such."

The Cherokee leader snorted. "So have I. So what motive might anyone have for murdering a prospector with a reputation for honesty? Nobody in the Indian territory is about to drill an oil well or sign any mineral lease that my council and me don't know about. Despite anything you've read about those proposals to divide up the tribal holdings between the family heads of the Five Civilized Tribes and grant us full citizenship, off the BIA rolls, it hasn't happened yet. It may never happen. There are vested interests on both sides and nobody is going to accept what he or she sees as the short end of any stick."

Longarm started to ask a question about gender. He decided it might be better to find out for himself. He said, "In sum, what you're saying is that I don't have to watch out for sneaky crooks creeping all about with one of them swamping oil well drilling towers. What about a slick talker asking folk to sign leasing agreements on salt domes yet to be drilled into?"

Bushyhead shrugged his broad shoulders and asked, "To what end? When and if individual Indian families get clear fee-simple title to those holdings they now occupy as common property of their tribe, they might or might not be dumb enough to sell *Tsan Equa* drilling or mining rights. As of now any such contracts signed by any Indian on the sly without his tribal council and the Bureau of Indian Affairs approving the same would not be worth anything."

"*Tsan Equa?*" Longarm asked.

Bushyhead said, "Big John, as in Rockefeller. I keep forgetting who I'm talking to, thanks to that deep tan. I was just now arguing about mineral leases with a Cherokee who doesn't get out in the sun as much."

The secretary gal had poked through her desk in vain and went off somewhere else for that map Longarm had asked for. So Longarm thought it would be all right to say, "I figured you might know who Big John was. What was the argument about? Wouldn't you all wind up better off if Standard Oil had to buy more of your rock-oil?"

The chief snorted, "How long do you think it would be *our* rock-oil if outsiders struck enough of it to matter? We don't *own* shit, as things now stand. We're on the books as wards of *Uba pike equa* and by our last treaty of '66 Our Great

Father reserves the right to set us back on the right path should we or our own elected government stumble or falter. Do I have to tell a federal lawman how easy it is to misread the fine print on some government regulation written half in Latin and only sent out to those law hawks who ask for them?"

Miss Old Path came back in with a rolled up map bound by a rubber band. As she handed it to him her boss rumbled on, "We have outside interests pestering us for coal and timber as well as more grazing leases than we've issued so far. We've been holding them off. But we know better than to make it worth their while to go over our heads with a better offer. You'll find the railroads already built and some planned rights of way we're still negotiating. We're not trying to turn the clock back to before the coward-chief Moytoy sold his mark on paper to the English. We know we have to move with the times. You don't see paint on my face or feathers in my hair and when I travel east to argue our case in Washington I ride the Pullman sleeping cars. But we have to move forward a step at a time. Planting each new footstep on solid ground. Every time we have moved in haste we have stepped in a bear trap our *Ontwaganha* brothers have set for us!"

He caught the bemused look in his secretary's big doe eyes and told her, "Don't laugh. I know what you're thinking. I know how much Scotch-Irish blood I have in me. That's what makes me such a good Cherokee. I know how some of my *Ontwaganha* brothers feel about Indians owning their own land and having money in the bank. I know what a tightrope walker feels like as the audience boos him, claps for him, or just laughs at him. But this is my tightrope and I will walk it as I think best!"

Longarm allowed an elected official, red or white, had call to run things as he saw fit. Then he left them to sort it out and went down to the street, where the brighter sunlight dazzled his eyes until he moved across the way to cut across that tree-shaded main square, with the bright rays lancing down through the leafy overhead branches to form puddles of sunlight on the sort of sooty bare soil.

He spied that full-blood in blue, Will Cash, supervising a game of mumbly peg some Cherokee kids were playing in the dirt at the base of a gnarly blackjack and mosied over. The

125

somewhat older and way darker Indian lawman didn't look his way. So Longarm knew Cash knew he was there. He watched the kid with the knife make his toss and draw a pie-slice line in the dirt with it when it stuck. Then he quietly said to nobody in particular, "I think it might be time for us to stop lying to one another, Will."

The Indian didn't answer for a million years. When he finally did he said, "I have lied to nobody. Nobody. My mother was a turtle. Turtles never lie!"

Longarm said, "I never said I was a turtle. I told you my name was Crawford and that I'd come this way to scout for rock-oil. That was not the entire truth. Is there somewheres we might go to finish this conversation in private?"

Will Cash said, "This place is private. These kids don't speak much English and did you pay attention to your elders when you were a kid?"

Longarm smiled sheepishly and said, "Mine had a fit when I run off to the war without their permit. My real name ain't Crawford. I'd be U.S. Deputy Marshal Custis Long of the Denver District Court and we figure that was me they thought they were killing with that Big Fifty the other day."

The Indian didn't change expression as he said, "I might have known Sergeant Deadpony was lying about you. His mother was a Deer. Why are you telling me the truth now?"

Longarm said, "I want your word as a lawman that you won't blab it about until I clear it with my own boss. I'm telling you because I'd rather have you working with me than shooting me dirty looks. I need to talk to Cherokee who might not admire Chief Bushyhead as much as Jim Deadpony and Miss Old Path seem to."

Will Cash shrugged and said, "Joel Mayes of the Downing Machine hates him and wants his job. But I have no more friends among that bunch than I do among Bushyhead's breeds and, by the way, we say *Tsalagi* when we mean our people. *Tseroki* was our old country. The country you stole from us."

Longarm said, "So I've been told and we ain't going to work together worth shit if we play kid games with one another. We're talking English. Irishmen showing off by shouting *Erin go Bragh* on Saint Paddy's day ain't convincing the rest of us they only speak Gaelic. You know who I'm talking about when I say I'd like to talk to some down-home Cherokee with a different political ax to grind. I won't insult your kith and kin by implying there's any such thing as a human being without any political axes to grind. Are you trying to follow my drift at all or should I just leave you to this game of mumbly peg and try somewheres else?"

The Indian said, "I have been listening. I know what you want. You want to meet some turtles with straight tongues. I don't know if any of my mother's clan will want to talk with you. I will have to ask them. I think they would be more willing if I could tell them there was a reason to talk to a lawman of your kind."

Longarm nodded soberly and said, "I have been sent here to catch a person or persons unknown making trouble, big trouble, for all of you Cherokee, red, white, or black. You've heard about those moonshiners running firewater to white drunks up Kansas way. I think it sounds silly, too. But if somebody doesn't catch them soon, the Kansas State Guard will be sending in a column to search high and low for them."

Will Cash growled, "That will mean empty saddles. Our own riders have too much heart to take that kind of shit!"

Longarm replied, "That's what I just said. When do I get to pow-wow with some more traditional Cherokee who might have more to tell me about political protection?"

The Indian answered, "*I* said I'd have to ask. When I find out I will tell you and we don't say powwow, we say *dega-lawivo*."

Longarm didn't argue. He asked the Cherokee to leave a note for him if he wasn't at the hotel as soon as they got any answer from the traditional full-bloods. Then he cut across the square to wire Billy Vail about a Miss Long's birthday party and suggest they just put all the candles on her cake, seeing everybody knew she'd been fibbing about her real age.

As he came out of the mottled shade to cross the sunny street in front of the telegraph office, that white man in black leather he'd seen earlier with Tulsa Tess was coming out the Western Union door. Their eyes met and the stranger looked away as innocently as a kid who'd put a tack on the teacher's chair. A big one.

Longarm looked through him and strode on into the telegraph office. He tossed the rolled-up map on the counter as he got out his wallet to flash his badge and say, "Hold this for me and show me out your back way! Now! We'll talk about it later, if I'm able!"

So in no time at all Longarm was alone in the alley with his .44-40 drawn and hugging the shady side as he made his way to that narrow slot between the Western Union and his hotel. He took a deep breath and let half of it out before he followed his gun muzzle around the corner with his eyes. There was nobody there. He'd already figured the slot at the far side of the hotel made more sense. He moved on in running crouch to keep the coffee-brown crown of his Stetson below the level of the top of the board fence behind the hotel. He stopped at the far end and tried the gap betwixt the hotel and the stage coach stop beyond.

The man in black leather was up at the far end of the shady slot, his back to Longarm as he covered the street out front with his own Remington repeater. Hoping to take him alive, Longarm eased forward into the slot on the balls of his feet. The dirt was soft where nobody had tossed a bottle or other crunchy trash. So Longarm figured his best move would be a rabbit punch before he grabbed for that Remington.

Then a voice from on high shrilled, "Elko! Behind you! Kill him!"

The man she'd called Elko might have, had Longarm hesitated. For the man in black was on the prod with his six-gun cocked as he spun like an ice skater showing off and fired at the same time!

But Longarm had had the edge of knowing where everybody was before the shooting started. So as the slot echoed to the dulcet roar of gunplay and the banshee screams of the woman above, the man called Elko staggered backwards from between the buildings to land limp as a dishrag on the sunny plank walk with six hundred grains of hot lead in his chest and no expression at all on his stone-cold face.

Then Longarm was out of the smoke-filled slot and running for the hotel entrance as fast as his boots could carry him. For old Elko would likely stay put, for now. But that bitch who'd warned him might not!

Chapter 18

It was a good thing he knew the layout of the hotel. As he tore in to head for the front stairs he heard high heels cascading down those back stairs! So he cut around to head her off and it was still close.

He was saved an alley chase when two Indian gals rolled down the last flight together in a flurry of skirts and tawny limbs, spitting and scratching like alley cats doused with cold water!

Longarm holstered his gun and reached for the handcuffs he'd kept in a hip pocket under the name of Crawford. As he untangled the two of them he told the Cherokee maid, "I got her, Miss Redbird. Let go her hair so's I can roll her over and cuff her right."

The petite Cherokee rolled free and smoothed her skirts way more modestly as the one under Longarm called him a boy buggering sister fucker with a little dick, if he recalled that much Lakota right. Her Osage dialect made it harder to say.

The Cherokee gal got to her feet and kicked Tulsa Tess in the ribs as she explained, "We met on the stairs and I asked her what was wrong. She tried to shove me down the stairs on my head. But I hung on to her, and how come you're putting those handcuffs on her and what is she yelling about? I don't speak Creek."

Longarm said, "Neither does she and I wish you wouldn't kick her, Miss Redbird. She's an Osage lady I'm charging with aiding and abetting, if not murder in the first degree."

He got off her and tried to help her to her feet. But the

Tulsa Tess he'd known, biblical, as Opal Standstall stayed put on her soft shapely rump as she glared up at them both and spat. "You can both go fuck yourselves if you can't find any dogs! I murdered nobody! Nobody! I just saw my sugar shot in the back and I'm going to tell them you raped me, too, Longarm!"

The man she'd accused so unfairly smiled thinly down at her to say, "I figured you'd figured out who I was. Was it something I let slip the other night or did somebody tell you?"

Before she could answer Will Cash and another Indian police roundsman came back to join them, guns drawn. When Cash spied Longarm he lowered the muzzle of his Schofield to a politer angle, saying, "They just told us you were the one who shot that *Ontwaganha* out on the walk. What was the charge and what are we holding this woman on?"

Tulsa Tess wailed, "Nothing! He has nothing on anybody! I should have come to you Cherokee lawmen when he raped me upstairs the night before last. But I was ashamed and he said he'd kill my *Wasichu* sugar if I told him. But I had to tell him and of course he had to defend my honor. But this coward who calls himself a lawman shot him in the back and now listen to him trying to say it was *me*! Examine his gun if you think my own charges are not true!"

Longarm grimaced and said, "Save yourself the sniffing, Will. I shot him three times. We'll leave it to your own coroner to say whether the bullets hit him front or back. I was trying to take him alive. She was up in their corner room and yelled a warning that got him killed whilst I was creeping up on him to take him alive. I'm still working on why I was trying to take him alive. He was set up to gun me as I came from the Western Union down the walk. I came by way of the back alley because I'd thought he might. I don't know who he was or why he was out to gun me. She called him Elko."

Will Cash stared soberly down at the woman seated firmly on her ass with her hands cuffed behind her back and spoke to her in Cherokee.

Miss Redbird said something in the same lingo and then switched to English so that both *Ontwaganha* could follow her drift as she told her own lawmen, "They were registered as a married couple named Watts. I thought she was skipping. Whores skip out on us a lot!"

"Pte!" snapped the Osage gal. "You were working with your *Wasichu* lover to frame my sugar and me! We have done nothing! Nothing! This big moose is cross with me because I laughed at his little cock while he was raping me the night before last!"

Longarm was too mortified to answer that. Will Cash nodded and said, "Elko Watts. Of course. He was wanted by his own kind in Utah territory as a range detective who went too far with a sheep herder. The Creek police had wired Judge Parker in Fort Smith that he was here in the Indian territory. We tribal lawmen have no jurisdiction on hired guns unless they gun an Indian."

Longarm said, "I spotted him and vice versa coming from Western Union just now. I'd be obliged if you'd hold her and post a guard on what's left of him whilst I go have a talk with the telegraph crew."

Will Cash said, "I already have two of my boys posted out front. What charge am I supposed to be holding this woman on?"

Tulsa Tess hissed, "Hear me! None! If Elko killed somebody out in Utah Territory I was never in on it. I can prove I have never been west of the Shining Mountains. Since when has it been a crime for a woman of the Osage Nation to be sinned against by *Wasichu?*"

The Cherokee shot Longarm a questioning look. Longarm shrugged and allowed, "Ain't no federal fornication statutes we could hold an Indian *woman* on. How about defamation of character and criminal impersonation?"

Will Cash soberly replied, "That sounds serious enough. But what are you talking about?"

Longarm said, "It was her grand notion to come knocking on my door. When I let her in and she had her way with my fair white body she told me she was Opal Standstall of the Cherokee Nation and suggested I look up a Miss Ruby Ridge of the same tribe if I enjoyed crimes against nature. So I submit she was defaming two Cherokee ladies whilst trying to get me killed by Sidewinding Walt Ridge, see?"

Will Cash nodded and said, "She could have got old Walter

killed as well. So I make that two defamations of character and two attempted murders and you'd better come along with us, now, Miss Tess."

She was spitting and banging her heels on the floor betwixt the two Cherokee lawmen and Longarm went out back by way of the kitchen to retrace his path to the back door of the Western Union.

Once he had, he tersely explained the situation to the telegraph crew, picked up that rolled map, and took a deep breath. He let half of it out so his voice wouldn't waver as he announced, "I have to know what the late Elko Watts was doing in here just before I shot it out with him. I know you've been told not to divulge the messages of your customers. I have this argument with you boys all the time and guess who's won so far, sooner or later."

The Swedish-looking gent in charge said, "Don't get your bowels in an uproar, Uncle Sam. If you're talking about that white man in black leather out on the walk he never told us his name was Watts and he sent no messages for us to hide or divulge. He gave *us* the name of Marx, Karl Marx, when he came in to pick up a Western Union money order, sent by a Mister Fred Engels from our Tulsa office."

Longarm smiled thinly and said, "I figured him and his pals might be out to redistribute the wealth of this wicked world. I read that manifesto they published a spell back. How much money are we talking about?"

The Western Union man said five hundred dollars.

Longarm whistled and said, "I suspect I know what such bounty was for and he must have felt it beat punching cows for a year. Is he on his back out front with that much on him in cash, or are we talking about company paper to take to a bank?"

The Western Union man said, "We cash money orders up to a hundred here. Anything more coming over the wire rates a bank draft made out to the payee against our business account. We're not in any shape to stand off bank robbers."

Longarm said, "Neither are some banks. But they do have more help and bigger vaults. What's to stop the wrong gent from picking up the money order meant for another?"

The Western Union man said, "Password. In this case any-

132

one picking up that money order for Karl Marx had to know his mother's maiden name was Vanderbilt. A lot of such passwords are as silly. Ours not to reason why. A Karl Marx came in to pick up his money and identified himself by offering the same maiden name as the sender suggested and we issued him the draft you'll no doubt find in his pocket out front."

"So how did this Fred Engels in Tulsa Town convince Western Union he was the real Fred Engels?" asked Longarm.

The telegrapher explained, "He never had to. When you want to send a Western Union money order it's more important to produce the money than any personal identification. Why should we care if you want to send your own money, under any name at all?"

Longarm sighed and said, "I follow your drift and I'll have to get the right names and the real reason for the pay-off out of the girl they left behind them."

That was easier said than done. Longarm went out the front way to find the Cherokee law wrapping the body in a tarp. They told Longarm Will Cash had the dead man's gun, the contents of his pockets and the Osage gal with him, headed for their police post near the local agency office.

Longarm stopped by his hotel to leave that light but clumsy map at the desk. Miss Redbird followed him back outside, asking, "What do you do to women to make them act so crazy? I know that Osage woman went to bed with you the other night. I heard her yelling how grand it felt. I know that other girl with red hair didn't want to go to bed with you. She told me so as she was checking out. But she couldn't tell me why this made her cry. Why haven't you said anything about kissing me the other night? Do you enjoy confusing women?"

Longarm truthfully replied, "You pretty little things confuse me a heap, too. It's hard to say who's working hardest at it. Sometimes I suspect we're just meant to confuse one another. I ain't forgot I kissed you, ma'am. You kiss swell and I'm sorry if it left you confused. But now I have to go over to the lockup and question another confusing gal. No offense?"

Did she kiss better than me?" the maid demanded.

Longarm said they'd talk about that later and lit out for the police post, feeling confused. He'd known what he was doing when he got shed of Pat Donovan. For no grown man with a lick of sense was about to ride the range unchaperoned with a recently orphaned young gal who demanded an "understanding." A man could get in enough trouble messing with an older gal who only said she wanted to get laid.

He found the log police post just past the white frame BIA compound. As he made for the weathered gray police post a gray-haired white woman came out the front door wearing a seersucker dress and an expression of disapproval. After that she was built young for her hair and not bad looking if you liked 'em tall and willowsome.

She brushed past Longarm with her nose in the air. He shrugged and went on inside to find Will Cash had the contents of Elko Watts's pockets spread across the booking desk. A wandering man could sure pick up a heap of library cards and voters' registrations made out to different names.

The money order draft from Tulsa Town read just the way the Western Union man had described it, save for those two bullet holes and a dab of almost dried blood. Elko could have cashed the draft anywhere. So the question before the house was the bank it had been drawn from, by who, legal or otherwise.

Longarm said he wanted to question the shemale prisoner in the back alone. The Cherokee lawman asked him if he thought that wise, seeing the gal kept accusing him of shoving it up her ass because he didn't have enough to pleasure a woman the regular way.

Longarm sighed and said, "Gee, I thought she liked me. She's just as likely to accuse us of gang rape and it's easier to make deals when the conversation starts out private."

The burly Cherokee said it was Longarm's funeral and had a turnkey take him back to the boiler-plate patent cell and lock him in with the Osage gal, alone. Her first move was a shrill cry of rape.

Longarm told her to button her damned bodice and listen tight. He warned her, "You're going about compromising me as the arresting officer to no avail. I'd be proud to admit under oath that I fucked you before I arrested you if I was asked whilst under oath in a court of law. But let's study on where I'd want to take you to stand trial. I can't charge you with trying to back-shoot me just now. I'd have a time proving that was you with a buffalo gun the day Moe Bradley got shot and Lord only knows how Donovan died. I can prove you checked into that hotel with another man before you told me you were staying with friends in other parts. It's up for grabs whether you were in that room or not when Elko fired from the roof and slithered down the slot in his leather suit and ducked back inside through that side window. So I suspect the Provost Marshal at Fort Gibson or Judge Parker at Fort Smith would ship you back to your own tribal council and let them deal with you in the good old Osage way. Is that where you want to wind up, Tulsa Tess?"

It must not have been. She heaved a sigh, sank down on her bunk bed, and proceeded to sing her sad song to him.

She hadn't been back in Osage jurisdiction for a spell and didn't want to stand trial for that one bitty knife fight over another man who could hardly matter to current events. She'd know the late Elko as well in Muskogee, closer to Fort Gibson, after she'd become Tulsa Tess the faro queen. She'd never pressed a known hired gun for details about his business dealings and hadn't seen him for a spell when she got in another jam in Muskogee.

She said she'd been aboard the stage from Fort Gibson when somebody else shot Moe Bradley. She'd met her old flame late that day and had no idea what might have happened to Pete Donovan before the two of them had checked into the only hotel in town.

She said Elko had told her he was waiting on a money order and that the two of them would be moving on as soon as it arrived. Then he'd asked her to see what she could fuck out of another hotel guest that made him nervous. She allowed she couldn't say why Elko hadn't bought her notion that Longarm was just some cuss called Crawford. Elko had never said a thing about pegging shots from rooftops or down in that shady slot.

Longarm allowed her tale made sense and advised her to stay calm a spell whilst he checked some details out. Then he had the turnkey let him out so he could bring Will Cash up to date.

But out front the burly Cherokee said, "Tell me later. They

135

just sent word from the BIA next door that they want to hear your side."

"My side of what?" asked Longarm with a puzzled smile.

The Cherokee lawman said, "Sodomy rape of a ward of the state. You know she's a lying whore and I know she's a lying whore, but they still have her listed on the BIA rolls as a dependent Indian!"

Chapter 19

When he got next door a smarmy white clerk who sort of reminded Longarm of the kid who played the typewriter out front at the Denver office told him the agent in charge was up Kansas way, meeting with other white officials about that pesky Indian moonshining. But when Longarm insisted they'd just sent for him the clerk allowed that had likely been Doctor Sternmuller, their health officer.

He rang a bell to summon an Indian kid, who led Longarm back to an office suite that smelled of antiseptic and rosewater. That tall gray willowsome gal in seersucker turned out to be Doctor Sternmuller. The BIA didn't pay as well as some fancy hospitals back east. So it had to take what it could get and Longarm was afraid Doc Sternmuller was one of those professional bureaucrats who took part of their pay in powers they got to abuse at will.

The severely handsome lady sawbones on the sad side of forty rose from her desk and told Longarm to follow her as she dismissed his young guide with a curt gesture. As Longarm tagged obediently after her into a smaller room set up with a scale, metal lockers, and a padded leather examining table the tall woman sniffed and said, "This isn't the first I've heard of your ways with Indian girls, *Wasichu Wastey*, or should I call you *Saltu ka Saltu*?"

Longarm smiled sheepishly and replied, "It depends on whether they're talking about me in one lingo or another, Doc. Before this gets one bit sillier, that Osage gal next door is likely going to be set free because I don't have anything certain to charge her with, and vice versa."

The shemale physician said, "I'll be the judge of that. Judith Buffalo Tail, as we have her on the Osage allotment rolls, is not in any position to drop anything, after charging you with forcing her to commit crimes against nature. Since you're a federal law officer, you surely know that under federal law she's a minor, with this Bureau of Indian Affairs acting as her legal guardian in any court of law, other than her own tribal courts, of course."

Longarm said, "She didn't want to stand trial before any Osage court on an old stabbing charge. That's how come she just came clean on the aiding and abetting of another white rascal. He's dead and if her tale of not being in town whilst some other white man were winding up dead holds together—"

"This bureau is not interested in white men killing other white men!" She cut in with an impatient wave of one hand, adding, "When I heard you'd arrested an Indian I naturally went right over to examine her. I'll admit I found no lacerations or contusions and she admitted she was neither a virgin nor unwilling to have normal sex with a white man who treated her decently. So we're left with the question of whether you did or did not handcuff her wrists to her ankles and ravage her rectum from the rear!"

Longarm had to laugh at the mental picture. He said, "I only have one set of cuffs handy and, even if I'd cuffed her in such a silly pose I ain't prone to treat any lady that rude, Doc. I don't want to brag, but I've never had call to rape nobody, front or back. I ain't claiming every gal I've ever asked has said yes. But enough of 'em have to keep a man from getting that desperate."

The white woman sniffed and said, "Whether she was willing or not is moot. It's against federal law for a white man to have intercouse with a treaty Indian and we both know it!"

Longarm said, "Aw, come on, Doc. Are you saying you want me to go out and arrest all the whites and for that matter blacks who might be openly cohabitating with Cherokee for miles around?"

She tried not to smile as she replied, "Don't try to confuse the Bureau of Indian Affairs with facts. The Five Civilized Tribes may be covered by different treaty details. The Osage are a sub tribe of the Sioux and—"

"Wrong!" Longarm cut in, adding, "No cigar on that guess, Doc. The Osage may talk the same lingo but they have never, ever, been listed as a hostile tribe, despite all the excuses they've been given by some whites. They signed a treaty with us way back when that's never been broken by either side. After that the Osage took up arms to fight for the Union against Cherokee and Confederate irregulars during the war. So whether they look or act as white as the Five Civilized Tribes or not, you can't call Osage wild Indians and I'd like a look at the small print on any treaty with any tribe before I'd plead one way or another to corn holing that false-hearted Osage gal next door!"

The agency health officer primly declared, "She never said you'd sodomized her next door. She said you forced yourself on her that way at the hotel. But why are we arguing about who did what to whom, or where, when we have forensic evidence to work with? Take off your clothes and hop up on that table, Deputy Long."

"Are you serious?" Longarm felt obliged to ask, trying not to laugh.

She said, "I am. Miss Buffalo Tail says you forced her to take it in her anal opening. You say she's a liar. I wasn't there. But, speaking as a physician, I feel qualified to judge what might or might not be the logical evidence. Do you want to take off your clothes and get it over with here and now or do we really have to bother Washington about her charges?"

Longarm laughed and proceeded to unbuckle his gunbelt. He hung it with his hat on one hook and sat on the table to shuck his boots before he shucked the rest of his duds while the shemale sawbones watched with clinical detachment. If it flustered her to see a naked man standing there with his old organ grinder dangling between them she failed to show it.

She said, "Get on the table and lie flat. I frankly can't see anyone of normal proportions taking anything that size against her will without more bruising than was evidenced by Miss Buffalo Tail."

Longarm felt an alarming twitch down yonder as he tried

not to think about any sort of tail while he calmly replied, "I was wondering how come she had her bodice unbuttoned, considering the mean things she'd been calling me. Can I get dressed again, now, seeing we both seem to agree I never shoved this old organ grinder up her ass?"

"I haven't finished my examination." The willowy woman in seersucker replied, stepping closer and reaching down to take the matter in hand as she added, "I've only seen this soft so far. I'd like to see what it looks like fully erect. You did say you wanted to make a liar out of that ward of the government, didn't you?"

As she proceeded to slowly slide her smooth hand up and down the shaft, as it rose to the occasion, Longarm gasped, "She was a liar when I met her and is that any way for a government official to act, Doc?"

Doctor Sternmuller kept stroking him with one hand as she fumbled a rubber condom from a skirt pocket with another. She demurely told him, "The fine print of both the Bible and Statute Law defines the sin of fornication rather exactly. The male organ inserted in the female organ and thrusting in and out until one or the other partner reaches orgasm would be my definition of the act of fornication. Would you go along with that, Deputy Long?"

He gasped, "I'm fixing to come all over your hand, Doc!"

She unrolled the condom on to his raging erection as she replied she wouldn't want that to happen. Then she hoisted her seerksucker skirts to show she had nothing on under them and forked a slender but shapely thigh across the table to impale her gray-thatched but lusty love maw on his rubber-sheathed shaft as he was coming with a hiss of confused pleasure.

As she settled on his throbbing erection to the roots she remarked in a matter-of-fact tone, "You were right. She was lying. She wouldn't have been able to take this up the rectum she showed me without a lot of lubrication and a willing attitude indeed!"

Longarm groaned, "Kee-rist, Doc! Could you move it faster or let me get on top?"

She primly replied, "No. To both questions. I felt that first spurt inside the rubber, you impatient child. I want to work myself up a bit before it comes in me a second time. As for letting you get on top, I am conducting a scientific experiment, here. What you suggest sounds like common fucking."

He laughed and insisted, "Damn it, Doc, we *are* fucking! Even though I'd be able to fuck you better if you let me get on top, with you out of them duds as well!"

She shook her gray head like a schoolmarm correcting a poor speller as she moved up and down with her seersucker skirts spread across her naked thighs and his bare belly. She said, "Don't be fresh-mouthed as I examine you, Deputy Long. We are not fornicating in the vulgar sense of the word. There is a thin but impermeable layer of rubber between us as I determine just what your level of virility might be. So your sex organ is not actually touching mine, no matter what it may feel like down there to either of us, see?"

He said, "I swear I won't touch the inside of your old ring dang doo any more than I'm already touching it if you'll shuck that seersucker and let me, ah, finish this examination right!"

She protested that allowing his naked body to press full length against her own would really feel like they were fornicating within the letter of the law.

He pointed out, "My cock would still be fully dressed inside of you. Ain't that the important thing? Come on, Doc, let's experiment on how it feels to fuck buck naked when we ain't really fucking at all because of that impervious barrier betwixt them few square inches of us!"

So she agreed that sounded like an experiment worth trying and once Longarm had her flat on her naked back atop the table to pound her his way and prove he could come more than twice in anybody built that fine, Doc Sternmuller thanked him for his lusty contribution to forensic science. That was what she called finding out all she could about the way folk fucked. Forensic science.

Longarm tried in vain to get her to take it without that rubber on him. She said she wasn't that sort of a gal and seemed to feel she was a poor old maid, doomed to die a virgin, since she'd never found a man who could keep up with her down yonder for any length of time.

The examining table was too narrow for the two of them to lie side by side and smoke, betwixt times. So they just lolled around her examining room bare ass, admiring one another's bodies as they smoked separate cheroots and chatted about that lying Osage gal next door.

Doc Sternmuller seemed more interested in why he'd arrested Tulsa Tess, now that he'd convinced her he'd never raped anybody in the ass.

She asked what happened next and how long he was likely to be in town, in case she wanted to examine him some more.

He said, "As you just found out, Doc, it ain't that hard to check out her unimaginative claims. The stage line and the hotel next door to their stop here in Tahlequah can make or break her story she wasn't witness to the deaths of a man who seems to have been mistaken for me for a moonshine expert from Fort Smith I was supposed to work with."

He took a drag on his cheroot and waved it for emphasis as she reclined like Miss Cleopatra on the table. He said, "She says she knew Elko Watts, a known gunslick from Muskogee, a few hours ride the other side of Fort Gibson. Elko was waiting here for money from Tulsa Town. But that Osage gal couldn't have been the only pal he'd made over by Fort Gibson and I suspect somebody wired from there that I was headed this way with a distinctive gray army mount. So that was the end of poor Moe Bradley when he rode in with the same pony ahead of me."

He took another drag, frowned thoughtfully, and decided, "I'll let the death of Pete Donovan simmer on the back of the stove until I know better. But whether he was poisoned or not, Elko was paid off from yet another party in Tulsa Town. So what if somebody in Tulsa Town knew a federal man was headed here to compare notes about moonshining with an expert on the subject, heard they were both dead and . . . that leaves a bum shot at another moonshine expert and . . . let's see. Pete Donovan's daughter, Pat, lit out for Fort Smith sudden, as if she might have been scared off, found nobody here to work with, or both. So, yep, somebody in Tulsa Town didn't want this child investigating that potheen they've been after making and who'd have thought they were that far south of the Kansas line?"

She asked if he'd like to try on another rubber and experiment a mite more. So Longarm suspected he was more interested in moonshining than she was. But if he had to mosey over towards Tulsa Town, where the borders of the Osage, Cherokee, and Creek reserves came together, he couldn't afford to cross any officials of the Bureau of Indian Affairs. So he put out his cheroot, put on another rubber, and they went at their affair dogstyle, with her remarking in a clinical tone that she somehow felt more naked with his fully dressed cock sliding in and out of her as the afternoon light streamed through the curtains while she watched herself taking it that way in the wall mirror across the small examining room. He thought it looked sort of sassy, too, as he watched himself humping a lady with gray hair.

They wound up the old-fashioned way and she even kissed him while she was coming, that time. But as they got dressed she warned him not to come courting her and allowed she'd send word if and when she cared to examine him some more.

He said there was a gal back at the Denver federal building with the same reservations about her reputation around the office. So he didn't kiss her good-bye, and it would have looked dumb to shake hands.

He consulted his watch on the way back to his hotel. He was mildly surprised to see how early it could still be. He went to the Western Union to see whether Billy Vail had wired a yes or no to his request. Billy hadn't. So even though most everyone for miles around seemed to know who he really was, he decided he'd best try to stay out of the public eye for the time being.

He went back to his hotel, picked up that survey map at the desk, and took it up to his room to study. But he'd barely taken the rubber band off when there came a knock on the door and he got up to open it.

It was Miss Redbird. Longarm gulped and asked what he could do for her, not sure he'd be able, if she'd changed her mind about him after all.

But she said, "There's a girl downstairs who wants to take you off somewhere with her. She's a full-blood and can't be more than fourteen. What on earth do you *do* to make women act so crazy around you? It felt nice when you kissed me the other night. But do you see me going crazy over you?"

To which Longarm could only reply, "Not hardly, ma'am. I reckon I'd best go on downstairs and ask that other gal what she wants of me."

Chapter 20

The Cherokee gal waiting in the lobby could have been younger than fourteen for all Longarm knew. She was dressed traditional in gathered home-spun skirts fashioned by a red sash, a thin cotton blouse and a red and black turban with her long dark hair cascading out the top to hang down her back.

She didn't answer when he asked her name. She said she'd been sent by the grandmothers to lead him somewhere. Her English wasn't as good as most Cherokee he'd met, so far. So he followed her outside and she led him through a series of back-alley dog-legs until he was as turned around as they likely wanted. They ducked through a hole in a thorn hedge and strode through sun flowers to the low side entrance of a low-slung windowless cabin.

It was dark and smoky inside. The young gal took him by one hand to lead him around the smoldering central fire and seat him with his back to the white-washed south wall. The east wall to his right was brick red. The logs to his left were painted stove-black. The north wall he was facing was painted blue.

Darker figures wrapped in turkey feather robes were seated all along the walls of the medicine meeting hall. A woman he could have seen a mite clearer if her face hadn't been painted red on one side and black on the other squatted closer to the fire in her own traditional garment of turkey feathers woven into netting to overlap like shingles or the scales of a fish while she chanted in a droning monotone. She seemed to be singing, or praying . . .

"Ogi-do-da galv-la-di he-hi, Galv-ghwo di-yu ge-se-sdi detsado-vi . . . " and so on as the young gal whispered, "We are not wild ones. She is saying the same Lord's Prayer as you people do, but she is saying it in *Tsalagi*."

Longarm allowed that sounded fair. The kid said nothing. So he never commented when, the Christian praying over, another old crone bent forward to trickle tobacco dust on the glowing coals. He'd seen other medicine folk test for secret enemies at a council fire that way. The tobacco dust flared evenly with no hissing or spitting occasioned by intended treachery, or a pinch of gunpowder added to the tobacco dust by a troublemaker with a political agenda or a hard-on against whites in general.

Once they'd evoked the Great Spirits of all concerned, another older woman he could barely make out spoke up in clear and pleasant English to declare, "We have heard of you, Custis Long. You have a good heart and a keen eye, so they say. You have dealt with other trouble at other agencies and you have pointed out the troublemakers without favoring red or white, so they say. The white man the government tells us we must obey as our paramount chief has sent for you, so they say, to hunt for those troublemakers making firewater out in the hills. What do *you* say?"

Longarm shrugged and truthfully replied, "I don't know who's making that moonshine. I don't know whether they're making it in the hills or smack dab in this town or another, ma'am. I have a pretty fair notion they've been moving around, filling a few jars here and a few jars there. I ain't sure I trust Dennis Bushyhead any more than you seem to. But I've yet to catch him in a lie and if he was in tight with those moonshiners it seems to me he'd have never sent for me."

The old gals mumbled and grunted in Cherokee for a spell. Cherokee sounded something like thick soup boiling over a low fire when it was spoken softly. The one who spoke perfect English hushed the rumbles and grunts to ask him, "Have you thought that maybe a chief who spends so much time with other *Ontwaganha* might have sent for someone like you because he thought that in spite of your reputation as a man hunter you would be helpless, helpless as a child without a blow gun as he hunts for birds in a strange thicket, where none of the birds sing songs he has heard before?"

Longarm nodded soberly and replied, "I ain't just thought of that, ma'am. I asked Dennis Bushyhead right out if that was his game. But he made one good point I'll pass on to you ladies. He asked how come him and his moonshining pals would want to have me shot the minute I got here if they knew I'd been chosen as a chump who wouldn't be able to catch them."

The Cherokee clanswomen bubbled and boiled about that for a spell and then their spokeswoman asked, "What if some of those troublemakers were afraid you were smarter than Dennis thought?"

Longarm replied without hesitation, "Same difference and it still lets the boys who sent for me off. No offense, ma'am, but we are having us a circular argument here. You don't ask somebody to guess which hand you're holding the button in, then kill him before he can guess the right button, when he never knew or cared about your fool buttons to begin with! They could have left me in Denver, minding my own beeswax in blissful ignorance and sent for some other chump they might have worried less about, see?"

She must have. The old gals didn't burble and bubble as long that time, before she decided, "Maybe you are right. Young Dennis has done a lot of things to make us cross. But he has never violated any of our blood laws and we have never allowed you young men to stab one another in the back when you are on the same path against a common enemy. We are very cross with the people making that firewater and getting us in trouble with the Kansas chiefs. How close do you think you are to catching them?"

To which Longarm could only reply, "Not close at all, ma'am. What you said about me hunting strange birds with one of them dart shooters your kids hunt 'em with described my feelings to a T. Will Cash must have told you I'd shot that one hired gun and arrested his Osage lady love, but—"

"They say you were fucking her, too," the motherly old gal cut in.

Longarm sighed and said, "News sure travels fast as one of them blow gun darts around here. I was about to say that regardless of who done what to whom, the late Elko Watts was paid off by a Western Union money order wired from Tulsa Town. That don't *have* to mean all that moonshine is coming from there. It's an awkward distance from the Kansas line to smuggle that many jars in bulk. But the mastermind who must have put all this together without either the assimilated or quill Cherokee getting wind of it . . . I'm sorry, ma'am. I forgot you'd rather be called *Tsalagi*."

She said, "Call us anything and get back to Tulsa Town. The place was begun as a trading post by a *Cusa* or what you would call a Creek on the Cusa side of the river-crossing where three nations come together. It was and is a good place to trade. Young men of all three nations go there to trade ponies, race ponies, and get in all sorts of other trouble. It sounds like a good place to do other bad things. The town marshal there is *Cusa* and so he would not be worried about firewater meant to travel north through Osage or *Tsalagi* country to be sold in Kansas, not in his own nation. When are you going over there to arrest somebody?"

Longarm said, "Not this evening. Still got me some fish to fry in these parts. But tell me something about the range due north out of Tulsa Town. You'd be traveling smack along the line betwixt the two Indian reserves, free to veer either way and would it be safe to say Osage police wouldn't cross over into your reserve and vice versa?"

She said that was obvious and added that the Cherokee and Osage left a sort of no-man's-land of unsettled range between them to avoid just the sort of situation he'd described.

He allowed he'd have to study that survey map some, explaining, "Most of the Kansas complaints have come from Coffeyville and points east, up Kansas way. I don't see why any moonshiners would smuggle a load across way to the west of Coffeyville and then circle around through the lawmen of Dry Kansas with a load of wet trouble. But, like I said, I might see something on paper that I just ain't picturing in my head."

She told him to tell Will Cash when he was ready to ride out of town and added, "We think you would ride our range better if you had some of our own young men riding with you. I am not speaking of the *Tsalagi* dressed in BIA blue. Will Cash and some of the other full-bloods have good hearts. But many who now call themselves *Tsalagi* are not what we true

148

Tsalagi call *Tsalagi*. Nobody who still honors his mother's clan would be making firewater and trouble for his mother's nation. Back when the blue sleeves and gray sleeves went to war it was not the full-bloods who wanted to take sides. None of us kept black prisoners. None of us saw any reason to get into it. But the breeds who had everything and still have everything chose to fight for the Confederacy, and when it ended we all owned less. All of us but the breeds who thought they were great *Ontwaganha* planters, that is! The Osage to the northwest had no slaves. They had no use for Confederate raiders. They fought them. When it was over the winning side praised the Osage and said they had never broken their treaty with Washington. That is why today the Osage have so much to say about their own affairs, even though it was only a few years ago they were squatting in skin tents and chewing the buckskins of their men to keep them soft. If the Kansas State Guard comes down this way, hunting those troublemakers, there will be much trouble. Some of our young men will resist them, so they say. Our young men do not remember how it was right after the big war, when columns or red, white and black riders from both sides came through to loot and burn while the people who had done nothing, nothing, could only hide or run for their lives! We hope you find out that firewater is moving north through Osage country. It would serve the Osage right for thinking they are in better with the BIA than we are!"

Longarm allowed he didn't want Kansas invading either nation if it could be avoided. So they burbled and bubbled some more, served him a bowl of corn mush with fresh-baked bread, or *kanahena* and *dugi*, as they said corn mush and bread, and had that little gal lead him back to his hotel.

Once she had he ducked into the dining room serving the hotel and stage line for some serious grub. The blander Cherokee grub had only served to remind him how close to suppertime it was getting and real ham and eggs filled the gas pockets left by the modest snacks back yonder. He knew most Indians tended to serve the best grub they had on hand to visitors. Unless he was missing something about Cherokee customs, the full-bloods weren't doing quite as well as those breeds who seemed to be running things now.

That was worth studying on, he decided, as he headed back to the nearby Western Union to see whether anything had arrived for him from Billy Vail. As he strode along the walk a voice behind him called out, "Longarm!" and he'd dropped behind a watering trough and drawn before he looked back. So it was just as well he recognized the blue uniform of young Jim Deadpony with a taller white man who looked less familiar.

Rising back to his own considerable height with a sheepish smile, Longarm called out, "Howdy, Sarge. I see you got back from Fort Smith all right."

The Cherokee indicated the white man with him as he replied in a laconic tone, "Heard I missed some excitement. This is Deputy Nat Rose from Judge Parker's outfit. We met on the trail from there today."

Longarm remembered the name. Nat Rose looked like dozens of tall tan riders. Longarm said, "You're lucky you didn't get here earlier, leading a dapple gray mare."

Rose said, "Sergeant Deadpony told me. Judge Parker will be pleased to hear that wasn't you they gunned after all. We heard you'd been shot in the back and they asked me to look into that, as well, when I got here."

Longarm said, "Aw, shit, I thought you might have been sent to avenge my ass, Nat. What's Judge Parker pissed off about this time?"

The deputy from Fort Smith said, "The ass of one Leroy Storch, bank examiner, recently out of Arkansas, murdered here in the Indian territory by a person or persons unknown. Before you say it, Sergeant Deadpony, here, told me all about the two of you being there when Storch bought it, just down the walk in front of the stage stop. I'd left Fort Smith by the time we met up. So I'll wire my home office to interview that Miss Donovan the two of you picked as the intended target. But as of now I'm still investigating his killing as his killing until somebody shows me that banker was the unintended target."

Longarm said, "I just this day had to shoot the only man who could say for certain who he was shooting at. But we do know somebody paid Elko Watts for something after another man who could have been me and a barkeep who was certainly working with me wound up dead."

He got back on the walk with them and added, "I was headed for the Western Union my ownself. What say we both send us some wires?"

They would have, too, had not a humming bullet drilled through the air just ahead of them to shatter the corner window of the hotel taproom and inspire the three of them to dive for cover.

As Longarm rolled back to rise on one knee behind that same watering trough Jim Deadpony called from behind the curbside cottonwood he'd chosen, "Church steeple! Just like before!"

Longarm peered that way but could only make out treetops from his own position and said so. The Cherokee insisted, "I don't have such a clear view from here. But I can make it out through the leaves and where else could the bastard be? They told us, last time, the way up was padlocked. For all I know it still is. But I'm still going up that ladder for a look!"

The man from Fort Smith leaped up from his own position behind a parked wagon and shouted, "Let's go!" as he dashed across the open street and into the shade of the square as Longarm and Jim Deadpony got up to follow. The square had cleared as if by magic. They didn't meet up with anybody until they got past that fried *kanahena* stand on the far side. Another Cherokee in blue was covering the side door of the church across the way from behind a blackjack trunk. As they got closer he shouted, "Stay back! We think there's a sniper up there in the bell tower. Will Cash just went inside to find out. Will thinks the rascal has been playing cute with padlock hasps."

Deadpony swore, broke cover, and raised both hands around his mouth to shout in Cherokee. Longarm didn't need any translation. He'd have been yelling the same thing if he'd been in command. But whether Will Cash heard his sergeant's orders or not suddenly became a moot question.

All of them at ground level were knocked flat by the shock wave as the belfry above them exploded in roaring flames to send the steeple soaring ass-over-teakettle as bells, shattered wood, and the bits and pieces of Will Cash and his bloody-blue uniform rained down from the smoke-filled sky for a hundred yards or more around!

Chapter 21

There was nothing like blowing up a church for attracting a crowd in a town that had no opera house. Longarm's ears were still ringing as most everyone he'd met in Tahlequah seemed to be converging on the still-smoldering confusion. Sergeant Deadpony quickly detailed all the Indian police in sight to police the area and hold back the crowd as they gathered bloody rags and gobs of what looked like their late Will Cash.

Nobody in police blues had the authority to stop Chief Bushyhead or Doc Sternmuller from the nearby agency, so they came crunching across busted glass and boards with nails sticking out of them as Longarm and Deputy Rose from Fort Smith were gingerly entering First Adventist with their six-guns drawn. When he spied the stout white Cherokee and the gray-haired gal in seersucker he waved them back, calling, "Will Cash just set off one infernal machine. We can't say for certain that was the only one!"

Deadpony came over to explain in more detail as he barred the open doorway as respectfully as he knew how. Deputy Nat Rose followed Longarm into the tricky light, drifting dust and dynamite fumes. The door to the ladderway stood wide open, but it was still padlocked. Some slicker with a mortice saw had fixed it so's a length of the jam swung out as easily as the door, and what had looked to be a padlock hasp held it securely shut.

Tapping the padlock with the muzzle of his .44-40 Longarm told Rose, "The sexton was likely telling the truth as he saw it when he said he had the only key to this lock. Anybody

153

who could lock or unlock this door at will would have had no call to act so sneaky."

Deputy Rose opined, "I wouldn't have had to be so sneaky if it had been me. I'd have just had a duplicate key made."

Longarm shook his head and said, "Not here in Tahlequah. How many locksmiths do you reckon there'd be? If our sneaky pal had to start from scratch after somebody wired I was headed this way with a dapple gray army mount this ingenious fretwork with a fairly silent saw blade in a deserted part of this church was more discreet."

He stepped into the ladder well and grimaced as he almost stepped on one of the shattered Cherokee's boots. Old Will's left foot was likely still in it. Longarm spotted something else amid the debris at the foot of the ladder. He hunkered down and held it up to Deputy Rose as he said, "Simple but nasty and almost foolproof."

Rose frowned down at the boxlike metal mechanism with a length of haywire dangling from it to ask if it was another lock.

Longarm got back to his feet, saying, "Action from a Hall breech-loader. Some old cap-and-ball Halls are still floating around, cheap. They were army issue during the Mexican War. So a lot wound up in Texas and some were issued to Confederate irregulars in the west. The Hall was chambered for paper cartridges, detonated by flint or percussion cap, depending on which was handy back in them days. As you can see, the whole action, trigger, hammer, and firing chamber, lifted up and, if you wanted, out, to load the rifle from the breech. Sort of. A lot of old boys in the Mexican campaign used to tote more than one of these actions so's he could reload fast or, in a pinch, used the action alone as a concealed weapon."

He tucked his six-gun under his armpit to pull the length of hay wire as he continued, "This here trigger was connected by this wire to something poor old Will made the mistake of moving, topside. The trap door itself most likely."

Deputy Rose brightened and said, "That must have smarted! Pulling the trigger fired the action and what'll you bet there was a quick fuze instead of a bullet in the chamber with the powder charge!"

Longarm nodded grimly and set the charred metal square

aside to move up the ladder awkwardly, with his gun hand occupied.

But there wasn't much ladder to mount, now. When Longarm found his head sticking up out of the truncated stump of the bell tower, with no place else for him to go. He holstered his six-gun and went back down.

Deputy Rose said, "I've been thinking. That poor redskin wasn't the one they were after. It was you or me they were after!"

Longarm nodded soberly and said, "I was wondering how long it might take you to notice. That shot they pegged our way through the treetops wasn't meant to wound anybody but to leave him alive to recover with the certain knowledge he had enemies in high places. It's possible that shot was fired from somewheres else, knowing we'd figure they'd fired from this tower they'd rigged earlier with dynamite."

Rose repressed a shudder and said, "Jesus! I'd have been the first one up the ladder if that poor Cherokee hadn't beat me to it. So that means they were after me, right?"

Longarm shrugged and said, "There were three of us as I recall. Jim Deadpony lives here and patrols after dark alone. So there wouldn't be much call to murder Jim so ingenious. You just got here this afternoon. They might have known you were coming or worked fast as all get-out after you arrived. On the other hand somebody pegged a shot at a man they took for me from this very tower and they've tried to gun me since then. So add it up."

Rose did, frowned thoughtfully, and pointed out, "You killed Elko Watts before I ever got here. Even if he was the one who wired this church to blow up. How could he have fired that shot to draw us here just a few minutes ago?"

Longarm answered simply, "He couldn't. And his only known accomplice is locked up at the moment. So that leaves an unknown accomplice and I was pretty sure I'd gotten all she knew out of Tulsa Tess. Let's go back outside and see if we can catch anybody lying to us."

They went. Chief Bushyhead and his young secretary gal were trying to comfort some full-blood women who kept tearing at their duds and keening like wildcats with toothaches. Doc Sternmuller was headed their way, looking as if butter wouldn't melt in her pussy as she asked Longarm if there were any wounded survivors, adding that she hadn't been able to make much sense of this mess, so far.

Longarm kept his voice as formal as he introduced her to the other white lawman from Fort Smith and said Will Cash seemed to have been the one victim and that they hadn't made much sense of things, either. Nat Rose seemed more interested in telling the older but handsome woman all about Hall rifle actions. So Longarm felt free to drift over to what seemed a thoroughly shaken Cherokee minister and his wife and daughter. All three almost as white as Chief Bushyhead.

When Longarm introduced himself as the law the minister accused the Baptist Cherokee of blowing up his church and confided darkly that old Dennis Bushyhead was a known Baptist for all his civilized manners.

Longarm said the U.S. Constitution forbade his taking sides in any religious arguments and said, "We're more worried about getting a line on the rascals who've been using your church tower as a sniper's nest cum infernal machine, Reverend."

The minister said, "I just told you. Baptists! Give me a traditional *ada-wehi* vomiting Black Drink at his *Galv-lati ehi* any time to a hard-shell Baptist! It may be hard for you people to understand, but we take our civilization *serious* out this way!"

Longarm said he'd noticed that and turned away with a tug of his hat brim at the ladies, hoping to find somebody less spiteful in the name of the Lord.

As he headed across the littered square through the dappled shade, with the light getting trickier so late in the day, the daughter who'd been standing by, shifting her weight from one foot to the other as if her high-buttoned shoes were pinching, caught up with Longarm to timidly tell him, "You mustn't think my poor father is always that way. Right now he's terribly upset. Will Cash was one of us, sort of. He didn't go to church very often and his women were traditionalists."

Longarm slowed down so's the pretty little thing could keep pace with him as he sized her up. He'd already decided she was at least three quarters white. She could have passed for a Greek or Roman goddess in a summer frock of red and white calico in that same checked pattern you saw in Eye-talian restaurants. After that she was still a minister's daughter and her dad had just said Christian Cherokee were serious as Hellfire and Damnation about the subject.

Pointing with his chin at the keening Indian women with Bushyhead and the equally fashionable but more Indian-looking Miss Old Path, he asked if those upset women were the women she'd just described as the traditional breed of Cherokee.

She sighed and said, "Yes. They don't speak English and Father's own *Tsalagi* is a different dialect. I know it's hard for outsiders to understand, but you see—"

"There are three ways to talk Cherokee," he cut in, adding, "Mayhaps four, if you count that earlier split when some of your nation moved out this way before they were asked and worked out their own simplified grammar. You folk sure have heaps of ways to conjugate a verb, ma'am, no offense."

She laughed. She had a pretty laugh and said, "*Gahlvi-ha. Gahlv-tsa. Agwahlv-lidi.* I am tying. I have just tied. I am about to tie. It goes on and on, in four accents, and you wonder why we'd just as soon speak English?"

Longarm smiled down at her and said, "I met this Chinee lady one time who explained why Chinee prefer to learn English over, say, French or Spanish. The Chinee agree with English speakers that a chair is a piece of furniture and a piano is a musical instrument. So they find it confounding to be told that in French or Spanish chairs, pianos, pots, pans, and such have to be male or shemale."

She laughed that skylark laugh again and agreed English had Cherokee beat all hollow when it came to simple rules of grammar.

Then her mother yoohooed her in *their* version of Cherokee and she said they'd talk some more about it another time, if he cared to call on them at the manse. So Longarm didn't get to tell her he'd observed that simple ways of life didn't always go with simple ways of talking. He'd tried to pick up some of that Uto-Aztec you heard the Paiute, Hopi, Shoshoni and such speak. He knew they meant a stranger who is not a stranger when they called him Saltu ka Saltu. But after that it got a lot tougher and the Na Déné the so called Navaho and

Apache spoke made other Indian dialects sound simple. You could ask a Lakota how to say "Horse," for instance, and he'd tell you it was "Shunka Wakan" when you meant horses in general or "Tashunka" when you meant a stud. But when you asked a Navaho how to say "Horse" he'd look at you blank and ask whether you meant his horse, your horse, a horse you could both see, or a horse only one of you had ever seen, and, in either case, was it male, shemale, running, walking, grazing, or just standing there, with a whole different way of describing each and every phase of horse until nobody else, red, white, or purple gave a damn!

Deputy Rose rejoined him, casting a knowing glance at the retreating form in checked calico as he said, "Now that's what I call a handsome young gal. But it's my own fault for getting here after you. You sly dog!"

Longarm felt no call to defend himself against such a silly charge. He said, "The son of a bitch who set that infernal machine is likely watching us from the crowd this instant and I hope he's sweating bullets. But the Cherokee lawmen have this situation under as much control as we could ever manage without knowing who to arrest for all this mess. So I reckon I'll go send them wires now."

Nat Rose said that made two of them. So they started across the square as the sun was painting everything orange and purple whilst it sank in the west. Longarm glanced up to see if there were any wishing stars out yet. Then he stopped in his tracks to declare, "Thunderation. Why didn't I consider that earlier?"

The other white lawman stared the same way through the tree branches and remarked, "I don't see nothing. Not unless you mean that big old barn over yonder."

Longarm said, "It ain't a barn, it's the Cherokee council house and it's what I mean. The tribal legislature ain't in session right now. So we're talking about a structure almost as high and just as empty as a church on a weekday."

Rose stared up at the big blur of shingles against the darkening sky as he volunteered, "Closer to where the three of us were when that shot rang out to lure us towards the higher church tower, too! But I don't see no cupola and any windows high enough to matter would face two wrong ways!"

Longarm moved on, saying, "Crawling up into a ventilating cupola set in the middle of that roof could be a bitch, even with a ladder set up smack-dab in the middle of the assembly hall. But let's not argue about it. Let's go look!"

So they did. They found a side door that seemed to be padlocked. Rose looked around and murmured, "Shouldn't be too big a boo to bust and I won't tell if you won't tell."

Longarm hauled out his pocket knife as he asked, "Might not have to. Somebody may have been ahead of us."

He drove the blade into the firm-looking jam near the padlock hasp and pried out a good six inches of wood above and below the brass to simply open the door like any other unlocked door.

Nat Rose laughed as he followed Longarm inside. Then he sniffed and sighed, "They told me you were smart. I was reserving my opinion up to now. But if that ain't gunsmoke I smell, some devils were just in here, farting in the dark!"

Longarm had no call to say he smelled the same faint odor of spent powder. He wanted to know where it had been spent. It was black as a bitch inside until he lit a series of waterproof waxed matches, found an oil lantern hanging from a nail, and lit that to shed more light on the subject.

They could have used way more. The ends of the big council house had been partitioned off for offices, cloak rooms, and the like. But the central council room was cavernous, with the truss roof so high the lantern light could barely reach it. So Longarm commenced to circle close to the walls as the other lawman tagged after him, asking what in thunder they were looking for.

Longarm replied, "Thunder was just what I had in mind. We had us a real gully washer out this way the other night, about the time they'd have been setting up to receive me."

He moved along the wall closer to that Western Union, and in no time at all he found the dried-out but considerable water stains he'd been looking for.

Nat Rose observed, "Looks like the roof's sprung a leak."

Longarm forged on, looking for a way up, as he replied, "I'll tell you in a minute whether that roof is leaking accidental or on purpose. There's a catwalk running from truss to truss along the eaves and I think I see a ladder down at the far end."

Chapter 22

"You must have been the intended target," Nat Rose said in a certain tone as he and Longarm stood side by side on the catwalk, taking turns to peer out through the gap left in the roof by a missing cedar shake or oversized shingle.

Longarm had already noticed the loophole offered a clear shot at the plank walk betwixt the door of his hotel and the next-door Western Union. Rose continued, "They couldn't draw a bead on you from here as you stood with that Donovan gal and Banker Storch further down and on the far side of that stage coach. So they had Elko try for you from the roof of your hotel, right?"

Longarm hunkered down to pry a dinky copper cap from between two planks of the catwalk they were on. He sniffed it and muttered, "Aw, shit, they used a Sharps or mayhaps an old Hawkin, chambered around .50 caliber, but not leaving any spent cartridges to trace. You can buy these detonating caps anywhere, by the gross, too cheap for anyone to remember doing business with you."

He stood back up to ask, "Where was the late Leroy Storch headed, to examine which bank?"

The lawman who'd been sent into the Indian territory to investigate the bank examiner's assassination had to think before he decided the Drover's Trust in Tulsa Town sounded about right. Then he added, "I don't see as it matters all that much. Seeing they thought they were gunning an expert on Irish whiskey."

Longarm shook his head and pointed out, "If that was the

original intent of the mastermind behind all this bullshit he, she, or it had every reason to believe I lay dead on ice and rock salt as the coach from Fort Smith rolled in. After that, if the mastermind knew anybody was coming from another direction entire to help me, he, she, or it had to know my second expert on the subject of Irish potheen was a young gal. Not a middle-aged man. So if Elko was aiming at Pat Donovan he was a piss-poor shot and, whether he was or wasn't, I can't see the mastermind paying him a year's salary for shooting the wrong victim!"

Nat Rose scowled out the loophole and muttered, "The Cherokee lawmen told me about that Western Union money order when I rode in with Deadpony this afternoon. They said you were next door at the BIA to answer charges from a she-male prisoner. How did that turn out?"

"Tolerable," said Longarm, soberly. He continued, "Doc Sternmuller decided Judith Buffalo Tail, a.k.a. Tulsa Tess, was a big fibber. I know she told me some whoppers and I reckon we'll let her stew in solitude for a spell whilst we see if we can't get a better line on the mastermind her boyfriend, at least, must have been riding for."

They started to drift toward the ladder without debating the matter as the Fort Smith lawman observed, "You keep saying he, she, or it. I wish you'd make up your mind and how come he, she, or it has to have such a *masterful* mind? Seems to me they've done a piss-poor job on you, so far. They've killed, what, three innocent bystanders trying to stop just the one of you?"

Longarm said, "Four, unless Pete Donovan died natural at a sort of odd time and place. I say he, she, or it because in my day I've wound up nailing masterminds of the male, she-male, and undecided persuasion. It ain't true that all sodomists are sissies. I tangled with one really deadly mastermind that everybody took for a horny old gal in powder, paint, and golden curls. I've had sweet young things and sincere-looking lawmen turn out to be deep-dyed villains on me. As for my conviction that some mastermind has to be behind all this bullshit, he, she, or it has done a pretty fair job of confounding the shit out of me, so far."

They got to the ladder and neither said much until they'd

made it down to the floor of the council chamber. Longarm raised that oil lantern to lead the way as they took the shorter route through muslin-covered seats and desks while Nat Rose protested, "Aw, come on. After laying out five hundred dollars only to see you kill the man he paid for killing you, I'd say you must have the mastermind even more confounded, old son!"

Longarm said, "I sincerely hope so. Up to now all the good moves I've made have been counter-punches. They swing, I block and throw a right-cross without having the least notion who I'm fighting in the dark! I've yet to make the first move because I've yet to figure out a first move. Have you ever had the feeling we'd be out of work if the wayward youth of this wicked world would just leave us the hell alone?"

Nat Rose chuckled and said he'd heard about the time Longarm had been minding his own beeswax in that bank, when unfortunate outlaws out to make their own withdrawals, made the mistake of pegging a shot at him, as well.

Longarm shrugged and said, "I met a gal masterminding a bank job who was cute as a button and looked as innocent as Miss Alice in that book by Mister Carroll. So keep an open mind about the one who ordered the shooting of your Mister Storch, or my Miss Donovan, as it may turn out to be. I just can't see the same villain ordering the killing of both."

Near the door they'd come in by Longarm hung the lantern back on its nail and pried two others meant for hanging things out of the plank partition before he trimmed the lantern and opened the door.

Sundown was about over and the square was about empty, save for free-tail bats chasing bugs against the purple sky. But there was as much light as Longarm needed to hammer those two nails, deep, above, and below the brass hasp with the butt of his six-gun, growling, "This ought to rattle anybody trying to sneak inside, quiet, in a hurry."

Nat Rose chuckled at the picture as he glanced back towards First Methodist. He said, "You'd never make out the stub of that bell tower from the Western Union, now. Wasn't all that much of it to see before they blew the top off. But I reckon what there was to see looked more likely a place to be shoot-

162

ing at us from than this old gray barn, even though this is way closer."

Longarm said, "Stage magicians call that misdirection. We all tend to follow flash with our eyes and pay no attention to that assistant stuffing rabbits in hats, off to one side. The question is whether they were trying to misdirect you from that bank in Tulsa Town or me from them roving moonshiners. Crooks cooking bank ledgers and crooks cooking sugared corn mash would be as likely to have the pocket jingle to hire paid assassins."

Nat Rose said he didn't see how the cowardly killer who'd wired First Adventist and then fired a wild shot from the council house to lure them toward the trap could be working for a crooked banker and a moonshine monger at the same time.

Longarm nodded curtly and said, "I was on my way to ask some questions in dots and dashes when we were so rudely interrupted. Why don't you finish checking into the hotel and meet me in the taproom in half an hour? I'll know better then whether we'll be riding for Tulsa Town together or not."

Nat Rose said he'd already checked into the same hotel and been given the room Pete Donovan had died in, with a fresh mattress on the bedstead. So he wanted to tag along and send his own wires back to his own boss. As they strode that way he added they'd be pleased as punch to hear the one and original Longarm hadn't been killed the way they'd heard.

Longarm said, "I wish you wouldn't do that, Nat. I ain't cleared my return from the dead with the old fart who runs my life, yet."

He explained further as they strode on to the telegraph office in the gathering dusk. The Fort Smith deputy followed Longarm's drift as soon as the obviously alive Denver deputy said, "I just don't know why Elko was wired that five hundred dollars. It works more ways than one. He could have thought he'd killed me, wired he had, and only begun to suspect the truth a few minutes before I had to shoot him. He'd sent a whore to sound me out the first night I got here. So he must have wanted to know more about me. She says she told him I was a nobody and he'd already told her he was waiting on that money. We locked eyes for the last time just after he'd picked up his bounty at yonder Western Union. So he never got to cash it and he never got to wire anyone on earth that he might have made a mistake."

As they crossed the dusty street together Rose suggested, "Leaves our banking friend, Storch, out of the running as an intended victim, don't it?"

Longarm said, "Not entire. He picked up his money order after Pete Donovan, Leroy Storch, and me were all declared dead. The only victim I can eliminate for certain is poor Will Cash. There was no way in hell the most cunning killer could have predicted Will Cash would be closer to the church than the rest of us when he fired that taunting shot our way from the council house."

They stepped up on the planks in front of Western Union as Longarm was humming an old Sunday-go-to-meeting tune. Nat Rose said, "I know that song. It's the called "Farther Along." My momma used to sing it to us when we asked too many questions."

Longarm didn't answer. They went on inside. Before Longarm asked the telegraph clerk said they had a day letter from Denver waiting on him. So he tore it open to scan whilst Nat Rose filed a field report by wire for his own federal district court.

Billy Vail advised Longarm to volunteer no answers but to tell no lies. Denver was quietly putting out a retraction on the sad story of his being shot in the back. They were hoping to hold off in the identity of the real victim until such time as somebody came forward to *ask* for news about the dead rascal. Old Billy was like that. What old-timers said about killers returning to the scene of the crime was easier to explain, as well as true, when you considered how a killer had to feel, waiting for news of his crime and wondering what the lawmen there might be thinking about him this very minute. So whilst kith and kin tended to come forward with questions about the dead or missing, it was almost as often that the killer came sniffing around asking how they were coming along with the investigation as he paid his respects to an old pal. The first one to report a serious fire was a likely suspect as well.

When it was his turn, Longarm wired Billy he meant to do some range riding, dressed cow, not being first to say much, as he tumble-weeded.

As they were leaving together they met Sergeant Deadpony on the walk. He told them things were quiet again, that Bushyhead wanted to see him again, come morning, and that there was another white stranger in town, asking about a long drink of water they call Longarm, as he put it without smiling.

Longarm and Nat Rose exchanged glances. Rose said, "Don't sound like nobody from my outfit. They still have you down as dead in Fort Smith."

Longarm asked the Indian lawman where the stranger might be at that moment. Jim Deadpony said he didn't know, but added, "Mosts all of you *Ontwaganha* wind up in the hotel taproom before the night grows old. It's the one place in town serving hard liquor, if they know you."

Longarm suggested they go have some. As he led the way he asked the lawman pledged to enforce BIA regulations where Cherokee might come by their own moonshine.

Deadpony said, "They don't serve moonshine at the facilities of a lily-white stage line. They don't have to. They haul the best bonded hard liquor along from Arkansas with the U.S. mail. It's *Kansas* as just went dry, not Arkansas. You can buy anything you fancy in Arkansas, if you have the price."

The three of them went into the hotel and entered the taproom from the lobby to find it almost empty. They bellied up to the bar, and if Jim Deadpony had heard it was against the law to serve full-bloods, he felt no call to arrest the barkeep when Longarm ordered Maryland rye all around.

He wasn't sure he'd want to make a habit of that when he saw how they were asking for the only real firewater within many a mile. It was good stuff, but he could see where there'd be a ready market for less formal whiskey.

He'd just said so when Deadpony nudged him and he turned to see a big burly white man in dirt-glazed batwing chaps, an old army shirt, and a sweat-stained four-square Stetson that had once been dove gray. He was heeled with a brace of Colt Lightnings as he paused just inside the entrance at point-blank range to stare at both white deputy marshals hard-eyed. Then he said, "I was told the one and original Longarm was a tall drink of water packing a heavy mustache and a cross-drawn six-gun. So now I see an Indian piss-ant and two tall drinks of water packing heavy mustaches and cross-drawn six-guns. So which of you pretty little things might I be after?"

Chapter 23

Jim Deadpony was first to answer. Stepping away from the bar with a dreamy smile on his face and a hand hovering near the grips of his side-draw Schofield, the Cherokee softly asked, "Would you care to rephrase that remark, cocksucker?"

Longarm quietly said, "Jim . . ."

But Deadpony had his dander up and sounded serious as he muttered, "Stay out of this. I'm the one he called a piss-ant and he's *mine*!"

Longarm insisted, "Be good children and don't fight and I'll introduce you to one another. Jim, you were fixing to draw on Pepper Palmer of the Pinkertons and, Pepper, you were way out of line when you called Sergeant James Deadpony of the Cherokee police a piss-ant. So why don't you just say so and have a drink with us, you asshole?"

The flamboyant rider in chaps and Colt Lightnings scowled at Longarm to demand, "Do I know you and have you gone out of your mind if you know me? I'll forget about this redskin being a piss-ant if you'd care to repeat that remark about assholes!"

Longarm snapped, "Jim! Don't! That's a direct order from a senior federal officer, and the poor asshole is suffering from the Ned Buntline disease that got Hickok killed. They published a fair likeness of him on a cover of *Detectives on the Rails* and it's gone to his head that old Edward Z. Judson, writing as Ned Buntline, the fastest typewriter in the west, described him as faster than the late James Butler Hickok."

"Are you daring me?" demanded Pepper Palmer, striking a

166

stance as he added, "You must be Longarm. They told me he thinks he's funny. But I like to make sure before I bury a man."

Longarm said, "Cut it out before I spank you for your own good. You are upsetting my younger companions, who may not know about your famous confrontation with the Thompson brothers."

Pepper Palmer blanched and protested, "Hold on! Let's not go raking up past misunderstandings. There was two of them, both reputed to be homicidal maniacs, and I didn't have warrants on either to justify a fight to the death."

Longarm nodded soberly and said, "I was trying to picture how any grown man could have talked himself in and out of the tense scene at the Dodge Alhambra. You're going to wind up dead as well as foolish if you don't learn not to carry on so wild and woolly around other men with guns and reps of their own to preserve. What are you drinking, and, by the way, you can't order hard liquor in these parts unless the sarge, here, knows you."

Pepper Palmer grasped the branch Longarm had extended him by smiling at Jim Deadpony to say, "Please accept my humble apologies and let's have some rye whiskey, Sarge. I'd have never intimated you were an Indian if I'd known they let you call the tune on serving around here!"

It wasn't good enough for Deadpony. The Cherokee lawman demanded to know what call the Pinkerton Detective Agency had to send anybody with or without a famous rep and mighty big mouth into his jurisdiction.

Longarm quietly pointed out, "The Pinks are mostly railroad dicks and you have railroads running across your reserve, Jim."

Pepper Palmer spoiled that excuse by admitting, "I don't ride the rails for Alan Pinkerton no more. The Scotch bastard fired me just for tossing a hobo off a reefer, like I was paid to do. How was I to know he was a runaway from a quality family? Did I ask him to land on his fool head and bust his neck? Kids who don't know how to land on their feet have no business hopping freights!"

Jim Deadpony said, "I never asked you about pushing kids

around in other parts, Palmer. I asked what you were doing around here."

Pepper Palmer said, "Bounty hunting. Cherokeee County, Kansas, has posted five hundred, apiece, on three known leaders of a moonshining operation down this way. Before he died of injuries sustained in a back room of the county lockup whilst he was trying to escape, this Indian bootlegger confessed he'd been buying his jars down here in the Indian territory off these three blue-eyed squaws, a mother and her two daughters. So, down the Neosho as far south as Locust Creek, and from yonder over this way have I rode, through canebreaks, bottomland tanglewoods, and upland peckerwoods, talking myself blue in the face with red, white, and black folk who kept telling me they were Cherokee but didn't know any blue-eyed full-blood with two blue-eyed daughters. When do I get that damned drink?"

Jim Deadpony nodded tersely at the white barkeep as Nat Rose, who didn't seem any fonder of Pepper Palmer, mildly observed, "You could have taken the train down from Coffeyville as far south as Wagoner and saved yourself and them Cherokee you pestered a heap of bother. Nobody who wants to get shit out of any Cherokee describes his womankind as *squaws*. Cherokee call gals something like *asgehyvas*. Ain't that right, Jim?"

Deadpony said, "Close enough. Both Cherokee County, Kansas and our Neosho River Valley would be a tad to the east of the rail line down from Coffeyville, right?"

Pepper Palmer shrugged and said, "If you say so. I wasn't out to insult Cherokee women. I've already explained as much to other thin-skinned Cherokee, and for some reason it's the breeds who seemed most upset about my search for three blue-eyed squaws. Like I told them all, the Indian bootlegger who confessed to buying moonshine off this family enterprise *described* them as blue-eyed squaws."

"Might the unfortunate cuss have been Arapaho or Cheyenne?" Longarm cut in, waving Pepper toward the extra shot glass on the bar as he explained, "*Squaw* is one way to pronounce the Eastern Algonquin word for woman. Western Algonquin pronounce it more like *Esquaw*. Nat's point is well-taken, though. Other nations speaking other lingos tend to

168

wonder why you called their mothers, wives, or daughters squaws, the way plain Americans might wonder why you called an American gal a señorita. Even when they savvy the meaning of the word they ain't too certain why you used it and some folk, red, white, or otherwise suspect you might just be out to mock them when you don't talk plain and simple to 'em."

Jim Deadpony didn't make any move to stop Pepper Palmer as the blow-hard bellied in between him and Longarm to reach for that shot of rye. But he couldn't help himself from dryly remarking, "We wouldn't want dumb Cherokee to think anyone was *mocking* them, right?"

Longarm said, "I thought we'd agreed not to fight amongst ourselves. I may have a line on how they've been making that moonshine, but this is the first description I've heard of anyone in the bunch. You say they've been running it across the state line, east of Coffeyville, Pepper?"

The bounty hunter shook his head and replied, "I said they'd caught this one bootlegger yonder. In case we're confused about our terminating, a moonshiner is a crook who makes the stuff and a bootlegger is the one who delivers it to the customer. You might call the two terms manufacturing and distribution. This old boy they caught with a wagonload of hooch just inside the Cherokee County line was as free as a bird about the destination of his jars. He just didn't want to say where he'd got 'em until he'd bled a mite from a split scalp. I was not the one who hit him that hard on his fool *head*! Confessions uttered in a state of delirium won't stand up in court, even when the poor son of a bitch *recovers* from a skull fracture."

Longarm asked if the bounty hunter had been there in any capacity.

Pepper Palmer shook his head and said, "They called me in after. They gave me what they wanted me to read of his full statement. Don't ask me why they thought it best to hire outside help after that bootlegger died on them."

Nat Rose asked anyway. "Wouldn't it have been faster to haul in the Kansas buyers that bootlegger confessed to supplying than to hire outside help and point him down this way?"

Pepper Palmer downed his shot, gasped, "Kee-rist, I needed that!" and asked Longarm, "Do you want to tell him or shall I? He looks old enough to hear the facts of life, up Kansas way."

Longarm grimaced and told the two younger lawmen, "The sort of country folk who write the laws of Kansas can write pissers. Kansas is the state where, when two railroad trains are approaching on separate tracks, each train is to stop and neither is to proceed before the other has passed."

"Tell him about the dry laws." Pepper grinned.

Longarm said, "I was getting to that. As of last session, the sale of alcoholic beverages in the state of Kansas is forbidden by law. The Kansas constitution providing that the sheriff of each county shall enforce the laws of state and county to the best of his ability, or as he sees fit. There's no oversight provisions that can be enforced. That's how come you can't get a beer in Abilene this summer whilst Dodge and many another cattle town further west is still wide-open-wet as ever."

Nat Rose, since he packed a federal badge, nodded sagely and said, "I can see why the sheriff of Cherokee County might not want to run in any registered voters in an election year."

Jim Deadpony said, "I can't. You Pink people sure write crazy laws and enforce them even crazier. I understand Kansas voting itself dry. People who don't think *Tsalagi* can't drink without acting silly may think *Ontwaganha* can't drink without acting silly and this taproom is living witness to the simple fact that passing laws are one thing and enforcing them can be another. But I don't see why thirsty Kansas *Ontwaganha* enjoying such a friendly neighborhood sheriff have to run that moonshine in across the state line. Why can't they just buy liquor from the other parts of Kansas where nobody gives a shit about the fool law?"

Longarm said, "Politics and economics. Local machines selling a blind eye to local pleasures don't let things get out of control, and anything your own lawmen don't have jurisdiction over, say one county seat away, tends to get out of control. Governor Lew Wallace, out New Mexico way, never would have had to put his foot down and drive both sides out of business if the Murphy-Dolan and Chisum-McSween-Tunstall factions had confined their war to Lincoln County and kept it down to a roar. Dodge City gets its hard liquor from Colorado, the same as other cattle towns that far west. Hauling the hooch the length of a dry state would call for more county graft along the way than any bootlegger might show any profit from in West Kansas."

Jim Deadpony asked, "What's wrong with buying regular bottled-in-bond in, say, Missouri for the going rate and bootlegging them into the dry east of Kansas to sell at a handsome profit?"

Longarm said, "You just answered your own question, Jim. I said it was partly economics. I've had more experience with white bootleggers running firewater to Indians, but in either case you can count on the crooks being greedy. This honest-to-God liquor we're drinking here in an officiously dry town seems to be selling at a handsome profit to the stage line, but I don't mind saying, it's straining my budget and I wouldn't pay more."

He pointed at his glass and signaled the barkeep for a refill as he casually asked the Indian lawman, "How much protection are they contributing to tribal charities, by the way?"

Deadpony shook his head and said, "Old Dennis has his faults, but he likes to deal with your rascals in black and white on paper. We've been screwed every time we trusted to a handshake with our *Ontwaganha* brothers. We know the stage line drops off some of the hard liquor bound for Fort Gibson at this midway stop where some of your people may be stuck overnight. What they charge, on their own premises, to their own customers, is none of our business as long as we don't see too many *Tsalagi* staggering out the door. You were going to tell us why somebody couldn't work something like this out with a wayside inn in Cherokee County, Kansas."

"Honest merchants who weren't greedy could," Longarm replied as he reached for his refilled shot glass and added, "Honest merchants who ain't greedy don't have to do business the hard way in dry Kansas. It ain't that hard to sell decent drinks at an honest profit in any number of wet states left. A crook who sets out to break the law when it ain't required is by definition out to make a crooked buck. They ain't about to get the cheapest grade of lawful firewater, anywhere, for less than three dollars a gallon. They ain't going to sell it to the most desperate drunks for more than say twenty, divided up into five-dollar jars or pint bottles selling for two-fifty."

Nat Rose whistled softly and said, "That wouldn't be a bad profit."

Longarm said, "They're doubtless shooting for more. The rough-and-ready moonshine methods we suspect would likely allow the moonshiners to sell to their bootlegging customers, down this way, at a dollar a gallon or less. Their raw materials cost next to nothing and they're paying neither tax nor rent that we know of. If them three blue-eyed squaws exist, and if they can wring out blankets as fast as Pat Donovan and me managed, the other night, they may be wringing out as much as fifty or more dollars worth of wholesale before they move on and start over at no greater expense."

The bounty hunter, Palmer, wrinkled his nose and declared, "It all seems penny-ante to this child. How come they're willing to pay such a handsome reward if we're talking about a band of wandering blue-eyed squaws and some trash white and Indian bootleggers running the shit into Kansas for other trash whites to go blind on?"

Longarm exchanged looks with Jim Deadpony. The Indian lawman said, "Same reason we've asked these federal men to help us track the sluts down. It ain't what they're doing that has so many upset. It's where and when they're doing it. A heap of local political machines up Kansas way would as soon let their regular bootleggers do things more discreetly and pay the regular protection. Our own chief is in the middle of some delicate negotiations, with bigger chips and our future as a nation on the table. The last thing anybody around here with a lick of sense might want is a headline-grabbing full investigation of some trashy backwoods crooks we primitive Indians can't seem to control."

He took a healthy slug of rye and slammed the glass down for another as he growled, "So far, we've been controlling the shit out of things, ain't we? Three white men and an Indian murdered while we, two deputy marshals and now a fucking bounty hunter, don't have any idea what the hell we're really up against!"

Chapter 24

Talking in circles whilst sipping rye whiskey wasn't all that educational and it had been a long day. So Longarm was as happy to be alone in his upstairs room with an empty bedstead inviting him to just lie down and die for a spell.

But he still had enough life left in him to go over that survey map he'd been aiming to get around to all day. So he stripped to the waist and shucked his boots to sit sideways on the covers with the map spread open but trying to curl up again until he thought to take his gold-washed watch chain from his vest and spread it on the thick springy paper with his watch at one end and the double derringer clipped to that end of the chain at the other. It worked pretty good.

He had to consider those blue-eyed squaws being described as neither Cherokee *asgehyvas* nor Osage *weyas* or *wenyas*, the Osage having different ways to say "women," the way white folk did. Pepper Palmer had only read a transcript of that Indian bootlegger's confession. He couldn't name the nation of the poor dead cuss. The small-town lawman taking his battered words down might have written *squaw* the way most army dispatches did for Indian woman. Squaw being five letters instead of eleven. But the fact that the banged-up bootlegger might have said squaw and meant squaw was a start, and there was a good-sized and right-new Arkansas-Cheyenne reserve around Fort Reno, as far out of the way as that seemed.

Longarm knew that country better. He'd herded cows up the Chisholm trail over yonder and had a gunfight in the roller skating rink at Fort Reno. The late Jesse Chisholm, not to be confused with the still sort of ornery Uncle John Chisum out New Mexico way, hadn't set out to blaze any cattle trail through the Indian territory. He'd been a Cherokee trader and wagon freighter who'd just drove where the driving was easy betwixt Kansas and Texas. The cow outfits aiming to drive their herds from Texas to Kansas found old Jesse's wagon ruts the best trail to follow over mostly open but sometimes tricky range. Jesse Chisholm had cashed in his chips back in '68, mourned by riders red, white, or otherwise, and gone to whatever just reward awaited a man who never let a stranger ride past him cold or hungry. The trail named after him had been closed more recent, when Abilene, Kansas, had voted herself out of the running as a cow town and business had shifted further west towards first Ellsworth and then Dodge. Folk in Kansas couldn't seem to get it through their heads that they couldn't enjoy the fruits of the cattle boom without the noise.

Longarm decided bootleggers following any of those western trails north to Kansas wouldn't work, no matter what Arapahao or, more likely, Cheyenne assimilates might call those blue-eyed moonshine gals. Neither breed of High Plains Horse Indian had been living as tame as the Five Civilized Tribes, but towards the end of their shining times Cheyenne dog soldiers had taken to reloading their spent rifle shells and devising percussion caps from trading post matchheads. So the notion of potheen didn't sound too tough for Cheyenne *esquas* to grasp. But Fort Reno was just too damned far west. The West Kansas cow towns were not in the market for cheap corn liquor sold at fancy prices. Longarm knew many a West Kansas town where you'd never know Kansas was supposed to be dry or that there was any liquor shortage to worry about.

Dismissing the old Chisholm Trail as it wound north through the far west of the Indian territory by Forts Cobb, Sill, and Reno, the bemused Longarm traced the routes of the two railroad lines running through the *eastern* reaches of the same. The Missouri, Kansas, and Texas line he'd ridden south from Kansas crossed into the same at Coffeyville, west of what was called the Grand or Neosho River, depending on whom one asked in these parts. In either case Pepper Palmer said that bootlegger had tried to run his load across east of Coffeyville and it stood to reason that nobody shipping moonshine as rail freight would be smuggling it by back roads in any wagon.

The other white-owned railroad, built with the permission and paying right-of-way fees to the Cherokee Tribal Council, was called the Saint Louis and San Francisco Railroad, even though it ended at Tulsa Town on the Arkansas River after cutting catty-corner across the Cherokee reserve from its northeast corner.

Longarm frowned thoughtfully and murmured aloud, "Now that's mighty odd when you study on it."

The somebody knocked on the door near the head of his bedstead and that seemed even odder as soon as Longarm consulted the watch on the map for the time.

It was pushing midnight. He rose from the bedstead to draw the .44-40 draped over a brass bedpost and trimmed his lamp to a faint blue glow before he opened the door to see that petite Cherokee maid, Miss Redbird, standing there with a candlestick in one hand and this ragged-ass envelope in the other.

He asked, "Ain't you been off duty for some time, ma'am?"

She said, "My friends call me Antonia and I thought you'd want to read this letter. That stuck-up Lorena Old Path, the chief's secretary and more, so they say, brought this over from their office earlier and I told her you were out."

Longarm accepted the envelope and stepped back to put his six-gun back in its holster as he dryly observed, "I reckon neither one of you could hear the four of us bragging in the taproom just off the lobby, eh?"

The petite Cherokee demurely replied, "She never asked who that was singing about O'Riley's daughter next door. She seemed anxious to be on her way, once I told her I'd see you got that letter."

Longarm noticed she'd followed him inside and set her candlestick on the end table near his lamp. He turned the wick up to shed more light as he sat on the edge of the bedstead to read the printed return address and Ohio postmark. Some typewriting allowed the letter had been sent to the late Moses Bradley in care of General Delivery at the Tahlequah Post Office. It was a safe bet the local postmaster was a member in good standing of the National Progressive Party. Since the letter had already been opened, in violation of U.S. postal

175

regulations, Longarm figured he and Chief Bushyhead were in the clear. He hadn't opened the U.S. mail in the first place and didn't ride for the postmaster general in the second.

Antonia Redbird shut the door to the hall and sat down beside him on the bedstead as he read the typed letter. It was from Moe Bradley's home office in Cleveland. They'd sent it well before he'd been killed a few days back. The letter instructed him to verify earlier indications along the Arkansas Valley Railroad's right of way and go as high as fifty cents an acre for exclusive drilling and producing options. Whatever the hell they were talking about.

Consulting the handy survey map, Longarm muttered, "Ain't no Arkansas Valley Railroad and wasn't that the line the folk around here don't want?"

The Indian girl nodded like a schoolgirl who'd done her homework and said, "We don't need any railroad down the Arkansas to Fort Smith. To begin with it would put the stage line this hotel belongs to out of business and *then* where would I be?"

"Ain't it past your bedtime?" Longarm asked her, recalling it was up in the air, downstairs, whether he was an oil man or a lawman and still feeling sheepish about the way that other Indian gal had spied on him in this very room, atop these very covers.

She said, "I'm not sleepy," in the tone of a petulant child who didn't want to be left out when company had come to call on her kin. Then she asked, "Why would the outfit you work for care about that old railroad, anyway?"

He started to say his outfit wouldn't. But he remembered she still had him down as a rock-oil man. So even though it hardly seemed likely Billy Vail would want him looking into mineral futures in pursuit of current moonshiners he told the maid, "I'm just scouting for Moe Bradley. You'd have to ask him the details. But I reckon they want us to sew up future drilling rights on likely sites along easy access to the tank cars a future railroad might roll in and out for us. In most stretches of unsettled western range the government encourages railroad building with land grants. Six hundred and forty acre sections checkerboarded alongside the tracks so's both the land office and the railroad can profit from settlements that follow the

176

rails. As I savvy that treaty of '66 hammered out by your Chief Ross, railroad outfits who wish to lay track through these Cherokee tribal holdings are allowed no more than a few yards either way from the tracks and just don't have to lay tracks if that don't suit 'em."

He saw there was a slip of paper down in the bottom of the envelope and fished it out as he muttered, "It sure beat all how the railroaders ran all that track to Tulsa Town or Fort Gibson and points south without the added incentive. That's what they called it when congress gave the Union Pacific and Central Pacific ten times the acreage of Ireland along both sides of the Transcontinental Railroad. Added incentive. Ross proved three years earlier that railroads were willing to just settle for enough land to lay their tracks across. But what's done is done, and if I follow the drift of these instructions our outfit wants old Moe and me to prospect likely spots to drill along the Arkansas Valley Railroad right of way and see how many suckers we can sign up for four bits an acre or less. It could sound less fair. A heap of hill folk back in the Cumberlands have sold coal futures under their land for less then four bits an acre. Most anything sounds reasonable when you're whittling on your porch and a slicker comes calling with a wad of ready cash and a paper for you to put your mark on. Let's see what this other slip of paper says."

It was a hasty note in a feminine hand, albeit the chief had likely dictated it. It had been tucked in to let Longarm know that no tribal lands could be bought, sold, or optioned without permit of the tribal council. He'd already figured as much. Under that same treaty of '66 the Cherokee got to manage their jointly held reserve as their elected legislature and governing council saw fit. Individual Cherokee families held recognized *tribal* title to such holdings as their tribe felt they had call to hold. So, being they were considered *almost* civilized, since they'd fucked up during the war, post-war Cherokee dwelt in their own homes on their own spreads, the same as white folk, until such time as they tried to sell it, mortgage it, or give it away to outsiders. The late Moses Bradley and his eastern rock-oil company had been way off base if they'd thought to sew up mineral options signed away at any price by individual Cherokee. Tribal Blood Law and the federal regulations of the Bureau of Indian Affairs agreed no dependent red, white, or otherwise Cherokee could sign away shit.

Longarm didn't care. Billy Vail hadn't sent him all this way to keep the Indians from getting slickered. He'd been sent to keep some Indians from taking advantage of desperate white drunks up in Kansas!

Antonia asked why he was grinning so mean. Longarm told her the joke wasn't on her or her folk. But when she wanted to know who the joke was on he figured it might be best to just scare her away, the way he'd managed the other night.

So he reached for the lamp to trim it down to a ghostly glow. He snuffed out her candle with his fingers, and said, "It's been a long day and I'm fixing to take off my pants and get under these covers in just one minute. You do whatever you've a mind to, Miss Antonia."

He meant it. He'd been screwed silly by Doc Sternmuller, almost blown to bits by dynamite, and the boys downstairs hadn't let him go before everybody had bought a couple of rounds.

He shoved his derringer and watch in the bed table drawer, rolled the map back up, and set it aside to shuck his boots. At that point he saw the petite Cherokee seemed to be peeling her maid's uniform off over her head. She unpinned her long black hair in the process and let it cascade down to almost shield her tawny bare breasts from his admiring gaze. Her perky nipples peeked out at him through the shiny dark strands. But, like most pure-bloods, she didn't have as much hair on her snatch as a white gal her age might have. Everything else she seemed to be offering contrasted considerable with the pale willowy health officer he'd had earlier. So he felt himself rising to the occasion as he shucked his pants. But she just seemed to be standing there, naked as a jay, pretty as a picture, and frozen as a statue. So Longarm grabbed a pillow to hide his hard-on as he assured her in a tone more calm than he felt, "It ain't too late to change your mind again. But I sure wish you'd make up your mind, Miss Antonia."

She sat down beside him, staring away into the shadows as she told him, "I don't know what I want to do. I liked it when you kissed me the other night. I always like it when boys first start to have their way with me. I get all excited and wet and then it's over and I feel excited and ashamed of myself. Every time I do it with a man I swear I'm never going to do it again. The whole thing is a big messy fuss over nothing! So how do you get those other girls so excited when you stick that mean old thing in them?"

Longarm sighed and said, "I'm just a natural man with no more, no less than I have to give. If you don't want any, you'd best leave now, before we both feel excited and ashamed."

She said, "You see, there was this old farmer I never would have married if my mother hadn't said he was the man for me. But when we drove off to his hog farm and he put that mean old thing in me . . ."

Longarm said, "Go tell it on the mountain, girl. I ain't writing a book on the subject like them doctors in Vienna Town. You've tried it some and you didn't like it. Next case and I sure wish you'd go tease somebody else with your considerable charms. You're built like a brick shithouse, and like most men I'd like to lay you. But since you don't want me to I won't and I sure wish you'd put your duds back on and let me get some shut-eye."

For some reason that inspired her to fling her bare body half atop his as she shoved the pillow out of the way to expose his old organ grinder in all its glory as he took her in his bare arms and kissed her, hotter than before, whilst she tongued him back and took the matter in hand as they fell back across the covers together.

But even as she spread her little brown thighs in wide welcome she was bitching with her moist lips on his, "Yes! Do it! Shove that wild and wicked thing as far inside me as it will go! But, I warn you, I'm probably not going to like it!"

Chapter 25

She was wrong, thanks to the science of old Doc Sternmuller. The BIA had sent the tall, gray, white lady west to be of assistance to the Cherokee and her orgy with Longarm, earlier that same day, seemed to tip the odds of making Antonia come in his favor.

He knew right off what part of her problem had to be. The pretty and petite Cherokee was built so tight betwixt her little legs that a grown man could barely get it in her, and, after that, she was hot and wet enough inside *before* she threw in those muscular pulsations. He'd seen bawdy gals smoke a cigar with their snatch to show off their inner natures. Little Antonia could have blown out matches with hers if she put her mind to it. So under the usual conditions of a man with a maid he'd have come in her fast, more than once, like those earlier victims. He'd been praised in the past for being too considerate to just roll over and go to sleep after he'd spent his wad in a pal. But he'd have never lasted as long as it finally took if he hadn't come more than once in good old Doc Sternmuller, and he'd have never kept it up that long if Antonia Redbird hadn't had such a delightful way of inspiring just another dozen thrusts.

Even so, Longarm was sure he'd never get there as they settled in for a mighty long ride along the primrose path. He'd gotten that pillow under her little brown rump right off and so he was bouncing in the saddle of love at a comfortable trot, even as part of his mind asked him just what in the hell he thought he was doing. Like most men, he'd usually gotten to the stage where it commenced to feel like a *chore* a mite farther along in a new romance with a nice lay. That was why they called that first month the honeymoon when a man was fool enough to go for signing away all rights to start over with somebody new. There had been times he'd been tempted. They called it the honeymoon because it was a mighty sweet time, when a man kept discovering new delights in a gal and she hadn't started to nag him yet. He got to thinking back as he sort of posted in the saddle with that sweet Cherokee love-maw sort of sucking his sort of tired erection. He recalled a night such as this with the Widow Stover from the South Pass County, when they'd been at it like this long enough for him to suspect they were both starting to show off as she kept pestering him for an answer to her proposal. He'd come close to proposing, his ownself, that time with the high-toned lovely who'd introduced him to the high-life of being served by her flunkies and sipping fizzy French champagne in bed together. But he'd held out to where, sure enough, it had started to feel like this. Like *work*!

"One Mississippi, two Mississippi, three Mississippi . . ." the man in the saddle counted silently as he thrust in and out with each Mississippi and promised himself he'd quit at a hundred whether he'd come or not.

But, somehow, by the time he reached a hundred Mississippis with the little Cherokee panting with pleasure and trying to wring him out with her innards, Longarm allowed he'd count to another hundred.

But before he got there, and he likely would have tried just one more hundred, the pretty little thing was all afluster, sobbing at him to blow out the lamp, only not to stop what he was doing and not to look at her whilst she felt so ashamed as she suddenly ran one hand down between their naked bellies to play with herself as he was laying her.

He bent closer to kiss her so's she wouldn't think he was peeking whilst, between the two of them, they brought her all the way to climax.

By the time they had Longarm had gotten sort of excited himself and didn't have to promise himself he'd stop when he got to the hundredth Mississippi to keep sliding it in and out. It had started to feel like he had to slide it in and out. So he did, as Antonia moaned, "Oh, stop! I can't take any more right now! I'm so hot and bothered down there that if you don't stop . . . Oh, don't stop! I can't believe it, but I seem to be coming again, with no hands!"

So that made two of them, and when at last he discharged his weapon in her he felt it all the way down to his toes and had to arch them up the other way to keep from cramping, and that felt grand as well. So he kissed her some more as he just lay there letting it soak in her pulsing innards until she suddenly commenced to buck and gasp about coming yet another time. So he managed to move just enough to let her before he just plain had to stop.

Once he had, Antonia asked adoringly if he'd made that Osage gal come that many times. Since her interest sounded more clinical than the naggings of a jealous heart, he told her honestly that he just couldn't say. He told the likely more sincere Cherokee, "Old Tulsa Tess was spying on me for somebody else. That gunslick I had to shoot out front sent her to find out whether I was really in the rock-oil business or a lawman looking into other matters."

She hugged him fondly around the waist with her muscular legs as she said, "They're still wondering about that downstairs. The manager told me not to tell the kitchen help anything I might have heard you and our tribal police discussing."

Longarm said, "The fewer who know the fewer they can gossip with. I might or might not be able to keep the other side guessing, if they ain't sized me up already. There's that deputy marshal from Fort Smith and a bounty hunter from Kansas if somebody's warned them about lawmen riding in from outside. Do you reckon you'd care to share a smoke with me as we try to get our second wind?"

She unwrapped her limbs from around him and he rolled off her to sit up and fetch them a cheroot and a light from the bed table. He got it going and handed it to her as she lay there smiling up at him with her dreamy sloe eyes. She took a deep drag and blew it out her nostrils as he took the smoke back. She said, "It was very kind of you not to laugh at me when I couldn't keep from jacking myself off at the last."

He gently replied, "It wasn't funny. Lots of gals need to help their clits along like so. I read somewheres that young gals who first learn to come that way have trouble learning to come more natural. Or to do so with a dick inside them, leastways. There's nothing unnatural about wanting to come, any way you can manage."

She said, "At the mission school they told us it was a crime against nature we had to be strong enough to resist."

Longarm chuckled fondly and said, "I'm sure the missionary folk meant every word and it must have mortified them every time they did it themselves."

She laughed but said, "You're awful! How can you accuse our poor physical education teacher of playing with herself when nobody was looking!"

He said, "She was likely too bashful to do it when somebody was looking. I think it was the prophet, Mohammed, who had the good sense to tell a disciple who asked about it that nine out of ten men did it and the tenth was a liar. Or mayhaps it was Confucious. One or the other. I know it was Confucious who said not to ask about life after death before you figured out what life was all about. Some of them prophets citing other revelations had more sense than to ask the impossible of their followers."

Then, to change the subject, he asked her how come she was named Redbird, adding, "We had redbirds around our spread when I was a boy back in West-By-God Virginia. But I ain't seen all that many, out this way."

She snuggled closer to say, "Silly, it's our family name, like say Smith or Jones."

He'd been told as much, earlier. He still found it odd how Cherokee could follow Christian practice with Indian-sounding names. When he said so Antonia insisted, "Most of us are Christians, too, you silly. Whether we take our family names from a *Tsalagi* ancestor or an *Ontwaganha* ancestor it's still an ancestor's name, handed down to all the brothers and sisters of the family, from the father's line."

He asked what about the mother's line, adding he'd heard the Cherokee in olden times had traced maternal descent.

She said, "Some of us still do, for traditional affairs like the green corn ceremonies attended by Christian and traditional *Tsalagi* alike. When you know a boy there bears the same maternal clan name as yourself you have to dance with somebody else. People would tease you, as if they saw you dancing with your brother, see?"

Longarm shrugged a bare shoulder and replied, "I reckon. Must make life as complexicated as recalling who goes to which church at an Irish gathering. You can't just go by last names. You just have to know. But I can see how you all would, growing up close together and all. What, ah, clan do you Redbirds belong to, Miss Antonia?"

She sounded sort of smug as she said, "Redbird was my daddy's family name. My momma was a turtle. Had daddy married a deer woman my clan would be deer. That would have been all right because his momma was a fox."

Longarm started to ask a dumb question, then nodded, and decided the last name Redbird could go with any clan as each generation avoided courting a member of one another's maternal, not paternal, descent. He was tempted to ask where that left a Cherokee descended from an Indian daddy and a white momma. But he was afraid she'd tell him, so he never asked.

He said, "Poor old Will Cash said his momma was a turtle, the same as your own. What did that make Will to you, Miss Antonia?"

She thought before she replied, "Sort of like an uncle or cousin on the turtle side. I don't have any other kin named Cash, though. I think Cash is a Scotch-Irish name."

Longarm dryly murmured, "It's just as well neither one of us has the Gaelic, then. He was a gruff old bird, but I was just starting to like him when they killed him. I don't reckon you've heard any gossip about the dynamite in First Adventist that us *Ontwaganha* lawmen hadn't?"

She said, "He'd had words with some *Kituhwa* riders, so they say. It isn't as easy to say who might be *Kituhwa*. They're a secret society. I know Will had taken to attending services at First Adventist even though he was Baptist with a traditional wife who wouldn't go to any Christian church. She was afraid they'd nail her to a cross. A lot of *Tsalagi* who cling to the old path feel that way. If they understood what the cross meant to us who follow it they would be Christians themselves, see?"

He did. He asked how serious the Cherokee who followed their old-time religion could get about, say, a favorite sister's man who'd upset her by running off to church and mayhaps scaring her.

Antonia said, "We've never had any religious riots among ourselves, if that's what you mean. Wasn't it some young *Ontwaganha* girls who told stories about evil spirits back east and got a lot of old women burned alive at the stake?"

Longarm said, "Touché! I'll keep the Salem witch trials in mind the next time somebody brings up medicine men. But in point of fact nobody got burned at the stake in Salem Village, not the town of Salem, and to their dubious credit it was the trial judges themselves who finally came to their senses and said they were sorry as all get-out. They hung just under twenty women and tortured one man to death when he refused to admit he was a wizard. But the whole thing was as disgusting a display of superstition as I've yet to catch an Indian at. Did you say *Old Path*, as in Miss Lorena Old Path who types for Chief Bushyhead, when you described the ways of them *Kituhwa* boys?"

He liked the little sass bettter when she said, "It wouldn't be fair to Lorena to say her family name meant any more than my own. I know for a fact she's Baptist, like the chief she works for, and most of the men of his National Progressive Party. I think Will Cash only went to First Adventist because he was sweet on Aura Purl, the minister's daughter."

Longarm blinked in surprise as he thought back to that short conversation with a pretty white Cherokee young enough to be the dead Indian lawman's daughter, even had old Will been single.

Then he shrugged and said, "Miss Aura seemed upset about the death by demolition of a man she only described to me as a member of their congregation. Are you sure folk weren't just mean-mouthing a man who'd backslid from both the Old Path and the Baptist faith of his party?"

She said, "I don't know. I only told you what they said about Will and Little Miss Refinement. When we were little she wouldn't skip rope with us full-bloods. Her momma dressed her in a pinafore and made her wear a sunbonnet when she went outside, lest she turn into a redskin like me. I never said anybody thought Will Cash was getting anywhere with Aura Purl. Those who said that was why he'd turned

185

Adventist said it seemed a sort of sad pathetic joke. Do you reckon it would count as self-abuse if you were to play with me down here while I played with you in return?"

He snuffed out the cheroot and held her closer in his arms as he felt her up, all over, whilst he tried to decide if he could possibly manage to get it up again. She snuggled and purred like a kitten anxious to be stroked and so he stroked her, not worried about his own pleasure as he simply worked to give her some more, the way you might pet a pup or scratch a pal's itchy back. He could tell she was itchy as hell down yonder as she commenced to wiggle and jiggle her hips while he rocked the little brave in the canoe for her. She felt hot and wetter than before as she shyly reached down to grab leather and hang on as they both found themselves moving at a brisk trot.

He didn't think he had another full orgasm in him. But, not caring whether he came or not, as long as she did, allowed him to just float with the current till he found himself really bobbing and discovered virtue was its own reward. For even as his unselfish ministrations got her to breathing harder and wriggling like an earthworm on an ant pile he found himself getting hard as a rock from her stroking.

She felt it, too, and begged him to shove it in her again. So he did, at a novel angle she swore was new to her, despite a short marriage and some doomed romances since. She really liked it when he lay beside her to shove it up under her wide-flung thighs with both her knees atop his own legs whilst he strummed her old banjo quick-step.

She moaned, "Oh, yes, yes, yes! This feels lovely and I just can't get enough of it and you did say you'll be staying here to the end of the week, didn't you?"

There were times for an honest answer and there were times a gal might cloud up and rain all over you if you told her the truth. So he didn't say anything at all as he whipped it out just long enough to roll his hips betwixt her spread thighs and finish right with the swell hard-on she'd inspired.

For she'd find out for herself he'd checked out by the cold gray light of dawn and parting was only sweet sorrow to a sissy poet. A knockaround rider with a tumbleweed job learned to avoid farewells as often as he could manage.

Chapter 26

Next morning at the municipal corral Longarm asked the colored Cherokee in charge what they'd done with that big dapple gray mare the famous Longarm had been leading when somebody shot him in the back out front. He wasn't ready to advertise who he really was before he had to.

The livery wrangler answered innocently, "Sold her as unclaimed stock. Read our rules and regulations posted in the tack room, you'll see we ain't required to feed and water stray ponies the police leave with us for more than forty-eight hours, see?"

Longarm said, "I see, but it seems a mite high-handed, no offense. Who might you have sold that lawman's mount to in such haste, just in case anybody asks?"

The older man said, "Another *Ontwaganha*. Last evening around sundown. He blew in from Tulsa Town with two spent ponies. A paint and a cordovan resting up out in the corral. We swapped and I asked a mite extra for that gray and a tolerable bay Barb. Why am I jawing about another man's business with you? Are you the law? I thought they said you were a rock-oil man."

Longarm said, "I'm just nosy by nature, I reckon. If you ain't sold that red pony I left in your safekeeping I'd like your hands to saddle and bridle him whilst I pick out another mount to trail after us. I'd as soon buy as hire. Returning mounts to where you started out with 'em can get complexicated in this neck of the woods!"

They went out back. The apparently colored man yelled in

Cherokee at two stable hands sitting on the corral rail. One went inside and the other dropped down inside the corral with his throw-rope as the dozen odd ponies penned up with Red Rocket milled about, wall-eyed, hoping the kid would rope somebody else.

Longarm was established by any identity as a man who's ridden in on Red Rocket. So those Cherokee commands had obviously involved the blue roan gelding with a blaze as the extra mount they aimed to sell him.

Unlike those assholes over at the Fort Gibson remount corral, the amiable colored Cherokee had picked him out a tolerable retired cowpony. A tad long in the tooth for cutting or roping but still good for steady trotting down a trail. His name was *Olata*, which was Cherokee for something like the wet ashes of a damped down camp fire and that was about the color of the brute's hide. When they saddled him for a ride around the corral he carried steady with no argument. So Longarm got to argue some about the price they were asking for a retired cowpony. Longarm knew he'd likely get his money back after he'd argued some about his travel expenses with Billy Vail. But he didn't want the old Cherokee or his hands to take him for a total fool just because he was white. So they were still arguing the price of horseflesh when Sergeant Deadpony caught up with Longarm and signaled trouble with his eyes.

Longarm told the hostler, "Leave the saddle on the blue and the lead line on Red Rocket. I'll settle up with you in a minute, as outrageous as your prices may be."

He followed the Indian lawman across the street to some shade and Deadpony told him, "A lawyer just rid in from Tulsa Town with a writ of *habeas corpus* on Tulsa Tess, a.k.a. Judith Buffalo Tail of the Osage Reservation Rolls. I don't know how much longer we can stall him. The chief is really down at Park Hill this morning, but the slicker won't have any trouble finding one of our own judges, or, failing that, file an appeal at the Indian Affairs agency."

Longarm grimaced and said, "May as well let him have her, then. It's a long ride to Tulsa Town and it might be interesting to see who Tulsa Tess winds up with, once she gets there."

Jim Deadpony brightened and asked, "You aim to tail them?

188

I thought you'd be riding north to scout those moonshiners, up closer to the Kansas line. Nat Rose and that bounty hunter, Pepper, just left for Tulsa Town. I asked them where they were bound. How come you didn't want to ride with them if you think those moonshiners are as far south of the line as Tulsa Town?"

Longarm smiled thinly and replied, "You sure are full of questions this morning, no offense. To answer backwards, my own boss, Marshal Vail, advises me to neither deny nor advertise who I really might be before I have to. Riding into a strange town with two known lawmen ain't the most discreet way to be taken for a harmless rock-oil man by any crooks who still don't know they gunned somebody else. As for how come all trails seem to lead to Tulsa Town right now, they just don't lead anywheres better. Them revenuers, some other federal deputies, and old Pepper Palmer have scouted the state line country at least as hard as I'd likely manage on my own. On the other hand, Tulsa Tess hails from that other crossroads town and now she seems to be headed back that way with a lawyer I doubt she ever hired."

Deadpony whistled softly and suggested, "Lawyer working for a gent who hires guns as well?"

Longarm said, "Too early to say. That's how come I mean to see where she winds up. The late Elko Watts works out more than one way. He might have been sent after me. He might have been sent to head off poor old Leroy Storch, the bank examiner. Like the old hymn goes, "Farther Along We'll Know More About It." Whether me or Nat Rose have been adding things up wrong there's still that Saint Lou and San Francisco Railroad, which only goes as far as Tulsa Town after cutting clean across this Cherokee reserve from its northeast corner, way closer to the Kansas line."

Deadpony objected, "Pepper Palmer said they caught that bootlegger with a wagonload of moonshine up yonder, north of any tracks."

Longarm nodded and said, "You may have just answered your own smart question. The SL & SFRR tracks don't get closer than ten miles from the Kansas line where they roll on into Missouri. That looks closer on the map than it would feel to tote jars of moonshine that weigh eight pounds a gallon.

After that you wouldn't want to unload just anywhere or cross the state line by broad day along a main road. I suspect them blue-eyed squaws we keep hearing so much about may be getting their backing or even their moonshine from some place nobody's thought to look, such as Tulsa Town."

Deadpony brightened and said, "Hanging around with you is catching. I just thought of something so smart I want to hug myself!"

Longarm dryly asked, "Were you fixing to share it with anybody? I was just talking to another fool Cherokee about self-love."

Deadpony said, "Nobody has even considered inspecting freight cargo bound from one rail stop to another within the Indian territory. But I don't see why we couldn't put a crew aboard at Tulsa Town to paw through any crates bound for local stops up the line. I could put it on the wire this very morning!"

Longarm allowed that sounded like a fine notion. Then he said, "I ain't sending myself to Tulsa Town by telegraph. I got to ride the better part of sixty miles, or at least two days in the saddle if I start right now."

The Indian lawman nodded and half turned to head for the Western Union. But Longarm said, "Hold on. I got a couple more questions. Your Miss Old Path delivered a letter addressed to the late Moses Bradley of Clevolium Incorporated, directing us to keep up the good work until such time as I flash my badge at anybody. What's the story on those mortal remains over to the undertaker's shed?"

Deadpony said, "Embalmed, on ice, in a root cellar. He'll keep for as long as we want to keep his death a secret. So they say."

Longarm knew the bodies of both Pete Donovan and Banker Storch had been pickled and sent back to Fort Smith by then. He said, "We just don't know whether anybody on the other side knows that ain't me they shot in the back my first day in town. It might be interesting to see who's willing to accept me in Tulsa Town as a rock-oil man and just who might not. Do we have any other paperwork about the real prospector's business in these parts?"

Deadpony nodded and said, "He had a bunch of papers in

his saddlebags when they shot him and I told everybody he was you. We impounded his saddle and possibles. They're in the tack room at our police post. I left the papers about oil well drilling and such with Chief Bushyhead and, like I said, he's down at Park Hill this morning. He ought to be back this afternoon, though."

Longarm thought, nodded, and decided, "Let's turn Tulsa Tess loose and give her and her lawyer a head start on me whilst I wait here in town for the chief to get back. I'd as soon trail a few hours back as ride into an ambush and I'd like to get my story straighter before I show up in Tulsa Town searching for rock-oil."

They shook on it and parted friendly. By that time the morning was half shot. He'd already given Nat Rose and Pepper Palmer a few hours' start. So he crossed back over to settle up with the livery wrangler and led the two ponies back to his hotel on foot.

When he asked if he could stable them out back they asked him if he wanted to pay up for another day, since checkout time was creeping up on them.

He didn't want to charge the taxpayers for a night's sleep in a Tahlequah hotel when, as near as he could figure from that survey map, he'd likely bed down for the night at Wagoner, a couple of rail stops north of Fort Gibson. The army post lay just south of midway betwixt the Cherokee capital of Tahlequah and the Creek trading center of Tulsa Town. The coach roads and telegraph lines dipped that far south to just follow the Arkansas Valley up to Tulsa Town. So in point of fact that would have been the easier riding, and for all he knew Tulsa Tess and her mysterious lawyer would be following it. But there was no way in hell a dead lawman was about to ride through Fort Gibson without being spotted by somebody there who'd met him before he'd been back-shot. So it made more sense to follow the rougher but shorter direct route and see if he could pick up that treacherous blue-eyed *weya*'s trail where she was the only one who knew him on sight.

Meanwhile he was stuck with two ponies as the sun rose higher. So he led them around the square to First Methodist where, fanning herself on the veranda of the manse next door, Miss Aura Purl in the flesh yoo-hooed him on over.

Tethering the riding stock to a curbside hitching post, Longarm went up the walk to doff his hat with one boot on the steps as he explained his problem.

The white-looking Cherokee gal set her fan aside and jumped up to declare his poor ponies were welcome to all the shade, cracked corn, and water they wanted, around to the back.

Longarm led the stock back by way of the gravel drive betwixt the manse and the church next door. He noticed some carpenters up in the dynamited tower, sawing shattered wood tidy. Aura Purl scampered over from the veranda steps to fall in beside him as she asked how he and the other lawmen were coming along with their investigation.

He warned her soberly, "I know your father had to be told what was going on, Miss Aura. I know I can't expect a minister's daughter to tell fibs. But should anybody ask you about me, could you just say you didn't know much about me?"

She dimpled up at him to declare, "You might be surprised by what a minister's daughter might or might not do. I'd be proud to lie right out if you thought it might hurt the villains who dynamited our bell tower and murdered poor Will Cash! What do you want me to say about you, Mister Crawford?"

He realized he'd never given the Purls any name at all as he covered his bets by declaring, "Saying you don't hardly know me would be the safest for all concerned. You see, we just don't know for certain who the rascals have been out to kill."

"Jim Deadpony told us that right after poor Will was murdered. He said somebody took a shot at you and that deputy from Fort Smith just before Will climbed up the bell tower to his doom. The one who shot at the three of you never fired from our tower at all, right?"

Longarm said that was close enough as he admired the way the sun played with her upswept hair. There was just a touch of reddish brown to her dark shiny hair, and he could see why her momma had made her wear a sunbonnet, growing up with other Cherokee gals. Aura Purl would have been taken for a striking brunette of, say, Eye-talian persuasion on the streets of Denver. But there was just a hint of darker ancestry in her smoldering brunette complexion. She flirted like a high-born

Latin gal as well, letting her big brown eyes do all the flashing as she smiled innocent and talked like you'd expect a minister's daughter to talk, except for those occasional and likely deliberate slips.

She led him into the carriage house behind the manse where a black pony that matched her hair nickered at them. Aura introduced him by the name of Nigger in the casual way most slave owners or recent slave owners used the word, meaning neither harm nor common courtesy to any colored folk. Longarm had no dog in that fight. It was up to the red, white, and black Cherokee to sort such matters out amongst themselves.

Aura showed him where to stall his own mounts and he was naturally the one to fill the water troughs and break out some feed. As he did so she warned him to water horses before feeding them instead of the other way around. A gal who'd name her pony Nigger was as likely to take a grown man for a fool kid. It was getting easier to see why Antonia Redbird had the minister's daughter down as a stuck-up snob. It was just as likely the pretty little thing was only dense. It was tough to tell whether some folk were insulting on purpose or just a tad stupid. She seemed hospitable enough. So he figured his ponies would be comfortable there whilst he tended some other last-minute chores in Tahlequah.

As they went around to the front together she allowed her folk were down at Park Hill, attending the same social gathering as Chief Bushyhead. When he asked her casual what it was about she sort of flounced her calico as she replied she hadn't asked and didn't care about the fuddy-duddy doings of her elders.

She said, "I'd rather ride my Nigger wild and free through the woods to this sweet little swimming hole I know. Have you ever gone skinny dipping, all alone, with an Indian maid, Mister Crawford? That's what they call girls like me, no matter how hard we try—Indian maids."

Longarm soberly assured her, "I was just now thinking to myself how tough it would be for you to get a job with a wild west show, Miss Aura. Chief Bushyhead told me being Cherokee is more a state of mind than a matter of blood lines and, at the rate you all seem to be going, nobody is likely to consider it any more unusual to be Cherokee than, say, French or Swedish or mayhaps Mexican."

She sighed and said, "You've yet to see our Indian cowboys full of black drink and bourbon at a *selu-itse* gathering. What makes you so shy about my invitation to go swimming on such a warm day? Is it some *gaktuna* you feel about my red skin?"

He paused on the front walk to turn and face her as he soberly told her, "I've indulged in more than a skinny dip with a pure-bred Quill Indian in my time, Miss Aura. I might even risk fooling around with a minister's daughter if I had the time and thought you meant it. But I ain't got the time, and if all you really want from me is my assurances that I find you desirable as a white gal, you got 'em."

He smiled down at her to wearily add, "As far as I can see you *are* a white gal and your elders ought to be ashamed of themselves for all this playacting at the expense of other white folk who have to pay taxes."

She stamped a pretty foot and said, "That's not true! We're not white people. Not *Ontwaganha* white people, anyway!"

He said, "Whatever. Come Saint Patrick's day a heap of Americans with one or more Irish grandmothers are fixing to wear something green and say rude things to one another in the Gaelic. But that won't make them real Irish and all this weeping and wailing about some Trail of Tears whilst you live tax free on more land than you can work don't make you real Indians. But that wasn't what they sent me over this way to look into. So I thank you kindly for the use of your stalls and I'll take you up on that swim some other time."

Chapter 27

Longarm took his time over a dinner of ham hocks, collards, and corn with two helpings of peach cobbler dessert and plenty of black coffee. But when he made it over to the chief's office Dennis Bushyhead hadn't come back yet.

But this time Miss Lorena Old Path seemed easier to get along with, now that she knew him better. When he told her what he was after she led him into a conference room and sat him at a long oak table with another mug of coffee and the saddlebags Jim Deadpony had left in her safekeeping.

One bag held changes of socks and underwear with a shaving kit, a bottle of brandy, a geologist's hammer, and a surveyor's compass. There was mostly paper in the other.

Longarm spread them out across the table to go through as soon as he had his own notebook and a pencil stub handy for taking notes. Like most men of action Longarm hated paperwork like he'd hated homework as a kid. Like most men who took his job serious, he was good at it because he made short work of it by starting at the top of the pile and checking off each infernal piece of paper as he built a second pile, neither making notes nor trying to remember anything he could dismiss, but making sure he understood every line on every slip he couldn't savvy at first glance.

He found a checkbook and some blank mineral futures agreements to be filled out and signed if you wanted Clevolium Incorporated to write you a handsome check for doing nothing at all. But there weren't any contracts filled in, let alone signed. So far, Clevolium Incorporated had yet to pay any Cherokee a cent to tie up any rock-oil underneath them. The most interesting find was a loose-leaf notebook filled with what seemed long lists of meaningless numbers until Longarm figured out the meanings of N, S, E, W, and °. They were compass bearings. In pairs. You didn't need to carry along a bulky map as long as you knew you were taking compass bearings from where you were on at least two prominent landmarks you'd find on any map of the country you were surveying. For once you did get to a map, you only had to draw lines backwards along the readings in your notebook from those known points on the map, and where they crossed was where you'd been when you shot them. So that meant each pair of numbers stood for some point on that overall survey map that the late Moe Bradley had wanted to remember. Lorena Old Path had said she couldn't let him carry off the papers left in her care. There were too many such bearings for him to record in his own field notes. He split the difference by recording one from each page, and that made for a whole page and a half in his pocket notebook. The numbers alone didn't take up much space, but each number had a name such as *Proctor's Mountain* or *Hino Crag* after it.

There was a leather-bound textbook on *Fossil Fuel Indications* that was filled with long words set in small print. Longarm took down the title, author, and publisher to look up again when he found himself locked inside a public library for the night. He was pawing through some expense account vouchers when Lorena Old Path came back in to ask how he was making out.

He told her, "They seem to have shot the poor cuss before he ever carried out half his orders. I'd say he'd spotted some likely indications on that earlier trip and they'd sent him back to sign property owners up for rock-oil leases."

She said she didn't follow his drift.

He explained how rock-oil outfits liked to tie up all the drilling rights in the neighborhood before they got down to serious business. He said, "Back in Penn State, where Colonel Drake sank the first oil wells back in the fifties, you'd barely get down to the oil and proceed to pump the same before some pest the next lot over would follow your lead and sink his own well. It must be mighty vexing after you've done all the hard exploring and, after that, you can sell such rights to a bigger outfit *without* much exploring on your own part. There's a heap of wheeling and dealing in mineral futures, Miss Lorena. Let's just say that's what poor old Moe was after, this trip. Futures on likely places he'd surveyed his earlier trip."

She pursed her lips like a schoolmarm spotting something naughty on the blackboard and said, "He never said a thing to Chief Bushyhead about drilling for rock-oil anywhere in this reserve."

To which Longarm could only reply, "Of course not. Somebody shot him in the back as he was riding into town. They thought he was me. Or at least we've been thinking they thought it was me. Let's go back over what you just said about him needing permission to sign anybody along the future right of way of an unbuilt railroad. What if he just asked folk holding title to Cherokee land with rock-oil under it to make a deal with his outfit on their own?"

She sounded sure when she replied, "They wouldn't be worth the paper they were written on. Lord knows we have plenty of squatters out in the peckerwoods. But they hold title to nothing. Individual families, known as Cherokee citizens in either tribal or federal courts, hold title to the lands they occupy under tribal rules, and Cherokee Blood Law forbids selling, leasing, or giving away joint tribal lands without permission of the whole tribe, see?"

He did. He said, "In sum, nobody could extract coal, rock-oil, or even building sand from anywhere in this Indian territory without leave of the tribal government involved. I take it you civilized tribesfolk as a group are paid by the gallon by that oil outfit pumping up near the Osage line at Bartlesville?"

She said, "We are and it's been paying almost as much into our tribal treasury as those grazing leases over in the outlet. They'd drilled other wells and dammed some natural rock-oil seeps up north of Tulsa Town, on both sides of the Osage-Cherokee line. Someday we may rival Penn State, so they say!"

He shrugged and decided, "Last time I read up on the subject they'd drilled over two thousand rock-oil wells since Drake's first one back in '59. Chief Bushyhead said he'd let Moe Bradley look for oil on his own spread down to

Park Hill. What would that have meant if Bradley had found some?"

The secretary who doubtless typed many a tribal legal ruling was able to answer without hesitation, "He'd have naturally gone on raising stock and produce above ground while the proceeds from the rock-oil was paid into the Cherokee treasury. Why do you ask?"

Longarm said, "They pay me to ask. So let me ask something else. I found this checkbook drawing on the Chemical Trust of Ohio. Where would I be able to cash such a check if Moe Bradley had handed me one for the rock-oil I had no right to sell him as a private owner?"

She answered just as surely, "At the nearest bank, if it was a good check. I imagine bankers would know more about such things. There's the big Drover's Trust, in Tulsa Town, operated by outsiders. Then there's an Indian-operated savings and loan association in each of our ... more organized capitals. The Osage weren't counted as one of the Civilized Tribes before the war. But one hand washes the other and so now they rate their own legislation, lower courts, newspaper, bank, and so on up at Pawhuska. But you said Moses Bradley was murdered before he managed to write any checks for anyone to cash, didn't you?"

Longarm made a note in his sort of crowded notebook and allowed that would be easy enough to check by telegram. It hardly seemed likely any teller in a small-town Indian-run bank would have trouble recalling such a transaction, and Nat Rose was on his way to Tulsa Town to look into the doings of that white-run Drover's Trust.

Young Jim Deadpony came in to join them, saying, "We just let Tulsa Tess go, like you said. She was last seen headed west along the Fort Gibson Road with her fancy *Ontwaganha* lawyer. Guess what she was riding sidesaddle."

Longarm said without hesitation, "Big dapple gray mare."

The two Cherokee exchanged thoughtful looks. Deadpony laughed and said, "They were right about this one. He has *orenda equa!*"

Longarm modestly replied, "If that's your word for medicine, they told me over at the livery that a stranger of my sort had swapped his jaded mounts for old Tabitha and a bay Barb.

198

Ought to make it easier for me to spot 'em at a distance, assuming Tulsa Tess lasts sixty miles aboard a mount that spooks unexpected. Me and Miss Lorena, here, were talking about the poor soul who led my strayed mount into town to get shot before he could explain about all this paper spread across the table."

Jim Deadpony frowned to ask, "What does rock-oil have to do with the moonshine being smuggled north into Kansas, way the hell east of Tulsa Town? Sorry, Miss Lorena."

She just nodded. Longarm said, "If I knew why so many roads seemed to lead towards Tulsa Town I'd likely have them blue-eyed squaws in the box! I don't *know* why somebody yonder hired a gunslick and a treacherous Osage gal to sneak over this way and shoot at two old boys I'm sure of."

Deadpony said, "You mean he surely shot that bank examiner and lay for you in broad daylight. Don't you think that unholy pair murdered Bradley, Will Cash, and that Irish barkeep, Donovan?"

Longarm sighed and asked, "How many times do I have to say that if I had all the answers I wouldn't have to ask so many questions! There just ain't no way they murdered Will Cash with dynamite after Elko was dead and Tess was locked up. Whoever wired that bell tower to blow at least one of us to smithereens must have known about that padlock not really counting."

The Indian lawman shrugged and tried, "Elko and the moll had somebody riding with them. Or the one who gunned Moses Bradley fired from some other vantage point. It was poor old Will who decided on the bell tower, both times. We know for a fact that shot they pegged at the three of us in front of the Western Union came from the closer Council House."

Longarm said, "Ain't nobody here likely to tell us who did what to whom from whence. I reckon I'd best be on my own way to Tulsa Town. I thank you for letting me go over these papers, Miss Lorena."

The dusky beauty dimpled at him to allow he was welcome and ask if they'd helped him cut any sign.

He sheepishly replied, "I still ain't certain why old Moe asked me to join him out this way and help him with his mysterious chores. I'm likely to look foolish, or suspicious, should I tell anyone who knows the business I just can't say what our business really was. But like the old song says, we might know more farther along."

He ticked his hat brim to the gal as he rose to take his leave. Jim Deadpony followed him downstairs and out front, casually asking where Longarm's riding stock might be.

When Longarm told him the young Indian chuckled sort of dirty and declared, "I might have known you'd have gotten to know our Aura Purl, you dog you!"

To which Longarm could only reply, "If that's meant in the biblical sense, I plead not guilty. She's the minister's daughter, for gawd's sake!"

The Cherokee who hailed from Tahlequah went on grinning but soothingly said, "Sure she is. And a ward of the state besides. My excuse is that we're both Deer Clan and for all her faults she ain't *that* wild. You say you're only headed over to the manse to fetch those ponies while Aura's parents are out of town? I'd better say good hunting, here, and let you saddle up over yonder without me saying another word."

Longarm started to ask more than one question. But there were both questions and answers no gent asked or answered about a lady. So they shook on it and Longarm strode on alone.

When he got back to the manse Aura Purl was waiting on her veranda sort of flushed and damp, as if she'd already had that skinny dip off in the peckerwoods. She followed him back and repeated her offer as he saddled Red Rocket and put the halter and lead on the untested blue roan. She said, "It's getting awfully hot and it's late in the day to head out for Tulsa Town. Why not cool off in the woods and get to know one another better while we have the chance?"

He repeated his offer to talk about skinny dipping later. She sobbed, "It's getting later and later even as we stand here listening to the big clock of Forever ticking the little time we have away, Custis!"

He found himself backing away from the frisky brunette as he told her this just wasn't the right time, whatever time it might have been. Then he asked her, "Who told you to call me Custis? Never mind, I might have known you gals would be comparing notes. Us boys have been known to do the same about you all."

She husked, "Make the time for me! Time is too precious to waste on stupid work! Time is the stuff our lives are made out of and when it's gone, that's all they gave us and we're gone forever in the Big Dark!"

Longarm gently but firmly held her at arm's length as he asked her if that was any way for a minister's daughter to talk.

She sneered, "Aw, shit, do I look stupid enough to swallow the pie in the sky that my poor scared daddy serves to other scared mortals? You know why Indian converts are so religious? For the same reason they beat those drums and shake those rattles as the night shadows move in all around their *adanaelvas*. They are scared of *Mauga*, the Big Dark Nothingness that's waiting down the trail of Time for all of us! But I'm not dumb enough to think you can drum or pray your way past *Mauga*! If I thought it would buy me an extra day on this earth I'd become a fucking nun! But it won't, and so I'm just fucking all I can in the time I have to enjoy myself!"

Longarm sighed and said, "I know the feeling. There's this Persian poet called Omar, or mayhaps the Irish poet who translated his stuff to English. Anyways, they advise us all to run off to the woods with a jug of wine, a loaf of bread, and somebody like thou because tomorrow may never come, and there's no argument with their logic. Only, nine times out of ten tomorrow does come, and there you are with all the wine drunk, all the bread et, and thou likely singing in the wilderness with some jasper who has a better job. So I'd best be on my way whilst I still have a job, and, Lord willing, the creeks don't rise. I may get back to you for some of that singing in the wilderness when it's less likely to cost either one of us as much."

She swore at him in Cherokee.

He sighed and said, "I'm likely to cuss myself harder when I find myself alone in my bedroll tonight. By the way, did you ever ask the late Will Cash to ride out to that swimming hole with you, Miss Aura?"

This time she slapped him.

That wasn't really an answer. But at least they'd established the sassy little brunette had *some* shame.

Chapter 28

Longarm rode west on Red Rocket, leading the bigger blue roan. He'd decided to just call the gelding Ashes because neither pony spoke any more Cherokee than he did and Ashes was close enough if the critter had been named for the color of his hide.

Avoiding the more traveled coach road, Longarm found himself out of town sooner, following the back road. Farms and stock spreads had been cleared to either side for a half-day ride or, say, fifteen miles out of Tahlequah. After that came mostly woods where thin topsoil or wood cutters hadn't left balds of big blue-stem and sunflowers. He knew this part of the Great American Desert tended to be wooded as far west as the north-south Neosho, say, a dozen miles ahead, where a change in the bedrock or earlier Osage firebugs had cleared the range almost total to rolling prairie. The Osage had always admired buffalo more than deer for supper. The professors working for the land office were still far from sure how much of the great plains between the Mississippi and the Rockies was natural and how much that poor primitive brute, the Horse Indian, had altered nature to suit his own needs. It was a simple fact that most prairie towns had commenced to sprout trees in backyards or along residential streets. The grass still growing all around seemed to change as Mister Lo and his buffalo herds moved on. Some said cows or, more notoriously, sheep grazed the native grasses out because they didn't nibble grass the way buffalo did. Others allowed the prairie changed from the way it had grown in Indian days because Indian buffalo hunters and Anglo-Mex stock herders managed their same prairie ranges different.

Early generations of New Englanders had grown up bragging about their glorious autumn sunsets without ever knowing they'd been the results of grass fires the size of whole New England states, set on purpose by prairie tribes to burn off the dead stems of late summer and make room for the next green-up, fertilized by the ashes of the summer before. Some white settlers in the Old South had allowed their ignorant darkies to manage their slash-pine plantations with controlled brush fires, learned from the ignorant woodland tribes. But most white settlers stomped out prairie fires as quick as they started, and some said that was how come they could tell where white folk had been grazing stock instead of buffalo. The Indians called the common plantain weed the white man's footprints and allowed they'd never seen tumbleweeds or "Kentucky Blue Grass" from Europe, in their Shining Times.

Longarm reined in to stare hard at another man-made change in nature down the road a piece as he thoughtfully drew his Winchester, levered a round in the chamber, and rode on at a walk with the rifle across his thighs and his free hand's finger on the trigger. For somebody in the not-too-distant past had planted themselves a thick hedge of what the French, who used to own these parts, had called *bois d'arc* whilst most white folk settled for Osage Orange. Left to itself the native shrub or brushy tree tended to just grow in groves a man or beast could go around. Nobody bigger than a rabbit went *through* Osage Orange. Its springy branches, just swell for making Indian bows, were armed with three-inch thorns and, if you planted the stuff close together in a row and pruned it back a few seasons, you wound up with a hedge that would stop most anything but a bullet.

Longarm was more worried about bullets coming out of that abandoned unkempt hedge than aiming at anybody he couldn't see on the far side. He seemed to be riding in on a deserted homestead that would make a dandy ambush. So he circled wide, through some thornsome but less dense honey locust on the far side of the wagon trace and, in the end, found out he'd spooked himself with no more than a *possible* ambush. But he never apologized to himself as he rode on. For as George

Armstrong Custer had proven to everyone's satisfaction but his own, you only had to ride into one ambush to wind up dead and, had old George paid attention to his own spooked scouts that summer's day in '76, he'd have never gone on to become such a fine example for other riders in Indian country.

Longarm reined in atop the next rise and stared back the way he'd just ridden as he wondered why he was thinking about Indians that afternoon. Most of the Cherokee he'd met in those parts had looked and acted more like Mexicans who'd been living north of the border a spell. The eastern newspapers who accused the Five Civilized Tribes of playing Indian in the backyard at the taxpayers' expense were motivated by populist politics. But fair was fair and it did seem a mite thick for an almost white descendant of almost white and literate grandparents to occupy more land than white homesteaders could file on as they pissed and moaned about past injustices. For there were heaps of Indians out this way who'd been forced to give up really different ways, and those colored slaves who'd been liberated at the end of the war hadn't been given shit, next to your average Apache or Comanche. Nobody had killed more white folk than the Comanche and there they were, down around Fort Sill, charging grazing fees whilst demanding bigger government handouts.

"Why am I so pissed off at Mister Lo this afternoon?" Longarm asked Red Rocket as he reined off the trail again to change saddles in a clump of blackjack.

Neither pony had any answers for him as he put the saddle and bridle on Ashes to let Red Rocket trail bareback for a spell.

Longarm decided there was something in the still summer air that reminded him of Mister Lo. He laughed at himself and declared out loud, "Well of course this feels like Indian country. It *is* Indian country! We're smack dab in the middle of the officious Indian territory, with Osage to the northwest, Creek to the southwest, and Cherokee all around us! Most anybody you meet along this wagon trace is more likely than not to be an Indian!"

But, just the same, the next time he came to some serious cover, a grove of box elder, an easy pistol shot off the trail, he rode over to it, reined in, and dismounted to tell the placid blue roan, "You just inhale some leaves whilst me and Mister Winchester make sure nobody's been following the three of us, hear?"

Both ponies commenced to browse boxelder leaves, as he'd figured they might. He chewed an unlit cheroot because it would have been a dumb move to light it with the occasional gentle breezes blowing mostly back the way they'd come.

After the three of them had been there a spell the grove's little critters got used to them and commenced to go about their regular chores again. Fence lizards skittered after bugs, a redwing chirred and what sounded like a cat but was really a bird commenced to meow at them from a top branch. Longarm glanced up at the sky and saw they'd do well to make it as far as the ferry north of Fort Gibson by moonrise at the rate they were going. He'd just said so when he spotted movement in the distance and over a rise came a dozen Indians on horseback.

Cherokee Indians, leastways. They were dressed more like cowboys, save for some head-flutter as they rode closer. Longarm resisted the temptation to hunker down behind the boxelders with his Winchester. He'd noticed before he'd ridden over to them that they grew too thick to see through, easy. But sudden movements could be spotted through fairly thick cover and experienced scouts avoided making any they could possibly avoid.

As the half-dozen Cherokee riders drew abreast of his position and then passed it whilst Longarm held his breath, he saw each one wore a squirrel tail and two white goose feathers on his otherwise civilized black hat, worn cavalry style. Longarm knew that back in their natural state the Cherokee, like other Iroquoians, had never gone in much for feathers. The full war bonnet, with all the symbolism of coup feathers, had been invented by Sioux-Hokan speakers and picked up with other bad habits by other nations. Left to their druthers, the old-time Cherokee had wrapped rags around their heads, Hindu style. It had been General Andrew Jackson, Old Hickory in the flesh, who'd ordered his Cherokee followers to wear those white goose feathers for identification when they'd fought under him against the Creek Confederacy at Horseshoe Bend in the wilds of Alabama. The squirrel tails had been their own idea. Jackson's Cherokee irregulars had made a name for themselves at Horseshoe Bend and those riders passing his position seemed anxious to preserve the tradition. Longarm's heart nearly stopped when one of them pointed at the roadside weeds he'd turned off through and yelled something in their own guttural lingo. But their leader, a lean-and hungry-looking cuss all in sun-faded denim, save for his hat, boots, and gun rig in matching shades of soot, yelled something back in the same lingo and some of the others laughed as they all rode on.

Longarm knew how the one who'd spotted sign felt. But for once he was pleased that the assholes in charge never seemed to listen.

They rode on towards the river until he'd lost sight of them. Longarm remounted the blue roan and trailed after, keeping his gait to a slower trot. He wanted them to reach the ferry across the Neosho well ahead of him. He didn't aim to join them for supper in the railroad town of Wagoner that evening, either. It might be safer to bed down in the woods once he crossed the river. He'd have made it a third of the way to Tulsa Town and an early start the next morning would get him there by broad day, in case anybody had beaten them there aboard a dapple gray mare.

The sun lay low up ahead. It was shining in his eyes as he reined in atop yet another rise to regard the blue Neosho winding from horizon to horizon as the trail took a shallow dive down a long grassy slope. He saw the log cabin beside the ferry landing and easily made out the ferry raft, itself, over on the far side, where they seemed to be letting off or taking on some other riders.

"That's one hell of an open slope to cover with no cover!" Longarm muttered aloud as Red Rocket, on the lead, lowered his muzzle to graze some trailside timothy. Longarm glanced all about, spied some more of that Osage orange, and decided to hole up and watch the ferry operate for a spell before he committed them to the uncertain service without the least notion where those mystery riders, likely *Kituhwa* might have been headed.

He rode in among the more loosely spaced sticker bushes some grown tall enough to call themselves shade trees over

206

that way. The so called oranges growing on Osage orange were indelible rock-hard balls that only *looked* like unripe oranges. But the two trees grew about the same height and cast the same deep shade.

But the shade wasn't deep enough to keep Longarm from spying that rider with two white goose feathers on his hat, quietly sitting atop his dark pony, yonder, as if waiting for somebody to come along.

Longarm didn't want to be that somebody. He swung Ashes back towards the wagon trace, even as he cursed himself for not having swapped mounts during their last trail break.

Ashes was in no shape to run too far with him. After that Longarm had nowheres much to run for on the east side of the river. His only chance was to get across and commence his run from there. It still figured to be close if it was him they were after. But close seemed better than hopeless. So he loped down the long slope toward that log cabin and its handful of log outbuildings. He hoped that once they saw he was in shape to fort up with his Winchester and a clear field of fire in all directions, they'd just be content to let him cross the damned old river and risk chasing after him through the coming night.

As he approached the ferry keeper's cabin he saw that out in midstream the ferry keeper or somebody working for him had headed back across the river, with the ferry raft empty. He hoped that hadn't been some but not all of the *Kituhwas* he was worried about. They worried him more if he had to worry about them being on both sides of the river as he tried to cross it, on a fucking open ferry raft!

As he reined in by the cabin he saw a young barefoot Cherokee gal in a cotton shift lounging in the open doorway. He called out to her that he needed to cross the river. She yelled back that he'd come to the right place. She pointed out at the oncoming ferry raft and invited him in for some coffee and cake, saying, "Pa won't feel like poling the other way until he's wrapped himself around some more coffee."

Longarm dismounted and led the two ponies closer as he casually asked if those riders her dad had just taken across might have been some good old boys he knew in the *Kituhwa* Society. She replied she'd heard that was a secret society.

There was something just a tad evasive in the way she said it. But as Longarm stopped, less than ten yards from the cabin door, he saw it was too late.

The gal had suddenly been replaced in the open doorway by that cuss in blue denim with soot trimmings. He had a Greener ten-gauge cradled casually over his left elbow with his right fist wrapped around the action as he called out in an amused tone, "It's about time you got here, *Ontwaganha*. Come on inside and tell us all about your pals in the *Kituhwa* Society. We can't wait to hear."

Chapter 29

Longarm had seen what Double O Buck could do to human flesh and a ten-gauge threw a heap of Double O Buck. After that another cuss was resting the muzzle of a .52 Spencer Repeater over the sill of an unglazed cabin window. So as the barefoot Cherokee gal came over to hold his horses, Longarm dismounted as if that had been his intent from the beginning and mosied over to the cabin with the muzzle of his own Winchester '73 aimed politely at the dirt.

As he followed the leader inside, a third *Kituhwa* politely but firmly took charge of the Winchester. But they'd made no attempt to disarm him of his holstered .44-40 or the double derringer in his vest by the time he'd been seated at an unpainted deal table in the middle of the one room making up that half of a dog-run cabin. The kitchen and such would be in the other half, connected only by the roofed but open dogrun between.

As his eyes adjusted to the indoor light Longarm saw there were only three befeathered riders in there with him. The one with the Spencer stayed put near the window as if to cover the ferry landing against all comers. The one who'd taken Longarm's Winchester was casually covering him with it from a far corner. The obvious leader sat down across from Longarm. He was a full-blood of around forty with the build of a younger athlete. After that he wore his hair in long black braids and you could see he'd had a mild case of the smallpox a few years back. Longarm asked if it was all right to smoke. The Indian shrugged and said, "Go ahead. Don't ask us to smoke with you before we've talked. The girl will bring us some Tennessee tea after she sees to your mounts. You can call me Echota."

Longarm nodded and said, "I heard *Kituhwa* came from the name of a *Tsalagi* town, too."

The *Kituhwa* leader looked pained and said, "You heard shit, from a gang of white kids playing Indian. That so called Cherokee capital a few miles south of the Ross trading post was named New Echota after a mythical gathering place in *Tsusginagi*, the ghost country of our older ways. *Echota* would translate as 'that which is unknown.' "

Longarm nodded and said, "I see why you chose it as a . . . professional name. Now tell me whether we're supposed to say Cherokee or *Tsalagi*."

The man who wanted to be called Unknown shrugged and said, "When we speak English it makes more sense to use the English word for my people, Cherokee. You do not speak *Tsalagi*. Neither do those half-assed breeds pretending to know baby-talk Cherokee over in Tahlequah. There was a time when real Cherokee ran things in a real Cherokee town. It was built around that real stomping ground, kept clear to play serious ball games with the rival teams from other nations. That fancy council house you see there today replaced our smaller but big enough *Degala-wiv* with open sides so the people could hear and see what was going on. But now the stomping ground has been turned into a pretty park and nobody can be sure what those carpetbaggers who claim to be Cherokee are up to!"

Longarm got out two cheroots and silently offered one, saying, "Carpetbagger seems a might harsh for your Chief Bushyhead. He struck me as a reasonable cuss looking out for his nation."

Echota sneered, "Who's nation, yours or mine? The asshole was born and raised a Baptist, went to fucking *Princeton* and doesn't even know his own name! Have you heard him say his Redcoat ancestor had a bushy head of hair, as if anything that insignificant would matter to our people when they were real people?"

Longarm saw the Indian didn't seem to want to smoke with him. So he put that one away and lit the other before he decided, "I wasn't there. Were you?"

Echota said, "I didn't have to be there. I follow the Old Path. A British officer named John Stuart was captured in a fight we had with the English, released unharmed when the fight was over, and made the King of England's supervisor to the Cherokee. That was what they called a resident trader, a supervisor, as if we had to take orders from the shits in those days!"

Longarm calmly asked, "Where does the family name come from, seeing old John married up with another white trader's daughter?"

The Indian said, "Susannah Emory had a Cherokee mother. *She* was the niece of the leader of the Husk Face or Bushy Head dancers. They dance in silence, wearing tattered cornhusk masks, during the visits of the False Face Society. Your students of our Old Path have written a lot of very silly things about the False Faces. They are not at all like those masked dancers over in the Pueblo country. Our False Faces do not dance at regular affairs such as the Green Corn gatherings. They never act as the regular spirits of the Old Path. They wear the crazy faces a sick person sees in fevered dreams. They come when invited, and only when invited, to dance around a sick person and make his other visions go away. The man who now calls himself Dennis Bushyhead knows nothing of these matters. Nothing. They do not teach about the False Faces Society in Baptist Sunday School. The Great White Father in Washington says Dennis Bushyhead is our paramount chief. They are always saying things like that in Washington."

The young gal came back in, by way of the side door from the dog-run, with a big bowl and some clay mugs on a wooden tray. She said she'd seen to Longarm's mounts and told her dad, the ferry man, not to come inside where he'd crowd things worse.

Longarm thanked her and asked Echota who might be the real chief if the full-bloods didn't recognize the same one as Washington.

Echota sighed, turned to the girl, and asked, "Can you still recite the names of our *Ugvwiyuhi Tsalagi*, little one?"

The girl nodded and began in their own lingo until she switched to English around the time of the Invasion of the Spaniards under De Soto.

She said, "That was when Queen Gwo-wa-tsi-gwi ruled and

so the bearded robbers were afraid to march north of the *Cusa*. Then Oo-la-dha-u-di-na was king for a long time because the people loved him. Later, Litsi made the people cross and they replaced him with Tsa-ma-gula. Then Moytoy became king and he was the one who made a mark he did not understand on some paper the English from Savannah showed him when they gave him presents."

The man who called himself Echota poured what they'd called tea in two mugs and slid one across the table to Long-arm as the Cherokee girl went on, "Later Moytoy told the people he was sorry and tried to take back the promises he'd made another king on paper. But *Ontwaganha* traders and missionaries were already among us, and when our kings tried to make war, some of the people always told the red sleeves what they were going to do and so we always lost."

She paused to watch as Longarm took a sip of his drink and somehow managed not to let his feelings show. It was Black Drink. He'd suffered this same hospitality further south among the Choctaw during an earlier track-down. The brew wasn't any darker than tea but the taste was black indeed, brewed from holly, persimmon, sassafrass, and such to be thrice as bitter and twice as strong as black coffee. The caffeine came from one variety of holly. When they wanted to throw in some real visions, at the risk of death, they tossed in some American mistletoe. But on this occasion the shit tasted as if it had been mixed as not much worse than double-strength coffee. So he didn't throw up and have a fit the way a polite Cherokee guest was supposed to on religious occasions.

Seeing he wasn't going to puke or cuss at her, the gal went on to pontificate, "After Lord Dunmore's war with us nobody was sure who the king was. Each town or sometimes a few towns together would follow one head man or chief while others thought it would be better to do what a stronger or richer chief told them to do. The chiefs with *Ontwaganha* blood were seldom strong as real *Tsalagi* but they could give presents and they knew how to get along with the *Ontwaganha* better. Sometimes they could get the *Ontwaganha* soldiers to back their claims against any full-bloods who opposed them. After a while it was the *Ontwaganha*, not the *Tsalagi*, who said who the *Tsalagi* chiefs were. Sometimes different *On-*

twaganha recognized different paramount chiefs. It was always best to be on the winning side when the *Ontwaganha* fought among themselves. The people who followed the red sleeves in the war between the red sleeves and the blue sleeves were forced to give away more land, and more rights. So they thought it was better to follow chiefs with *Ontwaganha* blood and let the grandmothers of the clans decide important manners. Chief Ross was not a bad chief for one of them. James Vann was a very cruel chief. Most of the others have just been assholes. Can I go out and help my father with his chores now?"

Echota dismissed her. As soon as she'd gone he asked Longarm whether he was starting to understand things better now.

Longarm replied, "Not hardly. They never sent me here to argue with anybody about tribal politics. The chief you seem to consider a white carpetbagger handed me the same sad shit about you poor oppressed and obviously starving Cherokee. If either of you expect me to feel guilty about the Trail of Tears it ain't working. I never voted for old Andrew Jackson. I've told colored folk not to blame this child for the cruel Triangular Trade. If we all get to blame others for sins committed by ancestors before they were born I have me a long list of grievances to present to Queen Victoria and, come to study on it, them Normans were never made to pay for treating the English so mean in 1066. Could you get to the infernal point and tell me what's eating you fucking full-bloods in the here and now?"

Echota smiled thinly and said, "Your straight tongue made a good impression on the grandmothers, too. They are afraid somebody else is going to kill you before you can catch those troublemakers selling firewater in Kansas. If somebody does not make them stop, it will give Kansas land-grabbers the excuse they have been looking for to send their state guard against us. If we fight them openly, they will call us wild Indians, and everybody knows wild Indians don't deserve to own any land. So we want to help you find out who those troublemakers among us are, and, once we know, they will make no firewater forever!"

Longarm said, "Hold on. I sure as certain could use some

213

help in tracking down them blue-eyed Indian gals selling fire-water to the cowboys. But when I catch 'em I mean to hand them over for trial in front of the nearest federal judge. No offense, but your own tribal courts don't have the authority to put moonshiners away as long as our own."

The Indian sipped more Black Drink and stared into space while he murmured in a dreamy voice, "That child mentioned a bad breed chief by the name of James Vann. Your government recognized him as one of three Cherokee chiefs because he was the richest Cherokee trader there was at the time. He owned a plantation and ran a tavern on the freight road so he could drink with his friends, the Georgia freighters, the Georgia Militia, and some riders who called themselves the Pony Boys. Your own people called them white trash."

Longarm took a cool sweet drag on his cheroot. Everything tasted sweet next to Black Drink. Echota sipped more and continued, "Vann was cruel to his colored slaves and beat his Cherokee wife when he had been drinking. He drank a lot. When his wife's brothers asked him not to beat their sister he laughed at them. When a colored slave girl was not willing to pleasure a drunkard in nasty ways he beat her, too, and then burned her at the stake out back to show everybody who was boss."

Longarm said, "He sounded like a true country gentleman. How come nobody complained to the government about him?"

Echota said, "They did. Many times. He just laughed and after he had killed two *Ontwaganha* in those duels your kind allows nobody wanted to argue with James Vann."

The Indian smiled like Miss Mona Lisa in that print and told Longarm, "His wife's brothers wanted to kill him and lift his hair as the Old Path blood laws said they had the right to do. But we had learned it always cost too much when somebody killed an *Ontwaganha* or anyone with *Ontwaganha* friends. So one morning they found Vann on the floor of his tavern in a big pool of blood. Some night visitors had shot him in his big beer belly so that he would take a long time to die, alone in the dark, screaming, with nobody wanting to come near a man who had taught them all to be afraid of him."

Longarm whistled softly and asked, "Did the killer or killers get away with it?"

Echota smiled innocently and replied, "Nobody could ever say who they were, for certain. Some said the night riders might have come from the settlement of Kituhwa. But, of course, nobody in Kituhwa could tell anyone anything."

Longarm asked, "Might this Cherokee town of Kituhwa been back east in them lands your folk were forced to give up?"

The leader of the riders now known as *Kituhwa* smiled boyishly and replied, "The grandmothers said you were quickwitted, for one of them. Where do you think we should look for those troublemakers selling firewater? Why are you riding west when Kansas lies to the north?"

Longarm said, "Federal revenuers, your own tribal police, deputy marshals from Fort Smith and Kansas bounty hunters have searched high and low along the Kansas line and as far south at Tahlequah without a lick of sign being sighted, so far. It's been my general experience that when experienced scouts can't seem to cut a trail, said trail has to be somewhere they ain't looked yet. An Indian bootlegger who might or might not have been telling the truth confessed he'd bought his jars off some blue-eyed squaws. The only suspect I've met who'd fit such a description was last seen headed for Tulsa Town with a lawyer who must have had some motive to work so hard. So that's where I'm headed and, no offense, I don't want you boys riding with me."

Echota shook his head and said, "The grandmothers want us to make sure nobody hurts you. When we saw it bothered you to have us follow, we circled around to meet you here. You have nothing to worry about in the Indian territory as long as we are backing you."

Longarm scowled and said, "I don't need your backing. I don't want your backing. I work better alone, and even if I didn't, I'm a federal lawman, not a vigilante. So if it's all the same with you, I'd like to ride on alone."

The Indian vigilante leader gently but firmly replied, "It is not up to us. It is not up to you. We have to do what our grandmothers want, and I just told you they want us to ride with you."

Chapter 30

Longarm suspected that the first philosopher who'd said a man ought to count to ten before losing his temper had likely packed a gun. So he got his Winchester back and got himself and his two ponies across the river by ferry raft without saying much to Echota and the fool Indians who'd crowded aboard with him.

Once he was back on dry ground Longarm rode Ashes and led Red Rocket as far west as the first road he came upon that seemed to follow the river south. When he swung his mount that way, the Cherokee riding at his side asked how come, adding, "Didn't you say we were headed for Tulsa Town?"

Longarm's tone was coldly polite as he replied, "I did. But I ain't. I owe the army remount service two ponies. So I mean to deliver these two to Fort Gibson. Then I mean to board me the first northbound out along the Missouri, Kansas, and Texas line. I have to transfer to the Kansas and Pacific to get on back to Denver."

Echota looked confounded and asked, "What about those troublemakers you were going to catch for us?"

Longarm snorted in disgust and replied, "If there is one thing you total assholes don't need any help with, it has to be making trouble to spare for your own fool selves. I tried, sincere, and not a fucking Cherokee I've talked to about them moonshiners has really wanted me to catch them."

Echota gasped, "How can you say that? Those breeds or squatters who sell firewater in the dry state of Kansas are going to get us all in trouble! If there is one thing the full-bloods, the mixed-bloods, the council Washington recognizes and the grandmothers we listen to agree on, it's those wicked moonshiners from somewhere else!"

Longarm just kept riding. Life was too short to waste time arguing with a woman set on having her way or a man who said he was following orders.

Echota insisted, "The grandmothers will be very cross with us. You have to go after that *Ontwaganha* woman you were following to Tulsa Town!"

Despite himself, Longarm said, "She wasn't a white gal. She didn't look as if she had much white blood in her. She looked Honest Injun with blue eyes. The late Crazy Horse had blue eyes. They just happen, now and again. But why am I telling you all this? You'd know better than me who's been making moonshine on the Cherokee reserve whilst nary a Cherokee gives a shit."

Echota insisted, "That's not true! We want them caught! We all want them caught! You have to catch them for us!"

To which Longarm dryly replied, "Did I ever tell you how you catch a side-hill-running unicorn? They call 'em side-hill-running because they have their legs on one side longer than the other, so's they can run along the side of a steep hill as fast as if they were running on the level."

"What am I supposed to tell the grandmothers when they ask where you rode after those troublemakers?" demanded the Cherokee, sort of desperate.

Longarm continued, "There's no mortal pony who can overtake a side-hill-running unicorn as it runs along the side of a hill. But where there's a will there's a way and so what you have to do is chase the side-hill-running unicorn until it's really running like hell, and then you just rein in, shake out a community loop, and rope the son of a bitch as it comes running clean around that hill at you from the opposite direction."

The Indian didn't laugh. He asked, "Is that what you think we have been doing with you? Do you think we have been playing jokes on you?"

Longarm shrugged. "Somebody sure has. On me and all them other old boys. Catching outlaws can be a bitch when the folk all around are out to help you. Catching outlaws in their own country amid their own kith and kin gets plain impossible. I got better things to do than hunt for Frank and Jesse in Clay County or search for Cherokee moonshiners other Cherokee just don't want caught."

Echota insisted, "Listen to me! You are wrong!"

But Longarm snapped, "No, you listen! If I ain't right, how come none of you are willing to let me do things my way? I'm sorry as hell about that Trail of Tears and it pains my ass you picked the wrong side in more than one war. But I've done all I can for you resentful rascals, and you can pull your own damn chestnuts out of your own damn fire!"

Echota rode beside him in silence for a time. Then he asked, "What if we were to go back and tell the grandmothers you wanted to hunt alone? Would you keep hunting?"

Longarm said he'd study on it. So a few minutes later he was riding through some cottonwoods alone. He rode on down the river until the trail forked, with one branch going on toward Fort Gibson whilst the other trended west.

He took that one, got turned around a time or more in the bottomland tangle of alder, cottonwood, elm, willow and such, but found his way to the railroad right of way running north and south across his path. By that time, the shadows had gotten ominously long.

There was a service road following the rails and telegraph poles and Longarm knew he was somewhere betwixt Fort Gibson and Wagoner. So he followed the tracks and poles north as he sang his ponies the sad old Irish folk song somebody had used for the tune of "The Streets of Laredo." The original version went . . .

> Oh, pity the plight,
> of a wayfaring stranger,
> with night coming on,
> and a long way from home.

But he spied lamplight ahead just after sundown, before the clear gloaming sky above had gone starry dark, and rode into the dinky railroad stop called Wagoner, after a Cherokee trader of that name. There was little more there than a trading post evolved into a general store that served the farm folk all around and provided livery service for anybody waiting to board a train or unload freight from the same.

Longarm tethered his ponies out front and went in to see about a place to bed the three of them down for the night. A little old lady with a face like a dried apple sent a full-blood kid out to tend his ponies whilst he sat by the cracker barrel near the unlit potbellied stove so's she could rustle him up some coffee and grub. He saw there were two old gents playing checkers on a box beyond the stove. Three younger locals lounged around them, watching. Nobody commented about the game or the stranger who'd just joined them. So it wasn't clear whether they'd taken him for one of their own or a total white man.

Everyone he'd seen so far, save for that one young boy, looked like they had various amounts of white blood. The old lady was wearing a calico print Mother Hubbard, and the men were just dressed country, the way most Cherokee, red, white, or otherwise seemed to dress.

When the old lady brought him a mug of coffee and a bowl of grits and gravy he saw they were living white as well as dressing and acting white alongside the railroad. It made sense. Indians scared of the iron horse tended to live over the horizon from any tracks. As Longarm was eating another local Cherokee came in, ignoring Longarm as he told the folk he knew, in English, "Well, Bushyhead's done her again. I just read it in the *Advocate*. He's turned down that offer for a third railroad. Says their offer for the right of way would hardly pay for the prime bottomland we'd lose along the Arkansas."

Longarm went on eating his grits and gravy in hopes somebody else might ask questions they might not answer for a stranger.

One of the Cherokee supervising the checker game said, "I wish old Dennis wouldn't dither about everything. We all know that sooner or later he's going to have to grant them that right of way or see them build on the *Cusa* side of the river and pay the damned *Cusa* all that money we could have had!"

The more grizzled of the checker players made a slick move, laughed, and said, "That game he's playing ain't as simple as this one. He has to dither about everything. The

219

conservatives and their grandmothers are on his ass every time
he gives outside interests an inch. The progress party is on his
ass every time it looks as if he's missed a chance to make a
buck for us. The *Ontwaganha* business tycoons are on the ass
of the BIA to straighten us wild Indians out no matter what
poor old Dennis does. The railroaders and cattlemen can be
held off. So can all those land-hungry squatters who keep
clamoring to be Indians. But, mark my words, them rock-oil
companies are going to have their way whether we agree to
let 'em drill here in the nation or they move us all to the Great
Sahara and sign mineral-future options with the mocking
birds!"

Longarm couldn't help himself. He piped up to ask whether
any of them had been pestered to sign anything with any rock-
oil scout.

The other old-timer playing checkers looked him over carefully and finally declared, "We ain't allowed to sign shit with
you gents. We are poor primitive Indians and the BIA don't
want nobody cheating any of us. Didn't you know that?"

One of the younger Cherokee stared harder at Longarm to
demand of him, "How come you didn't know that? Who are
you? What are you doing here? Are you looking for trouble?"

Longarm set his cup and bowl aside and rose to his full
considerable height as he softly but firmly replied, "I ain't
looking. But if you're offering, I ain't running. Now it's your
turn."

The crossroads tough laughed harder than the conversation
seemed to warrant and said, "Don't get your bowels in an
uproar, *Ontwaganha*. You was the one asking questions. Don't
we have the right to ask you why you want to know?"

Longarm said, "You do. I was making conversation. I don't
really give a shit whether anyone but me gets rich or poor on
mineral futures. I don't own one acre of tribal land. My tribe
was devolved by William of Normandy long ago. So we came
over here to fight you boys for land."

The Cherokee who'd started up with him laughed again and
said, "You admit right out you rascals took away our eastern
lands by right of naked conquest?"

Longarm said, "Sure. The same as your own officious tribal
history brags on how Cherokee took every hill and dale of

your eastern range from the Catawba who'd been there first. You still glory in how often you raided neighbors north and south, before and after the coming of my kind. The Georgia Slavocrats bullied anybody weaker. Just like you noble Cherokee sold them your war prisoners for black slaves who'd have more trouble getting away. You needed slaves because, next to war, your favorite occupations were two-sticks and dancing. Not chopping cotton."

One of the older checker players laughed and said, "We liked to hunt, too. Other men's women or deer, in that order. You must be that lawman they said Bushyhead had sent away for. They said you had a sandpaper tongue and packed a .44-40 to back it. Where were you fixing to bed down tonight, you ornery young cuss?"

Longarm allowed he was still studying on that. The older Cherokee got up and said, "You'll be staying at my house. That's final. A man with your brass balls ain't safe camping out in Cherokee country. You were right about how tough some of us can be."

So Longarm wound up spending the night with the Adair family of Wagoner, and if he didn't get to sleep with the farmer's daughter he was off to an early start the next morning and the day in the saddle passed without much excitement as the country got more open west of the Neosho.

He crossed the Verdigris fairly early in the morning, was coffeed and caked more than thrice along the way by folk who knew even less about those blue-eyed squaws, and finally saw the smoke haze of Tulsa Town above the prairie ahead by late afternoon.

Founded as a river crossing by Creek traders from the south, Tulsa Town had grown mostly on the north bank of the Arkansas after that ambitious Saint Lou and San Francisco Railroad had terminated on that side of the crossing. Situated as it was where the Cherokee, Creek, and Osage reservations met at a river crossing cum railroad terminal, the place had grown some and looked even less like an Indian town than Tahlequah had. As Longarm rode in on Red Rocket this late in the day, he saw kids of every complexion from Swedish blond to African brunette playing two-sticks in the vacant lots whilst men and women of all ages and races studied or ignored another

221

human being coming in from the east. So, first Longarm asked for and was given instructions to the nearest livery outfit.

As he rode on a city block and reined in before the big barnlike stable at one end of the unpainted but well-built pole corral he cast a casual glance inside to see how the ponies ahead of his own seemed to be faring.

A gal with long blonde hair in braids down either side of her Indian cheekbones and big sloe eyes came out of the stable in boots and a denim smock as Longarm was dismounting.

She said, "Howdy, I'd be Maria Garson, and what's the matter? You look as if you've just seen a ghost!"

To which Longarm could only reply, "Close enough. Where did you get that dapple gray Lippizan mare I see in your corral, Miss Maria? She looks just like a cavalry mount I used to know!"

Chapter 31

It only took a minute to make sure that was Tabitha out back with the rest of the stock. Longarm got to talk about her more as the breed gal showed him where to store his saddle and such in her tack room. He unlashed his frock coat and put it back on, seeing it would soon be sundown. He hung on to the Winchester saddle gun for the usual reasons. As he drew it from the boot, Maria Garson quietly warned, "Toting all that hardware into town is likely to occasion some discussion of your business here with the town law. We have a mayor and mixed commission government, all *wichasha* from the three nations that meet here. They frown on our own *pteole hoksilas* packing guns in town."

He had her nation pegged. Her casual use of the Sioux-Hokan term for plain old people when she meant Indians and describing a cowboy of any race as a *pteole hoksila* made her Osage, or an Osage breed, at least.

As he cradled the Winchester across an elbow he decided, "It might be less complexicated to come clean with you, Miss Maria. I'm neither a cowboy nor the rock-oil prospector I'd as soon be taken for by some. I'd be U.S. Deputy Marshal Custis Long, on a delicate field mission. Can I count on you to keep that under your hat?"

She gravely nodded and said, "I am not wearing a hat, but I have heard of you. The *Wasichu* call you Longarm and *Wichasha* know you as *Wasichu Wastey* or *Kola Wichasha*. We will take no *mazaska* to board either *shunka wakan* out back. Is there anything else you want from us?"

He smiled down at her, albeit not as far down as usual, since Osage ran to height, and told her, "You can start by talking plainer, ma'am. I never took you for High Dutch and if you're trying to find out how much of your lingo I savvy, I don't savvy enough to try any on a gal who's fluent in English."

The blonde breed blushed under her healthy tan and confessed she'd caught herself doing that with other *Wasichu*, or non-Indian riders.

She said, "It feels silly when some trail herder who takes you for a gal he'd like to bring home to mother suddenly stammers that you should have told him sooner you weren't really a white woman."

Longarm felt no call to ask if there'd been more than one such a swain. The hurt that still lingered in her dark wide-set eyes had a tale to tell he hadn't been sent all this way to investigate. So Longarm said, "That gray I was talking to in the corral out back was last seen leaving Tahlequah with another lady of the Osage persuasion riding her. The lawyer riding with her aboard a bay ain't accused of stealing either. He couldn't have known he was swapping spent ponies for state's evidence. I got his name here, somewheres. I copied it off the writ he used to get Miss Tulsa Tess, a.k.a. Judith Buffalo Tail, out of the Cherokee jail."

As he shifted the awkward Winchester to fumble out his notebook the Osage gal he was talking to said, "You must mean Mister Clark. He's one of our regular customers. He hired a paint and a cordovan Tuesday and returned the bay and the gray you're talking about. We allow that when the horses taken in exchange are covered by the deposit or, in this case, better stock than he rode off on. He told us he'd swapped the two jaded nags we'd hired him. It still seems up-and-up if you say he never stole either of the mounts he brought back with him."

Longarm checked his notes to be sure before he said, "Well, just to begin with, nobody in Tahlequah made any mention of a Mister Clark. The way I have it written down, a Lawyer Schreiber from here in Tulsa Town presented a writ signed by a Justice George Tallchief of the Pawhuska Tribal Tribunal and—"

"Stop right there," the Osage breed cut in, adding, "I don't know anything about any lawyer named Schreiber, but the Tallchiefs are a well-known Osage family. They breed ponies. Fine racing ponies. I know of no Osage named Tallchief who serves as a judge on our Tribal Tribunal."

Longarm lay the Winchester aside on a tack-room shelf and wrote all that down as he asked what Maria could tell him about that other Osage gal, Tulsa Tess cum Judith Buffalo Tail.

Maria shook her blonde head and said, "I've never heard of her by either name. I don't know any family called Buffalo Tail. But I guess they could be Osage. Our BIA rolls would have them listed as Osage if they really are. Since you are *Kola* you know how we who used to paint ourselves have started to hand down family names, the same as your own people, since most of us have become Christians and all of us have to be enrolled in a way the BIA allotment clerks can understand."

Longarm smiled at her and said, "That's a swell suggestion about the BIA, Miss Maria. Their office here ought to be able to clear up a heap about Tulsa Tess. Let's get back to your Mister Clark, who said he was Lawyer Schreiber. He left Tahlequah with them two ponies out back and a handsome blue-eyed lady of one Indian nation or another. How might he have arrived here?"

She answered simply, "Trail dusty and alone. Riding the bay and leading that dapple gray. He never mentioned anyone he might have been riding with. The gray was bareback. He must have dropped the lady and her saddle off along the way."

Longarm soberly observed, "There was many a mile of open range and a couple of swift rivers at their disposal, too. Let's hope he left her in Fort Gibson, put her on a train there, or just left her and her own sidesaddle at some other address here in Tulsa Town. You learn not to jump to conclusions in my trade."

She asked if it was possible a lawyer named Schreiber had somebody named Clark working for him.

He said, "That would answer a heap of questions, ma'am. I've heard your nation fielded mighty hunters and sharp trackers back in their Shining Times. I aim to follow up on both

225

your suggestions. Dropping by the local bar association as well as the BIA has to have running in wide circles beat. I've already caught both Tulsa Tess and her lawyer in big fibs. I reckon I'd better make sure either one of them exists as who they're supposed to be!"

She asked where he'd planned on having supper and spending the night. It might have been his imagination, but Longarm suspected he saw just a dab of disappointment in her big sloe eyes when he declared he meant to scout up a hotel closer to the railroad terminal and see if some other lawmen he knew might have made the same wise move.

She followed him out into the more amber sunlight of the dying day as she asked how come it was so smart for a lawman to bed down near a railroad terminal when his ponies were at a livery blocks away.

He said, "Two reasons, in case you ever take up my chosen occupation, ma'am. The knockaround drifters who commit more than half the crimes in this land of the free tend to hang around near the parts of a strange town they know best, and everybody starts the study of a strange town near the railroad."

"Unless he or she rode in on horseback," the livery manager pointed out with a wry smile.

Longarm smiled back and said, "The action to be found without effort in a strange town still tends to be found near the railroading parts of the same. After that, a wanted man who thinks he's been spotted tends to hop a train out before he hires a horse. For, no offense, the iron horse can take a man farther, faster, than anything else he could hope leave town on."

She said the Yellow Rose Hotel near the terminal was popular with his kind. He didn't ask if she'd ever been there with that trail herder who'd hurt her, and she didn't volunteer any more information about the fool place.

He said he'd give the place a try and asked her to send word if her mysterious Mister Clark came back to go for another ride aboard old Tabitha. He warned her to tell her stable hands about the dapple gray's tendency to shy and turn mean when you might least expect it.

When she said they hadn't noticed anything odd about the big gray he shared his suspicions about tin cricket toys with

226

her. She said a pony could be cured of such quirks, Osage style, if he had such a noisemaker on him.

He picked up his saddlebags with a sheepish smile and allowed there were limits to the possibles a man could pack for the field. Then they parted friendly and he headed on west into the center of town with his more awkward than heavy load. He had to carry the saddlebags and his frock coat over his left elbow so he could walk with the Winchester in his gun hand, his finger on the trigger with the action on safe.

As he asked directions to the railroad depot he saw the residents of Tulsa Town tended to look more Indian, albeit hardly anybody wore Quill Indian outfits. Tall gents with tawny diamond-shaped faces under high-crowned hats with straight brims and occasional feathers struck him as likely Osage. He'd gotten surer about Cherokee of late. To begin with they dressed more white and as often as not *looked* more white. The Creek riders from across the river dressed as white as Cherokee but seemed to look more Indian when they didn't look colored. There were no signs posted, as in Texas where the horns grew just as long, saying whether colored customers were welcome or not as he passed barbershops, set-down beaneries, and such.

He found the Yellow Rose near the raiload terminal and Western Union in a business center that looked right for any trail town that far west. He traipsed into the hotel and asked the mighty dusky Indian desk clerk whether Deputy Rose and Pepper Palmer had proceeded him.

They had. The desk clerk said they'd both checked in earlier in the day. But he hadn't seen either since around noon, when they'd gone off together. So Longarm hired a room for himself, carried his rifle and baggage up to it, and hung the frock coat in the closet with the awkward but tempting Winchester. He figured the saddlebags would be safe enough draped over the foot of the bedstead. He wedged a match stem in the door crack as he locked up, anyway.

The long lonesome ride from Tahlequah had given him time to mull recent confusion over in his head. So he had a heap of new questions to ask and he commenced by asking directions to the Tulsa Town Bar Association.

It was just down the street. After that, a motherly old reception gal with Indian features to clash with her pleated bodice and pince-nez had no Lawyer Schreiber currently listed as licensed to practice anywhere in the Indian territory. But after she'd pawed through the file cards a second time she allowed they'd had a Franz Schreiber, Esquire, a spell back. She said he'd died of the galloping consumption in the winter of '76, adding, "The poor man had been told the climate out our way might help his delicate lungs. It didn't. He only tried a few civil cases before his health gave out."

Longarm asked if it would be possible for him to get some transcripts of the legal briefs the late Lawyer Schreiber might have filed.

She said it was possible but might call for some tedious dusty work in the back. He followed her drift and said, "A man who said he was a lawyer called Franz Schreiber sprung a suspect from the Cherokee jail with a writ signed by an Osage judge who don't exist. I suspect such a rascal must have known the real Lawyer Schreiber wasn't going to be popping out of nowhere to ask him who he really was. A dead lawyer who never had too many clients might have inspired the deception on the part of such a client and—"

"We'll get right to work on it!" the smart old law clerk with Indian features cut in. So Longarm said he'd be at the Yellow Rose if they had anything that looked interesting before he came by again in the morning.

The Tulsa Town BIA wasn't far, but, being a government installation, it got to close before sundown. So he went over to the Western Union and got off a progress report to Billy Vail and some night letters to everyone else he could think of to ask about an increasingly tangled ball of yarn.

Marshal Billy Vail called what he was doing the process of eliminating and he'd taught the same to all his deputies. It was sort of like when you went deer hunting and came across more tracks than you could ever follow. You eliminated rabbit tracks, turkey tracks, and even fox tracks so you could track down the damned deer.

He suspected local politics, tribal feuds, and Lord only knew what all had left him and those other lawmen with more sign to read than a sensible tracker needed. But having sent his wires he set the whole can of worms aside to wriggle as he saw about finding something to eat.

He spied a beanery across the way and, next door, as he headed for it, a toy store. That reminded him of something Maria Garson at that livery had said. So he went inside and, sure enough, they had plenty of those tin crickets you could click at gray mares to drive them loco.

He bought one, put it in a vest pocket, and went next door for some grub. Being it was a transportation hub, serving travelers of all the persuasions, he was able to order a T-bone smothered in chili with two fried eggs on top. He washed his mince pie dessert down with an extra helping of black coffee, which still tasted sweet when he thought back to that Black Drink. Then he stepped outside as the sun was setting and started back for his hotel with said sunset in his eyes.

So he didn't recognize the two figures coming his way along the walk, both black and blurry against the scarlet sunset. But they could see him, and beyond. Pepper Palmer shouted, "Longarm! Behind you! Duck!" as both of them seemed to be slapping leather.

Longarm dove sideways into the open doorway of a notions shop as shots rang out and big lead hornets buzzed through the space his spine had just occupied. He'd naturally drawn his own .44-40 as he'd ducked for cover. A little old lady was beating him with a broom and yelling at him to get out of her shop as he crawled back to her doorway for a look-see. A haze of gunsmoke, painted pink as cotton candy by the sunset, obscured the walk he'd just traversed from the east. When he looked the other way he saw by those chaps that the black outline bending over another sprawled half off the walk had to be Pepper Palmer. When Longarm called out to him, the bounty hunter yelled back, "They got Nat Rose! I made it one gunslick with a Spencer .50 seven-shooter. He let fly and ducked betwixt buildings this side of that toy store sign!"

Longarm sprang to his feet, tersely told the old lady he was sorry for knocking her on her ass, and ran up the walk with his unfired and mighty hungry six-gun leading the way.

Once he got on the right side of the sundown's ruby light, he could see at a glance they'd got Nat Rose indeed. The other federal deputy was missing half his head as what was left of it lay in the dust off the walk. Longarm told Palmer, "Stay here and tidy up with the town law and such. I'll be back directly, Lord willing, and he don't get me, too!"

Chapter 32

Longarm got a city block north of the bigger east-west street he'd been on and chased his lengthening shadow across the crimson dust of gloaming toward that livery run by Maria Garson. He knew he was only playing a long shot, but at least it was a shot. All bets were off if the killer who had to know Tulsa Town better holed up in the same. But the rascal had run for it after gunning one lawman and leaving two more alive. So there was a chance he'd keep running and there was no train standing in the terminal just now.

Longarm saw he'd guessed smart when out ahead he spied what seemed a pink pony coming his way at a lope as its rider lashed its rump with the rein ends. Longarm recognized Tabitha despite the tricky red light. He'd never laid eyes on the jasper riding her his way. If the man on horseback knew Longarm on sight, the red sky at Longarm's back made him tougher to recognize. So Longarm had the edge, if all he wanted was yet another dead gunslick to question.

So he stepped to one side, as if to get out of the galloping mare's way, and reached in his vest pocket as if for a smoke instead of going for his gun.

Then, just as Tabitha and her strange rider drew abreast of him, Longarm clicked that tin cricket more than once.

Once might have been enough. At the first sharp click the dapple gray dropped her muzzle betwixt her front legs, threw her big gray ass at the sky, and proceeded to imitate a hula dancer doing a handstand until her rider parted company with her to land flat on his back, spread eagle, as Longarm drew and stepped forward to calmly call out, "Easy, Tabitha! Easy, old gal! I'll kill the cocksucker for you if he moves a fucking muscle!"

The spooked mare crow-hopped half a furlong on and paused by a water trough across the way to slake her thirst as Longarm strode over to the man sprawled in the red dust to calmly ask, "Are you listening to me, cocksucker?"

The stranger didn't answer. He couldn't answer as he tried in vain to suck air into his stunned chest. Longarm suggested, "Don't try so hard. Try little shallow breaths as the numbness wears off."

He hunkered down to disarm the stranger. He said, "This .38 Colt Lightning never done that deed on Nat Rose. Just take it easy whilst we see what sort of saddle gun you favor. I meant what I said about moving a muscle and you doubtless know who you were just shooting at."

He strode slowly and calmly toward Tabitha as the spooked mare eyed him warily and raised her head from the water with her reins dragging.

Longarm crooned, "You don't want to trip over them reins and have to be put out of your misery, old gal. I'm sorry I had to spook you like that. I won't do it no more, hear?"

He heard voices behind him. He turned to see Maria Garson and one of her Indian stable hands running down the street toward them. Some others who'd noticed the bucking contest were headed his way as well. So he holstered his .44-40, broke out his badge, and pinned it to his vest before he moved in to gather Tabitha's reins with a sudden swoop and steady her with a palm over her flared nostrils by the time the blonde Osage gal got as far as the man on his back in the middle of the road.

Maria pointed down and called, "This is that Mister Clark we were talking about. I sent one of my other hands to your hotel just now. But I couldn't stop him from mounting his own pony, could I?"

Longarm drew the downed man's saddle gun far enough from its boot to see it was a Henry .44-40. He swore softly and led Tabitha back to rejoin her more recent rider at the booted feet of Maria Garson. He told the breed gal she'd done

232

the right thing. Then he kicked Clark in the ribs to gain his undivided attention.

As the man who called himself Clark winced in pain Longarm said, "I know how long it takes to get your talking-wind back after a fall such as that. You may find this hard to believe, but I have been bucked off in my own time. So before you start lying, let me count the ways I have you. I can doubtless prove you were the last man seen with Tulsa Tess or Judith Buffalo Tail whilst she was still alive. So for openers I can charge you with murdering her to shut her up, somewheres betwixt the Cherokee jail and your arrival in Tulsa Town without her!"

Clark groaned, "You're crazy! I never harmed a hair on that whore's head! I left her alive and well in Fort Gibson. She has kin in Muskogee. I was only doing some Indian pals a favor, see?"

Longarm said, "If it turns out she was fibbing about being Osage, and if you'd care to help us find hide or hair of a material witness anywhere on the Creek reserve I'll take it back. But as things now stand, I'm charging you with murdering her on the Cherokee reserve to help out some friends Miss Maria, here, would define as *Wasichu*. I can prove Tulsa Tess was shacked up in Tahlequah with Elko Watts and there's no doubt Elko Watts gunned at least one innocent bystander. So what's it going to be, states evidence or a solo rope dance? Old Judge Parker over to Fort Smith is going to hang *somebody* for the killing of Nat Rose just now."

The man at their feet, having recovered his breath, seemed to have recovered some grit in the process. He told Longarm to do something to himself that was not only impossible but a mighty nasty suggestion to make when ladies were present. So Longarm kicked him again and warned, "Next time you say anything that rude you get to swallow some teeth. I was only offering you a way out. If you don't aim to talk, don't talk dirty!"

A tall dark gent with a badge of his own and a Schofield .45 to go with the feather up the back of his high-crowned Stetson came through the gathering crowd to calmly but firmly ask what in blue thunder was going on. Maria Garson said something to him in Osage. He nodded but replied in English, "I was asking the *Wasichu*, Miss Maria."

So Longarm explained his suspicions that the man at their feet was the same man who'd just gunned a federal deputy near the Western Union and might have killed Tulsa Tess after springing her from the Cherokee jail with a forged Osage writ of habeas corpus.

The Indian lawman said in that case he'd be proud to run the cuss in and hold him until the matter could be sorted out. Clark protested his innocence as Longarm and the Indian got him to his feet. It was the Indian lawman who put his own cuffs on the prisoner. He seemed to be enjoying himself. Indian police had to be careful about manhandling white prisoners without white comrades-in-arms to back their play. As he got a better look at the upright Clark in the tricky light, the town lawman decided, "I've seen this one around the railroad depot. Somebody told me he was a lawyer."

Longarm nodded and replied, "He's told bigger fibs. I'm still working on what I said to restore his confidence, just now. I'd ask him, but, as you see, he's suddenly acting as if I've been barking up the wrong tree. So I reckon I have been."

Maria told her young hand to take charge of Tabitha. She might have tagged along after the two lawmen and their prisoner if Longarm hadn't assured her he'd come back later and tell her all about it.

That left him and the Indian, who said they called him Jerry, free to march the tight-lipped cuss called Clark all the way into the middle of town, where Longarm had to go over it all again at the town lockup, run by a mixed bunch who rotated the position of Head Marshal amongst Cherokee, Creek, and Osage assimilates.

Longarm's chore was somewhat eased by Pepper Palmer having beaten him there to dictate a deposition. For all his swagger, Pepper was well versed in the rules of evidence and so he'd known better than to say anything that would be easy to challenge in court. When he saw the man Longarm and the Osage lawman brought in, at close range, Pepper said Clark looked like the jasper who'd popped out of that slot behind a fellow lawman to fire a fusilade of .50-caliber slugs at Longarm, Nat Rose, and himself. So when Clark sneered that Pep

234

per couldn't prove a thing Longarm said, "We don't have to prove nothing tonight. All the places we could ask about you have shut down for the nignt, as well you know, you smug bastard. But we can hold you seventy-two hours on no more than suspicion, and I suspect you of murdering that Indian gal as well as old Nat. Farther along, as the church song says, we'll understand why."

The town lawmen said they'd be proud to hold a white man in their patent cell for as long as a white arresting officer wanted him held. The Osage called Jerry said they had liaison with the tribal police off the three surrounding reserves. It was his suggestion they check with Muskogee as well as Fort Gibson. He said, "No gal living high here in Tulsa Town would glory in the name of Tulsa Tess. *All* the whores in town are Tulsa gals, and it ain't no novelty to be Osage on this side of the river, when you study on it."

Longarm nodded and said, "Her story was that she'd taken up with the late Elko Watts in Muskogee after being run off the Osage reserve. A Creek gal under a cloud works as well when you consider all the other lies I caught her in."

They put Clark away for the night. Pepper told Longarm they had Nat Rose at the nearby town morgue and that he'd already wired Fort Smith about him.

Longarm grimaced and said, "They're doubtless finding it tedious to haul dead Fort Smith gents in from this Indian territory. Poor old Nat was sent to look into the killing of Banker Storch and now I got to look into the killing of Nat Rose! Did you ever get the feeling you were pitching hay against the wind?"

Pepper shrugged and said, "Such feelings go with the job. If it was too easy to catch crooks nobody would be a crook. I vote we just keep plugging till we catch them blue-eyed squaws. It's obvious that whoever the mastermind behind all this moonshine bullshit may be, the reason they keep shooting at you is to keep you from catching them. You must have said or done something to make then think you're getting warm."

"How do you know it's me they've been shooting at?" Longarm asked in a thoughtful tone as he stared out the window into the gathering dusk.

Pepper said, "You've been in the line of fire every time

somebody or other's been gunned. Neither Nat nor that bank examiner had any connection to that rock-oil prospector or the Cherokee peace officer they blew up. You're the only common demon eater."

Longarm muttered, "I suspect *denominator* is the term you had in mind. Like you just heard me tell the turd, I can't ask anybody all that much about him tonight and I promised another pal I'd come back as soon as I had anything at all to say."

Pepper and Jerry followed him outside but didn't chase him through the dark streets to the livery run by Maria Garson. So he found Maria had done her hair up fancier and splashed on some violet-water since last they'd spoken. Her quarters were above the tack room, off the hay loft, and it appeared she dwelt alone. Her tidy but cramped two rooms might have been about right for a weekend shack job, since she wasn't a bad-looking gal. But Longarm was already starting to feel hemmed in as she sat him on a sofa bed and fed him coffee and cake in spite of his protests that he'd just had supper in town.

She made him tell her all about the arrest and the events leading up to the same. When he got to the part about Clark starting to whine for his life and then suddenly clamming up with a knowing sneer, Maria said, "I was there. It was right after you said his pal Elko killed an innocent bystander in Tahlequah."

Longarm nodded absently, then brightened and said, "Lord love you; Miss Maria, you should be riding with us against the denizens of the owlhoot trail!"

She sat down beside him to cut some more cake for him as she quietly said she'd like that. Then she asked what she'd said that made him and his Lord love her so much.

Longarm said, "Tulsa Tess told me, while she was singing for her own supper, how Elko Watts had told *her* he'd been sent to Tahlequah to gun somebody for five hundred dollars. He never told her it was *me*. So I may have had too high an opinion of myself. The man Elko did shoot, a few feet away from me and another expert on moonshining, was a bank examiner on his way here to Tulsa Town to . . . examine a bank, I reckon."

Maria asked, "Didn't you say you *Wasichu* lawmen were

after Indians selling *mni wakan* up in Kansas?"

Longarm shook his head and said, "Pepper Palmer and me were. Nat Rose was here to look into the murder of that bank examiner and what if we haven't been talking about *missing* anybody? Hired guns are by definition supposed to know how to shoot. So you have to wonder when first a bank examiner and then a lawman investigating the death of the same bank examiner get shot before either can make it to the Drover's Trust here in Tulsa Town! Thanks to your prodding my memory I'm sure Clark clammed up right after I accused him and his pals of gunning an innocent bystander instead of me. He knew I wasn't even warm. He knew there was no way anyone in front of a judge and jury could offer a halfway sensible motive for anyone in his bunch to be gunning for *me*! None of them *have* been gunning for me, and you're so smart you ought to hug yourself, Miss Maria!"

To which she coyly replied, "Why would I want to hug myself? Isn't that what friends are for?"

So it only seemed natural for him to shove his coffee and cake aside and take the dusky well-built blonde in his arms for a friendly hug.

This seemed to lead as naturally to the two of them leaning back a tad farther on the cushions as she reached up to skim his hat across the room so's they could swap some spit, and it was Maria who made the first sassy grab for the buckle of his gunbelt, as if she wanted that out of the way as well.

Longarm could see she knew how to unbuckle a man. So he ran his free hand down her denim-clad flank, feeling nothing under the smock but her firm feminine flesh till he got halfway down her thigh and commenced to gather her skirts up above her knees.

When she grasped his intent she twisted her lips aside from his enough to murmur, *"Kannst ich auch ein bischen Haut-deutsch ver'stehen!"*

To which Longarm could only reply, "You sure can! Is there any point for us to be speaking High Dutch, Miss Maria?"

She got rid of his gunbelt and grabbed for his fly as she passionately confessed, "My daddy was Scotch-Irish and my momma was only half Osage. She'd learned High Dutch as well as Osage and taught them both to me as a child. So I'm three quarters *Wasichu* and doesn't that count for anything in your eyes?"

Longarm didn't answer. He had his free hand up under her skirt and he really didn't give a damn what all that warm moist lap-fur might or might not strike his infernal *eyes*!

Chapter 33

Longarm really liked women and he tried not to hurt them even if it meant hurting his old organ grinder. So even as he got it out and in position to plunge, he felt obliged to warn her he wasn't sure how long he'd be in town.

Maria threw her long legs wider apart as she sobbed, "For God's sake, nobody's asking you to respect me in the morning! Stop teasing me like this! *Tawitan yo!*"

Longarm sincerely doubted that was how you said "Let's fuck!" in High Dutch. But it was close enough to similar remarks he'd heard in a Lakota teepee so he just followed her suggestion as deep as it would go and she was begging for it deeper as she proceeded to try and buck him out of her love saddle.

She'd have likely done it, too, if she hadn't been hanging on to the horn with her hot tight innards until she suddenly shuddered all over at the top of a rise and then sort of fainted under him as he pounded on to glory.

It was even better in her bedroom, a few minutes later, with all of their duds off and more room to wrestle. A man could have gotten the distinct impression old Maria hadn't been getting any lately, from the way she kept coming and bawling for more.

She said she was sorry she'd gone so *witko* as they shared a smoke in the soft afterglow of a really swell session of slap and tickle. He assured her he'd felt as loco up yonder among the stars. He was hoping like hell she wouldn't tell him the sad story of how she'd got to be such a great lay.

But of course, being a woman, she had to, and Longarm had to pretend he gave toad squat as she went on and on about some trail boss with a High Dutch handle who'd taken her for another immigrant when she noticed he was having trouble with her English and threw some High Dutch she knew at him.

She snuggled closer and commenced to toy with Longarm's limp dick as she sadly explained, "Wolfgang was on shore-leave off a clipper out of Emden when they drafted him for the Hood's Texas Brigade in Galveston. By the time he'd learned enough English to tell them he'd never ridden a cavalry mount before, he'd gotten pretty good at it. He came out of the war a cavalry sergeant and that led in turn to his meeting me as he was bossing a herd up from Texas."

Longarm didn't care to hear about her losing her cherry to the Texas trail boss. So he blew a smoke ring at her papered ceiling and observed, "There's been heaps of immigration from them High Dutch countries since old Bismarck has been wadding them all together as that new Germanic Empire. Do you know Doc Sternmuller from the BIA, over to Tahlequah?"

Maria shook her blonde head and replied, "No. Why should I, and what a funny name!"

Longarm blew another smoke ring and said, "I just thought you might. Seeing you have so much in common. Being part High Dutch, I mean. What's so funny about her name?"

The Osage breed said, "It means someone who mills or grinds *stars*. How on earth could anyone's ancestors have done a thing like that?"

He shrugged his bare shoulder under her head to reply, "Old country names can suffer a sea change by the time they wind up on this side of the main ocean in English. I know some Irish folk in Denver named Coin and they still say that means Wild Goose in Gaelic. What might the name Schreiber mean, seeing it sounds High Dutch?"

She said, "That's easy. Schreiber would translate as Scribe or Clerk in English. Are we talking about that dead lawyer, dear?"

Longarm said, "The real Franz Schreiber, Esquire, is dead A cuss who says his name is really Clark served a phony wri

240

as a lawyer named Schreiber, and Clark is just another spelling of Clerk!"

Maria brightened and said, "That must mean he made *both* names up! Do you think it means he speaks High Dutch as well?"

Longarm replied, "I don't know. I aim to find out. Remind me before you throw me out in the cold gray dawn to take down something really mean to say in High Dutch. You do know how to cuss a gent out in that lingo, don't you?"

She began to stroke the part of him she'd been working up again as she said, "Of course. You've no idea how I cursed that silly Wolfgang when he said he could never bring a *Halbnegerin* home to Texas!"

Longarm started to ask if that had meant "half nigger" as it sort of sounded. But then she'd suddenly cocked a long tan leg across him to part her own blonde crotch hair on what she'd wrought. So he had to rise to the occasion again and it was hours before she ever dictated him an awful thing to say to any man who savvied the lingo.

They managed to catch a few winks of sleep before a blamed rooster was crowing outside and she rose first to wash up, serve him a cold breakfast in bed, and wind up needing another douche before she just couldn't get out of going downstairs to open up for the day.

Longarm took his time and joined her later in the corral, where she had old Tabitha tethered tightly to a corral post. Longarm saw the gray mare could barely move her head up, down, or sideways as she just had to stand there, like a naughty child stood in a corner.

Longarm ambled over to join them, resisting the impulse to lay a hand on such a great lay as he quietly said, "Your Lakota cousins do that much the same. It seems to work. Albeit good old boys of my own persuasion have been heard to opine it breaks a mount's spirit."

Maria went on petting Tabitha's dapple gray hide as she replied in an annoyed tone, "Our Osage irregulars rode circles around those Kansas Jayhawkers on their spiritless Indian ponies. This poor thing has been proving for some time that she won't be taught not to buck by letting her buck!"

She took the tin cricket Longarm had bought from a pocket

of her denim smock to suddenly click it as she went on petting Tabitha.

The big gray mare tried to fling herself high in the sky, of course. But she couldn't move her head enough, either way, to buck serious. So Maria just went on petting her and telling her how pretty she was until the mare calmed down some more.

Maria turned to Longarm to say, "We'll let her just stand here and miss our company for an hour or more. Then I'll be back with a nice carrot or a bunch of lovegrass to give her as I click this cricket at her again."

Longarm said, "I know how horse Indian gentling works. Most cavalry or cow outfits don't want to spend the time you folk do. They figure it's best to just let a mount fight a good rider until it's established who the boss might be."

Maria said, "Tell me something I've never been told. Some of our own full-blooded cow hands have started to break *shunka wakan* that cruel way. It only works when nobody gets bucked off. Tabitha and me understand one another. She just doesn't know it yet."

So Longarm managed not to kiss her, allowed he'd be back late to see how she might be coming, and strode back into town in the morning cool with his frock coat back on. He had some officious calls ahead of him.

At the BIA they confirmed his suspicion that no such dependent Indian as Tulsa Tess or Judith Buffalo Tail was enrolled as Cherokee, Creek, or Osage. That might or might not mean she'd been raised as a ward of the state under some other name. The old geezer he talked to at the BIA was inclined to answer more questions than anyone asked him. So Longarm had to gently but firmly inform the nice old fuss that he'd already known that much about the current Indian policy

Folk back east and all too many Indians out west seemed to think reservations were prison farms with the white agency staff acting as wardens. But things weren't half that simple.

Despite newspaper headlines about hostile Indians jumping a reservation and having to be rounded up and brought back to their agencies by the army, they were only talking about renegades.

A Hostile was an unreconstructed Quill Indian who'd never

242

signed a treaty with the U.S. Government, the Florida Seminole being the most famous example. Many a nation, such as the Osage, Pawnee, Pima, and most Pueblo had never fought the U.S. Government and been given a good part of their original range as their reserve. Anyone who expected the government to grant all the ground wandering hunter-gatherers had roamed in their Shining Times just didn't grasp the realities of politics. The nations who'd fought the government before agreeing to settle some fool place or another hadn't been offered the generous terms of the Friendly Nations to begin with and their agents had often been corrupt or just plain stupid. But when an agency was working right the Indians assigned to it received rations, trade goods, and such cash as they seemed able to manage in return for their peaceable behavior.

Indians who didn't like reservation life were free to leave any time and go most anywhere to do most anything as long as they obeyed those federal, state, and local laws imposed on other free citizens. Breeds or even full-bloods who chose to declare themselves white were seldom challenged by anyone, as long as they *behaved* white. It was the notion you could loll about your reservation, nursing your grudges whilst you spent your government allotment money on booze and ammunition until it seemed a swell time to go wild some more than resulted in most of the recent headlines. Victorio was off the reservation again, after being forgiven more than once for past raids, and those Lakota were still up Canada way, trying to horn in on the Blackfoot and Cree hunting grounds. But in point of fact this fair-sized town, where three big reservations met, was closer to the way most Indians had commenced to get along.

Those eastern Cherokee were far from the only former tribes folk who now lived fee-simple on their own farms, didn't ask for any handouts, and didn't have to take any shit off the Great White Father.

He'd read in papers published by Indians that a heap of Indians had been feuding and fussing about such notions. Some Indians wanted to just fold a bad hand and get on with life as regular Americans whilst others, including many a breed who'd tried supporting himself on the outside, liked things just the way they were.

243

When he got to the police post he found Pepper Palmer already back in the cell block with the rascal who kept insisting he was Frank Clark. Palmer had been threatening to kick the shit out of him if Clark wouldn't talk. From the way the prisoner just sat there on his fold-down bunk, hugging his own knees, it was a safe bet he'd been through the mill before and knew how the game was played.

The Indian turnkey had been too smart to let the big bounty hunter inside the bars with Clark. Longarm joined Pepper there to tell Pepper, not the prisoner, "There's no call to waste further breath on him, old son. *Wir habt die Leiche begründen.*"

It didn't work. For all the coaching old Maria had offered earlier in bed, he might as well have tried Osage on the cuss who'd used the name of Schreiber.

Pepper Palmer asked him what in thunder he'd just said. Longarm had memorized another phrase to redden the face of anyone who spoke High Dutch. But he kept a sharp eye on the man in the cell as he replied in English, "Oh, I forgot you don't follow my drift when I get excited. I was just saying we found the body. So there's no call to question the *Arsesauger* further."

Clark jumped up and came over to the bars, protesting, "You're full of shit! You never found no body! There ain't no way you could have found her body!"

Longarm ignored him and told Pepper, "Let's go. Now that he's told me who he was working for, we may as well arrest the mastermind and wrap this up for poor old Nat Rose."

Pepper followed Longarm outside, chaps flapping as Longarm picked up the pace, and almost yelled, "Where in thunder are we bound in such a hurry? I thought you and me were both working on them moonshiners. Are you saying that rascal back there told you who they were?"

Longarm said, "Not hardly. The son of a bitch I'm after right now never sent Elko Watts to intercept this child or that Irish gal in Tahlequah. Elko got the bank examiner he'd been paid to head off. But poor Nat Rose kept coming, aiming to examine the same bank, and it was him, not me, they were aiming at last evening. It's all simple as duck soup as soon as you do some of that *eliminating*. I don't see any bounty in ol

Nat's case for you, Pepper. But you're welcome to tag along if you care to."

Pepper said, "I care to. They told me you were good, but this is a thundering wonder I got to see. That tight-lipped son of a bitch back yonder never told us who he was working for, pard!"

Longarm said, "Not in so many words. If my hunch is right the old boy who hired Elko and made up both names we have for Clark, is the smart-ass who told me. That Drover's Trust is just down the way and so farther along, as the old song goes, we'll know more about it!"

They did. Posting Palmer near the front entrance of the Drover's Trust, Longarm strode in wearing the expression of an old store cat who's just spied a mouse in a blind corner with no way out. So even the branch manager, a Banker Graves of the white persuasion, looked uneasy as Longarm flashed his badge and announced he was there to clean house.

Graves offered him a seat by his desk in the back and lowered his own voice as he confided, "We've been expecting somebody. Hardly a federal deputy. The main office in Omaha wrote us to expect a Mister Storch from our Fort Smith branch. I thought Storch was an accountant, not a lawman!"

Longarm said, "He was. To save us some time. Which one of your own officials goes with a High Dutch name such as Hans or Fritz?"

Graves looked confused, then gazed in the direction of a portly bullet-headed individual who was staring back, uneasy, before Graves could say, "Well, there's our Mister Huber in charge of secured loans, over there by that pillaster."

So Longarm rose to what must have seemed an ominous height to the bank official staring their way. The loan officer called Huber was suddenly on his feet and headed for the door.

Then he saw Pepper Palmer standing in the doorway with his gun hand hovering and hesitated, fumbling nervously at the holstered .32 under his left armpit as Pepper purred, "Go for it, Pilgrim. Pretty please?"

The portly banker seemed to deflate as if he'd been punctured. So Longarm just came up behind him to say, "You're under arrest. The charge is murder and bank fraud. Thanks for backing my play, Pepper."

The big bounty hunter grinned sort of goofy and replied, "Think nothing of it. Glad I was able to help. Now will somebody please tell me what in blue blazes the two of us just did?"

Chapter 34

Longarm wasn't about to explain what he was trying to pull in front of the suspect he was trying to pull it on. So once he'd shoved Huber against a wall, disarmed and handcuffed him while the other employees looked away, embarrassed for the protesting loan officer, Longarm tore a page out of his notebook and handprinted a few words, asking that his prisoner be held as a fresh-caught *Shunka Wakan*.

He handed the note to Pepper Palmer and said, "I'd be obliged if you could frog march this cuss to the town lockup and make sure you give this to an Osage peace officer. I ain't sure how to write what I just wrote in Cherokee or Creek."

Pepper scanned the note and asked what a *Shunka Wakan* was.

Longarm said, "If I wanted the whole world to know I'd have writ in plain American. I'll be along directly to tell you all more about it. What are you waiting for, a kiss good-bye?"

Pepper took Huber by one arm and growled, "Let's go, little darling. If I don't get no bounty money out of this I'll be sore as hell!"

As soon as they were on their way Longarm returned to the ashen-faced Banker Graves and said, "So much for who done it. I still ain't sure what he done. I ain't the bank examiner he ordered assassinated. But I reckon a look at his books are still in order."

Graves rose from his desk, turning out to be shorter than he looked sitting on the throne, but said, "There must be some mistake. When we learned the main branch was sending an

247

accountant to go over our books we naturally burned some midnight oil over them ourselves. So I can assure you not one red cent is missing from any of the accounts our Mister Huber handles!"

Longarm shrugged and said, "Had your main branch thought anyone was just dipping in their cash drawer they'd have never assigned old Leroy Storch the task of examining your paperwork, tighter than you might know how. Let's just go over them accounts Huber was personally riding herd on. If he hadn't given himself away, just now, Lord knows where a green bank examiner like me might start."

So they showed him to a side room and sat him at a table so's a nice-looking older woman who allowed she was part Muskogee, as most Creek preferred to be called, could bring him ledger after ledger, kept in the foreign-looking handwriting of their Mister Huber.

When he asked her, she said she thought Huber had been raised back east in York State, but she'd noticed his handwriting favored his High Dutch name. He'd likely learned to read and write from a schoolmarm of the same persuasion. Immigrant folk tended to cluster in small towns or big city neighborhoods.

The Muskogee lady tried not to admit it. But he finally got her to allow she'd sometimes had to take the loan officers word on some of his scribble scrabble when she was typing up loan transactions, making out checks and so forth.

After he'd gone through the first two ledgers and she was putting another one before him, Longarm asked her to set across the table for a minute.

Once she had, Longarm chose his words carefully before he told her, "I'm having trouble with our current Indian policy, ma'am. You may have noticed the BIA ain't exactly consistent in its rules and regulations."

She sighed and said, "I've noticed that, growing up on what they've designated as the Creek Reservation. Depending on recent elections back east, they've wavered all my life between containment and assimilation. Right now, under Secretary Schurz, they want us to stop playing Indian and start paying taxes like everyone else. You've heard what Senator Henry Dawes has been proposing, back east?"

Longarm read the *Denver Post* and *Rocky Mountain News* from time to time. So he nodded and said, "That proposed General Allotment Act sounds swell until you consider some of the nations who still live in the Stone Age, no offense. That Dawes Act has been turned down and rewrit more than once. But that does take us to one of the things that's bothering me about some fair-sized loans your Mister Huber authorized. The proposed legislation, giving you folk the right to own, buy, sell, or mortgage your own family homesteads is still proposed. Until such time as all or part of your Five Civilized Tribes get fee-simple title to private land I fail to see how this bank can offer secured loans to any Indian applicants."

She said, "We couldn't issue one red cent on any regular mortgage agreement. But thanks to our having been literate Christians, for the most part, for some time, the BIA allows residents of this territory to engage in private business provided we are not receiving government allotments in cash or kind."

Longarm glanced down at the ledger to pick out and examine before he said, "All right, I can see how this William Adair of the Cherokee Nation borrowed eight hundred dollars to expand his freight business with more mules and rolling stock. I can see he's put up said mules and Conestoga wagons as security and, after that, he seems to have been making his payments with interest. But what happens if such an uncertainly defined businessman fails to pay back the loan and runs off with all that portable security?"

She simply answered, "That's never happened. We keep trying to tell people that we're *civilized*. But should any member of any tribe behave in such a way his own tribal council would deal with him the way the courts in any outside county would deal with a crook. He might or might not get away with it. No bank could stay in business if it never took a chance on any loans. What makes you suspect Freighter Adair is planning to skip out on our loan to him?"

Longarm said, "On the face of it, nothing. On the face of it these books seem to be in order, like your Mister Graves said. So how come Leroy Storch was shot before he could go over them? It has to be something that would take a real pro to spot."

"Unless there's nothing there to be spotted." She sniffed.

Longarm shook his head with certainty and replied, "Innocent loan officers don't hire guns to have bank examiners killed. Innocent men don't bolt for the door when a lawman they've been dreading for weeks shows up on their doorstep. But I ain't enough of a bookkeeper to see what even your branch manager's been missing. So I'll have to skin my cat some other way."

Longarm put his own notes away and rose to go back outside. As he did so Banker Graves jumped up to ask if he'd found anything amiss.

When Longarm allowed he hadn't Graves said, "We've been over *all* our books with a fine-tooth comb since word came in about poor Mister Storch being murdered on his way out here from the main office in Chicago."

Longarm almost let that slip by him. But he whipped his notebook out again to demand, "Leroy Storch was from your Chicago headquarters? I have him down here as a bank examiner from Fort Smith, Arkansas."

Graves explained, "That was where he last cleared the accounts of another branch of Drover's Trust. Most of our business, as you might guess from our name, is with white men in the cattle industry. But our Fort Smith branch has made some loans to breeds and self-supporting Indians for the same reasons we have. A sound loan is a sound loan and we're smack in the center of the Indian territory."

Longarm made a note and asked, "Tell me if I have this straight. Leroy Storch was out this way from your main office to go over the savings and loans of prosperous assimilated Indians, right?"

Graves said, "I think so. You'd have to ask poor Leroy Storch just what might have struck him as irregular. As I just said, he went over the books in Fort Smith and didn't find anything amiss."

Longarm grimaced and replied, "I could hardly ask him what he thought he might find in them ledgers I just looked at. Somebody shot him to keep him from finding what neither you nor me has been able to spot!"

Graves asked, "What if there's nothing there at all? Storch

must have suspected he'd find something amiss at Fort Smith. Yet we know he didn't."

Longarm shook his head and said, "Nobody shot him before he could go over the books in your Fort Smith branch. They shot him to keep him from checking your guilty-acting Huber's accounts. It's a safe bet old Huber knew nobody else at the main office could tell us exactly what poor Storch suspected. I'll wire them. Letting them know we're holding Huber for the murder of Storch might shake somebody in Chicago awake. Meanwhile I got a few more tricks of the trade to try. So I'd best get cracking."

He did. He was able to pick up an old Spencer repeater, cheap, at the first hock shop he tried. Finding a new-fangled Bell telephone set in Tulsa Town took some doing. They didn't have any telephone exchange yet. But hope springs eternal and Longarm was able to get a marked-down interoffice set with the wires and wet cell he'd need at a hardware a few doors down from the Western Union.

He sent some Western Union telegrams whilst he was at it and toted his load back to the town lockup.

He found Pepper Palmer out front, jawing with that Osage lawman they called Jerry. As he set most of his load on the floor near the desk, the Osage asked, "Why didn't you tell us right off you were *Wasichu Waste*? We locked that banker alone in one of the cells we use for women on wilder nights. That is what you meant when you said to treat him as if he was an unbroken *shunka wakan*, wasn't it?"

Longarm nodded and took the telephone set out of the bag, saying, "I'm going to need the loan of a brass lantern to stuff with the mouthpiece of this set. I mean to play a trick on them that some Mex Rurales tried on me in a Sonora jail one evening. Might you have two adjoining cells we can put Clark and Huber in, separate and alone?"

Jerry talked to their desk man in Osage for a minute, then said it was as good as done. Longarm said he wanted to hang the telephone receiver disguised as a lantern betwixt the cells, first. He told Pepper Palmer what else he wanted and then Jerry led him back to the cell block and he got to work with the screwdriver blade of his pocket knife and a hammer borrowed from the bottom drawer out front.

Once he had the empty cells set up to receive his two prisoners he whistled and had Jerry and a Creek turnkey join him in front of the cell they'd been holding the banker alone in. He told Longarm he was planning to have him fired for false arrest. Longarm told him it was a free country and, meanwhile, they wanted to put him in a cleaner cell down the way.

As they were leading him to the end of the cell block Pepper Palmer caught up with them, holding up that hock shop Spencer as he chortled, "This surely looks like the murder weapon to me, and we found it right where he said we might!"

Longarm made himself sound more worried than he felt as he quietly told Pepper, "Let's talk about all that up front. Little pitchers have big ears and I gave my word."

Pepper looked sheepish and dropped back as Banker Huber twisted to stare at that Spencer as if it was about to explode and kill them all.

They put him in the last cell and took their time fetching the suspect who called himself Clark. They locked him in the second cell from the end and told him he'd missed noon dinner but might get supper if he behaved his fool self.

Then everyone but the turnkey went down and crowded around the other half of the ruptured telephone and its battery, at the far end of the wire Longarm had strung along the top bars.

Longarm sat on the cell bunk with the earpiece, not hearing much, as Pepper Palmer insisted, "You keep saying later and this is later, damn it! What led you to believe that banker was backing the play of the cuss called Clark?"

Longarm tersely replied, "Clark ain't his real name. Somebody told him to use it when he dealt in horseflesh at that livery. When he got to the Cherokee jail in Tahlequah he posed as a dead lawyer by the name of Schreiber, which means the same as Clerk or Clark in High Dutch. I tried some High Dutch on Clark. He didn't seem to know any. I figured somebody he was working for did. Somebody who'd changed Schreiber to Clark on the spur of the moment without thinking. Huber even *writes* like an infernal immigrant."

Jerry was the one who said, "I understand that much. What made you think he was riding for anybody of any background at Drover's Trust?"

Longarm said, "Nat Rose from Fort Smith told us Leroy Storch was on his way to examine the books at Drover's Trust. Nat said *he* was aiming to ask some questions at Drover's Trust. Pepper, here, was with me when a lawman finally showed up to ask some questions at Drover's Trust."

Pepper grinned and said, "That was one damned Dutchman that didn't want to talk to the law!"

Longarm hissed, "Pipe down! They're talking at last!"

He had to strain. The connection was weak or they weren't talking as close to the mouthpiece as Bell's patent called for. But he made out the voice of Huber almost sobbing, "Why did you tell them where you'd hidden that Spencer, you dumb ox? Did you think giving me away would get you off? I told you and Elko that if anyone arrested you your only chance was to sit tight, keep quiet, and let me work on the outside to get you out!"

Another voice Longarm recognized as that of the first one he'd nailed that day replied in anger, "What are you talking about! Nobody told them shit, unless it was you! How could they have found that gun unless it was you who told them you'd told me to toss it up on that damned roof! I have been keeping quiet. I figured right after they grabbed me that they didn't know who you'd hired Elko and me to deal with. How in the hell did they find their way to you, dad blast it! I never told them. Elko never told them. That blue-eyed squaw of Elko's never told them. So who's left?"

Huber snarled, "Who indeed? You let that cunt live in spite of our deal. I warned Elko not to get mixed up with anyone we didn't know and I see she got to you as well. So you let her go. She turned you in, and now you think you can save your neck by turning State's Evidence? Let me tell you something, Dakota Dave, there is no way in hell the man who pulls the trigger is going to save himself by turning in his comrades!"

Longarm looked up at the other lawmen down at that end with him and murmured, "Jackpot. Clark is Dakota Dave Morrison, a known killer for hire. Huber hired him to kill three people that I might be able to hang on him and make 'em stick. Only takes one to hang him when you consider he'd be standing trial in front of Judge Parker of the Fort Smith Federal District Court. After that the fucking banker has a point. Any lawyer worth his salt would be sure to say Dakota Dave was just saying all those mean things about Huber to save his doomed ass."

Pepper Palmer insisted, "Come on, pard, you just said Dakota Dave gets *paid* to kill folk! All you have to prove is that he's been working for old Huber all along and—"

"How?" asked Longarm bleakly, before adding, "We need the *motive*. Without a motive Huber would have no call to hire any killers to kill a fly, and I doubt a man that desperate to cover something up would have shared such secrets with other crooks!"

Chapter 35

Pepper Palmer tagged along as Longarm headed back to the Western Union. The Kansas bounty hunter wanted to know where they might be headed. So Longarm said, "I got to see if there's any answers to a mess of questions I've sent out along the wires. After that I'll be headed over to the BIA. Why don't you mosey over to the railroad and see if they'll let you have a look through their recent dispatches and bills of lading."

Pepper demanded, "To what end? I thought you and me came over here to Tulsa Town in search of them moonshiners. So far, all we've worked on is that mysterious banking bullshit neither one of us was sent to look into! What do you expect me to uncover about bank fraud at the infernal railroad terminal?"

Longarm kept walking as he said, "How should I know what you might find before you've found it? You used to be a Pinkerton railroad dick. You'd know better than me if there was any unusual railroading going on. I know I've been sidetracked. I still aim to crack the case Nat Rose gave his life for. In the meantime, this is the business center of the Indian territory and the terminal here gets more through freight in bulk than Treasury could shake a stick at. After that carlots of most anything a moonshiner might use might be broken up here to distribute in less suspicious amounts as wagon freight or the combined passenger way-freight locals running back and forth inside the Indian territory, see?"

Pepper Palmer did. He said, "Hot damn! You're talking

255

about stuff like bulk grain and sugar by the ton, right?"

Longarm said, "I'm talking about distribution patterns of the same. An honest jobber here in Tulsa Town might break up bulk shipments and supply many a crossroads general store with reasonable amounts of feed grain, table sugar, flapjack syrup, and such. See if you can find a way-freight dispatch calling for delivery of more moonshine makings than an honest merchant could sell, local. Close to the northeast end of the line would be even more suspicious."

Pepper nodded and said, "Right, that Indian bootlegger confessed to buying his jars off them blue-eyed squaws just south of the state line."

They shook on it and parted friendly. At the Western Union they'd been holding a wire from Marshal Billy Vail, cussing him out for the time he was wasting in Tulsa Town and asking if she was pretty.

Longarm was more interested in the night letter from Clevolium Inc. of Ohio. They confirmed Longarm's suspicions that some papers seemed to be missing from the late Moses Bradley's saddlebags. He'd brought those blank mineral leases west along with a list of likely properties his outfit wanted him to confirm as their best bets for drilling. They said they'd searched in vain, so far, for the field notes Bradley had made on his earlier visit. Unless they were buried in the files somewhere the rock-oil whizz had taken them.

The only bright spot was that nobody in Ohio could see how anybody else would have any use for the missing notes. Nobody was about to drill anywhere or lay out one red cent until such time as Bradley's earlier thoughts on the subject could be confirmed and new deals made with the Cherokee Tribal Council because they, not any individuals of their nation, had the final say.

Putting the telegrams away Longarm moseyed on towards the BIA. Then he saw a sign over a corral across the way and walked on over. He entered the frame shed near the corral gate and asked the young red-headed Cherokee gal if this might be the Adair Freight Line run by a William Adair of the Cherokee persuasion.

She nodded brightly, allowed she was Uncle Will's niece, in charge whilst he and her cousins were hauling some cooperage and a windmill kit down the Arkansas towards Fort Gibson.

Longarm asked if she could tell him anything about that loan her uncle had taken out from Drover's Trust. He wasn't surprised when she just looked blank. He thanked her for her time and went back to the BIA, where they told him he had to start over with a new agent entire.

Longarm had discovered in the past that some Indian agents were as wrong-headed about Indians as old Nate Meeker, over Colorado way, who'd riled his Ute charges enough to get himself and a whole lot of other white folk killed, whilst others, such as John Clum at San Carlos, could be said to be too soft by half the unreconstructed Apache. Most agents were in-between and he'd found that old timer better than most.

But the younger squirt in charge that lazy business day in Tulsa Town made a good first impression on Longarm. After he'd sat their visitor down and offered him a good cigar he said, "Banker Graves and that bookkeeper have already thrashed this out with us, Deputy Long. None of the Indians making business loans have put up tribal property as security. The loans have all been simple and short-term at lower interest than many banks lawfully demand. Nobody has fallen in arrears, and some of the loans have already been repaid in full. Banker Graves told us that bank examiner seems to have expressed doubts about their secured loans department, just before he was murdered by a person or persons unknown."

Longarm got his mild claro going and blew some sweet fumes out his nostrils before he flatly stated, "We know who killed that bank examiner. We're working on the motive now. I read those bank ledgers the same way. The only thing at all unusual about a heap of safe simple transactions seems to be the complexion of the borrowers. So let's talk about that. To begin with, I find it confusing that this agency seems to oversee the doings of three separate tribes."

The Indian agent shook his head and said, "It's not unusual at all. Over to the west you'll find one agency for the Arapaho and Cheyenne, another for the Comanche and Kiowa combined. We just set up another branch to the east for the Delaware and Shawnee who just moved out here from a more crowded east. You have to understand, and I wish some Indians would, that our job is to ease the transition between a lost way of life and the way life has to be lived, these days. Each group requires different services. It would be silly as well as needlessly expensive for us to issue bags of flour and pin money to the English-speaking literate Christians around this agency as it would be cruel to order an Oglala Lakota to go out and get a damned job."

Longarm decided the kid was all right. He said, "I've noticed some Cherokee dress better than I can afford. You're telling me an Indian's rights to do business varies with his level of education, right?"

The BIA man shook his head again and said, "It's not that simple. Members of the Five Civilized Tribes have been . . . well, civilized for three or four generations. Many members, or let's say former members of those five tribes and others have long since moved off the Great White Father's blanket to get on with life as unchallenged American citizens. We don't track people down and demand they prove they're not secret Indians. Our clients here in the Indian territory hold treaty rights granted by the U.S. Government. We *have* to look out for their interests or their interests as defined by Act of Congress. Some Indians agree this is a pain in the ass and a drain on the taxpayers, but there you have it. The Muskogee or Creek have applied for full self-rule under territorial status. They want to become full citizens in a territory called Oklahoma, meaning Red People in Muskogee. Maybe some day they will. In the meantime here we are, with one shoe off and one shoe on, as in the poem about my son John."

Longarm said he'd heard tell about that Dawes Act and asked what might be holding it up, seeing both the *New York Herald* and some Indians wanted to just divvy up their tribal holding and get on with life as regular folk.

The BIA man made a wry face and replied, "Other Indians, and some of our time-serving white bureaucrats. A lot of pencil pushers, red and white, would be out of work if the Indian territory became something like Montana territory with a few reservations set aside for the very few Quill Indians who really need them. Chief Bushyhead likes things just the way they are. He'd only be a prosperous white man, like his brother out in California, the other way. The opposition party led by Lew

258

Downing are running on a platform calling for redistribution of Cherokee tribal holdings. Whether they'll change their mind and soak it to us for more handouts, once they've been elected, is anybody's guess. To call a man a crooked politician is redundant."

Longarm blew a thoughtful smoke ring and declared, "Bushyhead's position might not be that simple, no offense. I'm sure a heap of his Cherokee, red, white, or black, would as soon sink or swim on their own private spreads. There's other Cherokee, called *Kituhwa*, who'd argue they're being pushed into modern times too fast for comfort."

The BIA man asked what Cherokee tribal politics had to do with the mysterious doings at the Drover's Trust.

Longarm sighed and said, "Nothing, as far as I can tell. If I've followed you correct, you're saying there ain't a thing irregular about the business Banker Huber has been having others killed to cover up."

It had been a statement, not a question. But the BIA man still felt obliged to say, "Think of our duty to Mister Lo as the duties of a legal guardian to an immature ward. The amount of freedom allowed to said ward would depend on your ward's mature behavior. You might allow a young lady of sixteen to attend a ball with an escort of good character. You'd think twice if the same white boy wanted to ride off overnight with a six-year-old child. We'd have the power to step in if we thought somebody was taking advantage of a dependent Indian. But as I told you, we've been over the books and there seems to be nothing at all shady about that loan officer's transactions with any Indian."

Longarm had hoped the cuss wouldn't say that. He hated legwork on a hot dusty afternoon. But he had to do what they paid him to do. So he consulted his notebook, found a street number that didn't seem too far, and headed over that way.

The establishment was a small hardware shop with a lumberyard and other building supplies out back. Their sign read, "LENAPE LUMBER."

When he went into the shop a bell tinkled and a friendly enough old full-blood came out front to ask what he could do for him.

Longarm flashed his badge and said, "I'd be U.S. Deputy

259

Marshal Custis Long. I'd like to jaw with you about your loan with Drover's Trust, if you've a minute, Mister . . . ?"

"Wachung, Elmer Wachung of the Lenape Nation, or what you might call the Delaware. What loan are you talking about, Deputy? We ain't borrowed anything off any bank. We used to borrow money and buy on credit from you boys. That's how you wound up with the state of New Jersey without a fight."

Longarm went over his notes again and insisted, "Says here that an E. Wachung of Lenape Lumber borrowed eight hundred dollars from Drover's Trust to set this new business up. Am I right in guessing you ain't been out here long?"

The Indian lumberman nodded and said, "Less than a year. The BIA just relocated us out this way, along with some pesky Shawnee. This town is handier to the railroad. So we set up here to supply Lenape or anyone else the wherewithal from flooring to finish coat as they build their new homes in the Golden West."

"But you say you didn't borrow any money at all from Drover's Trust?" Longarm insisted.

The Indian said, "Nary a penny. Grubstaked this business with the help of other full-bloods. Doing business with your kind can cost a Lenape his red hide! Are you trying to accuse me of something crooked, Deputy Pale Face?"

Longarm smiled agreeably and said, "We got the white man accused of three or four murders in jail, Mister Wachung. According to his own records, Banker Huber has never accused you of anything but a swell credit rating. Says you've just about paid off that eight hundred he loaned you, with six percent interest!"

The older man insisted, "Never heard of any banker called Huber. Never borrowed shit off that Drover's Trust. They must have me mixed up with some other wild Indian. You know how we all look alike."

Longarm thanked the cranky old cuss and got out of there before he had to hear any more about Mister Lo, the poor Indian. The Shawnee had been pissers in their day. The Delaware hadn't been as famous because they'd calmed down a heap by Daniel Boone's day.

He forged on, removing his frock coat and toting it over his left forearm as the sun got ever warmer on his back. He found the dress shop, run by two nice little old ladies of the Creek persuasion, and they insisted in taking him in the back and serving him some coffee and layer cake before they'd talk about their business with the law.

He noticed members of the Five Civilized Tribes put sugar and cream in coffee. It was the Horse Nations of the High Plains who served it with white flour stirred in. Their quarters in the back smelled of lemon oil and violet water instead of buckskin and smoke. Cherokee tended to say the Creek had been less civilized, back east, because the Creek had held out against white ways a generation longer and seldom kept slaves, once they'd started growing and selling their own cotton to the mills of Manchester.

He liked the dithersome old gals more than the outwardly friendly but sarcastic Elmer Wachung at the lumberyard. So he found it a lot easier to believe Miss Lizzy, the elder of the pair, when she told him they'd never borrowed any four hundred dollars from Drover's Trust to buy yard goods and Paris notions at a discount.

Miss Lizzy said, "There must be some mistake, young sir. We've never had any dealing with that bank. We take our trade to our own tribal savings and loan. Are we going to have to prove that in any court of law?"

Longarm said, "No, ma'am. According to a loan officer who's had others killed to cover his tracks, your debt has been repaid in full with forty-eight dollars in interest and a Class A credit rating."

The two honest Indian ladies exchanged puzzled glances. Miss Lizzy said, "Well, I never!"

Longarm said, "That seems obvious, ma'am. Neither has anyone else on my list, so far. I only took down names and addresses within easy walking. But I still have eight to go, and even thought it only takes three strikes in a baseball game, Judge Parker over to Fort Smith is inclined to want an airtight case before he hangs anybody."

Chapter 36

Longarm figured they had one by the time he trudged into the Tulsa Town lockup with a list of one likely and ten sure witnesses who were willing to swear they'd never taken out the bank loans recorded in their names.

That blazing sun in a cloudless cobalt sky had really done a job on him and Longarm was glad to get out of it before he saw his Osage pal Jerry, Banker Graves, and some Indian lawmen he hadn't met yet gathered around another Spencer repeater and an open overnight bag on the desk.

Jerry called out, "We found the real murder weapon where the killer said he'd tossed it. It ain't hard for us redskins to track down a rifle on a flat roof, once we know we're hunting for it. We got a fatter cow here, when we searched Huber's quarters. This bag of *mazaska* was under his bed!"

As Longarm moved closer to admire the money, nothing smaller than a sawbuck, that occupied over half the stout leather bag's square bottom, Banker Graves insisted, "I just don't understand this at all! Huber's salary was only fifteen hundred per. There was no way on earth Huber could have saved this in the two years he's been with us. But we're not missing any money at the bank!"

Longarm finished shaking with the moon-faced Creek Jerry had introduced as the head marshal pro-tem before he told the banker, "You just hadn't figured it out yet. Leroy Storch at your main office must have smelled a rat and written Huber about it. Maybe Huber will be willing to tie up some loose ends as he waits to hang in Fort Smith. Maybe he won't. I don't matter. We got him on enough. He was playing a brass-balled variation on the old robbing-Peter-to-pay-Paul credit-kiting scheme. He should have run for it with what he already had in this bag as soon as he learned that bank examiner was on the way. But, as you see, there's room here for a few thousand more and he could have hired turds such as Elko and Dakota Dave for hundreds."

The banker struck his own forehead with an open palm as he sort of sobbed, "Oh, my God! That old credit-kiting chestnut, right under my nose, and I never suspected a thing!"

The moon-faced head marshal grumbled that he still didn't know what the suspects in the back had been up to.

Longarm let Banker Graves explain, "Huber was our loan officer. He got to approve and pay out bank loans. Nobody should have and nobody did question his wisdom as long as the loans he approved seemed to be being repaid on schedule. To keep it simple, suppose you have control of the cash drawer and you loan a hundred dollars to nobody at all at six percent interest. Then suppose you put *some* of the money back, on the dates agreed to on the forged application. Then suppose you loan some more money, and then some more, to the same good credit rating on the same terms?"

Longarm said, "He was planning a real kiss-off at the end. He'd paid off some of the smaller loans in full. He figured nobody would have made a fuss if he'd approved even bigger loans to those Class A credit risks. Once he had as much cash as he could carry in this bag he meant to simply quit his job in the middle of the month and be on his way to anywhere with nobody suspecting a thing for at least two or three weeks, see?"

The Indians didn't. The banker groaned, "He'd had more like a full month before we even suspected anything was wrong! When none of those payments due by the tenth of the month came in we'd have sent a polite notice that the loan was overdue. Lord knows how long I'd have taken to really go after anyone. Most of our Indian clients have been unusually honest about their just debts!"

Longarm brightened and said, "I suspect you just solved the mystery of what prompted that bank examiner in Chicago to head this way! He was at your Fort Smith branch, too, if you'll remember. He was unsettled by honest Indians."

"Thank you," said the head marshal, adding, "What in the hell are you talking about? Are you saying we're too dumb to cheat in business?"

Longarm soothed, "Nope. I never said you weren't the civilized tribes. Huber did. He approved a whole slew of business loans, then shuffled the money around to make it seem each and every loan was being repaid on time every month!"

The moon-faced Creek looked relieved and said, "That would be asking a heap from human nature. The crook fucked up by making everyone else look too honest!"

Pepper Palmer came flapping in to unbuckle his chaps and hang them on the coatrack before anyone with more sense on such a day could say he ought to. As he turned from the rack he announced, "I struck out at the railroad dispatcher's, pawing through way-freight orders for moonshine makings. The only regular bulk shipments to any of the local stops has been barn paint. They sure have been building a heap of new barns up around Wyandotte."

One of the Indian lawmen said, "That's one of those raw settlements around the new Delaware-Shawnee agency. Those eastern sissies whitewash fence rails. They need a little time to get used to the climate out our way."

Longarm asked if by any chance those Delaware barn builders might be buying their supplies off Lenape Lumber, there in Tulsa Town.

Pepper said, "I think that might have been the firm on some bills of lading. Why do you ask?"

Longarm said, "We can ask old Elmer Wachung more about that when we talk to him some more about this. You eat the apple a bite at a time and I'd like to have those boys in the back wrapped tidy before I wire Fort Smith to send somebody to pick them up."

Banker Graves frowned and asked, "Don't we at Drover's Trust have anything to say about where our own loan officer stands trial for all this money he's stolen from us?"

Longarm shrugged and asked, "How are you going to prove he stole it? It's all here and any lawyer worth his salt would be sure to intimate he was just saving funds at his disposal in an unsual place. Those folk whose names he forged to phony loan applications ain't out a plugged nickel. On the other hand, Judge Isaac Parker and old George Maledon, the Fort Smith hangman, want those boys in the back on at least two counts of murder in the first!"

Banker Graves soberly allowed it might be best to let Fort Smith deal with the sons of bitches.

Longarm nodded at his Osage pal, Jerry, and said, "*Wastey.* Like I said, I'd like to wrap them tidy. My deposition to Judge Parker about them phony loans would hold more water if it was witnessed by other lawmen. Who'd like to tag along as I retrace my steps and get each and everyone of those folk who never borrowed any money from Drover's Trust to repeat what they told me in front of at least two witnesses."

Jerry and another Osage said they'd go. When Pepper volunteered Longarm felt obliged to point out, "This ain't your fight and you've already backed my play a heap, for no bounty money at all, Pepper."

The raw-boned bounty hunter shrugged and said, "Let's just say I'm queer for you. I want to ask that one cuss on your list why he's been selling so much red paint, anyways."

Nobody else cared to go back out in that hot afternoon sun without a better reason than that. So Longarm, Pepper, Jerry, and a younger Osage called Shasapa, likely because he seemed to have some colored blood, stepped out again into what felt like a bake oven, even though it was the main street of Tulsa Town.

Nobody Longarm talked to a second time in front of witnesses wanted to take anything back. The two Indian lawmen allowed they'd be willing to bear witness in front of Judge Parker if Fort Smith sent them any such summons. Old Isaac Parker was more likely to settle for that overnight case full of money as material evidence that somebody had surely been lying about all those secured loans.

As sheer good luck had favored them on such a scorcher, most of the places they had to call on had been on the shady side, but they saw they'd have to cross over to where a half-loaded delivery dray and a miserable team of mules stood out front of Lenape Lumber in the blazing sunlight.

Nobody had to invite Pepper Palmer to take the lead, or swagger out ahead as if he thought Longarm and the two Indians worked for him. Halfway across Longarm saw someone had posted a sign in the glass of their front door, allowing they were closed for the day despite the hour.

Pepper spied it, too, and called out, "What the hell? How could they be closed this early with that wagon only half loaded and them mules hitched up to go?"

His answer came when someone inside shoved the muzzle of a repeating rifle through the glass beside the mysterious sign and commenced fire before the first shards of glass had hit the plank walk!

Generations of infantrymen and other gunfighters had been advised over and over to advance on the enemy guns when caught in the open. It worked more often than anything else you could do at such a time because it went against human nature and wasn't as expected. It worked that day for Longarm and the two Indians, who'd likely been told the same by some Osage war vet. Old Jerry shouted *"Heyoka yo!"* as he tore ahead, slapping leather. Young Shasapa not only tore across the street but busted clean through the plank gate of the side-drive leading back to the lumberyard behind their office shed.

Longarm couldn't tell what Pepper was up to until he'd made it to the cover of that dray loaded with building supplies. As he glanced back the way he'd just come, .44-40 in hand, he saw Pepper was down in the middle of the dusty street. Whether he'd turned to run back, frozen in place, or just lucked out as the apparent leader, he sure lay still in the glaring sunlight.

The rifleman who'd nailed Pepper pegged a shot Longarm's way to puncture a paint drum and spatter him with dots of Barn Red. When that didn't seem to work the sly dog pegged a shot at the mule team and, sure enough, they bolted, hauling Longarm's cover with them!

But Longarm fired even smarter, aiming not at the shattered glass of the door but through the pine siding to his right or the same as he pictured how an unseen man with a rifle would naturally be firing around the jam to his own left.

It worked. The rifle muzzle trained his way swung up to fire at the cloudless sky as old Jerry, who'd flattened out against the pine siding closer to a front window, smashed the window glass with his Schofield to empty it into the smoke

266

filled interior, even as Longarm shouted, "Hold your fire! See if we can take somebody alive!"

Old Jerry held his fire, risked a peek inside, and called back in a voice that didn't sound at all ashamed, "We don't have to waste our time questioning *this* old fart! If he ain't on his way to Old Woman's Lodge he's giving one hell of a performance!"

Longarm moved in gingerly behind the smoking muzzle of his own six-gun to kick the door inward. It wasn't easy. Old Elmer Wachung lay just inside full of lead and pine splinters, still looking pissed at white men.

Jerry joined Longarm in the doorway, whistled, and said, "We sure cleaned *his* plow. But how come? I thought you said he wasn't in on anything with Banker Huber."

Longarm said, "I didn't think he was. I don't see how he could have been."

The other lawman insisted, "He must have been up to *something!*"

To which Longarm replied, "I noticed. He'd have likely gotten away with it if he hadn't thought we were on to him and coming to arrest him! I'd be obliged if you'd go back and see to Pepper. I'll go on through the back and see how our pal Shasapa made out."

He suited his actions to his words, threading his way back through shelves and piles of hardware, paint, and painter's supplies from tools to turpentine. He'd just found the back room where the old Delaware had been reading the *Police Gazette* on a sofa when he heard more gunplay, out back, and once more advanced on the enemy guns.

Having more cover this time, Longarm dropped low and cracked the back door to see if he could tell what he might be getting into. So he saw young Shasapa crouched behind a pile of lumber with his back to the gate he'd shattered.

Longarm called out, "Where is he, Shasapa?"

Before the Indian lawman could answer a shot rang out and gunsmoke rose above a more distant lumber pile. The bullet spanged into the jam above Longarm's head, showering splinters to stick to the dots of red paint on his poor Stetson.

Shasapa yelled back without turning, "Young full-blood. Winchester. I got him pinned in that corner, a stack this side of the back fence and the alley gate. But I just can't drill through all them one-inch planks laid sideways to me with anything this side of a field gun!"

Longarm called out, "Give it up, old son! We got your boss! He's the one we were after! Come out and talk to us and we may be able to make a deal!"

The kid behind the stacked floor planks answered Longarm's mild suggestion with three rounds of rapid fire before Shasapa bounced a bullet of his own into all that smoke to silence the surly rascal.

"Did I get him?" the colored Osage called out, hopefully.

Longarm called back, "I can't tell. Keep your head down." Then he tried, "Hey, Lenape boy, are you still sore at us? This ain't the way you want to end it, old son! You're surrounded three to one and I'd be proud to say it was Elmer, out front, who gunned our only casualty. Give up before anybody else gets hurt and I can promise you won't hang and might not draw much time at all!"

The desperate Delaware fired at the sound of Longarm's voice from around a lower corner of his lumber pile.

Then the alley gate to the lumberyard crashed open and Longarm was set to shoot old Jerry before he realized just in time that the Osage wasn't throwing all that lead at him or Shasapa.

Striding farther into the yard through his own cloud of gunsmoke the Indian lawman called, "Pepper's dead. I circled the block. So now this shitface over this way is dead, too. Ain' you boys proud of me?"

Longarm was too steamed to speak until the three of them loomed over the sprawled remains of a teenager in a bloody shirt behind that other lumber pile. When young Shasapa allowed he'd seen the kid at a stomp-dance earlier, Longarm managed to sound polite as he said, "I sort of figured he and the old Delaware he worked for were up to *something* here in the Indian territory. I only wish at least one of 'em was in any position to tell me what it might have been, dammit!"

Chapter 37

What with one damned deposition, telegram sent out or received, and the longer letter he had to write to Pepper's kin,
Longarm never got back to Maria and Tabitha before the sul-
len shades of evening were falling.

He found the blonde Osage and the gray Lippizan out back
in the last ruby light of the gloaming. Tabitha's head was still
tightly tethered to that same post and the droppings around
her hind hooves read that she'd been standing there all day.
The Horse Indian way left a *shunka wakan* or Medicine Dog
plenty of time to think betwixt human contacts. After enough
meditating, even a wild mustang full of piss and vinegar commenced to notice the only relief from hunger, thirst, and sheer
monotony came in the form of a two-legged critter who talked
soft, petted gentle, and offered you a sip of water or a sweet
nibble as long as you behaved yourself. When you acted up,
your two-legged pal went away for a long tedious spell. If you
had the brains of a gnat you decided on your own not to act
up any more. It took Indians longer, but they could get most
ponies to do amazing tricks for them. They ate the ones they
couldn't teach any tricks.

As Longarm strode over with the baggage from the hotel
room he'd gotten tired of paying for, Maria called out, "Watch
this, Custis!"

So he watched as the Osage livery gal clicked that tin
cricket right next to Tabitha's head.

The big gray flinched, but didn't put her back into the effort
and Maria quickly called her a *wichinchala wastey* and fed

her another piece of apple. A lot of small rewards were easier to remember than one big favor when you were born a horse, or a human being, according to old Nick Machiavelli, who'd surely met some riders of the owlhoot trail in his own time.

Maria ran a friendly hand over the both of them and suggested they talk about Tabitha's bad habits up in her quarters whilst she whipped them up some supper.

Along the way she opined he'd been right about somebody teaching the big gray to shy to that one odd sound alone. She said she thought a quirt or spur rowel applied along with a tin cricket click, over and over when no officers were watching, would surely produce a cavalry mount that would buck on demand and be bought cheap as condemned stock.

Longarm said, "Remind me to mention all this to the provost marshal when I return old Tabitha to Fort Gibson. I told their remount sergeant about another crook who carried away what seemed to be soiled army grub he could sell off post once he'd washed off some joke-shop stink."

Maria didn't notice what had spattered on his Stetson until they were up in her quarters and she'd lit a lamp while he put away his saddlebags and Winchester.

He told her how he'd been spattered with barn paint, pine splinters, and such in that shoot-out at Lenape Lumber. She took the hat from him and said she'd try to clean it after supper and some slap and tickle. She said she liked to scrub out stains and such in the nude.

He told her she was welcome to try, but added, "I tried some turpentine on it, over to the lumberyard before we left. It just seemed to smear it deeper into the felt. I was about ready for a new hat in any case. That paint was mixed to stay stuck to a barn through fair weather and foul, honey. They were selling a lot of it. So it must dry serious."

She wanted to hear more about the shoot-out, of course. So he told her all he knew, adding, "The late Pepper Palmer suspected they were up to something because they made a heap of mixed-lot shipments back up the line to the Delaware Shawnee agency, which seems to be where a mother and two daughters described as blue-eyed squaws have been selling moonshine, if not making it, Irish style. I know you Osage call a gal a *weya*, but squaw is as polite in Algonquin, which both Delaware and Shawnee speak."

Maria got her banked stove going and commenced to mix cornmeal and eggs in a stirring bowl as she allowed a Delaware merchant so far from the Delaware agency struck her as suspicious, too.

Longarm admired her from the kitchen chair he'd straddled as he told her, "Hell, girl, we *know* Elmer Wachung was *up* to something. He went down in a blaze of gunfire to prove that much to us. But after that we're stuck. We can't connect him in any way to Banker Huber and those other gunslicks. There's no evidence he ever heard of either Leroy Storch or that rock-oil man, Moses Bradley. Bradley's company back in Ohio just replied by wire and they haven't even *thought* about rock-oil up in the northeast corner of this Indian territory. Such wells and seeps as anyone's found lie due north of here along the Osage-Cherokee line."

Maria poured her batter in a cast-iron skillet as she dimpled and said, "I'm glad. I've always wanted to be rich, and our tribal council shares any windfalls with us all, even Steven. I've already gotten some modest but welcome checks on my share of grazing and mineral fees."

Longarm said he'd heard as much from the BIA and asked how her tribe felt about that Dawes Act.

She said Osage opinion, like Cherokee and Creek opinion, could be best described as argumentative. She said, "I wouldn't mind being called a white woman with some Indian blood. That's what I feel I am. But some of my kin, with no more Indian blood than me, feel more comfortable on the Great White Father's blanket. As a dependent ward of the government you get to bitch when your allotments are late and holler for more when they ain't. Most of us no longer take allotments because you have to prove you're really poor as Mister Lo to apply for them. But a lot of people are afraid to take that last big step and have to think for themselves if times get tough."

She tossed in some shredded beef and diced dried apple to make one hell of an improvement on the usual corn meal *papwasna* staple of her nation. Her lusher version looked like a Denver omelet and tasted . . . like *papwasna*. She served it to him with Arbuckle brand coffee, made fancier than most cow camp coffee, and asked as they were supping how he liked the late Elmer Wachung as a member of that moonshine ring.

Longarm sighed and said Pepper Palmer had suggested as much, but they'd found no evidence pointing that way.

He explained, "As a jobber who bought wholesale and distributed all over the territory retail, in smaller lots, Wachung could and did buy two hundred proof industrial alcohol, as shellac thinner. You mix flakes of solid lac scraped off Hindu fig trees with alcohol to make shellac. There ain't no practical way to distill the alcohol back out of such a mixture and if there was it would be dumb. A jar of shellac costs more than a jar of moonshine. Pepper noticed they were stocking and shipping an unusual amount of that barn paint I got on my hat in the shoot-out. But such paint is a mixture of linseed oil, turpentine, and pigments. A high tones form of plain old iron rust in the case of barn red. Neither linseed oil, turpentine, nor iron oxide can be used to make moonshine. I wish I could think of something else as crooked you could do with paint, shellac, turpentine thinnner, and such. Old Elmer never shot Pepper Palmer just for the hell of it."

Maria served him some cake she'd baked and a new position she'd thought up for dessert. It sure felt swell to lie there nibbling marble cake with her blonde head bobbing up and down like that betwixt his knees.

He didn't have to tell her he was leaving until after they'd done it the old-fashioned and sweeter way in her narrow bedstead. He was braced for a fuss, but Maria took it like a member of a warrior race when he said he had to get on back to Tahlequah in the morning.

Being a woman, she naturally asked why. So he lit a smoke for the two of them and told her as they cuddled atop the covers on such a night, "I followed poor Nat Rose and Pepper Palmer over this way in hopes a case of bank fraud might be moonshining. I'm glad I got sidetracked. Tabitha thanks you too."

Maria refused the offer when he put the cheroot to her lips. She told him, "Please don't say you hope to get back this way before you leave the territory for good, Custis. I thought yo

272

said you'd run up a blind alley in Tahlequah. I thought you said all the sign led over this way."

He took a drag on the cheroot and said, "This away and that way, up by the Delaware-Shawnee agency. But there's a couple of loose ends I want to tie up in Tahlequah. Starting with that rock-oil man, Moses Bradley, who just won't tie in with Huber and his hired guns no matter how you twist the pieces."

She said, "I thought you thought they might have mistaken him for you because he was leading Tabitha."

Longarm shook his head and said, "I thought so until I did me some thinking about that easy answer. If somebody shot Bradley on sight because they thought he was me, how come nobody's gone out of their way to shoot at me since?"

She blinked and asked, "Didn't you just live through a gunfight at Lenape Lumber? Didn't you have it out with that Elko Watts earlier?"

Longarm said, "Elko was afraid I might be the law. He wasn't sure at first. So why would he have had any call to shoot anyone as me, way earlier? Nope. I was *there* when others were getting shot at or blown up with dynamite. But there's not a lick of proof I was the target of any of them murdersome attacks. Somebody prepared the locked doors of both a church tower and a meeting hall in advance for whatever in blue blazes they were planning. I don't see how it could have been me they were really after. I got to go back and find out who it was, if he, she, or it is still alive by the time I can get back there!"

So she let him smoke his cheroot down and then they made love some more and she got up restless and bare ass, to carry his Stetson into the kitchen with some spot remover. He dozed off before she could say how she was doing. But the next morning, as she served him in bed, in every way, Maria seemed mighty proud of the way she'd cleaned his hat good as new.

He meant it when he said he hated to leave her. Then he did, riding Red Rocket and leading Tabitha until they were well out of town. Once they were, he tested the big gray with that tin cricket, more than once, as the three of them made their way back to the Cherokee capital without incident, or a lick of interesting sights or sounds to break the tedious hours on the long weary trail. It seemed to take longer, even though they made better time. So after close to eighteen hours in the saddle and another lonesome night in a sleeping bag, Longarm was as pleased as punch to see Tahlequah still there where he'd left it as they rode in well before noon.

He left the two mounts and his saddle at the same municipal livery and headed for that same hotel with his saddlebags and Winchester. As he approached the nearer shattered tower of First Adventist he spotted Sergeant Jim Deadpony talking with Miss Aura Purl, the minister's white-looking daughter, on the steps of the next-door manse.

Longarm knew better than to horn in on another man's sparking. But Deadpony hailed him. So Longarm went over, ticking the brim of his new-looking Stetson to the pretty brunette in lilac organdy.

They both seemed surprised to see him. So he put his own boot up on a step and told them what he'd been up to in Tulsa Town, leaving out a few juicy parts.

When he said no leads had panned out as far as the moonshining went, Deadpony sighed and said, "I just hate it when you have to start all over from scratch. Is there anything I can do, pard?"

Longarm said, "I could use a list of all your tribesmen the late Moe Bradley called on the last time he was out this way. The chief did ask you to ride around with him, didn't he?"

Deadpony nodded but said, "I'd have to get my field notes to be sure of every stop we made. Are you staying over by that same hotel?"

Longarm allowed that was where he was headed. Deadpony said he'd be proud to drop a complete list off there later. He said something polite in Cherokee to the minister's daughter and lit out, as if anxious to be of service. Longarm would have ticked his brim again and done the same if Aura Purl hadn't asked him to stay, saying, "Come inside and have some lemonade I just made. It's already warming up and we're going to have another scorcher, I fear!"

Longarm couldn't argue with that and her offer sounded tempting in more ways than one. But when he followed her inside and along a dark hallway to the kitchen out back there was a colored lady in a more traditional Cherokee outfit at work. Aura spoke to her in their own *Tsalagi* and led Longarm on out the back door, to where some wicker chairs were set up around a tin table with a big parasol on the shady side of the manse.

She sat him down and allowed he could smoke whilst they waited for the lemonade. She asked him more questions than he had answers for about bank frauds, rock-oil leases, and moonshiners and then the cook brought the lemonade, with some butterscotch shortbread besides, and Longarm had to allow this beat any comforts he could think of at the hotel. Antonia Redbird wouldn't be getting off duty until after dark.

Aura regarded him thoughtfully as she sipped her own lemonade whilst leaving the pastries untouched. She said a gal had to watch her figure. Longarm knew he was expected to say her figure looked just fine to him. So he said it.

She demurely replied, "You're just saying that. You've never seen me with my stays unlaced."

She let that sink in, then purred, "There's no way I could offer a gentleman caller such a view, here on church property. But do you remember what I said about that dear little swimming hole, way out in the pines where the breeze blows sweeter and cooler?"

He had to admit he had. That was the simple truth. But he was still jarred when she came right out with, "Goody. Let's ride out yonder in my pony cart and go for a skinny dip before we just melt away in this heat!"

Longarm gulped and asked, "You want us to go swimming together, ah, without no duds on, in broad daylight, Miss Aura?"

She asked in a defiant manner for a minister's daughter, "Why not? It's going to get hotter before it gets cooler. I like to swim, and I like you. So why don't we just cut out all this hemming and hawing and get out of our clothes and this ridiculous vertical position? What's the matter? Surely a man with your reputation isn't too shy to go for a dip with little old me?"

To which he could only reply, "It was your reputation I was concerned with, ma'am. But if you ain't worried, I ain't worried, and I sure wouldn't want to be taken for a sissy by such a handsome offer!"

Chapter 38

It appeared you could say more in *Tsalagi* than you could with the same number of syllables in English because that black Cherokee cook came out the kitchen door with a picnic hamper and a folded blanket when Aura yelled for them. The older woman didn't look surprised when her young mistress said they were going for a pony cart ride. It seemed possible the household staff was used to such sudden whims.

Longarm followed Aura with the blanket and basket. When they got to the carriage house a full-blood kid was hitching a paint pony betwixt the shafts of a wicker-sided pony cart. Folk rich enough to afford such service smiled graciously but didn't have to tip their help as things just seemed to go their way before they had to ask out loud.

They got the pony cart out in the drive for them and steadied the paint whilst Longarm helped Aura up in the two-wheel cart so she could take the ribbons already wrapped around the buggy whip in its handy socket.

Longarm put his saddlebags and her stuff on the floor betwixt the two benchlike seats facing one another with their backs to the big red wheels. You drove such a cart sideways, seated on the bench of your own preference. Being right-handed, Aura sat with her right arm towards the paint's rump. Longarm took the usual passenger's seat with his back to the left wheel of the cart. Aura grunted something in *Tsalaki*. The kid let go and stepped out of the way. Aura grunted at the pony and it got going down the gravel drive as if she'd flicked it with the buggy whip. Longarm recalled what Maria had said about horse brains. You didn't need to take your buggy whip from its socket when your draft critter knew it was there. A man could get the distinct impression Aura Purl was used to having her own way with man or beast. But he hadn't had any since the night before last and as he sat there contrasting the two amazingly different gals the BIA had classified as Indians, he found his old organ grinder rising to the occasion already.

Aura turned out onto the street. Then swung the next corner as if to avoid the center of town as she drove on, a vision in organdy that looked cooler than it could have felt with the sun climbing ever higher in the cloudless sky above. Aura's blue-black hair and lightly suntanned skin would have worked on any pure white gal of mayhaps Latin kith and kin. Her features were more Celtic than any other cast. She looked as Irish as that lighter complected Pat Donovan he'd sent back to Fort Smith. Of the two, Aura had the finer bone structure. He felt sure a man could have invited her along on one of those high-toned Irish fox hunts and nobody would have suspected her of being a Cherokee in disguise. That book he'd read and some of the Cherokee he'd talked to agreed the lighter blood lines of the nation seemed to be Scotch-Irish and earlier Creole French with a dash of more recent High Dutch mission folk. Darker Cherokee, like the cook back yonder at the manse, seemed to still hew wood and carry water for their erstwhile owners. They kept *saying* they were civilized as most white folk.

Aura drove along a tree-lined street that turned into a country lane in no time as they passed some older Cherokee women hanging wash out to dry near a low rambling log cabin. From the looks they got as they passed by at a trot Longarm got to wondering how often they'd seen the minister's daughter driving past with any number of others.

But a man who pictured others with too much imagination was likely to lead a celibate life. Since few if any women were easy lays when they'd never been out with anybody before you. He felt at least as embarrassed for himself, knowing he was becoming fairly well known in a small town without having tried half this hard.

They drove through alternate strips of cultivated and wooded land, the wooded parts thick second-growth this close to a town. He'd already noticed how abruptly the eastern reaches of the Indian territory went from rolling prairie to wooded hill country. He was still surprised when they turned off the main wagon trace, up a narrower lane betwixt popple and blackjack, then suddenly into no bullshit slash pine, denser than an old growth pine forest would have been because this particular tract had been burned out and left to reseed itself. Longarm knew the space betwixt the pines would get wider as any slower growers got left behind in the shade. But when Aura turned to him and asked him to just smell that air Longarm allowed her piney woods were just swell.

He moved over to sit beside her and put an arm around her as they drove on. She didn't seem to mind. But when he moved to kiss her Aura pulled away and said, "Down, boy! I can't drive with my eyes closed and your big mush in my way!"

But at least she was smiling as she said it. So Longarm leaned back and let her have it her way, the way she seemed to like things.

As if she'd sensed she'd irked him, Aura reined in and turned to him, saying, "Oh, go ahead and kiss me, then. But no groping till we make it to that swimming hole, you impetuous thing!"

He chuckled fondly and said, "Sail on, oh ship of state. I'm sort of looking forward to . . . that *swimming* hole."

She laughed, dirty, and flipped the ribbons to urge the pair on up the trail through the pines. Longarm was just about to ask how you managed a swimming hole on a slope when they crested a rise and drove downhill through the piney woods until, all of a sudden, they were out of the pines on a narrow crescent of gravel beach, with a good five acres of calm water reflecting the blue of the cloudless sky.

Longarm said, "This sure is a pretty place. And you say nobody else ever comes here, Miss Aura?"

As she wrapped the ribbons around the buggy whip Aura demurely confessed her family owned the whole pine forest. Longarm helped her down and handed her the hamper and blanket. As she spread the blanket on the gravel, there being no grass, Longarm led the pony a few yards off to the one dead pine in sight and unwrapped the ribbons again to teth it. As he turned around, expecting to see his gracious hostess spreading picnic grub on the blanket, he saw Aura Purl was shucking her lilac organdy outfit off over her upswept black hair. The black hair on her head, that was. She hadn't been wearing a stitch under her frock, despite all that talk about laced stays, and her hair seemed as black all over.

As she tossed the organdy dress aside, Aura laughed and turned away to dash into the water until it was rippling up around her perky breasts when she turned again to call out, "Come on in! It feels divine on my poor overheated fanny!"

Longarm tossed his hat and coat aside, but called back, "I'll be with you in a minute. Got to . . . ah, heed a call to nature!"

As he turned away he heard her calling, "Oh, come on in and piss in the water if you want to! I won't tell if you won't tell!"

He just kept going as her lewd laughter pursued him through the pines. He knew he didn't have much time to work with. How long would most gals expect a man to take, crapping in the woods?

He forced himself to run on another furlong before he began to circle. He knew he had to circle wide enough in the time he had, as quiet as he could manage.

That was fairly quiet, thanks to the spongy carpet of pine needles underfoot as he forced his way through the feathery almost interlocking pine branches. Then he'd made it around to that narrow trail they'd followed in and, sure enough, a second set of pony tracks led towards the pond, where Aura was still splashing and calling out how cool it felt.

Longarm felt it was fairly safe to jog down the sandy path toward the merry tempting sounds of the naked Cherokee siren because, with any luck, everybody had him taking a shit on the woods around on the far side. But he slowed to a walk when he spied where that second pony had turned off the trail to the left. He moved that way himself and eased through the thick woods until he spied the brown rump of another rider's tethered mount.

Longarm circled in, letting the tethered pony see his silent form so it wouldn't spook when he moved closer. He moved just close enough to cut the line of heel prints leading toward the water's edge through the pines. He drew his .44-40 as he eased on after them, taking a step and pausing to listen before taking another until, crouched ahead of him to cover the open water beyond with a Winchester in hand and his Schofield on his right hip, was the man in BIA blue Longarm had hoped against hope not to see there.

Since he did, Longarm quietly said, "I got the drop on you, Sergeant Deadpony. Now drop that rifle and get slowly to your feet, facing away from me, unless you'd like to be one dead pony indeed!"

The Cherokee lawman lay his Winchester on the pine needles and slowly rose, hand held polite, as he calmly asked, "What's this all about, old pard? I only followed you and Aura out this way to make sure you would be safe, see?"

Longarm said, "Unbuckle your gun rig and let that six-gun fall anywhere it has a mind to. I ain't arresting you as an armed and dangerous peeping Tom."

The Indian did as he was told. When the gun rig dropped softly to the forest duff Deadpony stepped clear and turned around in a natural manner, a puzzled smile on his face and a nickel-plated derringer in his brown right fist.

So they both fired at the same time. The range was just a tad far, or that derringer pulled to the left. Because Longarm got off with what felt like a spook tugging at his right shirt sleeve, as the six-gun he was holding just below it drilled a little blue hole over one of Jim Deadpony's eyebrows and shot blood, brains, and hair all over the pine needles betwixt him and the water's edge!

As the treacherous Cherokee sprawled limply betwixt Longarm and the treacherous gal out yonder in the water, Aura called out in *Tsalagi*.

Longarm called back, "If you're asking if he got me, Miss Aura, the answer is no."

Aura screamed like a witch with a busted bottle up her twat and waded rapidly ashore to run for that cart without stopping to dress. But of course by the time she could untether her pain and drive back along the one trail in or out, Longarm had cut over to the trail to block her, grabbing her pony's ribbons closer to its bit as the naked fury in the wicker cart lashed at him with her buggy whip.

Longarm caught the end of the whip around a free forearm

grabbed it, and yanked it from the wild-eyed gal's hand. She jumped out of the cart to run back toward the water, screaming for the literally dead Deadpony to come help her.

Longarm caught up with her and gave her a good shaking as he told her firmly but not unkindly to shut up and listen. When she tried to scratch he slapped her on her ass in the shallows of the swimming hole and yelled, "Cool off and listen tight or you'll be sorry, girl!"

She hissed, "You can't arrest me, white cock! I haven't done anything to any of your kind. You have no power over me! None! I am *Tsalagi!*"

To which Longarm calmly replied, "So are the grandmothers and the *Kituhwa* riders who enforce the old blood laws of their nation. Their *real* nation, not this half-baked excuse for an Indian reservation ruled by the likes of you."

She got back to her feet in the ankle deep water, unashamed or not thinking about her state of dishabille as she pouted, "Poo, I haven't done anything to offend those old crones in feather robes. I don't even know why Jim asked me to bring you out here today. He never said anything about you killing him, or vice versa!"

Longarm said, "Close, but no cigar. Let me tell you what I think the two of you were up to and you can tell me about anything I've left out. Keep it in mind that your only chance is a trial before old Issac over to Fort Smith. I doubt he'd hang a woman for aiding and abetting. Lord knows what your tribal council would give you, if it had to try you. But they won't get the chance, will they? Them night riders will carry you off somewhere private as this and . . . Say, do you reckon it's true about that Cherokee whore who got gang raped by fifty men in the hopes it might cure her? I hope it ain't true. I'd hate to think what they might do to a white Cherokee they blamed for the murder of a full-blood like Will Cash."

She dropped to her naked knees in the shallows and covered her face with her hands as she sobbed, "That wasn't supposed to happen! One of the *Ontwaganha* lawmen was supposed to climb up in the bell tower and die. How were we supposed to know Will would get there first?"

Longarm smiled down at her and said, "He did. That's all the grandmothers are going to care about. I know you mean kids didn't give toad squat who died, that time. It was all to cover the one murder Jim was worried about. But I digress. Let's start at the beginning and you can stop me if I'm getting cold."

She said, "Please let me go. It was all Jim's idea. I swear I meant no harm and I'll suck your cock if you let me go!"

Longarm ignored the tempting offer and said, "In the beginning a rock-oil man named Bradley ran a survey out this way and chose a few likely spots to drill. Jim Deadpony was riding with him. So he was in position to know when Bradley marked sites owned, or more accurately, controlled by your family. Like these woods, you don't really own them fee-simple. You *hold* them at the discretion of your tribal council."

She didn't argue. She just knelt there, shuddering or pissing in the water. It was hard to tell. He said, "Jim Deadpony knew, being the law, how things are likely to start changing in these parts within the next few years. As your tribe disbands of its own accord and you all turn into regular folk with some Indian blood, you'll really get to own your own private holdings and lease the mineral rights as private citizens. Jim knew tribal taboos wouldn't keep the two of you from being more than pals and let's not get into how he knew about this swell place to get bare-ass in your daddy's woods. He knew some day all this, or any other holding with rock-oil under it, would be all yours, and thus all his. Only Bradley had spotted drilling sites premature. He was fixing to spoil it all by offering to lease from individuals or, failing that, the Cherokee nation. The Osage are already selling rock-oil as a tribe and sharing the profits. You two didn't want to share no profits. Jim shot that prospector to keep your secret. Then he said it was me just to make everybody think I was the intended target. He must have been a real worrywart. He set that trap in the tower and got you to peg that wild shot at us whilst he was with us, not to kill anybody in particular but to make us think he was innocent. All that crap with the church lock was to cover the fact that you two had to get into the *council house* that way. The two of you were stupid not to quit whilst you were ahead, but other crooks dragged red herrings across your dumb tracks and now we've eliminated like anything and you'd best put your dress back on so's I can turn you over to the Fort Smith jurisdiction, if you know what's good for you, you naughty kid!"

Chapter 39

They drove back to Tahlequah with Jim Deadpony's mount hitched to the rear of the cart, Deadpony's body on the floor with that blanket over it, and Aura Purl handcuffed in her wilted lilac frock and begging him not to turn her over to the *Kituhwa* Society.

Chief Dennis Bushyhead agreed the treacherous young thing wouldn't last until a white deputy from Fort Smith could come out to fetch her if they locked her up in the Cherokee jai. So the chief, Lorena Old Path, and the police corporal who'd be replacing Deadpony worked something out for her, cuffed to a cot in a root cellar with a pot to piss in and some hours ahead in the dark to consider her own wicked ways.

Longarm sent needful telegraph wires and then, the blazing sun having slowly vaulted over to the western reach of the sultry sky by then, he headed for his hotel, looking forward to his supper and the night ahead with Antonia Redbird, bless the way her petite dark form would contrast with good old Maria's, back in Tulsa Town.

But once again that Scotch poet's warning about the best laid plans of mice and men panned out when that bitty young gal in the traditional tribal costume popped out of that same slot Elko Watts had been lying for him that other time and told Longarm to come with her.

He wasn't about to come with anybody that young, but he followed the skinny little thing through more slits and alleyways until, once more, she had him turned around as to just where he might be in that town of modest dimensions. But it didn't feel as if they were headed for that medicine lodge or whatever, this time. The young gal led him through a shady apple orchard to the back of another log house entire and a slanty cellar door of sun-bleached planks. The kid opened one leaf to point down into the darkness and murmur, "She waits for you."

Longarm shrugged and gingerly moved down the steps fashioned from split logs imbedded in the solid earth. The kid above shut the cellar door after him. But he could just make things out by the ruby glow of a candle burning in the red glass chimney of a railroad lantern.

One of those old Cherokee ladies in a turkey feather robe was seated on a mattress against the far wall in the cooler albeit musky gloom. As Longarm moved closer and doffed his Stetson he saw she'd painted the left half of her face bright red. The other half was jet black. It was hard to say what she really looked like, save for spooky.

Her hair was covered by a twisted turban of red and black calico. She patted a space on the mattress beside her and announced, "They call me Split Face. I am their *Agewehi*, or you might say medicine woman. When the followers of the old path need Black Drink or other medicine they ask me for it. When they want to know what the fuck is going on, they ask me for it. So what the fuck is going on, *Ontwaganha*, who knows more than I do?"

Longarm brought the spooky-looking gal up to date, only leaving out where they were holding Aura Purl. It took some telling and she said it was all right to light up if he'd give her one of his three-for-a-nickel cheroots.

After she'd heard him out and smoked a spell, the painted crone said she'd always known Jim Deadpony would come to no good with his fancy outside ways and his messing with that honorary *Tsalagi* brunette.

Blowing an expert smoke ring in the dim light, the medicine woman said, "Those damned breeds have grabbed all the best land and mean to make it their own, as white ranchers who've recovered their senses, as soon as that unjust Dawes Act is rammed down our throats. You know as well as I that nobody cared about this western scrubland they moved us to before they found out it might be valuable!"

Longarm nodded soberly and said, "When you're right you're right, ma'am. The Osage tribal council has already commenced to share mineral rights found on Osage land even Steven. Whether you folk follow that plan or another, look on the bright side. In another generation or so this Indian territory figures to be a prosperous state or regular territory, with you members of the Five Civilized Tribes considered free and equal to other American citizens."

She stared into space and muttered, "I wish you hadn't said that. I know your words are true. My grandchildren will be *Ontwaganha* who may boast of some Cherokee blood or try to hide it, depending on how much of your sort of wealth they end up with!"

He said, "I know it ain't fair, ma'am. No matter what the Good Book and the U.S. Constitution says, Mother Nature doesn't hand out equal shares and Lady Luck can be even more fickle. But if you're asking my advice about the way things seem to be going, I got some to offer."

She turned to him, her big brown eyes filled with desperate hope as she murmured, "My people come to me for advice. I have little to offer these days. Things change, change, change, faster than anybody can keep track of! I wish things would stay the same. We knew what we were doing in the days of our grandmothers' grandmothers!"

Longarm gently said, "No you didn't. Your opposite number amidst the Navaho nation tell of a great spirit called Changing Woman. I've often thought if I had to start all over and choose one faith over all the others I'd go with Changing Woman. They say she appears in visions as a handsome young gal, a motherly older woman, or a scary old hag with death in her eyes. The one thing about Changing Woman and this old world is that nothing stays the same for very long, save for stars, rocks, and dead folk after they've had time to rot some. Those of us still alive have to change and then change some more for as long as we may get to before we turn to permanent dust. In my travels I've found you Indian folk ain't the only ones trying in vain to live in a past that gets more golden as they fail to get anywhere in the here and now. You meet still-young vets of the Army of Virginia, clinging to the myth that they ever had a chance, as that plantation they lost turns ever more grand in the misty past of a Dixie that never was."

He took a drag on his cheroot to let that sink in before he continued. "Old Irish drunks sing songs about an Emerald Isle they remember more like kids picture Fairyland than anybody ever lost to the awful English. If they ever drive the English out they'll still be mooning over the way things used to be as they find themselves working for a living in the few years Changing Woman gives anybody. Up on the Rosebud Reservation, even as we speak, men living on BIA allotments instead of buffalo are spending their little cash on firewater that takes them back to that Happy Hunting Ground where nobody ever went hungry, nobody ever lost his own scalp or pony, and real men were free, free, free to rob and scalp others, as they lived forever without modern medical advances to slow them down."

She must have known where he was headed. She must not have wanted to be taken there. She said, "Tell me about the firewater those evil women with blue eyes have been making to get us all in trouble with your own drunks, *Ontwaganha*."

He said, "My friends call me Custis. I wired the Delaware-Shawnee agency about them blue-eyed squaws from Tulsa Town. That one witness who said he'd bought a wagonload of moonshine jars off blue-eyed squaws was just a Delaware or Shawnee telling the simple truth."

She said she knew squaw was an Algonquin word for woman and asked him to tell her something she didn't know

He said, "For openers the BIA informs me there are more blue-eyed squaws of Delaware extraction than you might shake a stick at for the same reason some of your own folk could pass for regular Americans. The Delaware or Lene Lenape lived along the Delaware River betwixt Penn State and New Jersey. They tended to get along well with white settlers I reckon the ones who went on calling themselves Indian thought that beat working. More than half the original tribe just melted in with the newer Americans all around. The one up in the northeast corner of this officious Indian territory asked to come out here and live with you other real Indians A self-supporting Delaware called Elmer Wachung moved on to Tulsa Town and went into lumber and building supplies

We think but can't prove he was masterminding that moonshining up along the Kansas line. We ain't figured out how Elmer and his fellow tribes folk at the other end of the shortline through Indian territory has been doing it. We found no still or sour mash around his lumberyard as we tidied up and searched for sign. But now that I've wrapped up a heap of distracting side issues, I mean to find out. My fellow lawmen in Tulsa Town are waiting on my wired say-so before they fill some mailed-in orders from the Delaware-Shawnee agency. I need time to deliver two cavalry mounts to Fort Gibson and have one remount sergeant arrested by his own military police. From there I can hop the Missouri, Kansas, and Texas line to Vinita and transfer to the Saint Lou line we suspect the moonshiners have been using. I'll wire to have another shipment sent to Wyandotte. I'll intercept it and ride along to see who picks it up, to do what with it, when it's delivered a few days late."

Split Face said, "If those Delaware women have any brains they won't accept delivery. They tell me you have been sleeping with that Sternmuller woman at the BIA and the *Tsalagi* maid from your hotel. Have you fucked Aura Purl, and which of the three did you enjoy the most?"

Longarm gulped, grinned sheepishly, and said, "It don't matter whether we round up every member of that moonshining bunch as long as they stop moonshining. Save for old Elmer Wachung, who can't hardly hang for it now, we don't have anything more serious than moonshining on anybody left. I told you how other crooks entire were behind all those other crimes."

She nodded sagely and insisted, "You haven't answered my other and more interesting question."

Longarm took a deep drag to give himself time to choose his words before he said, "The answer as regards the murdersome Aura Purl is no. It's tough to get a conviction when a crook you arrest can say you had your wicked way with her guilty hide."

"And the others, red and white?" the medicine woman insisted.

Longarm sighed and said, "No offense, but it's none of your beeswax, ma'am. How would you like it if some man made love to you and then told everybody how your charms compared with those of another lady entire?"

She smiled, a mighty weird sight with her face painted half red and half black, and then she shucked her turkey feather robe to show she'd been wearing nary a stitch under it as she softly replied, "Make love to me and never tell anybody else about it. I have heard some very strange stories about you . . . Custis. I have to find out if they are true. I am a medicine woman. I have to know everything that's going on."

Longarm had to allow that sounded fair, once he'd seen the body that went with her grotesque face. He'd been taking her for fifty or more. As she snuffed her smoke in the dirt by the mattress and lay back across it to spread slender thighs in welcome, he figured she couldn't have made it past thirty yet.

As he started to undress she husked, "Hurry, hurry, hurry! I have wanted to since first I saw you in another place when I was wearing another face!"

To which he felt obliged to reply, "I don't want any of that face paint on this shirt when I have to face other folk with other faces, ma'am. I'd ask you to wipe that paint off, but I follow your drift. But what if we were to blow out that ruby light and you could wipe it off in the dark for me?"

She began to fondle herself betwixt the legs as she pleaded with him to just get on with it. So he knew she was one of those gals, bless 'em, who liked to see what she was doing when things got down-home on a mattress.

Having shucked his duds and snuffed his own smoke, Longarm mounted her with mixed emotions, delighted at her lovely shape and the tight wet depths of her sweet brown flesh. But it sure beat all how funny a gal looked with her adoring eyes gazing up at him from a face half fire-engine red and half locomotive black!

She commenced to gyrate her shapely pelvis and promised she'd get the paint off for him if he wanted to kiss her. So he did and she kissed swell for such a traditional Indian. Left to themselves they have never learned to ride horses or do anything but pant in one another's faces and rub noses.

Old Split Face proved to be a real hostile Indian after he'd come in her missionary style. Like the old joke went, she'd take it hoss style, dog style, any style, as long as he wanted to keep humping.

But, to his mild surprise, the sun was still shining outside when she finally let him out of there. She'd washed any paint she'd smeared on him away with cotton waste dipped in some other shit. He left her cellar with more than sweet memories of Cherokee medicine, however.

He'd asked her if she could get him as strong an extract of that Black Drink they brewed from leaves and such they gathered and cured. She said she'd send him some before he left town.

So he went back to his hotel, walking sort of stiff, and had that supper. He was pretty saddle sore and not sure he ever wanted to meet another Cherokee gal for as long as he lived. But somehow, later that evening, after Antonia Redbird got off work at the hotel, he was able to do what a man was expected to do at such times.

There was a heap to be said for the way Changing Woman had created all her loving daughters, and good old Antonia liked to get on top to begin with.

Nobody ever came to the hotel with the herbs and such he'd need to brew his own Black Drink. He reflected in the perfidity of womankind as he got ready to ride out the next morning.

Chief Bushyhead and his secretary gal, Lorena Old Path, came down to the municipal corral to see him off. They'd agreed when he'd brought Aura and the remains of Jim Deadpony in that his visit to their nation had turned out needlessly interesting, thanks to other crooks entire and the likely natural death of old Pete Donovan adding up to a more complexicated puzzle than a man could fit into one sensible picture.

As they were saddling Red Rocket and putting Tabitha on a lead line for him to ride over to Fort Gibson and catch the train to Wyandotte, Dennis Bushyhead told him they were sending someone from Fort Smith to carry the penitent Aura the opposite direction.

The chief said, "I wish they hadn't given us a divided reservation with coal and rock-oil under it. If only they'd just left us alone in our higher and greener hills back east—"

"You'd have never come back from the California hills to run for the job of Cherokee Chief," Longarm soothed as he swung himself up in the saddle, adding, "The Chinee have a blessing, or a curse, that goes 'May you live in interesting times.' Consider how interesting you'd have all found life if Columbus had never happened."

Bushyhead laughed sheepishly. Lorena Old Path suddenly held up a brown paper package to say, "Some child in traditional dress asked me to give this to you. Do you have any idea what it might be?"

Longarm smiled down at her and innocently replied he'd asked a way-older Cherokee lady for some herbs to experiment with.

Lorena looked away with a Mona Lisa smile. So she must not have known he'd spotted the smudge of red face paint she'd missed under her left ear.

Chapter 40

They had Sergeant Mulholland in the guardhouse by the time Longarm rode into Fort Gibson. So he left Red Rocket and the hopefully cured Tabitha in the charge of a hopefully more honest remount sergeant and hopped the next northbound train with his saddle and other baggage.

They made good time as far as Vinita Junction, where he had to get off to transfer to the northeastbound Saint Lou line.

The single tracks crossed, there, on open cast-iron X frogs nobody needed to switch. But since simple rail crossings could lead to mighty complicated pile-ups there was a semiphore tower to signal who'd have the right of way. The tower arms were operated from a shed set no more than half a story above the long L-shaped open platform serving both rail lines, along with the hamlet of Vinita Junction itself.

Longarm introduced himself to the friendly white railroad man in the shed and explained, "I have to run just up to Wyandotte and back, Lord willing, and I've guessed right for a change. So I'd be obliged if I could leave this bulksome saddle and my possibles with you until I get back to catch another northbound MK&T. I move faster with just my saddle gun."

Before the older man could ask, Longarm nodded at the dinky town outside the dusty window glass and added, "I'd leave all this shit with somebody who has more room if I wanted anyone wiring up the line that I might be coming. I'm working with the advice and consent of the Cherokee powers that be, officious and sneaky. But I'd like to be sure nobody else could be expecting my arrival in Wyandotte and I see you

291

do have a telegraph wire running that way, no offense."

The railroader told him to store his saddle over a rafter and added, "You've timed it right, Deputy Long. For yonder comes your train from Tulsa Town, that local passenger and way-freight combination bound for Wyandotte."

Longarm dropped down from the box he'd stood on to store his shit, his Winchester in hand, to peer through that window as, sure enough, a Baldwin 2-4-2 came puffing at them under a plume of that ugly smoke you got from burning coal instead of wood for your boiler.

He felt obliged to offer the railroader a nicer smoke for his time and trouble. So he did and it was well he was still in the shed with the signal man when the train pulled in and naturally paused for such time as it took to load or unload some way-freight. Because some of the passengers got off to stretch their legs along the platform, just yards away at a somewhat lower level, and Longarm recognized a blonde in a summer straw boater and a tan poplin travel duster he'd known in the past, in the Biblical sense.

Longarm moved back from the grimy glass with a weary curse. The railroader asked how come, adding, "That's a mighty handsome young gal out yonder, Deputy Long. What have you ever done to her, you sly dog?"

Longarm confided, "It's what I don't want her doing to me. They call her Sparky and she considers herself an ace reporter for this big newspaper chain. They have to let her. Her family owns it. Last time I met her, up to the Omaha State Fair, she wrote some wild west shit about me that would make Buffalo Bill Cody blush. Lord only knows what she'd put in her papers if she knew what I'm still trying to tidy up discreet in these parts. I promised both Chief Bushyhead and some other Cherokee I'd see how quiet I could keep the rest of my mission."

The railroader laughed and repeated the old saw about the three most rapid forms of communications being telegraph, telephone, and tell any woman. So they just smoked on behind the grimy glass until the engine bell commenced to clang and Miss Sparky got back aboard her passenger coach.

Longarm let the combination start up and ran to throw himself aboard the forward freight car. He'd asked his pals in Tulsa Town to chalk mark the one he was interested in. They'd left the door open for him for the same reason.

Setting his Winchester aside and placing the package of herbs from Split Face atop a coffin he hoped nobody was inside as yet, Longarm found the crate from Lenape Lumber, addressed to Pequest Paint and Hardware in Wyandotte, the Delaware agency. Crates were made to be pried open and so were gallon paint cans when you had a screwdriver blade on a good pocket knife. But the top layer of cans marked Barn Red seemed to look and smell like cheap outdoor paint. So he lifted them out and set them aside on the swaying freight car's flooring. The layer below looked as much like barn paint but smelled different. Having a heap of time to kill in any case, Longarm broke open that packet of Black Drink makings and rolled the dry leaves finer to drop a handful of the concentrate in each can and stir some with a stick of dunnage off the deck before resealing each can and putting it back.

All but one. He considered how he'd been spattered with the same paint mix that Maria had managed to clean off his hat with soap and water and elbow grease as he set that sample aside. By this time Elmer Wachung's Delaware pals had to know about that gunplay at Lenape Lumber and a missing can or two would doubtless get by as logical.

After that there was little to do but sit in the doorway and smoke with his legs hanging out and his Winchester across his knees. He hauled himself inside each time they stopped, of course. But there were only a handful of stops and then, still on the bright side of sundown, they were slowing down for Wyandotte and Longarm dropped off running lest he spook anybody taking delivery on that paint they'd ordered.

So he was off to one side, strolling in the shade of some backside cottonwood, when what looked like an Irish washwoman of the black hair and blue-eyed persuasion rode in with a colored kid driving her buckboard. Longarm watched a safe distance as the kid and a couple of freight hands loaded that one big crate aboard her flatbed wagon.

He let them drive off before he drifted over to the platform and asked the way to Pequest Paint and Hardware.

They told him he'd just missed the owner, Horticia Eaglefeeder, and gave him easy directions to her nearby shop.

Longarm passed it on the far side of the one main street,

hugging the shade as, sure enough, across the way, that same
buckboard stood out front, already unloaded.

Longarm strode on with his Winchester cradled and that can
of paint he'd stolen from them in his left hand, deeper in the
shade. He found the Wyandotte branch of the BIA easy
enough. Nobody else painted anything but a church white, ou
this way.

He almost walked into a trap. But just as he was fixing to
cross the sunny street Longarm spied that reporter gal coming
out on the steps with a skinny white man in a snuff-colored
suit.

Longarm waited across the way until Sparky had left for
wherever such an overactive child might be headed next. Then
he crossed over and went in to show the Indian agent wha
he'd wrought.

The agent was named Needham and seemed decent enough
considering how hot he looked in that wool suit. He led Long
arm out back where a Delaware housemaid served them ice
bourbon highballs on the shadier back veranda while Longarr
brought Needham up to date.

When Needham swore and said, "I'll have my Delawar
police arrest Horticia Eaglefeeder and her sluttish daughte
this very afternoon!" Longarm shook his head and replied, '
wish you wouldn't."

The Indian agent stared thunderghasted at him. So Longar
explained, "I'll be proud to show you what they've all bee
up to. I'm sure you'll agree I have enough on 'em to make a
arrest. But then what, aside from newspaper headlines abo
Lo, the poor Indian, not understanding our white ways ar
blah, blah, blah until even Judge Parker, down to Fort Smit
keeps letting Sam Starr and his white squaw off with yet a
other warning. I promised Chief Bushyhead I'd *end* this moo
shining, not discourage it for a spell. Are you ready for me
show you what they've been up to, yet?"

Needham allowed he sure was, so they carried their drin
to the toolshed attached to the agency stable and Longar
showed him.

Borrowing a saddle blanket which he said he wouldn't r
ally ruin from the tack room, Longarm found a milk buck
and spread the thick wool across the top, allowing the doub

294

thickness to sag some as he asked the agent to hold it in place.

Needham took his coat off and rolled his sleeves up first. He was no fool and it sure looked as if Longarm meant to pour a bucket of red barn paint into that bucket through the saddle blanket.

Longarm did, slowly, as he explained, "We thought at first they'd been distilling Irish style with wool blankets. In either case alcohol will pick up a hint of wool-oil."

Needham gasped, "I thought you said you weren't going to ruin that saddle blanket!" as he saw the thick barn-red goo accumulate like the leavings of a hog butchering in the depression over the milk bucket.

Longarm soothed, "Don't get your bowels in an uproar. Alcohol mixes with either oil or water. In this case we're straining iron oxide paint pigment out of a mixture of alcohol, water, and a shot of glycerin to smooth the rawness. The late Elmer Wachung was breaking even in the lumber and hardware business because the freight charges from back east were eating into his profits. He was in a position to order two hundred proof industrial alcohol as shellac thinner. So he did. He even sold a jar or so as shellac thinner. But thanks to Kansas going dry this summer he was in a better position to dilute it with Arkansas River water and sell it as moonshine. He knew he'd be the most logical suspect if he operated openly this close to the Kansas line. So he set up that dummy paint and hardware outfit, here in Wyandotte, and the rest we know."

Needham said, "No we don't," as Longarm took charge of the blanket and removed it from the bucket. Then he laughed. "Yes we do. You've bled almost all the red out and I'd say one or two more passes through any filter would do it."

The agent stuck a finger in the almost clear contents of the bucket and cautiously tasted. He nodded and marveled, "Not bad. A little rusty and inclined to smell like sheep dip, but I've known drunks who'd pay for worse."

"Twenty dollars a gallon, up Kansas way," said Longarm, adding, "We don't want the Kansas State Guard getting any more upset than they are already, so here's what I'd like to do, with your permit, of course."

Longarm told Needham what he'd done as they carried the

pigment-stained blanket out to the pump yard. As Longarm rinsed the course oxide out as easily as if it had been red clay, he asked what that reporter gal had wanted before.

Needham laughed and said, "She seems to be lost. Says she's out to do a scoop on that Myra Belle Shirley shacked up with young Sam Starr down by Fort Smith. She's staying over by the railroad depot if you'd like to meet her."

Longarm repressed a shudder and said, "Already have. Don't want her printing whoppers or even the truth about what I've been up to here. I just told you why we don't want any of this moonshine story to get out if we can help it."

He shook the rinsed blanket out and draped it over a rail to dry as he said, "Having given the last of the fools enough rope, I need to give them a little more time. So how am I to hole up here in Wyandotte without that pesky reporting gal finding out I'm in town?"

The Indian agent said that would be easy and it was, as soon as he talked to some Indians he had beholding to him. A pleasant old Shawnee couple fed him a swell supper and put him up for the night in their new frame house on the far side of town.

Like other assimilated Indians, the Thompsons lived the same as most farm folk of their income. So the feather bed was soft and the flannel cover was just right for the balmy night air through the open window. So Longarm fell right off to dream about a white reporter gal with red and black pain on her face as she played the French horn.

After a hearty breakfast of cornmeal waffles Longarm wer calling on Pequest Paint and Hardware with Agent Needham It felt sort of dumb to face one fat old white lady and her tw darker and more hawk-nosed daughters after all the excitemer he'd had hunting them.

When Longarm flashed his badge old Hortense insisted sh had nary a drop of moonshine on the premises and invited hir to search the place if he liked. There wasn't much of the ding little shop to search.

Longarm nodded soberly and said, "We know you and yor kids strained Elmer Wachung's moonshine mixture overnig and sent that colored boy off this morning with them last jar ma'am. We wanted you to do it. So we let you do it. Would you care to know why?"

She said she didn't know what he was talking about.

He said, "Yes you do. What you were doing was so simple and so easy that nobody looking for moonshine still or even a potheen fire thought to look smack in town at a regular business address. But we just put you out of business, if you know what's good for you. I spiked that last load of jars with Cherokee Black Drink. Any former customers who ignore such a bitter taste are fixing to puke their brains out. You won't ever be able to make it up to them when they demand their money back because Elmer Wachung won't ever mix you anything better or worse. So if I were you I'd start packing."

Agent Needham told them they were fired as Indians unless they'd care to argue their case in front of the Delaware tribal council.

They must not have wanted to. As they commenced to weep and wail Longarm nudged Needham and suggested they give the ladies time to sort things out and decide where they meant to move. He doubted they could be dumb enough to hang around long enough for their disappointed moonshine customers to come calling.

So they shook on it and parted friendly. Longarm wired his own boss and Chief Bushyhead the trouble was over and headed for the railroad stop with his gear to get out of there whilst the getting was good.

But there she was, waiting on the platform with her own carpetbags and there was nothing a gent could do but tick his hat brim to the lady as she gasped, "Custis Long! What are you doing here and where did you go that time in Omaha when you told me you'd be right back?"

To which Longarm could only reply, "Howdy, Miss Sparky. They told me you were doing a story on that infamous Myra Belle Shirley of Younger's Bend."

The perky little blonde grabbed his sleeve and said, "She claims she used to go with the famous Cole Younger. But I just found out it was a tinhorn gambler called *Bruce* Younger and you're not getting out of my sight until you've told me all you know about that bandit queen!"

She meant it. But he didn't mind helping a pal with newspaper scoops that didn't count as they transferred later in the day to a train that had a private Pullman compartment. For he'd forgotten how Sparky could move her pale shapely bottom in broad daylight, or how much she liked to, as often as he could get her off the subject of her wild west stories.

**Explore the exciting Old West with one
of the men who made it wild!**